ONE SHILLING.

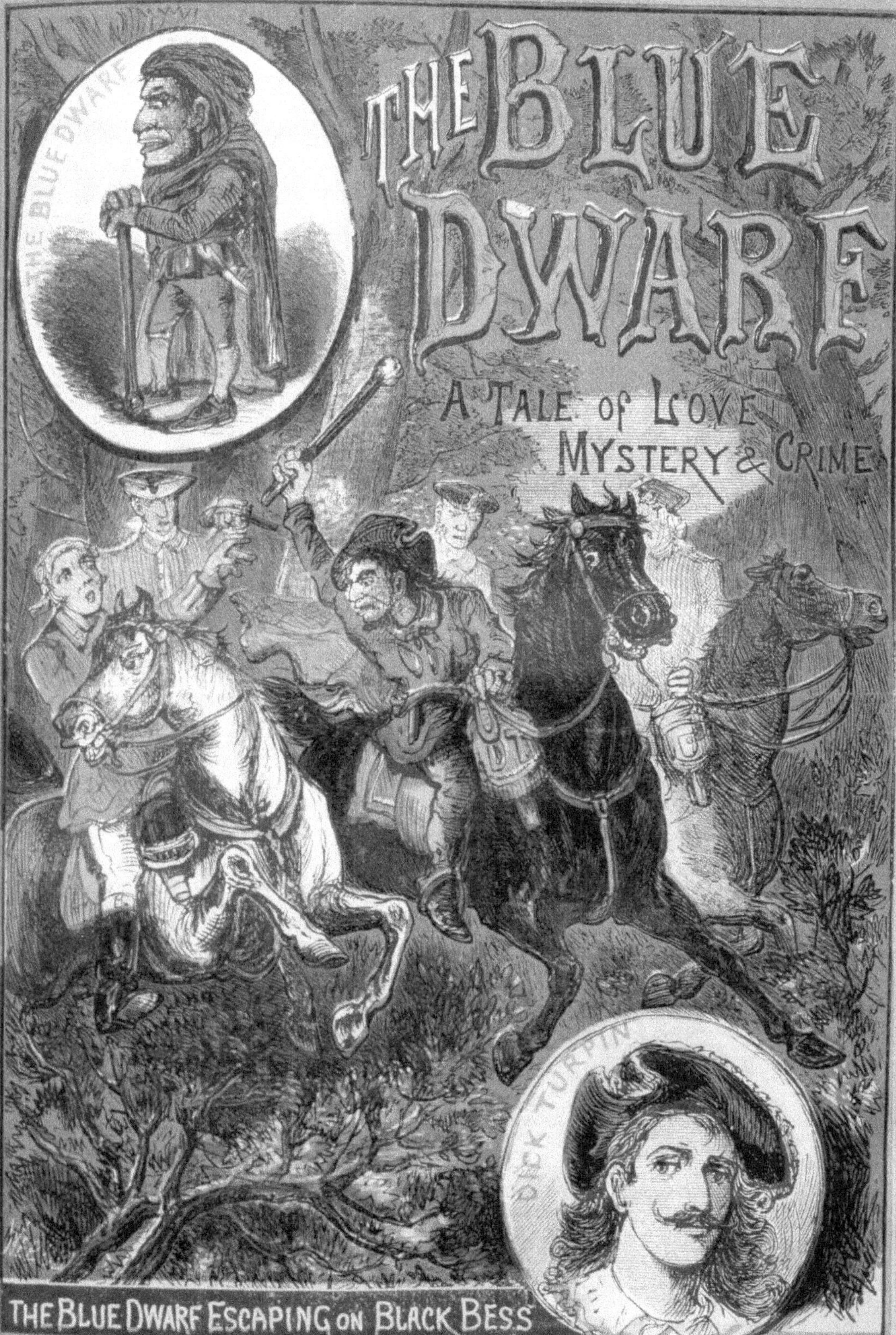
THE BLUE DWARF
A TALE OF LOVE MYSTERY & CRIME
THE BLUE DWARF
DICK TURPIN
THE BLUE DWARF ESCAPING ON BLACK BESS

LONDON: HOGARTH HOUSE. BOUVERIE STREET. FLEET STREET. E.C.

THE TWO TERRIFIED RUFFIANS FELL BACK IN THEIR CHAIRS.

THE BLUE DWARF;

A TALE OF LOVE, MYSTERY, AND CRIME.

By PERCY B. ST. JOHN.

VOLUME II.

CHAPTER LXXI.

We now revert to Seabright Hall, where Lady Stanley Seabright and four others, one a gawky youth of eighteen, and three girls, stood in the drawing-room.

Though the girls were charming, the mother only cared for the youth, Edward. Nineteen years before she had been married to Stanley Seabright, and about a year after a son had been born. Then it turned out that Lady Seabright had a husband living.

The matter was hushed up. But there was one that knew all, and that was Morris, the steward.

Sir Stanley had a belief that Falkland also knew, for one day when he had grossly insulted him, that personage turned and said—

"Never mind, my cousin, now; but your bastard will never inherit!"

Still, he believed that whatever suspicions Falkland might have, he had no actual evidence.

This will sufficiently explain what was the state of affairs in the drawing-room of Seabright Hall that day.

Dick and Tom rode up to the door of the mansion and asked to see Mr. Morris, the steward. They were at once admitted to the sanctum of the dapper little elderly man.

"Are you quite alone?" asked Dick.

"Quite alone!" said Morris.

"We come from Sir Falkland," said Dick Turpin.

"Is Sir Stanley dead?" gasped Morris.

"Yes."

"Thank heaven! then the king will have his own again. Tell me all about it. Has he written to me?"

"Yes; there is his letter."

And he handed the document to the honest steward, who read it carefully through.

"Gentlemen," said Joseph Morris, after reading the letter, "my master bids me trust you. I will. Lady Stanley is a hard woman. But I would spare her even as much as I could."

"Mr. Morris," replied Dick Turpin, "have you forgotten how grossly Lady Stanley insulted the master's wife on one occasion?"

"No," replied Morris; "I have not forgotten."

"We must act up to our instructions, neither more nor less," replied Dick. "The insult to his wife rankles in his bosom."

"I presume you wish to carry out your instructions without delay?"

"Certainly," replied Dick.

Morris bowed his head, and still led the way into the drawing-room, where Lady Seabright was.

"My lady, two gentlemen from London," said Morris, in cold, dry tones—"Mr. Hardwick and Mr. Johnson."

"What is the meaning of this intrusion?"

"If you will dismiss the young ladies, we will speak," said Mr. Hardwick, alias Dick Turpin.

The governess took the hint, and retired.

"Now then," cried Lady Seabright, haughtily.

"As we have a good deal to say, we beg to take our seats. Morris, while lunch is getting ready, will you send us up wine and biscuits?"

"Morris, these men are mad," gasped the mistress of the house, while the boy came forward, with a dazed kind of look, which seemed to say that, if there was only one man present, he should like to punch his head.

"No, my lady, not at all mad. I am going to obey their orders," said Morris, bitterly.

Lady Seabright looked at him aghast.

"We are here, madam," began Dick, "by the command and instructions of Sir Falkland Seabright, to request you and your family to leave these premises at the very——"

"Madman! scoundrel! where is my husband?" she shrieked.

"Dead as a door-nail—broke his neck on the racecourse," was the answer.

She was appalled, but only for a moment.

"If my husband is dead, there is no Sir Falkland. My son here, Sir Edward, is heir to all."

"*Bastard!*" said Mr. Hardwick, mildly. "Here in my hands I hold the certificate of your marriage to William Howard, the certificate of your marriage to Stanley Seabright, the certificate of the death of William Howard, when Teddy yonder was four, and the certificate of your *second* marriage with your late husband."

"What does it all mean?" shrieked the boy.

"That we have to leave—that your father's cousin turns us out," said Lady Seabright.

"But is it not your fault? Have I not been brought up to believe myself master of this place at my father's death?"

"You are not," said his mother, who was terrified at the storm she had raised.

Morris now entered with refreshments.

"It was never a secret to me, my lady," he said quietly. "My old master told me never to lose sight of Mr. Falkland's interests, and I never did."

"Serpent! snake! had I but known!" shrieked Lady Seabright; and then turning to Edward, "Remember, there is my dowry."

"But I shall be a beggar," gasped Edward.

"No," said his guilty mother; "your father made a secret will, in case his cousin discovered the truth. Let us go."

"Pardon me, madam," said Hardwick, with polite urbanity, "but my orders were to ask you to remain until after the funeral."

But Lady Seabright sailed out of the room without making any answer. As a matter of fact, she intended to go, as she could not face the neighbourhood, before whom Edward had been paraded as the heir to the title and estate.

Next day a carriage drove up to the door—

the body had been brought early in the morning—from which alighted Sir Falkland, his wife—a pale but still beautiful woman—and a bright little boy in deep mourning.

The servants had been prepared by Morris, and, the departure of Lady Seabright and her family fully confirming the rumour, accepted his words as true, and Sir Falkland was received without a murmur.

There is little more to be said.

After the funeral the will of Sir Stanley was read. It intimated that, apart from settlements on his wife and daughters, all was to go to his son and heir.

This was heard in silence, Sir Falkland's solicitor intimating that he would have his say presently.

The solicitor who had made Sir Stanley's will now produced a second document.

"'My last will and testament,'" he read, "'to be opened only in case of any question about my son Edward's claims.'"

Everybody looked deeply interested, as, with a preliminary cough, the attorney read, in clear and distinct tones, as follows :—

"'In the event of my boy Edward's right being disputed and his claims upset by any legal quibble'"—"a-hem!" from the lawyer—"'I hereby bequeath to him the sum of twelve thousand pounds, the interest to be paid to him for the rest of his natural life.'"

Sir Falkland's lawyer now explained.

"When Sir Stanley married Mrs. Howard, formerly Emily Granby, he believed her to be a widow," he said. "Shortly after this son was born the supposed dead man turned up, so that Lady Seabright had unwittingly committed bigamy. Two years later her husband really died, and Sir Stanley secretly re-married his wife. The whole thing was kept from the world, in the hope that nothing would transpire."

"But it did transpire," cried Morris, the steward, hotly. "When my good old master, Sir Ronald Seabright, was on his death-bed, he called me to his side and expressed his deep regret at his injustice to his nephew, Falkland. He had been grossly deceived by Sir Stanley. He had discovered the whole story of Mr. Falkland's marriage, which he highly approved and commended.

"He expressed his utter abhorrence of the deceit practised upon him by Stanley, whose marriage he found out only a few hours before his death. He was too ill to alter his will—in fact, he was dying; but he bade me never to lose sight of the interests of Mr. Falkland.

"Mr. Stanley knew I was Mr. Falkland's friend, and on the morning of the funeral he gave me notice to leave that afternoon. I laughed in his face, and said 'wait until the will is read.'

"The will was read, and it contained this proviso—'To Walter Morris, my attached and faithful steward and friend, I leave five hundred a year, with permanent residence in Seabright Hall. All rents are to be collected by him, and paid over half-yearly to the titular owner; he is to have power to restrain mortgages—none to be valid unless with his written consent.'

"I need not say," continued Walter Morris, "that I never allowed one penny to be raised on mortgage, or there would have been little left for my beloved master, Sir Falkland. All would have gone to that cub of a boy, Edward ——"

"I thank you, Morris," said Sir Falkland, rising and crossing the room to where he stood near the open window to shake hands with him; "may you live long to be my friend and faithful steward."

"Die, miserable cur!" cried a harsh voice from without, and two pistol shots were heard, the discharge filling the room with smoke. When this cleared away, Walter Morris lay on his back, Sir Falkland bending over him.

A medical man was immediately sent for, and he speedily arrived at the hall.

"This way, doctor," cried the baronet; "for heaven's sake see what can be done."

"A narrow escape, Sir Falkland," replied the doctor; "but the bullet only grazed his temple and slightly stunned him."

This was quite true, and in a few minutes he revived, drank a glass of wine, and was led to his room. Everybody present congratulated Sir Falkland and retired.

When they were gone the baronet looked round for the supposed Mr. Hardwick and his companion. When the shot was fired they had rushed to the window, and, getting outside, had started for their horses.

———

CHAPTER LXXII.

THE CHASE.

It was true. Even before the smoke had cleared away, Dick Turpin and Tom King had dashed through the window and seen the retreating form of a man.

"The cub!" said Dick Turpin, with a terrific oath. "Keep him in sight, Tom."

And Dick started for the stables. He returned in a few minutes with the horses, which, as a matter of precaution, were ready saddled always. Both mounted.

The window opened on a lawn leading to a flower-garden, beyond which, separated only by a hedge, was a field, and then another hedge and the king's highway. The two started gallantly, and in a moment were in the field.

"There he goes!" cried Tom, with a wild view hallo, which struck terror into the heart of the fugitive. "I see a hollow in the hedge—let's over!"

He turned his horse with his whip as he spoke, sitting the animal straight as a dart, his fingers holding the reins lightly but firmly. As he reached the hedge he patted the mare, and the pretty creature gathered herself for the leap, then went over like a bird, Dick following.

The fugitive had just turned a corner, and was going off at a rapid pace. Perhaps he might have gone faster had he known who "the avengers of fate" were who were coming up behind.

On! on, went the eager highwaymen, determined, after the way in which they had been trusted by Sir Falkland, to capture the evil-doer and bring him back to suffer whatever punishment the baronet chose to inflict.

The road was well known to them, and they were aware that there were no paths, alleys, or cross-roads, for some distance. Then there was a green, where the road forked in order to meet again a few miles further. These roads were made to suit the convenience of certain farmers.

For a moment, when they reached this fork,

they halted and conferred, listening all the while. But no sound was heard.

"We will meet at the 'Cross Keys,'" said Dick, taking the right road, while Tom King took the left.

On they galloped, until they reached the "Cross Keys;" neither had seen anything of the fugitive. The night was coming on and looked threatening. They determined to give their horses breathing time, at all events. Throwing their reins to the attendant ostler, they entered the parlour, where they ordered something to eat, something that was either ready or could be got ready in a few minutes.

"Bacon and eggs, sir?" said the waiter, and, satisfied with a nod, went out to give his orders to the cook, which he did with the remark, "they looks hungry ones."

At which the cook laughed, and prepared a dish accordingly. When it was brought up the two highwaymen smiled. It was a meal after their own hearts, and necessitated a good supply of ale, which they ordered. It was brought at once.

"You seem very quiet," remarked Dick, just for something to say. "Nobody in the house!"

"Very few—leastwise, none but yourselves—except one gent, who ordered a fowl and ham, in the bar parlour, but went away without eating it just after you came in."

"Very strange!" said Dick, looking significantly at Tom.

"Well, sir, we know him, and he threw down a guinea, saying he remembered he had to dine at Luton Hall, and must not spoil his appetite," replied the garrulous waiter, little thinking what a web he was weaving round the stranger.

"Where is Luton Hall, and who does it belong to?" asked Dick.

"It belongs to Sir Charles Granby, uncle to that Lady Seabright whose son was cheated out of his inheritance by an impostor," the waiter went on; "the rightful heir, Sir Edward, it was who just left. Sir Charles means to take up his cause. He's a wonderful peculiar man, sirs; builds cottages on his estates, forgives poachers, cuts down his farmers' rents. Some call him a fool, and some think he's mad."

"How far is it to Luton Hall?"

"About twenty miles," remarked the waiter.

"You go through Chirling to reach it!" carelessly remarked Dick.

"Yes, sir," was the reply.

"Let us have a stiff rummer of brandy and our bill. We go on to-night, but shall probably return to-morrow," said Dick.

"Going to be a bad night," urged the waiter; "better wait until morning."

"We know our business best," retorted Dick, with solemn gravity.

"Going to be caught in the storm and claim Sir Charles' hospitality," replied Dick, laughing.

"They'll sure to know us," said Tom King.

"Oh, no!" said Dick; "leave that to me."

Having paid their bill and mounted, they started on their journey. It was about seven in the evening. It was very hot, the flowers hung their heads, the leaves upon the trees doubled themselves up as though in pain, and even the brazen-faced sunflowers hung their heads, instead of staring up at the sky as usual. But now and then a faint and distant rumbling broke the silence, and when that died away you might have heard a leaf fall.

For a long time there had been intense heat; the sun had shone unblushingly, ripening the harvest and scorching up all else. Tall and straight the corn stood, a field of brightest gold stretching away and away up hill, down dale. The earth was split asunder; its fissures opened and gaped with their great mouths for rain.

But now, as the distant rumbling grew nearer, a shiver seemed to pass over the ground, the grass bent, the leaves fluttered faintly, the stronger flowers seemed to lift their heads as if listening, and a darkness crept up from behind the hills where the sun had not long set, coming on and on against the rising wind.

They were in sight of Chirling, and hastened their speed, reaching that town and an inn ere the storm broke.

Putting up their horses, they ordered dinner, and hurried out to where a Jew lived well known to Dick. They kept their capes over their heads in the inn, and only spoke to the waiter in a dark passage. When they returned they were clothed like country gentlemen, with each a heavy great coat and a slouched hat. Thus accoutred they returned to the inn. Their nearest and dearest friends would not have known them. What hair they had was jet black, while both had small silky Vandyke beards. Their complexion was completely olive.

"Waiter," said Dick, in an affected tone, which he thought might pass muster as a foreign accent, "we have to go to Luton Hall. The evening is not promising—can you lend us a covered cart and a horse? We can't ride through this weather. We'll leave our horses, and pay for supper, bed, and breakfast."

About a quarter of an hour later in came Boniface, all of a bustle (he had assured himself of the great value of the mares to be left in the stable), to say that if they must go out that night they could have a covered cart and a stout, reliable horse.

Dick thanked him and put down five guineas, adding that they would settle in the morning.

Ten minutes later they started. They had only six miles to go, but what a six miles! Few men would willingly have been out that night. Just after they started, the grass and leaves stirred once more, and the rain came pattering down.

How the earth welcomed it! how nature rejoiced at it! Again and again the lightning flashed, again and again the thunder crashed overhead and rolled away in the distance; each moment the wind grew stronger, tearing away at the tree-trunks and waving their branches high in the air. The clouds had utterly darkened the sky, and the rain poured down in torrents.

They found the lodge gates open, and drove as fast as their heavy horse could take them towards the house.

"It's time we had shelter," muttered Turpin.

As he spoke, once more the clouds were rent asunder, once more the fork of fire gleamed across the darkened sky, darting downward, playing along the earth like a serpent of electricity, coming nearer and nearer, till, with a cry which was almost human in its agony, the horse rose upon its hind legs, beating the air for a moment with his hoofs, and then fell heavily on one side, dead.

The two men had hardly scrambled out when once again the angry lightning poured down, striking a great oak, splitting it from branch to root, scorching and burning it, licking up the sap with greedy, fiery tongue. They paused to see no more, but, rushing for the door, rang two loud and ringing peals.

They were quickly answered, and ushered into the hall, the door being closed hastily behind them.

"What has happened?" said a fine, tall, old English gentleman, coming to the door of the principal room.

"Well, Sir Charles," said Dick, speaking suavely, "you have lost one of your finest oaks and we have had our horse killed. We were bound on a journey of necessity to Malden Castle, and dreading the storm, left our horses at an inn at Chirling, and came on with a horse and cart. We were driving up to your door to ask temporary shelter, when the two terrible flashes split your tree and killed our horse."

"Come in, gentlemen," cried Sir Charles Granby, warmly. "I'm thankful you thought of coming here. My niece, Lady Seabright, her son Edward, and her three daughters——"

"You ought to know our names—Ledger and Ford, of the firm of Grimshaw, City," said Dick, with his usual unblushing effrontery.

"No occasion for names," chuckled Sir Charles. "On a night like this I wouldn't turn a thief away—if we could help it. Sit down; Townsend, a steaming tankard for each gentleman. We sup in less than an hour."

They were at once made at home, and beds ordered. Dick and Tom explained incidentally that they had been absent in Italy for three months, to account for their tanned skins and beards.

"We have only just come home, Sir Charles," said Dick, "and feel loth to get rid of the signs of travel."

Sir Charles laughed, and the conversation went on between the baronet, the strangers, and Lady Seabright. The girls had retired shortly after their arrival, and Edward, as usual, was sullen. As a matter of fact, except among stable boys and such like, he never had anything to say.

When supper was announced, Sir Charles took in Lady Seabright, the men following in the rear. The supper was plain but substantial, and the travellers did ample justice to it. After supper Lady Seabright retired, the men remaining to drink a bowl of punch.

When this had been finished, Sir Charles suggested another; but the two highwaymen declined.

"Edward," said Sir Charles, "these gentlemen sleep in the blue corridor. The servants are all gone to bed save Peter. Will you show them their rooms; they are one on each side of yours?"

"Certainly, sir," was the answer, in a rough and surly tone of voice, of which, however, Sir Charles took no notice.

He left them at their respective doors, each with a lamp, and with a muttered "good night," entered his own room.

———

CHAPTER LXXIII.

COMPLICATIONS.

The highwaymen did not go to bed. As soon as the door was closed behind Mr. Edward Seabright, as he called himself, they entered the same room, and closing the door, sat down to converse.

The clock in the tower of Luton Hall struck eleven. Dick put his hand into the pocket of his great-coat, which he had brought up with him, and took out first a pocket pistol, then a flask called by the same name, and then a pipe and tobacco. Tom King did the same.

They then lighted their pipes, and held a brief conference, after which they lay down on the bed together for an hour or two's rest. They trusted to the clock in the tower, which was very loud to those who were not used to it.

They woke with the dawn, and as soon as they had imbibed a drop of brandy, prepared for action. Dick Turpin had contrived, in his bold, rather boyish, handwriting, to scrawl a few lines, which he left on the table in his bedroom.

"Mr. Edward Granby last night having attempted to assassinate Sir Falkland Seabright and Mr. Walter Morris, we have taken him away to be dealt with as the baronet shall direct."

They put no signature.

Having done this, they went out into the passage and entered Granby's room. He slept soundly. They at once took measures to wake him.

He soon opened his eyes, to find the two guests of the previous evening standing by his bed side, pistol in hand. He looked literally appalled.

"Dress," Dick Turpin said, quietly; "no harm will be done you if you obey us. Resist, and I must put a bullet through your head. No shirking."

Edward was in an agony of terror; the presence of these two men at his bed-side at that hour of the morning, armed, resolute and determined, was too much for him. His fear was abject, and he could scarcely dress.

Still he had to obey. As soon as he was ready they bade him lead the way to the stables, where there were horses in plenty. Three were quietly saddled, and then mounting they rode off in the direction of the inn.

How to get Black Bess and Tom King's horse was now the difficulty. The death of the borrowed horse and the loss of the cart would enable the landlord to charge them any price he thought proper. Now both the highwaymen were disinclined to part with more cash than was absolutely necessary.

They must have recourse to stratagem. Both their horses were admirably trained, and had learned to obey signals quite as well as any circus horse. They were to be made to do anything their masters wished by a curious number of whistles. They would stand still as death on hearing one signal, or come to their masters on hearing another.

They determined to try the latter. True, they were fastened in their stables, but both had left strict injunctions for them to be ready saddled.

Both uttered a series of shrill and vibrating whistles, then waited.

Not many minutes had elapsed when a terrific uproar was heard. The horses were snorting and stamping their feet against the door of the stable. Dick and Tom concealed themselves behind a tree. The stable-yard was only separated from the street by a low wall.

"There'll be fun in a minute," whispered Dick, "you keep your eye on the youngster, Tom."

Dick was right. In a few minutes an ostler who slept over the stable came down a ladder cursing at being awakened in this untimely manner. He was not at all choice in his language, and in his right hand he viciously clutched a riding whip.

He lifted the bar of the stable door, and as he did so two shrill whistles rent the air. The doors were dashed open, the ostler sent sprawling on his back, and away bounded the faithful and intelligent animals, leaping the wall and joining their masters with every expression of delight.

The ostler rose with a round volley of oaths, and ran to the stone fence, just in time to see three mounted men riding off, while two horses galloped off on the road towards London.

"Won't maister be wild," said the ostler, scratching his head.

And he was wild, especially when he heard of the death of his best cart-horse, which he had lent to the strangers on the faith of their liberal payment, and on the strength of their leaving two splendid horses in pawn. It was a long time before the event was forgotten. It was much commented on, but not in the presence of the landlord.

Meanwhile, without stopping, the three men dashed along the road, Edward Granby in the middle. He remained sullen and silent, never speaking a single word. He had nothing particular to fear, he thought, from Sir Falkland, who, for the sake of the family name, would subject him to no public prosecution.

In this mood he reached Seabright Hall, and the trio rode into the forecourt. The servants were about, and when asked about Mr. Morris said he was doing nicely, but had been ordered several days' rest. Sir Falkland was not yet down, but the breakfast-bell would ring in half-an-hour.

Dick asked to be shown a room in which to place his prisoner, where there was no chance of escape. The servants readily showed him a room near the library, a sort of muniment room, with nothing but loopholes to light it. Here he was fastened in, after which the highwaymen saw to their horses.

Sir Falkland had heard the trot of horses, and looking out of window had seen the arrival of Dick and Tom, guarding Edward Granby. He was very much surprised, and dressing hastily, went down stairs. They awaited him in the breakfast-room.

"Beg your pardon, Sir Falkland, for acting without orders," said Dick ; "but we have brought the attempted murderer of yourself and Mr. Morris back, for you to do with him as you may think fit."

"I am much obliged," replied the baronet ; "it will do him good for him to learn that his murderous intentions are known. We will breakfast first, and think of what is to be done afterwards."

This view was readily acquiesced in. The three breakfasted together, Lady Falkland, not yet strong, rising later, and breakfasting with her little son.

When breakfast was over, Sir Falkland went up to see his wife, leaving the others to their own devices. Under pretence of asking after Mr. Morris, they sauntered to his rooms, where they found the deputy-steward, who reported well of him. He would be out and about in a few days.

"Will you try a nip of brandy after your ride, gentlemen ?" asked the urbane subordinate —who already knew the habits of the two mysterious visitors.

Neither had any objection, so a bottle of brandy and glasses were put before them. We may premise that in passing through they had removed their disguises and resumed their natural appearance.

Then they rejoined Sir Falkland and briefly told the adventures of the night, to which he listened with an amused kind of gravity, which showed that he quite enjoyed the narrative.

Dick had scarcely finished his story when Sir Charles Granby was announced. Dick and Tom rose confusedly.

"Be calm," said Sir Falkland, with a smile, "remember you have put off your disguises—and will not be recognised until it is necessary.'

"Ah ! Sir Charles, it is many years since we have met. I was a mere boy then. Be seated."

"You have done nothing rash ?" cried the baronet, anxiously.

"I have done nothing at all. I am glad you have come. Mr. Hardwick here will explain, after I have said a few words."

The baronet explained the reading of the will, with the result, laying particular stress on the secret will.

"I was crossing the room to shake hands with Morris and to thank him for all his kindness to me and mine, when two shots were fired, one hitting poor Morris, luckily, not dangerously," said Sir Falkland, "the other whistling past my ear. Mr. Hardwick here will tell you the rest."

"I was looking at the window as Sir Falkland crossed the room," continued Dick, "and distinctly saw Mr. Edward level two pistols. I had no time to prevent the pistols being fired, but I and my friend here rushed after the would-be assassin, mounted our horses, and dashed in pursuit, scarcely losing sight of him at all. How he eluded us, matters not. We at once decided to follow him up and obtain entrance to your house is disguise—which we did."

"Then, I presume, you are Messrs. Ledger and Ford, lately returned from Italy ?" asked Sir Charles, grimly.

They bowed demurely, contriving to conceal the smile that illumined their rubicund countenances.

"Under the circumstances, I cannot blame you," said Sir Charles. "And now, Sir Falkland, what are your intentions ?"

"To thoroughly frighten the young cub, and bid him go hang elsewhere," was the stern reply.

"I won't have any more to do with him," said Sir Charles, gravely ; "the secret will upsets all false assertions that have been made to me."

"Would you like to see it, and all the other documents ?" asked Sir Falkland.

"Yes. Let us get it over."

"Come to the library," said the master of the house, motioning to the two others to follow ; and having reached that room and locked the door, he added, "bring him in."

They opened the door, and found 'the cub' fast asleep. They speedily roused him and led him into the presence of the two baronets. At the sight of Sir Charles he turned chalky white and fell back in an arm chair.

In a few moments, however, he seemed to recover himself, and sat up, defiant and insolent.

"Why am I dragged from my bed and brought here by two midnight ruffians ?" he asked.

"You are before two magistrates," said Sir Falkland, quietly ; "you are accused on indisputable evidence of the attempted murder of Walter Morris—of your wretched desire to kill me I say nothing. Do you wish to hear the evidence ?"

"No ! Suppose I did do it. What then ? Have I not been cheated, defrauded and robbed in the most iniquitous manner ? Brought up as acknowledged heir of Sir Stanley, when he is dead—killed, it appears to me, under very suspicious circumstances—a cock and a bull story is raked up, and I am, to suit a purpose, proclaimed a bastard."

"Which you are," said Sir Charles; "the second will proves it. Will you be committed for trial, or submit to our sentence ?"

"I don't care," he sullenly replied.

"You must decide. If you do not, I must send for my clerk, and make out your committal," remarked Sir Falkland.

"Do with me as you will."

"Then go your way; but beware how you come near either of our houses again. The charge of murder can always be revived," sternly added the master of the house. "You have ample means, take care you do not squander them."

"Yes ! take care you do not," said Sir Charles, "for not one penny of my money will you have, or your mother either. I shall leave all I can spare to the girls—the rest will go with the title and estates to my heir."

Edward Granby muttered something under his teeth, rose, and was ushered by Tom and Turpin out of the house. They did not return to the library. When they saw Sir Falkland again the other was gone. They were now thanked and liberally rewarded.

"Remember !" said the baronet, "to me you have acted fairly and honourably. I will say nothing of your profession ; but if at any time I can be of use to you, count on me."

Dick and Tom, much affected, shook hands respectfully, and took their departure—to meet again, perhaps.

Meanwhile, to end for the present with Edward Granby, we will follow Sir Charles home. He found Lady Seabright very anxious about her son.

"Where is Edward ?—he was not in his room," she gasped.

"I am very sorry," said he, "to speak harshly, —but if your son had his deserts, he would be in Newgate. He attempted last night to murder Sir Falkland and Walter Morris. He wounded the one and missed the other. I have just left the baronet, who, on condition of his never appearing in these parts again, has let him off."

"And you have deserted him ?" gasped his niece, wildly.

"I have forbidden him to come near me— forbidden him taking my name," the baronet went on, sternly. "I shall not place it in your power to help him out of my money, so shall leave what I have to leave to your daughters."

"You turn against me ?"

"Not at all. I will educate and bring up your daughters, if you like," he said ; "but I wash my hands of that boy."

CHAPTER LXXIV.
STARTLING ADVENTURES.

Dick and Tom having kept so quiet, for them, for such a time, determined to have a pull on London awhile. As they often said, there was no place like it for a gentleman. He could move in just what society he liked.

With regard to our friends, this was not exactly true, as though they had once or twice, under peculiar circumstances, been able to creep into fashionable resorts, it was always under false pretences.

They were hail-fellow-well-met in all the flash resorts of the metropolis, where men of more elevated position came occasionally to unbend ; but these men could go into higher resorts when they willed it.

Ben Duffy's, commonly called Moll's Retreat, was a very flash crib, where all the fastest girls about town did congregate. It was a place where you could dance, flirt, eat, drink, or play cards. The moment you entered and paid your money, you were free of the crib, and no questions asked.

Dick and Tom rather affected it, as they had many pals there, both male and female, and the free and easy style of the amusement suited their tastes. One evening, afer their return from Seabright Hall, having a few guineas to spare, they went thither, and were soon amongst the thickest of the fun. They were dressed in style, with no affectation of disguise.

The authorities never interfered with the den, for a very good reason. Its owner was in their pay, and gave them many a hint, without his connivance being known or suspected. He had made it a condition of his treachery that nobody should ever be arrested on his premises.

After a dance, the two high tobies sat down at a table with two 'blowers,' and ordering a bowl of punch, began singing ribald songs to popular airs. While they were so doing three men entered, with a swaggering air. Two of them were our old acquaintances, Brian Seymour and Robert Woodstock, while the third, who walked between them was Edward Granby. Yes, this unfortunate youth, the victim of the faults of others, had been picked up by these two sharpers, who were showing him life. Heaven help the youth with the silly ambition of seeing life—that is, launching into vice and crime of every kind,—who falls into the hands of two such men !

They had discovered that he had money, how much they neither knew nor cared ; but while he had any they would stick to him. They were utterly at fault about the earl, and were satisfied that Joe Askew had turned traitor. At all events they could no longer get any information from him. It was, therefore, only natural they should seek to make money elsewhere.

Edward Clancy—he had dropped the Granby —was tolerably sober, a rather rare occurrence, and looking around saw the two highwaymen. Retreating behind Brian Seymour, he whispered in his ear—"Who are those two men ?"

"Do you know them ?" asked Brian.

"I hate, I loathe them. They have been my curse, my bane, my ruin ; but for them I should be a baronet with a rich rent-roll."

"You would like to do them an ill turn ?" asked Brian.

"Yes ! at the risk of my life !" he answered.

"Come this way," continued Brian, and led him to a table where, a waiter following, they ordered drink. "Now listen, and keep your own counsel. Those two men are Dick Turpin and Tom King. Yes ! you needn't look so incredulous. They are well known here, but the runners never interfere. Besides, they wish to take these two men red-handed."

"But, could Sir Falkland have known?" gasped Edward.

"Who may he be?" asked Brian, and when the other explained, continued, "oh, yes! the mad gambler, whose cousin was so mysteriously killed at Hopwood. Ah! you know him. Well, I dare say he and Dick Turpin are well acquainted; he is employed by men of higher rank. Would you like to make a good pot of money?"

"Wouldn't I? it is just what I do want!" said Clancy. "Fun and money, money and fun; that's my motto."

"Well, we'll do a little flutter here, just for amusement, and then we'll go back to my lodgings. You will have to keep quiet for a while if you come to our house, but you will spend no money, and, on the contrary, earn some."

"All right," said their dupe, and, their drink finished, they went to the table and played for an hour, Edward Clancy as a matter of course losing.

They then rose and left. Brian's lodgings were at no great distance. Supper was ordered, and then Brian unfolded his plans.

"These men are leagued with a relation of mine, to do me out of both a title and estates," began Brian; "to thwart this nefarious plot we have for a long time been watching these two. The other members of the conspiracy have disappeared, it is believed, with a view to produce a sham heir-at-law. We have employed spies and agents without end, but all have been defeated or got tired. If you will watch them, track them, enable us to find them when they communicate with our incarnate foes, we will pay you well, and guard you against the dangers of London. You are a novice, and could easily be taken in; be known as our friend and none will dare to harm you."

"Command—I obey," said Edward, who had an inordinate idea of his own qualifications.

"Well, we will keep you on the track of Dick and Tom," continued Brian. "What we want to find out is, when he is in communication with our foes. The principal agent is a hideous cripple, a dwarf, all indigo-coloured, but a keen and consummate rascal. We will obtain you entrance to many of Dick and Tom's resorts. You must be a sleuth hound. Should Dick and this wretched dwarf meet, watch where the latter goes. Track him on foot or on horseback, and let us know the result."

"I will," he answered.

After this a copious supper was discussed, cards indulged in, and, towards morning, the party broke up, each going his own way, with an agreement to meet at twelve o'clock on the morrow.

Brian and Robert chuckled. They had secured a new tool, and one who would not be too expensive, as what money they paid him they could easily win again; so they promised themselves to be exact to the rendezvous.

Edward was there, and received his instructions. After considerable discussion he was provided with a disguise, which made him look like a travelling apothecary—one of those men who used to go about the country on a lean horse, with a box of simples, drugs, and pills, a kind of itinerant laboratory.

They went to a costumier, and, after half an hour, came forth, Edward so disguised that his own mother would not have known him. Thus apparelled and disguised they introduced him to one or two of Dick's haunts—made him free of the house.

"Be careful," said Brian, "while you are at this work of what you drink. If you should betray yourself to Dick he will have no mercy."

Edward promised. This last threat had more effect upon him than anything else. He had a great respect for his own carcase, and a great fear of Dick Turpin's prowess. He had already seen enough of his prowess, determination, and readiness of wit. He resolved, therefore, to run no useless risks.

Four evenings passed, and then, wandering about from place to place, he suddenly found himself following the Blue Dwarf, and saw him enter one of Dick Turpin's haunts. He retreated into the background and looked for a place of concealment; but he could see only some very inferior shops. One was a milk shop, and here, calling for a glass of milk, he waited.

Very soon he saw both Dick Turpin and Tom King enter.

He hurried to a corner public-house, where he had an hour before left Brian.

He had not gone, but had been joined by Robert Woodstock. He hastily told his story. They were jubilant.

"Now that horrible Blue Dwarf in no way knows you—stick to him—follow him. I will have a horse ready. Now go back."

Edward did, quite warming to the excitement. He had not waited ten minutes when the Blue Dwarf came out, wrapped in his cloak. Edward followed, finding his comrades at the corner of the street with a horse. Edward received some whispered instructions and went on. A hundred yards further on a boy waited with a horse. This the Blue Dwarf mounted and trotted off, wrapped in his cloak. He was in the Strand in a moment, and going in the direction of Fleet-street.

It was not late, and both pedestrians and horsemen were about. There was no danger of losing sight of Sapathwa. His peculiar figure identified him. After reaching Fleet-street he trotted quicker, and kept on until he arrived at London Bridge, which he crossed, and took the direction of Greenwich.

Edward kept him in sight without difficulty, the more so that the man he was stalking turned not to the right or left. The young man kept as far as he could in the background, so as to give no chance of his errand being suspected.

But the foremost rider showed no sign of stopping for a long time, indeed, not until he had reached an inn beyond Gad's Hill. Here, to Edward's great delight, he halted, dismounted, and hurried in, leaving his horse in the hands of the ostler.

Edward did the same, and, going in, entered the public room. It was empty, and the young man at once ordered something to drink. With this he placed himself near the window, whence he could see when the other left.

Half an hour passed, and then, riding as if for a race, up came two men, who at once shouted "House!" and were attended to without alighting. They ordered drinks, and gave some directions.

As they did so Edward Clancy recognised Dick Turpin and Tom King, the much-dreaded highwaymen.

Then he heard a shuffling in the passage, and the Blue Dwarf joined them. Then, with lightning-like speed, all three darted off in a southerly direction.

Edward Clancy was furious and afraid. What did it mean? But he must lose no time. He hurriedly paid his score and, mounting, followed. But his quarry was out of sight.

Still, he determined to follow them in the hope that something might turn up; like the man in the play, he never threw a chance away.

But, though he rode hard and fast, he could make no discovery. They had disappeared as if they had been swallowed by an earthquake.

Disconsolate and angry at his failure, he turned towards London, when two mounted men darted from under some trees.

"Who and what are you?" said Dick Turpin, clutching his bridle. "Show the glim, Tom; let's see what he's made of."

Edward Clancy shook with terror at the lamp being produced. Dick pulled off his wig and goggles, and burst out laughing. "So you've turned spy, Master Edward Clancy. Take that!" cutting him across the face with his heavy riding whip, "and tell your rascally employer, Brian Seymour, I did it."

With which he started the horse and sent Edward flying along the road, his feet out of the stirrups, and himself yelling with pain and fury.

He went away, however, only a hundred yards, and at a turning in the road halted to reflect. His personal chastisement had only exasperated him, and filled his mind with fury and bitter hatred.

He resolved to return on his way at any risk or peril.

He did so, and soon had the satisfaction of getting within sight of the two highwaymen, who were jogging along, laughing—at him doubtless. He ground his teeth with impotent rage and fury. Still, he would discover their secret. It did not take him long to do so. After riding two miles they turned down an avenue leading to a house, and disappeared through the open gates.

A sign-post stood at the corner house, and on this he contrived to read, "To Heathcoate House." Satisfied with this, he turned back, went to the roadside inn, engaged a bed, gave directions to be called early, and retired, after drinking a quart of old ale with half a pint of rum in it.

Next day, when Brian Seymour rode up in disguise, he found a large board up with "To Let" on it. On enquiry, he found that the family had left on the previous night, the woman thought for the Continent.

Brian returned to town, sick with rage, to be shown a paragraph in the *Weekly Tatler*, to the effect that the Earl and Countess of Elphick and party had started for the Continent. The countess, who had recently presented her lord with a son and heir, was ordered change of climate.

We leave Brian Seymour and his coadjutor to their thoughts.

CHAPTER LXXV.

THE ORPHAN'S FRIEND.

It was time. To the delight and rapture of the earl, and the intense joy of the countess, a male child had been born unto them. Colonel Grant and Lord Jermyn were intensely delighted.

Lord Jermyn, though comparatively a young man, was very proud to be a grandfather, as in fact most men are.

The child, which was in perfect health, had been born three weeks ago. Lady Elphick was in perfect health, but the removal was the consequence of excess of precaution on the part of the father and mother of the child. At the same time, the doctor, seeing that the mother was anxious about something, did what most doctors would do under the circumstances, recommended change of air.

As a rule, it is one of those remedies which, if it does no good, certainly does no harm. So they started for a village which, under another name, has become famous. But at the time of which we speak, it was known to a very few. Its name was Brighthelmstone.

Its proximity to Lewes was, perhaps, the first cause of its being unearthed. First a rich banker bought some land there and built a country house, one or two followed, and then a few more followed suit. The doctor was from Lewes and knew of a residence at Brighton which had been empty some years. It had once belonged to a large estate, but of all its acres only two remained.

It was a rambling old building, incongruous in its combination of stone, brick, and framework. The house was for the greater part gloomy and antiquated. It was originally an oblong stone structure, with massive jail-like walls and narrow windows. Money will do almost anything, and the Blue Dwarf had sent down artificers who had made great changes.

Partitions were pulled down, bay-windows and verandahs superseded dark porches, halls and staircases were widened, folding-doors, plate-glass, cornices, panellings and gilding, made a wonderful transformation. Furniture, too, had been sent down for the rooms that were to be occupied, the rest being left to mould, damp and rust.

To this house, early in the morning after Heathcoate was abandoned, came a travelling carriage. It contained the earl, his wife, the nurse, and baby.

It was guarded by two stout men in rough coats, who rode one at each window. A little distance behind came another carriage containing Colonel Grant and Lord Jermyn. Both drew up at the entrance to Penshere Lodge.

"A queer old place," said Shelton Seymour to his wife, "but picturesque."

"It looks gloomy enough," laughed Laura; "but I dare say dear old Sapathwa knows best."

The door was opened by one of their old domestics, and the earl, his wife, nurse, and child, hurried in.

Laura was delighted at the preparations made for them. The inhabited rooms were elegant in the extreme, while the countess went into raptures over the nursery, which was next to her room. But the journey had made them all tired and hungry, and the first thought of all was breakfast, which was quite ready. A good look out had been kept, and the instant the carriages were descried in the distance, the servants were on hospitable thoughts intent.

A hearty meal was consumed, and then all retired to seek well-earned repose. Dick and Tom took their matutinal repast with Sapathwa, who had been working hard all night to have the last finishing touches put to the house. As soon as they were satisfied, they too retired, and all was silent in Penshere Lodge. At one, however, every one was on foot again, and after some attention to the toilette, were ready for dinner.

Dick and Tom dined with the Blue Dwarf, from whom they received a handsome reward for past services. They settled a code of messages on both sides, in case they required to communicate. After this the highwaymen took their departure for Lewes, it being their intention to return to London that way.

There was a main road from there, and they would be on the king's highway, when perhaps they might do a stroke of business.

They were, however, not to see London as soon as they expected. On reaching Lewes they put up at the Castle Hotel, a house well known to both, and which was frequented by some of the upper ten. They selected the parlour, which at that time of day was empty.

They simply ordered grogs, and, these being served, began conversing of their prospects. These men never thought of how brief their career might prove, and how they might at any moment be cut off in the prime of life.

They laughed, joked, and were merry. Presently there was a lull in the conversation. Tom King was about to break the silence, but Dick put his finger to his lips. His head was leant against the wall, near a square-cut aperture, which communicated with another room. Two persons had just entered the latter apartment, and Dick had heard their first words.

"We are private enough here," said one, "and now let me hear what you have got to say."

"Let us have a bottle of wine, first," replied the other, in a harsh, grating voice.

"Do you think I'm made of money?" asked the first speaker, petulantly. "But I suppose we cannot occupy a private room without drinking. Ring."

The order was obeyed and the wine brought in. Both filled their glasses.

"I presume, Mr. Rochford, it is unnecessary to recapitulate the past, and to say how by my instrumentality you have become rich," began the other.

"Whatever you may have done for me in the past, you have been paid for," was the supercilious reply.

"I have not, as you will learn. Allow me, Mr. Rochford, to recapitulate events, and you will find yourself singularly in error."

"What mean you?"

"If you do not interrupt me, you will soon know. When Mr. Henry Armstrong died, nearly two years ago, by the terms of a will unexpectedly produced, you, Mr. Henry Armstrong's wife's brother, were left executor and guardian."

"I recollect, perfectly."

"I presume that you have not forgotten that will was a rank forgery?" continued the other.

"Yes, Mr. Joe Stammers, you are a very good hand at that," the other sarcastically replied. "For your forgery you had five hundred pounds."

"And you over a thousand a year—the widow only getting two hundred, while the rest is to accumulate in your hands!"—with a curt laugh—"until her son Henry is of age."

"It is accumulating," retorted the other.

"But will Henry Armstrong ever see a penny of it? Long before the eight years are up, Mr.

Richard Rochford will have left for parts unknown."

"That is my business," drily retorted the other.

"Say, rather, mine," responded the other, in a menacing tone. "To cut a long story short—I have the real will in my possession—the real will, I say."

"*The real will!* There never was a will. My brother-in-law died intestate."

"No. When you sent me to search the desk, I found his will and I O U's for three thousand, signed by yourself," was the deliberate answer.

"Scoundrel!" gasped Rochford.

"I am speaking the plain truth, and unless you consent to give me a thousand guineas in hard cash and notes, I shall go to Widow Armstrong, who lives close here, and tell the whole story. Don't think to get away, for I am desperate, and my mind is made up."

"You will give me the will and the I O U's for a thousand guineas?" asked Richard Rochford, musingly.

"Yes."

"When?"

"Whenever you like."

"It is now five o'clock," replied Rochford. "You know where I live; come at eight, bring the documents, and I will have everything ready."

"No tricks upon travellers," said the other. "I shall leave word where I am going, and if not returned by nine, I shall be looked for."

"All right," laughed Rochford.

"Stop where you are," whispered Dick. "Wait till I come back. Such a game!"

Tom nodded. He knew his partner and companion too well to doubt any of his actions.

Dick in one instant was in the bar, and asking about supper and beds. While he was so doing, a portly-looking man, of sanctimonious aspect, followed by a thin, wiry little man, passed.

"Isn't that Mr. Rochford?" asked Dick, when the man's back was turned.

"Ye'sir," was the prompt reply.

"Well, I've come from London on business of his," replied Dick—"his and Mrs. Armstrong's—can you give me their addresses?"

"Certainly, sir!" replied the waiter; "shall I put them on paper?"

"Yes, if you please," said Dick, and in a few minutes he returned to the public room with the addresses in his pocket.

"I have ordered supper and beds," he told Tom. "I'm going out for a little while; when I return I will explain."

In the course of his strange and chequered career, Dick Turpin had done many kind and generous actions. He had pretty well decided to do one now. If he could make anything out of it, well and good.

He went outside, and, once in the street, asked his way to Vigo Street, where resided the widow Armstrong, at No. 10. It was easily found. It was a quiet, neat street, with gardens in front, not at all ill-kept.

Dick knocked smartly, a right correct London knock, and was answered by a smart maid.

"Is Mrs. Armstrong at home?" he asked; "if so, say a gentleman from London on business."

"Come in!" said a pleasant voice from the parlour, and he was ushered into the presence of a pleasant-looking woman of about five-and-thirty, who still wore widow's weeds.

"Be seated, sir," she said, pleasantly, "and then you can tell me your business."

"Are we quite alone?" asked Dick, "as my business is both important and private."

The door was closed.

"Will you take a little brandy? it is all I have in the house," and, without waiting for an answer, she went to the door, opened it, and called down in the direction of the kitchen, "Hot water and glasses!"

"Yes'm," was the answer.

The refreshing beverage was mixed, Dick taking a very stiff dose, and the widow a very mild and modest portion.

"My dear madam," began Dick, "before entering on business which may terminate pleasantly, I shall have, I am sorry to say, to slightly hurt your feelings. I am compelled to allude to your late lamented husband."

Mrs. Armstrong put her handkerchief to her eyes, and wiped away the semblance of a tear.

"I have no objection to speak of him," she said; "he was a good husband."

"Well, so I have heard," continued Dick; "but, now, have you any particular opinion about that will of his?"

"I thought it very unkind. A mother is the best guardian of her son," she replied, very quickly, and in a determined tone.

"Now, my dear Mrs. Armstrong, would you be surprised to hear that that will was a forgery?" he asked.

"Great heaven forgive me! but that was my thought all along. But who could the forger be?"

"Who benefits by it? Who, by its means, is able to defraud the widow and the orphan?" asked Dick.

"No! no! not my brother," she gasped.

"Well," said Dick, in a hem-ing, ha-ing way, "he did not, perhaps, forge it himself; but he paid a man, bribed him to do it, paying a heavy price."

"Merciful creator!" she exclaimed, clasping her hands, while tears welled from her still handsome eyes. "But how do you know?"

"All in good time," he answered; "I will explain presently. In addition to this will being forged, there is a real will, in your husband's writing, leaving everything to you in trust for your son. Now, Mrs. Armstrong, I have particular reasons for not telling you how I learned this; but you must trust me."

"I will, sir, and thank you for the task—you are very generous."

"Not so generous as you think," observed Dick, drily. "I will explain. Now the man who forged the will is very hard-up, and has, by threatening to come to you, induced Mr. Rochford to promise a thousand pounds for the real will, which, doubtless, he will at once destroy."

"Heaven forefend!" gasped Mrs. Armstrong.

"Now, if I bring you the real will, and a confession of the forgery, with the money itself—or the securities—may I have that thousand guineas? I am a poor man, and may as well have it as that scoundrel forger."

"Certainly! and may the gratitude of the widow and orphan be yours," she cried.

"Wait awhile," he said; "it is not done yet; but I believe it will be done. Have you any male friend you can trust?"

Mrs. Armstrong's face flushed a little.

"I have a friend, a Mr. Crowder, a distant cousin, who is very kind to my boy," she answered, colouring up. "Well, everybody knows, I am going to marry him. He is a rich man to me—a man in good business."

"Can you trust him?"

"With my life!" she replied. "He is good and true, and could marry a heiress if he chose."

"Will you ask him to be here at nine to-night!" he said, rising.

"He generally comes in of an evening after business," she responded, frankly.

"I will be with you—at least, I hope so. My task is not without danger, but nothing venture, nothing have. Don't tell Mr. Crowder too much until I come. You can simply say you are told the will is a forgery, and that the real one has been found."

"I will do as you say, sir," and she attended him to the door herself.

CHAPTER LXXVI.

AN ADVENTURE.

On his return to the inn, Dick at once ordered up supper, and as soon as the waiter was out of the room, told his story to Tom.

Tom laughed heartily.

"You are a regular Amadis of Gaul, a knight-errant," said Tom, who had been well educated, but turned out of Rugby for some act in which love and larceny were strangely mixed up; "a regular squire of dames. What part am I to play in this little comedy?"

"As you will share the danger, so you shall the profits," replied Dick; "we'll divide. It will be dark at eight, quite dark, and we must put on our slouched hats, and take our pistols with us."

Tom nodded, and went on with his supper. Dick had found that the address of Mr. Rochford was his office address, where he invariably remained until eight or half-past, an hour after the clerk had gone. He then went to an inn, where he had a horse, and rode out to an outskirt about a mile distant.

At a quarter to eight, muffled up to the eyes, Dick and Tom stood in an archway, watching. There was a light in a window on the ground floor, in the front office, and presently they saw Mr. Joe Stammers approach the door and knock and ring.

A light flickered in the passage, and then the door was opened quickly, and as quickly closed behind the visitor. The two highwaymen crossed over at once, Dick with a skeleton key in his hand. Without the slightest noise or difficulty the door was opened and the two men entered.

We will precede them. Not a word was spoken until the two men were in the front office. The evenings had begun to get chilly, and there was a cosy fire, while on a small table near was a bottle and two glasses.

"Your old weakness," said Rochford, with something like a sneer—Joe Stammers had been his articled clerk once—"used to be Hollands. Help yourself," he added, after filling up his own glass, which he drank off without leaving a drop.

After a moment's hesitation the other did the same.

"Is this story of the will true, or is it another concoction of your own?" continued Richard Rochford.

"It bears the signature of the late Henry Armstrong, is drawn by Taylor and Knight, and witnessed by James Nelson and Walter Stebbings, all alive. Here is the document. It does not go out of my hands until I have the money."

"But it does, though," said Dick Turpin, "by your leave," and he snatched it from his grasp, putting it in his capacious pocket.

Both rose with an oath, to find themselves confronted by two fierce-looking men with cocked pistols presented at their heads. The two terrified ruffians fell back in their chairs, to which, in the twinkling of an eye, they were strongly attached by cords.

"Now, Mr. Richard Rochford, and you, Mr. Stammers, are you not a pretty rascally couple—thieves, forgers, and robbers of the orphan?" said Dick, sarcastically. "One moment."

And he examined the will, which was to all appearance correct. At all events, it seemed so to him.

"That's all right."

"Villains! burglars! what are you going to do with it?" gasped Rochford, while Joe Stammers writhed with terror.

"Take it to Mrs. Armstrong," replied Dick; "but we have no wish to do anything illegal, you know—oh, not at all—not in our way. If you like, we'll send round to the Town Hall for an officer and the magistrate's clerk—Mr. Crowder, if you wish so."

"What do you want?" sullenly asked Richard Rochford, who knew that that course meant hanging for both himself and Stammers.

"Wait a bit! Jim," addressing Tom, "open that drawer," pointing to one marked "Armstrong trust and cheque books."

Tom did as requested, and pulled out two cheque books and two bankers' books. One was marked "Armstrong Trust;" the other "R. Rochford's private account."

"How much to the Armstrong trust?" asked Dick, while Rochford glared, and the craven Joe Stammers cried.

"One thousand eight hundred guineas," was the gleeful highwayman's response.

"And the private account?" continued Dick, with great glee.

"Three thousand."

"Very good," Dick went on; "tear one cheque out of each and give them to me. I will put one before him."

"Now, sir, sign that cheque for one thousand six hundred guineas, re Armstrong trust."

"And if I refuse?"

"There is no compulsion. You will do just as you like. Jim, we'd better do things straight. I'll stop here while you go to the Town Hall."

"I will sign," hissed Rochford, and he did sign.

"Now," presenting the other cheque, "sign for one thousand guineas on your private account."

Rochford turned pale, ghastly pale, then green.

"Would you ruin me?"

"Not at all; there's no compulsion, eh, Jim?" laughed Dick, and again the man signed.

"Am I free now?" gasped Richard Rochford.

"No; in the first place I must see that these cheques are correct. Besides, I want you to sign something else. Jim, just write a few lines I shall dictate. Ready?" "Yes." "Then write: 'I Richard Rochford, and I, Joe Stammers, acknowledge having forged the will produced at the funeral of Henry Armstrong.'"

"Do you want to hang us?" groaned Richard Rochford.

"No; as soon as you have signed you will be free until eleven o'clock to-morrow. You can settle your affairs in that time; your sister will not prosecute you—but leave Lewes."

The paper was ready. The two wretched men signed, and then Tom King signed his name as witness, James Young, while Dick Turpin put his scrawl on as Edward Carlton, the name in which he had told Tom to fill up his cheque.

"I shall not be half an hour," he said, as he rose; "keep guard, Jim. Sha'n't keep you waiting long."

And he went out, hurrying as fast as he could to Vigo Street, No. 10, where he knocked, and was at once admitted. He found a nice little supper waiting, and Mr. Crowder seated by the fire. He was a sensible, honest-looking man, of about forty—exceedingly good-looking.

"My cousin has told me part of what is happening to-night," he said, as he placed a chair for Dick. "I await your further communications."

Dick seated himself, and pulled out a handful of documents.

"Please to read this one first," he said.

Mr. Crowder opened it, and glanced his eye down it.

"Yes; it is Henry's will," he cried, "made some two or three years before the poor fellow's death. I had forgotten all about it. He leaves everything to you as guardian and executrix for your life, and then to your son. So you see, Ellen, I don't come in for much," he added, laughing.

"Will you read this?" continued Dick, handing in the confession.

"He and Joe Stammers forged the will," exclaimed Mr. Crowder, "and they have signed a confession. Where are they?"

"I left them safe in the charge of a friend. I promised Mr. Rochford perfect safety until to-morrow, in your name, Mrs. Armstrong."

"Quite right," she said, sobbing; "tell him to get away—he's my brother."

"Certainly, Mrs. Armstrong," continued Dick. "I have a little more business to transact first. You must excuse me for entering into a few particulars. I cannot tell you how I discovered all this, except that I did discover it all. Mr. Richard Rochford was to pay Mr. Joe Stammers a thousand guineas for that will, and had not I overheard the plot, it would have been reduced to cinders; while before Mrs. Armstrong's son came of age, Mr. Rochford would have fled."

"We are deeply beholden to you," said both; "in what way can we reward you?"

"Without spending a farthing of your own," Dick went on, "you can reward me. The thousand guineas he promised to Joe Stammers he has given to me. First, however, here is a cheque for the Armstrong trust money," putting the bank-book and cheque into Mr. Crowder's hand, who looked at him in amazement.

He was thoroughly frightened, and only remarked; "what do we not owe you, Mr. ——?"

"Mr. Edward Carlton," said the highwayman, bowing, "and here is a cheque for my thousand guineas. Will you go with me to the bank in the morning?"

"Certainly; with the greatest of pleasure," exclaimed Mr. Crowder; "and now you will sup with us?"

DICK TURPIN AND TOM KING PUNISH THE SPY.

" I as much as promised to release Mr. Rochford, whom I have left at his office under the guardianship of a friend of mine. I pray you will pardon me to-night. I will be at the bank at ten, and you can introduce me to the manager. You must have a great deal to talk about to-night."

" You must have a sup of Hollands," exclaimed the worthy widow, as she hurriedly poured out half a tumbler, which Dick at once drank down without the addition of water. He then wished them good evening, and retired.

He found faithful Tom guarding his quarry.

" It's all right," said Dick, jauntily; " Mr. Crowder and Mrs. Armstrong have endorsed my promise that you shall have until eleven o'clock to-morrow to settle your affairs. After that Mr. Crowder will give notice to the authorities. Take my advice, and lose no time."

With which Dick and Tom unfastened them, and left them to themselves. Going over to the inn, Dick told his story to Tom, and made him laugh heartily.

" You always were a Paladin, Dick, and always will be," he said; " imagine being the friend of the widow and the orphan!"

" I often rob the rich to give to the poor," grinned Dick; " in my own home, where I am called Jack Palmer, I am looked upon as the most charitable farmer in the parish."

" You must take me to see your family, some day," replied Tom.

" I must go soon," answered Dick; " they must begin to fear I am lost. As soon as we reach London we will go; you must pass as another cattle dealer. Now, then, for a stiff last glass. This place seems very slow. Not a traveller here to-day but ourselves."

The waiter came in for orders, and Dick ordered a bowl of punch—hot, sweet, and strong.

" Our horses have been seen to, I presume?" asked courteous Dick Turpin. " I should think you had plenty of time. You don't seem to be very busy here."

" Well, sir, not just now; but market days our house is that crowded you can scarce get served, and also when 'sizes is on," said the waiter, proudly.

And he went out to fetch the bowl of punch, with which he soon returned. It was steaming hot, smelt delicious, and Dick, in the warmth of his heart, poured out a tumbler for the attendant, who drank it without even winking, strong as it was.

Half an hour later they took their little lamps and went to bed, giving strict orders to be called at nine.

They did ample justice to their breakfast, and at ten o'clock precisely started on horseback for the bank. Tom remained outside, while Dick went in. He found Mr. Crowder awaiting him.

He had already seen the manager and made everything all right. All they had to do was to walk in and take the money.

" I have transferred the trust cheque to my account, while your money awaits you," said Crowder. " I have told the manager what I owe to you."

And they went straight to the manager's room, where Dick took his money, drank a glass of wine with the urbane banker, and then retired to join his comrade.

Mr. Crowder, however, insisted on their coming round to 10, Vigo Street, to receive Mrs. Armstrong's thanks, which they could not very well refuse to do. They had evidently saved her son's fortune, which the false trustee would have made away with when it suited his purpose.

The friends alighted and went into the house, where Mrs. Armstrong awaited them with extreme impatience. She would not be denied, and, though they could not breakfast, they had to indulge in several drinks before they were allowed to depart.

They at last got leave to go. All this time they had heard no news of Mr. Richard Rochford and Joe Stammers. But this mystery was soon to be solved.

A clerk came in with the fearful news that the principal and clerk were both dead. There had evidently been a fearful struggle. Rochford had been strangled by Joe Stammers, who in return had, while dying, stabbed him to the heart.

They were found on the floor, still clutched as in the death struggle.

" You will stay to the inquest?" said Mr. Crowder. Mrs. Armstrong had fainted, while the clerk had rushed back to be present when the authorities came. " All must be exposed now, all explained—the real will, the forgery, everything. Your evidence will be invaluable."

" Mr. Crowder," said Dick, in an earnest tone, " do you feel grateful to us?"

" Most deeply so. You have saved my future wife and stepson from comparative ruin. How can you doubt our gratitude?" asked Crowder, warmly.

" Then do not detain us. I will trust to your honour and generosity when I tell you a secret which explains our fear of detention. We have acted fair and square to you, because I was indignant at the rascality of those rogues. If we were detained it might prove awkward. My name is Dick Turpin, and my friend's Tom King."

Crowder started back, incredulous. But for the solemn occasion he would have laughed.

" Why this joke?" he said.

" It is no joke, Mr. Crowder. We are now wholly in your power."

" Go—in heaven's name!" cried the other, shaking both their hands, " and in the hour of your greatest need may this generous, noble deed be remembered to you."

" Thanks," was the quiet and simple reply; after which they went out, mounted their horses, and rode off, leaving Mr. Crowder petrified with horror.

All the villainy of Rochford and Joe Stammers came out on the inquest, while the strangers were spoken of as the innocent means of their discovery.

Dick had told Crowder just at the last how he had overheard them at the inn.

When Mrs. Armstrong heard the truth with regard to her benefactors she was wild with surprise, and, we fancy, retained a sneaking regard for highwaymen for the rest of her life.

CHAPTER LXXVII.
RETURN TO LONDON.

The two highwaymen had made so good a use of their Lewes adventure that they seemed to feel at peace with all the world. They determined, therefore, to go direct to London, have a night's enjoyment, and then pay a visit to the home of Dick Turpin, where they could well afford to spend a week.

Meanwhile there was deep distress in the house of Jack Palmer. He had never been away so long before, and both his wife and daughter were exceedingly distraught about him.

They began to fear that on his long journey he had fallen ill or met with some mishap. He was known to have carried large sums of money about him, and in those days highwaymen abounded.

Lucy's wedding day had been fixed for the following Thursday, and it was now Monday. All the preparations had been made, but, unless the head of the family turned up, they would be useless.

The lover was rather sulky about the matter. Still, though he was in the dumps, he did not go to the length of expecting Lucy to marry in her father's absence. Still, when Jack Palmer did come home he meant to have it out with him, and beg him to stop at home. He had a comfortable farm, had put a goodish bit of money in his wife's name in the bank, and could well afford to retire on his laurels.

It was nearly dinner time at the farm, which was also a dairy, and the labourers were coming in to their meals, with that steady regularity which appertains to your true Briton.

Frank and Lucy were seated in the portico, where there was a bench on each side. They were talking, as lovers will talk, and have talked since the earliest days, that which is utter nonsense to everybody else, but which is sweet to them.

"Here's father!" suddenly cried Lucy Palmer, jumping up, "with a stranger."

In an instant the farm was in an uproar, Mrs. Palmer leaving her workpeople to the tender mercies of a deputy.

Mr. Palmer rode up, submitted manfully to embraces and reproaches, and then introduced his friend as Mr. Markham, who had come to spend a day or two.

"And now let us have something to eat," he said; "we've ridden a goodish way this morning, and feel hungry."

The dinner was ready. In those days there was no stint at English tables, and what was provided for three would generally prove more than enough for twice as many.

Mrs. Palmer asked for five minutes to see to the cloth being laid, which was given her, and then the party filed in. The meal was well cooked, the ale splendid, and the conversation pleasant.

Mr. Markham wondered that, with such a haven of rest, Dick should be tempted to go wandering about the land risking his life at every venture, knowing full well how some day the matter must end.

When dinner was over, more potent liquors were put on the table and the glasses filled.

"One moment, my man; do you know what next Thursday is?" asked Mrs. Palmer.

"No; somebody's birthday?" asked Jack.

"Father!" cried Lucy, in accents of mild, but sad reproach.

"Well, what's up; what have I done?" asked the bewildered head of the family.

"Don't you know it's Lucy's wedding day?" observed Mrs. Palmer, demurely.

"Dang it, but I'd forgotten," said Jack Palmer, slapping his thigh with a hearty bang;

"well! well! it's a good job I've come home. Markham, you must stop to see them turned off!"

And Jack Palmer winked atrociously at his companion, who grinned all over his face.

"Certainly," said Mr. Thomas Markham; "couldn't think of going away until that interesting event is over."

"I wish, Palmer," said his future son-in-law, "you'd stop at home altogether. You're comfortable enough, and ought to be happy here. Come, father."

"It isn't that I aint happy, Frank; but I'm too young to settle down yet. I like an active life, and seem never to be so happy as when on horseback. A canter over a heath is to me the greatest pleasure in life; but I'll think about it. And so it's Thursday, eh, lassie?" chucking his daughter under her chin; "so he was afraid it might be put off, eh? Well, here's to the health of the bridegroom; fill a fresh glass, Markham."

He was obeyed, and the toast being drank, conversation turned on the events of the coming Thursday. Dick almost wished he had saved some of the jewels that had passed through his hands; but on reflection knew that this might have proved dangerous. He resolved, therefore, to buy some presents.

After dinner the women retired to attend to household duties, leaving the men to grog and pipes.

"I say, Frank, I'm sorry I forgot the day," said Jack Palmer, "or I'd have brought some trinkets. Will you buy her a watch and chain?" he added, putting down twenty guineas; "bring it on the morning, or when you like."

"And allow me," remarked Thomas Markham, putting down five guineas, "to ask you to buy the young lady the best ring you can for the money."

"With great pleasure," responded the honest young farmer, wringing their hands in his frank delight.

It was a pleasure, indeed, to be son-in-law to such a fine, generous fellow.

"I wish, though," continued Frank, "you'd stop at home. Mrs. Palmer is main anxious when you're away. She dreams that you will be robbed and murdered some day; we've heard rare stories, of late, of Dick Turpin, Jack Sheppard, and others, and you often have a goodish bit of money with you."

"We aint afraid of those sort of people, are we, Tom?" said Palmer, with a rather constrained laugh; "but I'll think the matter over. The next time I make a big haul, I'll stop at home three months, and see how I like it."

With this promise his future son-in-law was compelled to be satisfied, and shortly after took his leave to attend to business, principally to purchase presents for his bride.

Little did Frank imagine how the few words he had said about Turpin rankled in his father-in-law's breast. At home, in that atmosphere of innocence and peace, he wished always to forget.

"Smart young fellow that," remarked Tom King, drily; "he'll make your daughter happy, I fancy. Really, if I was you, I'd be half inclined to take his advice."

"No, no! It may be it'll come to that some day," replied Jack Palmer, rather sadly; "but not yet. I should die of weariness. No, no! Perhaps when I'm old and stiff it may come, ut not now. Let's go down to the 'Cock and Bottle' for an hour."

Dick went to the kitchen, where his wife and daughter were at work.

"I'm going for a stroll," he said, "with my friend. Have supper at seven, and let my London friend see what a farmer's wife and daughter can do."

Miss Palmer smiled, kissed her father, and then with a smile said, "don't be late and spoil the supper. I know what the 'Cock and Bottle' is."

"No, my dear, we won't be late," said Jack Palmer, laughing; "but who said anything about the 'Cock and Bottle?'"

"As if I didn't know what your strolls meant!" she said, saucily.

"Mrs. Palmer," he continued, in a grave but bantering manner, "is this the way you bring up your children?"

"Dear old dad!" said Lucy, and pushed him out of the kitchen.

A few unbidden tears came into his eyes, which he hastily wiped away, and Richard was himself again when he rejoined Mr. Thomas Markham.

The inn was at no great distance. It was the scene of the great single-stick fight, and need not, therefore, be described again.

At that hour of the day it was not much frequented; but Jack Palmer found one or two ready to welcome him, and all became jovial. Presently Frank joined them. He was on his way to supper at the farm, and thought he might, by looking in, secure the attendance of his future father-in-law and his friend.

The parlour gradually filled. It had gone abroad that Jack Palmer had returned, and he was so popular, and his presence so infrequent, that every one rushed to have a drink with him and a shake of the hand.

Everybody was jolly, when the door opened and Brian Seymour and Robert Woodstock entered. They were handsomely dressed, and, having been riding along the road, one of their horses had got a stone in his shoe, which had so lamed him that they had to halt while it was being seen to.

Dick Turpin shivered, turned ghastly pale, drank off a glass, and then grew stern and determined. He had made up his mind.

"By the way, Jones," he said, in strident tones, which were heard in every part of the room, "I have not been in these parts for so long that I am behind hand with the news. Has anything been heard of the murderers of the two old ladies in Chelsea?"

"No, sir," replied the village constable, respectfully; "the officers have pretty well given up the case."

"Well, it's no business of mine," continued Mr. Jack Palmer; "but if I were a Bow Street runner I'd have spotted them long ago. Who gained by their death? who knew the old house and its ways? who was seen in the neighbourhood with a bundle that very night?"

"But, sir," remarked Jones, "if you know so much, why not spot them?"

"I'm not of the sort to turn informer," said the other, loftily; "but if I ever do come across the fellows I'll spot 'em. It's a crying shame that men who hold their heads high should escape, when a poor pickpocket is hanged for five shillings."

Brian Seymour and Robert Woodstock sat spellbound in the corner. They had recognised Dick Turpin, and were planning how to take advantage of their discovery, when they heard his words and were appalled. That he would carry out his threat if they in any way interfered with him they firmly believed.

He was evidently here among friends. Little did they suspect the truth, or adieu to Jack Palmer's peace of mind.

They finished their drink and summoned the waiter, asking if their horses were ready.

"Yes, sir," was the quick reply; "quite ready."

"Then we'll continue our journey," said Brian, rising, and going out without looking to the right or left.

Jack Palmer's object was attained. They departed without even asking the name of the very loud speaker. He chuckled as they went out.

"Drove those heavy swells away!" said one.

"Did you know them?" he asked.

"Well," replied Jack Palmer, "they're the kiddies as benefited by the murder, that's all I know. Yes, my lad," addressing Frank, "I know time's up. One moment, Smith," addressing the waiter, "glasses round!"

These were brought in very rapid fashion, having, in fact, been ordered for a quarter to seven.

"Thursday, friends all, my daughter will be married to my friend here," tapping Frank on the shoulder. "They will be strung up and turned off at eleven, and at twelve there will be dinner for all friends and neighbours. I shall fit up the old and new barns, and then, after dinner, those who like to dance, shall. Drink to their healths!"

And everybody did. This is the way Dick Turpin spent his money at home. Many a good, honest, plodding man does not do half so much good with his allotted wealth; storing it while alive, and leaving it to spendthrift heirs to make "ducks and drakes" of.

Meanwhile, terror-stricken and appalled, Brian and Robert had ridden off.

"That villain knows too much," muttered Brian, with a savage curse. "What infernal unlucky wind brought him there? He seemed cock of the walk. Up to some of his tricks. We must get rid of him. We can't denounce him, he would have us on the hip. Though known as a highwayman, his testimony in this case would be taken. Suspicion must be diverted; we must hang someone. Why not old Martha, or the boy?"

"How can we do that?" asked Robert.

"We can have sudden suspicions—I can shake my head—then some of the plunder, or similar plunder which we can swear to, that will enough," continued the vile and unscrupulous plotter.

And with this monstrous scheme in their heads, the two ruffians rode off to London.

<hr>

CHAPTER LXXVIII.

WEDDING BELLS.

After supper that evening, Frank handed over the watch and chain to the master of the house and the ring to his friend, Tom Markham.

"Here, Lucy," said Jack Palmer, "I didn't mean to give this to you until Thursday; but it's safer in your custody than mine. My friend, Tom, here, has something for you, too."

Lucy was delighted. Her father was always liberal; but though she had many trinkets, she had none like these.

"You are kind, papa," she cried; "and you, sir; I'm so much obliged. Frank, arn't they nice?"

"Yes! but not so nice as their owner," said Frank, gallantly.

"Nonsense, Frank," said the pleased and gratified girl. "Don't be foolish."

Such is young love. How often does all this foolish fondness end before a year is out, and the stern realities of life take its place!

"Jerusa!" says a new-made American bride, "ain't you going to take me out to-night to eat ices and sweets?"

"Molly, I'm surprised at you," replies the amazed husband; "you forget we've been married six weeks."

"I don't think we're wanted, Tom," remarked Jack Palmer; "let's take a stroll for an hour."

Mrs. Palmer pouted, Lucy smiled, Frank laughed, and away the men went.

"That was a risky thing for you to do," observed Tom, when they were out of hearing, "to beard those fellows."

"The cravens know themselves guilty," replied his friend. "I was at the 'Grotto' on the night of the double murder, and saw them sneak off in a hackney coach with a bundle. This would be enough to set the officers on their track, and to cause inquiries to be made. The servants of the old women would prove their presence there that night."

"True!" remarked Tom, and the subject dropped—to be revived in a most startling manner.

*   *   *   *   *

Time passed swiftly, and Thursday morning came, bright and sunshiny. All were astir betimes and at work. Everybody had a holiday from anything except what was connected with the marriage festivities.

They were of the usual rural and rustic character. The church was decked with flowers, the children and young people brought bouquets, and the elders other presents.

At eleven, the wedding procession started in a waggon, decked for the occasion. drawn by four horses, which made a grand floral show, supplemented by ribbons.

Frank met them at the church, as did all their friends, except the bridesmaids, who were rosy, apple-cheeked girls, dressed in every colour of the rainbow.

The ceremony was duly performed, and then the important business of the day began. What was a wedding, indeed, without feasting? In modern times fashionable and town weddings generally are rather shorn of their resplendent hospitality.

In the country, however, where it can be afforded, everything goes on pretty well as usual.

The dinner in the barns was a great success. Jack Palmer had outshone himself, and the meal was resplendent. Nothing was wanting that any heart, young or old, could wish for in the way of meat, poultry, pies, and puddings, with beer and spirits galore.

These people were not educated up to wine at this time.

The dinner was a long and ponderous affair, but at length even the most hungry appetite was appeased. The tables were cleared, and the musicians began to tune up.

The tables were brought outside, and supplied with seats, liquor and tobacco for the elders, who made up their minds to enjoy themselves with material comforts, while the younger ones danced.

This they did until, at seven o'clock, with renewed appetites, they sat down to supper, at which Mr. Jack Palmer and others made some rather confused speeches, which, however, were uproariously applauded.

The meal ended at nine, after which both Jack and Tom were carried to bed, muttering certain anathemas, which, luckily, were not understood.

The jolly party soon broke up, the young husband and wife slipping away on horseback quite unnoticed, to the disgust and disappointment of some who had intended to give them a salvo of rather coarse bucolic humour before they departed.

Dick and Tom remained until Monday, Frank insisting on their paying himself and wife a visit on the Sunday. Mr. and Mrs. Palmer found their child both happy and contented, and Dick in his heart rejoiced that his daughter was so well provided for, so that whatever might be his fate, she would be well cared for.

This Mrs. Palmer was, amply, as far as money was concerned, while she was in everything qualified to manage a farm.

A very jolly day was spent, and next day, after breakfast, the two highwaymen started for town.

They had enjoyed themselves thoroughly; but both were eager for London and its delights, while, as they expressed themselves, business must be attended to.

Dick used all his usual precautions as to leaving his home, passed through the wooded pathway as usual, changed his clothes at the hiding place, and then cantered on to London full of health and spirits.

Dick's first duty was to go to the address he had given to the Blue Dwarf; but found that no message had been received, which assured them that all was well in that quarter.

Now Turpin was too shrewd a judge of human nature not to know how bitter Brian Seymour and his colleague would be against him. While he lived they were never safe. He rightly judged that, while seeking to trace the hiding place of the earl and family, they would try to remove from their path one who, like himself, was a thorn in their sides.

It behoved him, therefore, to constantly keep his eyes about him, for fear he might fall into some well-laid trap.

Open violence he despised, as he had too much confidence in his own powers to fear any man that ever lived. Treachery was what he had to fear upon the part of these two villainous schemers.

When they entered into any of their old haunts, they looked keenly around for any sign of their foes.

On the second night of their arrival, they strolled into "Paddy's Goose" for a night's joviality. They found the usual crowd there of every sort, but on this occasion went at once to the gambling end of the shop.

Here they found Joe Askew, sleek, well-looking, in the act of playing for small sums. He winced at sight of them, but when Dick beckoned to him, came at once at his call.

"Down on your luck?" observed Dick.

"Not particularly," replied Joe; "but I never play for high stakes except against a flat, and there ain't many here."

"No," said Dick, laughing. "Well, here's a guinea. I only want to ask a question, but you must answer it truly."

"I will if I can," was the reply.

"Have you seen Brian Seymour and Robert Woodstock lately?" asked Dick Turpin.

"I saw them yesterday," he answered, "and they were asking the same question about you."

"Well, that is funny," laughed Dick. "Now look you, Askew; let byegones be byegones. You keep straight and fair, and you shall lose nothing by it. Don't answer these questions about me, but give me a hint now and then of their movements. You need never want a guinea."

"Well, sir," replied Joe Askew, "they think me safe still, and have set me to watch for the Blue Dwarf. He and his friends were last seen, they say, somewhere Gad's Hill way. They gave out about going abroad; but Brian, he don't believe that, so he's ordered me to go down that road and make all the inquiries I can."

"Do just as you like," retorted Dick Turpin, carelessly; "but, I tell you, you will find nothing. I know all about them; but that's my business."

"He's got a young fellow who is up to any rascality," continued Joe. "He calls himself Teddy, and he's been poking about. I believe he's gone somewhere to the sea side, in that direction, in search of them."

"Thanks," said Dick, handing him another guinea. "Don't go anywhere for a day or two."

"All right, sir;" and Joe Askew, touching his hat, returned to the gaming table.

Dick Turpin at once determined to send off a warning to the Blue Dwarf to beware of Teddy, the spy, who might, in the chapter of accidents, stumble on their retreat.

This determined on, both sat down among the herd of gamblers, with varying success. Towards morning they got level, and went off to some place where they could get creature refreshments.

They went to the nearest house, where we have already accompanied them, and having fed gloriously, went home.

Here, on rising, Dick wrote a letter to the post office, Lewes, where a messenger was to call every day.

*   *   *   *   *

While Dick Turpin's letter is on its way through Lewes to Brighthelmstone, we will return to Brian Seymour and Robert Woodstock.

What Dick Turpin had said at the "Cock and Bottle" was of itself appalling enough, but with other little hints the consequences might be dreadful.

The two men met one evening at the lodgings of Brian Seymour. They had talked the matter over, and resolved that, by fair means or foul, Dick Turpin and his companion must be got rid of. Both were too well aware of the character of the officers not to know of the existence of some compact amongst the runners.

To capture the highwaymen in London in one of their ordinary haunts would not suit their ideas. They wanted not only the reward, but the glory.

They must, if they would be safe, get rid, at all events, of Dick Turpin. Of course, in his anomalous position he could not very easily appear against them; but he might put the officials on the right scent, and inquiries at the house, by proving their presence in the house.

But the idea of forestalling any suspicion by accusing the two servants in the house still rankled in the cold-blooded villains' minds. Should everything else fail, this must be done.

The family at Brighthelmstone lived, of course, in great seclusion. Had there been anybody living in that quiet place suited to their rank and position, still the necessity of privacy would have prevented them from making any acquaintances or friends.

Until the hour came when he could make his will break the entail, and exclude Brian altogether. Once of age, it was his intention to seek the protection of the law.

The whole of Brian's machinations would be disclosed to view unless he left the country, or abstained from any molestation. All this was agreed on.

Shelton and Laura, with the baby and the servant which had charge of the precious treasure—of course, like most parents, they thought the little one a *rara avis*—were out one morning, at about twelve, sauntering about a green lane near the house, when the servant from Lewes came in sight. He rode up, touched his hat, and said there was a letter for Sapathwa.

"Go on," replied the earl, "we will follow."

The domestic obeyed. When they reached the house they found their three friends closeted together. Sapathwa held up a letter.

"It does not contain pleasant news," he said; "but there is no cause for immediate alarm, but that young cub, Brian's new agent, thinks we are somewhere down this way."

Shelton sighed. His wife had gone to the nursery with the nurse and baby. Was his wretched and miserable persecution never to cease? In the pride of his heart he had announced the birth of his son and heir. Had he not been unwise, for might not Brian Seymour in his utter unscrupulousness aim at him through his child?

If anything did happen through Brian's grasping avarice and vindictive hate, he would not hesitate to slay him with his own hands.

He awaited the arrival of Dick Turpin with some anxiety. The highwayman was not much of a letter-writer, and his personal explanation was much desired.

But all that day they looked out for him in vain, nor did he turn up that night. They waited until midnight, and then retired to rest, taking care to fasten every door, window, and shutter.

What had detained Dick Turpin? We shall see.

CHAPTER LXXIX.
THE SPY'S FATE.

When Dick Turpin and Tom King left London on the way to Brighthelmstone to report in person to the Blue Dwarf, about half way the two friends determined to separate, and enter every house they passed in search of the young sleuth hound.

Dick Turpin took the direct road to the sea-shore, while Tom King diverged to that one which led to Lewes.

We will follow Dick Turpin, who went along at a leisurely pace, entering every inn and tavern he passed, and examining those in the bar and in the parlour.

When about fifteen miles from Brighthelmstone he entered a little, old-fashioned public-house, whose very appearance satisfied you you were miles and miles away in the country, and had found a real village hostelry. That it was old, its porch, low windows, and high-pitched roof undoubtedly proved. More than this, infallible sign, on entering you had to descend two steps; and even then, if you were not careful, your head would bob against a protruding beam, unless, indeed, you were a dwarf or a mannikin, producing an effect which was, to say the least, undesirable.

The proof that it was far from the busy haunts of men was supported by the poultry, ducks, and geese that rambled the place with an air of conscious authority and fearless of molestation. Again, a few trees surrounding it cut off any evidences of other dwellings; and at the back was a real old-time smithy, where you could see the red glow of the cinders and hear the roar of the bellows, accompanied by the clinking of the hammers all day long.

He entered; the landlord, fat, jolly, and red—so red that his face seemed to radiate heat, and materially enhance the dazzling brilliance of his clean white apron—stood behind the bar with one hand resting lovingly on a pull of the beer-engine, and an inviting smile rippling on his rubicund features, as much as to say—"Come in and drink my ale, and be as jovial as myself."

Dick, who had got a boy to hold his horse, went up to the bar and ordered a pint of the best ale. Having seated himself on a bench, he nodded to the company and put the measure to his lips.

As he did so, he scanned the visitors in the bar. They were five in number, four undoubted natives. The fifth was a nondescript. He was shabbily dressed, with old top boots, corduroy breeches, a seedy coat that had once been fine and fashionable, a face slightly scored with scars, and a scratch wig of the ugliest make.

Dick, having half-finished his measure, put it down on the bench and made some observation about the weather. Being always of a jovial and merry disposition he soon "set the table in a roar," so to speak, and won all hearts by standing treat all round. He took very little notice of the stranger in the corner, who himself was reticent and silent.

Presently, Dick Turpin rose, tossed off a small mug of brandy, after which he went out, mounted, and rode off. He had scarcely disappeared when the stranger also hurried out, called for his horse, and being attended, rode off in the direction taken by the highwayman.

Dick cast his eyes over his shoulder and smiled. The other was just falling into the trap which he had set for him.

Dick never attempted to quicken his pace for some time, indeed, for several miles, when suddenly he loosened the reins, touched his horse with his whip, and started at a gallop.

For a moment the pursuing horseman appeared to lose his presence of mind, but then spurred up his steed and started in pursuit.

His mount was a good one and soon he was moving with great rapidity along the road.

But the foremost horseman had already gained considerably on the rearward one. He could occasionally catch a glimpse of him, and when he could not see him could still hear his hoof-clang on the stony road.

He hurried on, fearful of losing the track. He already knew enough of Dick to be aware of his artfulness and cunning, and feared he would play him some trick.

On! on! he went steadily, urging his steed forward. There were some turnings and windings in the road, which, as a rule, however, was tolerably straight, and then he reached a part of the highway where it was lined on each side by a thick growth of forest, while on each also was a strip of greensward.

All sound of the horse in front had ceased, but that probably was accounted for by the sward.

He kept on, therefore, pressing his horse to its utmost and highest speed. The road was now quite dark, and he had to use considerable caution as he moved along.

Another mile he went, and found the road narrow rapidly until in one place the overhanging branches were down so low as to nearly brush off his hat.

Still he plunged onward, to be brought to a sudden stop by two outstretched arms, one on each side, which caught his bridle, and brought his horse to a stand still.

"Hands off!" he cried.

"No, my frolicsome kiddy," said the sarcastic voice of Dick Turpin, "you have thrust yourself into a hornet's nest, and you don't get out without being stung."

In another moment his two captors—for Tom had rejoined Dick but a few minutes before—were hurrying him along. He would have struggled, but knew that it was useless. He was in the hands of two powerful and merciless men, and submission was his only course.

After trotting about half a mile, they halted just where a sign-post stood on a small green, and, dismounting themselves, made him do the same. They now carried him to the post, produced some cords, and one propping him up, the other tied him to the square piece of wood with knots, which not even the hangman could have improved on.

Teddy, for it was the irrepressible Teddy, the agent and spy of Brian Seymour, resisted and bellowed—all in vain. They only laughed and jeered, which was perhaps very cruel, but quite natural; and having successfully prevented him from spying on them for the future, they gave him each a cut on the back, and rode off.

With many a wild and savage oath, with many a heartrending curse, did Teddy pursue them, wishing all the time he had never mixed himself up with the affairs of Brian Seymour.

Presently he pricked up his ears. He could hear the heavy lumbering trot of a cart-horse coming his way.

"Help! murder! help!" he yelled with loud and piercing cries that rent the welkin.

Still the lumbering trot continued, and presently up came a farmer's boy, mounted on a big horse, who rode up to where the unfortunate spy was bellowing more like a bull than anything else.

"What's oop?" asked the yokel.

"Been assaulted by highwaymen and tied here to starve," was the answer.

"Then you ain't got no money?" the simple bucolic replied.

"Yes, I have; and I'll give it you if you cut me free," exclaimed Teddy.

The boy dismounted. Teddy. whose arms were free, fumbled in his waistcoat and produced a guinea.

"Make haste," he said, holding up the coin between his finger and thumb; "cut me free, and it is yours."

"Noa!" answered the boy, grinning with the genuine simplicity and innocence of the country bumpkin, "give it I to see first. It might be a bad un."

Teddy had no choice but to give it up. As soon as the boy got it he squatted down on a convenient milestone and began to examine the coin. He rubbed it, he bit it, he spat upon it, and then, hesitated.

"Are you going to cut me loose?" gasped Teddy, frantic with rage.

"You ain't got another of these 'ere things?" asked the boy, with a drawl.

"No! but if you cut me loose quick and take me somewhere where I can get a bed——"

The youngster grinned.

"Not such a fool as I looks," he said. "You wants to take t'other from I."

And turning towards his horse, the yokel took his departure, chuckling. He left Teddy in a frantic state of mind, which he manifested by curses and oaths.

Suddenly he gave a great start. Close to his feet the boy had dropped a clasp knife, with which he had originally intended to cut his bonds. His foot touched it, and after superhuman exertions, for Dick had securely fastened him, he was able to clutch it.

With a wild war whoop cry, he cut himself loose, and mounting, followed in the track of the boy.

One mile further on was an inn, and here Teddy at once determined to put up.

He entered, and the first thing he saw was the boy, intent on bread and cheese and beer. He had recognised the boy, but the boy had had no real opportunity of seeing him.

He was half choked in his endeavours to eat, drink, and tell the story of the flat he had diddled out of a guinea.

"Yes, you scoundrel," said Teddy, catching him by the ear; "you miserable little cur, if you don't give me back my guinea I'll send for a constable."

And to the astonished labourers and the landlord he told his story. The boy looked very blue, but, fumbling in his pocket, produced the guinea and returned it.

"Now, my lad, another time you'll reflect that honesty is the best policy," said Teddy, sententiously. "I offered him another half-guinea if he would cut me loose and bring me to where I could get a decent bed."

"Eh, Bill, but you're a pretty rascal!" observed the landlord, "you deserve to be hung for serving a gentleman so."

Bill made no reply, but, finishing his cheese, rose and went sullenly out of the house, a dark and furious scowl upon his brow.

Teddy thoroughly enjoyed himself, and after supper went to bed, ordering one of the servants to call him early.

When they knocked at the door, there was no answer. The door was not fastened, and, going in, the chamber-maid was horrified to find the unfortunate Teddy lying stone dead, with his throat cut.

An alarm was at once given and the landlord summoned.

His first impulse was to search the clothes. Not a penny was to be found.

"It's that boy, Bill Hayward!" cried the landlord; "he's been and killed him—and all for a few guineas."

It was true, and Bill Hayward was arrested with the blood on his clothes and the money in his pocket.

He was found guilty, condemned, and hanged.*

————

CHAPTER LXXX.

MEANWHILE Dick Turpin and Tom King were utterly ignorant of the terrible fate which had befallen Brian Seymour's unscrupulous spy, and had ridden on to Brighthelmstone.

There was no inn there, but at a small farmhouse refreshments were to be obtained in a kind of barn. Hither the two men went, got some refreshments, and passed the night on a pile of straw.

In the morning, leaving Tom King to do the best he could, Dick Turpin sauntered across the downs in the direction of Penshere. He reached it about eight o'clock, and was at once admitted to the presence of the Blue Dwarf, to whom he explained what had passed.

He could not but smile at the way in which they had served the spy, little imagining the terrible and fatal end which had been that of Teddy.

A brief conference was held, and then it was determined that the two highwaymen should return to London, passing where they had left their unfortunate victim.

"I shall be in London in a few days," said Sapathwa, "and then you can let me know what has happened. Brian Seymour is near the end of his tether. I have made up my mind, rather than that he shall continue to persecute Shelton Seymour, to cut the ground from under his feet."

Dick Turpin knew his place too well to ask questions, and shortly afterwards took his departure, as usual well rewarded for his services.

After making a plain but hearty meal in the shape of breakfast at the farm, the two started. Their intention was to try back, calling at every inn for news.

When they reached the "Fortune of War" they noticed a crowd hanging about, and went in, a kind of presentiment actuating them both.

It was almost as crowded inside as out, but the people made way for two respectable-looking travellers.

Finding all other places crowded, they made their way to the bar parlour, where the landlord was with some of his cronies.

"What's the matter?" asked Dick, when he had given his orders.

"Murder's the matter, sir!" said the master of the house. "A poor traveller, sir, as slept here last night, murdered by a boy."

And he told the whole story, to which Dick

* Even as late as 1881, a boy of thirteen was murdered by another boy of fourteen for the sake of nine shillings which he had in his pocket. He was duly hanged.

and Tom listened with apparently deep interest, but in reality with awe and terror.

Of course it was no fault of theirs; but still it was errible. The spy was bent on aiding and abetting crime, but still it was a fearful ending.

Of course there was no doubt about the identity, as the young man had told his own story, putting his misadventure generally upon highwaymen. There was no necessity, therefore, for further delay; and, finishing their glasses, they remounted and rode off.

On reaching London, Dick managed to scrawl a few lines to the Blue Dwarf, giving brief details of what had happened, and promising fuller details when Sapathwa came to town.

They now resolved to amuse themselves. Dick did, however, pay a visit home to see his wife and family, but he only stopped from Saturday until Monday, leaving some money behind, and urging pressing business. He, however, threw out a hint that, perhaps, after a few more journeys he might make up his mind to retire.

On the Monday evening, on his return, he and Tom went to one of their haunts, where they knew a lot of the loose riff-raff of London.

Here they amused themselves with cards, dice, and drink.

Presently conversation turned on topics likely to interest the class who were collected there. The murder of a traveller by a boy was talked about, and some other atrocity.

"But what do you think?" asked one. "You remember that there murder of the two old women in Chelsea?"

"Yes," said the other.

"Well, a old woman and a boy is taken up for it," continued the other; "their own servants. I don't believe it. That was a put-up job."

"You don't mean that, Rasper," put in Dick; "why, I don't believe it either. Somebody as gained by it did that, mark my words."

And all nodded. The conversation went on; and, after awhile, Dick Turpin and Tom King left.

"What infernal scoundrels Brian and Robert must be," mused Dick. "But it shan't be; I'll save those two."

"How can you do it?" asked King.

"Well, I must think it out," said Dick, musing; and the two went to their several lodgings.

Next day Dick was out betimes, and went at once to the residence of a notorious Old Bailey lawyer named Bill Scroggins, who was under some obligations to him.

He paid him a fee, and then intimated that he would pay him further moneys in the future. After this he told him the charge against the old woman and the boy.

"You must see them and take up their defence. I'll find all the funds; and, what's more, I'll appear in the witness-box," said the highwayman.

"What?" gasped Bill Scroggins.

"Yes, I have no fear. I shall appear as a farmer, give my evidence, and then retire. It's no use talking to me, I mean to do it," firmly rejoined his strange client.

"A wilful man will have his way," said the other; and so they parted.

Next day Sapathwa sent for Dick, and asked for further explanations about Teddy. Of course the murder of the boy was a matter to be regretted; but it removed a troublesome instrument from their enemies' hands.

Dick then told him about the Chelsea murder, all his suspicions, and the determination he had come to to appear as witness for the accused.

Sapathwa applauded him warmly, and signified his intention of paying all expenses.

Dick expressed his deep gratitude; and so they separated, and both returned to their mutual occupations.

Two or three days later, Dick Turpin, having found out the day of the trial, which would take place three weeks later, went out on an expedition.

CHAPTER LXXXI.

"FIVE HUNDRED POUNDS REWARD."

The two highwaymen, as we are aware, seldom commenced operations near any of those places where they were generally or personally known.

Innkeepers, ostlers, and men of that kidney were excepted.

The place selected now was almost new ground. They had done a little stroke of business on the road once, and been sheltered at the "Royal Oak" inn, a busy place enough for a country village, which did, in fact, a very good trade, being frequented, one day a week, by farmers, on others, by stray bagmen and other travellers, and in the evening by gentlemen's servants and the usual small fry of the village.

Dick Turpin and Tom King were well aware that in these reunions gossip predominated quite as much as in any drum at the West End, or coterie at a club.

Mrs. Marsham was a host in herself, and quite ready to tell all the news of the neighbourhood. She was rather stiff, and hard and angular in appearance, but, in truth, she was kindly, buxom, and hearty, while her success in the hostelrie had long existed, irrespective and without any reference to her personality. It was the scrupulous cleanliness of the rooms, and the order, the well-aired beds with snowy covers, and the well-cooked, well-served meals, that visitors to the "Royal Oak" inn rejoiced over.

Dick Turpin had always appeared to her, personally, as a well-to-do commercial traveller, who aimed at marrying a rich widow.

Only Josh Parkins, the ostler, suspected the real character of the man who owned that spanking mare, and interest, as a matter of course, kept him quiet.

It was about four o'clock of a clear, bright, frosty afternoon, when the two high tobies rode along the road in the direction of Wickham, near Doncaster. Both were in good spirits, and, as usual with men of their character and pursuits, took little heed of anything but the immediate future.

When within a mile-and-a-half of the village, the sky, a dull grey, save where it warmed to lurid copper in the west, indicated that somewhere in that region—somewhere far away behind the thick gloom—a sun had set.

It was not an afternoon when anyone would care much to be out for a walk, it was rather one for homes and firesides; yet a young girl was just opening the green gate that led to a plain uncompromising white house.

"What house is that?" asked Dick, with his politest bow.

"Elm House," she answered, and went towards the residence.

It was an old, square house, among a lot of elm trees, with here and there dark evergreens, rank and overgrown, pressing round the house in solemn rows. It was by no means a cheerful place, and the two travellers seemed glad to escape the gloom which hung over it.

Half-a-mile further they came in sight of a very different place. A sudden turn in the road brought some great iron gates into view. Behind these was the house—large, low, red brick. It was, in fact, a perfect Elizabethan mansion, surrounded by as many hundred acres as Elm House had roods.

This was Ferrers Lodge, a place Dick had seen and heard of once before. It belonged to a great absentee nobleman, Lord Ferrers Leigh.

"Nice place that," remarked Tom; "some rich old curmudgeon, I suppose, owns it."

"I think not," replied Dick; "but Lord Ferrers Leigh is, I believe, a man of great wealth."

"Ah," said Tom; "that's the sort of crib to crack."

"If he's at home it might be," Dick went on; "but he generally sends all his plate and jewellery to the Doncaster Bank."

Twenty minutes later they arrived at the inn, ordering dinner and beds, and then adjourning to the public room.

It was early, and not one visitor had, as yet, entered the public room or parlour, as it was always called.

Dick and his friend were quite satisfied. They knew that someone would turn up in time for them to hear all the gossip. They, accordingly, enjoyed their dinner with the appetite of hearty Englishmen who want no adjuncts to eat the beef and mutton of ordinary life.

When the cloth was cleared, and a bowl of steaming punch, with pipes, brought in, the two travellers prepared, complacently, to spend the evening. They, however, quietly summoned Josh Parkins, and bade him to see carefully to their horses, which were to be kept saddled.

"House closes early ?" asked Dick.

"Half-past-ten," replied Josh Parkins.

"Be in the yard at eleven," continued Dick, with a peculiar wink.

Josh nodded, and went out; not a minute too soon. From that moment a stream of visitors and idlers came in, ordered grogs and pipes, and began to talk. For a time Dick and Tom kept their conversation to themselves, listening. Suddenly, just as they were about to join in the general hubbub, a man lounged in, and nodded to several present.

He then gave order for several drinks for himself and personal friends, and then rose and went out.

"What ails Gerald Blount," asked one; "he seems uneasy."

"Just what has ailed him since he left his wife for that ere Lady Rochford," replied one.

"May I ask," observed Dick, "who that gentleman is ?"

"Well, his name was mentioned just now," said one, glad to air his superior knowledge, "Gerald Blount, but his history is not so well known. Some years ago he inherited Elm House, and meeting a very wealthy, excellent girl, married her for love. They seemed very happy, and the charming picture made by Ethel Lester and her bridesmaids was not soon forgotten; the beauty of the girl, and the presence of her stalwart, handsome lover.

"It was not a happy marriage; things progressed but badly with the young couple; he soon spent his money, raising mortgages on Elm House. Then he left his wife in poor lodgings, and went among his loose associates.

"The papers were full, one morning, of a fearful fire at the West End, and of the gallant rescue of a lady of rank and fashion, snatched from her very bed and borne through the fire and smoke by the strong arms of a man, whose personal appearance and bravery were much dilated upon by the sensation-seeking chroniclers, who did not fail to descant in more or less glowing terms, upon the insufficiency of her drapery to hide from indiscreet eyes the voluptuous charms of the rescued beauty.

"From that moment Gerald Blount was lost. These two were equal in beauty, and still more alike in their ill-regulated, ungovernable passions; she forsook her husband,—he forgot his neglected wife, and they eloped together.

"The Divorce Court made short work with the countess, but Gerald Blount's wife disappeared.

"Since then, the man who came in here just now and the repentant countess, lead, it is said, a cat-and-dog life, especially as his money and hers too is exhausted. What he wants near Elm House, I cannot say."

"Perhaps Lawyer Lamson may lend him some more money on the mortgage of his acres," observed one.

"No," answered the other, with a shake of his head, "he will not gammon him to that extent."

And the conversation changed to other topics, amongst others, the grand doings at Ferrers Lodge, where, in honour of Lord Leigh's return from a continental tour, with his young wife, a select party were being entertained.

Dick and Tom listened, making no remarks. A little after ten the company began to move. Except in the haunts of fashion and vice, in London, our ancestors were early birds, at all events among the middle classes, whose hard work and steady habits so conduce to the wealth and prosperity of our country.

Dick and Tom, who, as usual, occupied a double-bedded room, retired at half past ten. They locked themselves in, and waited for the house to be closed, and until the inmates had retired to rest. They proceeded meanwhile to array themselves for their night expedition, looking to their pistols, dark lanterns and masks.

At a quarter to eleven, they heard a faint, low whistle in the yard. It was a signal from Josh Parkins that the coast was clear.

They opened the window and found the ladder as directed, and went down cautiously. At the foot of the ladder stood the ostler with their two horses ready.

Dick put two guineas into the man's hand, and bade him look out sharp for their return.

The man gave a nod, and led the way to the side gate, by which they could leave. Passing through this, they found themselves in a lane, leading to the king's highway, and trotting along this, soon found themselves on the edge of Ferrers Park. It was in a ring fence, and two men with sharp knives and chisels soon made a gap, through which they led their horses, which then they fastened to the projecting bough of a tree.

Passing through a dense thicket, they soon found themselves at the rear of the mansion.

We must here pause a moment, to record a brief episode in Dick's life which occurred about a year before, when he was not in constant partnership with Tom. Hotly pursued for a more than usually audacious escapade, he left Black Bess with a horsey friend, and, hiring a quiet cob, had disguised himself as a physician wearied with long and arduous practice, and taken up his abode for the benefit of his health at the Royal Oak.

Here he remained for ten days, in fact until the hue-and-cry was well over, and appeared thoroughly to enjoy himself. Liberal, pleasant, chatty, he had made himself agreeable to all, and through the landlady had been introduced to the steward in charge of Ferrers Lodge. Under his guidance he had visited the whole of the house, and knew the use of every chamber.

The rather garrulous steward, having to deal with a gentleman from London, an able physician, had shown Dr. Freeman everything, even to the library, where, in a secret place known only to a few, the heirlooms and family jewels were kept.

Dr. Freeman was very much complimented, and smilingly bade Croxon be very cautious with strangers as a rule.

We will precede the audacious burglars to the house.

Next night was to be a ball; the gala had already lasted three days, and all the guests had retired early. The servants had done the same. Nearly all the reception rooms were on the ground floor, and the best bedrooms on the first; the house being very long and wide, without being in any way lofty.

Over the library were two small bedrooms, in one of which slept Lady Ferrers Leigh's own woman; in the other, a woman of about thirty, known as Mrs. Charlton, an assistant housekeeper.

She was very superior in appearance to her station, handsome, though sad-looking. She was silent in her manner and quiet in her habits, moving about with so soft a footstep as to make some of the servants feel quite creepy.

Not feeling very sleepy on the night in question, she loosened her hair, removed her dress, substituting her dressing gown, a relic of better days, and took up a book which proved interesting.

Presently she thought she heard a noise in the library. She listened intently, holding her breath, and presently she became aware that somebody was getting in at the window. It might be a belated guest, or a servant who had gone out on some night adventure, but still she felt as if she must satisfy herself. She simply twisted up her hair, wrapped her shawl closely round her shoulders, unlocked her door softly, and stole out upon the landing. She had a small night lamp in her hand.

She began slowly descending the stairs, and as she did so, heard the hall door creak. It was opened when she reached the third step by a man from the inside, a servant she knew well. He was a new importation from London, and had been strongly recommended to the butler.

He let another man in.

The servant, too, had a small lamp in his hand, by the light of which the woman made out the face of the intruder.

Then there was a wild scream which rent the very air as it rang through the corridors, and a woman with dishevelled hair—it had got loose—rushed down the remaining steps.

"Gerald, my husband!" she cried. "What wicked errand are you bound on?"

"My wife!" gasped the terror-stricken burglar, who was about to rob the jewel safe, with the connivance of Joe Nibson, a man he had contrived to get into the house with a false character, such as is so easily obtained by dishonest servants.

Shrieks were now heard from above. Aroused from her first sleep, the lady's maid came rushing out.

Gerald Blount knew the game was up. He knew that in his wife's recognition of him lay utter ruin and the loss of the Circe that had so bewitched him. One bound and he was beside her; two quick, dastard blows with a heavy iron instrument he had brought with him to prize open the safe, and the fearful deed was done! His horrified accomplice had already fled, and he hastened to follow his example.

By this time cries were heard from different parts of the house, bells were rung, and a general commotion ensued.

Meanwhile what had happened to Dick Turpin and Tom King?

They had found no difficulty in getting into the library, and had been there some time before Mrs. Gerald Blount, who had obtained a home and occupation through the kindness of the housekeeper, a countrywoman of hers—both were Wiltshire—had heard anything.

Once inside, Dick had walked up to an old-fashioned oak chest with iron clamps, the lid of which he easily opened. He at once took possession of several jewel cases and thrust them into his capacious pockets, Tom King helping him.

"Eh! What's that?" suddenly whispered Tom; and both, standing still, listened.

They heard the street-door open, and Dick, peering out, recognised the man of the early part of the evening.

He was about to close the door when the shriek came, and the highwayman was witness to the cruel deed perpetrated by Gerald Blount.

"Let's clear out of this," he said, in a low tone, and made for the window followed by Tom King.

Having reached the spot where their horses awaited them, they halted and held a conference.

Dick told all he had seen.

"That fellow, Gerald Blount, will get the credit of committing the burglary as well as the murder," said Dick, "so that we need not be in a hurry. There will be a pretty hubbub and hue-and-cry to-morrow. We will take it coolly. I should like to see the end."

With this they mounted their steeds, rode quietly back to the inn, were let in by Josh and at once went to their rooms, where they consumed a stiff rummer of brandy and water and went to sleep.

Long before they were down to breakfast, the murder and burglary was the talk of the village, and those who had seen Gerald Blount on the previous night in the inn parlour, were looked up too with something like awe and admiration.

The burglary, the cruel murder, were the one topic of conversation. Before midnight, men had been sent out in every direction to warn the officers of justice and search for the criminal.

When Dick Turpin and Tom King came down to breakfast, they passed through the bar, the window of which looked upon the road, on the opposite side of which was a dead wall, with a few old bills scattered here and there.

Our two high tobies were told the news. at which they pretended to be terrified and appalled.

While still speaking they were surprised to see enter the bar, a short figure in a cloak and hood, whom they recognised at once as the Blue Dwarf. He had arrived the evening before on one of his mysterious journeys, and had seen them ride up during the night.

Tom King retreated in alarm, but not so Dick; neither made any pretence of recognition, but allowed the local people to go on with their conversation.

"The officers have been sent for from all directions," said the landlady's brother; "and they do say some Bow Street runners aint far off. Oh, there comes Sam Atkins and Jim Newton in a cart, the village constable and a bill sticker," nodding to the two guests; "they aint got a bill out yet. Noa! Dang it, but they've stopped at the old wall."

It was true. The cart was drawn one side, and then the constable and the bill sticker proceeded to business, the latter using a short ladder. This he ascended, and proceeded to unfold a poster.

"Oh!" said the disappointed villager, when it was posted; "that's a old one as Jimmy sticks up when he aint got nothing else."

The two highwaymen turned and saw—

£500 REWARD

IS OFFERED TO WHOEVER SHALL FIRST BRING INTO THE HANDS OF JUSTICE THAT NOTORIOUS CRIMINAL,

DICK TURPIN,

&c., &c.

"I think I've seen that before," put in Dick; "let's have another toothful of schnaps, and then to breakfast."

Two hours later they were riding off by devious ways to London, all too intent on the local tragedy to care for what, to many, was a very common event.

The Blue Dwarf, after a brief interval, left them to pursue his way alone.

We may as well finish this episode, it will not be referred to again.

The friends were very careful in disposing of the jewellery they had taken from the library of Ferrers Lodge, and it ultimately found its way back to its owner, who never could comprehend how Gerald Blount could have got rid of his plunder.

He was taken, and six weeks later he was condemned to death. Yes. There he sat, a living, breathing man, whose stalwart frame and manly beauty had been their own destroyer, their own curse, to be in a few hours huddled, after a shameful death, into a hideous grave, dug by night within the precincts of a common gaol.

This miserable history, with that of the lady whose beauty ruined him, and the sufferings of his unhappy wife, created a tremendous sensation at the time.

We spare our readers the details of the execution, which were of the usual sombre character.

CHAPTER LXXXII.

THE CHELSEA MURDER.—THE TRIAL.

The trial was fixed for the Monday, at the Old Bailey.

One curious thing about the matter was that the prosecution had been instituted on a very slender basis. The more immediate neighbours had been talking. The truth was that Brian Seymour and Robert Woodstock had set a lot of false rumours afloat, which had reached the ears of the authorities.

These in their turn had applied to Brian Seymour, who professed to be very horrified and astonished, but hemmed and ha'ed, and said he had never suspected them.

"They may have had confederates," he said; "if so, they must have carried off the plunder. If any of it could be traced——"

The officers shook their heads. There was no chance after such a long period had elapsed. Still, they would arrest them and put them on their trial.

The horror of the old woman and the lad was great indeed when they found themselves accused of this foul and wicked crime.

Still they had to submit, and on the day coming round were arraigned and put in the dock.

The indictment was read, and then the prosecuting counsel made his statement. No one seemed to think in a crowded court that there was much evidence against them. Still, they were the servants of the deceased—they were found in the house on the morning after the murder and robbery.

It looked suspicious. The judge shook his head, the jury whispered, and the general public were divided.

Then the counsel for the defence rose. He made a very clear and lucid speech. But that which struck the listeners most, and made two hearts beat with dread and fear, was one sentence.

"If we are to judge by motives, I should unhesitatingly accuse the person who gained by the death of the two old ladies—Brian Seymour, their nephew. He spent the evening with his maiden aunts, leaving them about eleven. At half-past eleven, he and a friend were seen at the 'Priory Tavern' in the neighbourhood, and the friend was in a hackney coach with a parcel."

Profound sensation, as modern reporters would say, now prevailed in the court.

"I shall call a witness who saw them," resumed the counsel, "and I must ask the court to weigh his evidence."

He now beckoned to a man in court, a stout, farmer-looking personage, with a grey wig, spectacles, and a brown rough coat.

"Swear William Graham," said the counsel, while the attorney looked on uneasily.

"My lord," said the counsel, "will you allow the witness to tell his own story? He is not much used to courts of law, and questions may puzzle him."

"Let him speak," remarked the judge.

The man was sworn as William Graham. His

DICK TURPIN PREPARES TO POUR THE SLEEPING DRAUGHT DOWN THE LAWYER'S THROAT.

No. 16.

evidence was brief and to the purpose. He knew nothing of the two ladies who had been robbed and murdered. It was only afterwards, from the papers, that he knew of Brian Seymour having two aunts. On the night of the murder he had business at the " Priory Tavern." It was a little past the half-hour after eleven when he saw Brian Seymour come in, select a hackney coachman, take one drink, and go out. He watched him into the hackney coach, where a man he knew by sight was waiting for him. This man was Robert Woodstock, a shady man about town, a constant companion of Brian Seymour in cheating at cards and other nefarious actions.

"My lord!" yelled Brian Seymour, who had hitherto lost the power of speech, "the man is an infamous liar. Besides, there is a reward for his apprehension—he is the notorious and infamous highwayman, Dick Turpin. Arrest him!" —turning to Pooly.

"Touch him at your peril!" roared the Lord Chief Justice. "The man is here as a witness —he is under my protection!"

The cheer that followed was perhaps the most ringing cheer ever heard in a court of law, No questions were asked Mr. William Graham; the jury, without waiting to hear another word, rose, crying, "*Not Guilty!*" During the confusion that ensued, Dick Turpin made good his exit. Nobody was more astonished than the counsel for the defence; the attorney knew all about it.

The prisoners were at once discharged, and many wondered that Brian and Robert were not taken at once into custody.

When the judge was asked to do so, he shook his head, speaking in a low tone.

"We can't expect that honest fellow—scoundrel I mean—to risk his neck a second time," remarked the judge to one who sat beside him; "the fact is, I admire pluck wherever I find it. I'm afraid if he ever comes to be tried before me he won't be hung."

And so Brian Seymour and Robert Woodstock escaped for the time scot free; at all events, they had nothing just then to fear from human justice, as represented by the law.

But every man of honour cut them dead, while even roués and blacklegs fought shy of them—at all events in public.

CHAPTER LXXXIII.

DICK TURPIN DRINKS THE HEALTH OF THE LORD CHIEF JUSTICE!

Tom King had done all he could to dissuade his friend from his Quixotic enterprise, but in vain. Dick, with all his faults, had a dogged sense of right and honour. The fact that two innocent persons were being accused of a crime which, in his own mind, he knew to have been committed by others, was far too much for him.

Before going into the court, he and Tom King with others entered a tavern near the court, very much frequented by the fancy, and called for glasses round.

"Shan't see you again, Dick," said Tom King, sorrowfully, "it aint likely. They won't part, once they get you."

And the gay highwayman seemed almost as if he were going to cry, so certain was he of never seeing his friend again.

Dick departed. The others remained, smoking and drinking for about two hours, beguiling the weary minutes by conversation. No allusion was made to what was uppermost in their thoughts.

Still Tom King kept glancing up at the clock.

Then suddenly a man, a tout employed to get witnesses when *alibis* and that sort of thing had to be found, rushed in.

"He's in the witness box," he said, "and speaking as calm as a lamb as doesn't know it's going to have its throat cut."

All held their breath. It was too astounding to be believed. Not one had ever heard of a parallel case.

"Let us drink!" suddenly said Tom, pointing to the empty punch bowl, which the tout at once took up, went outside, and returned. It was now full and steaming.

Scarcely were their glasses all replenished, when an authoritative voice bade them "stop!"

All leaped to their feet in utter astonishment. It was Dick Turpin, free and alone.

"Fill your glasses," he went on, "and I will give you a toast."

For a moment all were too astonished to speak. Then one and all filled their tumblers and prepared to drink.

"Gentlemen, the toast I have to propose is one that will surprise you," he went on; "it is —The Lord Chief Justice. No heel-taps."

Now, everyone knew Dick Turpin too well to hesitate when he spoke. Everyone drank the toast, and emptied his rummer right royally.

Then Dick told his story, to which the others listened with amazement. They could scarcely credit it, such firmness and generosity on the part of one who was generally considered hard and cruel.

"But," observed Dick, "I mustn't abuse his kindness. He can't protect me after the court rises. I must be off!"

"One more glass," cried one of the party, "and then, if you take a fool's advice, you'll mizzle."

"I thank you, Jack," replied Dick.

The glass was drank, and then both Dick and Tom hurried out, sought their horses, and rode away. Not a minute too soon. Ten minutes later a man, whom all knew to be a spy of the Bow Street runners, sauntered into the room as if in search of an acquaintance.

"Who do you want, Soapy Sam?" observed one of the company.

"Not you," replied the other, in a surly tone; "you aint worth having. I shouldn't get a groat out of you."

"No matter, Sam," said the first speaker, drily—

> "'Good Mr. Knave, give me my due,
> I like a tart as well as you;
> But I would starve on good roast beef,
> Ere I would look so like a thief!'"

The laughter was so loud and general at this sally, that Soapy Sam beat a hasty retreat, and appeared no more in their company that evening.

Meanwhile, Dick and Tom determined to pass a night in their safe retreat in Epping Forest, where they had no fear of being followed.

They reached their lair about eight, and easily summoned Half-Hung Smith, who was at once despatched in search of such creature comforts as could be procured for money in that benighted district. But our highwaymen were not very particular. They liked luxuries when they could get them, but they could put up with plain, even coarse food, when it was necessary. Their henchman, however, knew what he was about, and took care to bring them the best he could procure at farm-house and inn.

They were perfectly satisfied, and after a few merry hours, went to bed jolly, that is, in a high state of physical happiness, arising from a not unusual extra drop of the best ale and spirits the local inns could supply.

They were in no hurry to rise, but when they did, soon found a copious and well-cooked meal of bacon and eggs, which they thoroughly enjoyed.

They then indulged in a chat, and promising Half-Hung Smith to return a little earlier next time, mounted their horses and took their departure. Previous to starting, they arranged to get a long way from London to a certain rendezvous, where messages from the Blue Dwarf would reach them, before they commenced business operations.

They kept strictly to this resolution, travelling openly in the daytime and putting up at night at comfortable inns.

At length they reached the rendezvous, the "Leather Bottle," an old posting-house near Retford, where they arrived in the evening, and straightway secured a room for the night.

There was a letter for Dick from Sapathwa. It told them that all was going well for the present. The family remained undisturbed, and was likely to be so, unless Brian Seymour, through some new emissary, traced their place of concealment.

Dick and Tom were, therefore, free to do as they pleased, and determined, if possible, to do some daring and successful stroke of business.

Highway robbery was, however, a very chance affair. Men who travelled much were apt to carry with them only money enough for necessaries; while the stage coaches were provided with an armed guard and coachman, who generally, if aided by one or two plucky passengers, would beat off one or two highwaymen.

They occupied the coffee-room, as it was called, supped, drank, smoked, and chatted freely with the other guests. In this way they heard a good deal of the local history, the residences of the nobility and gentry, and the habits of their owners.

"Old Peters any better?" asked a farmer-looking personage of the doctor—there is always a doctor in these reunions.

"Not much—can't make him out. There does not seem much the matter with him," replied the local Æsculapius; "but he is sinking in an extraordinary way. I can't quite make it out. His widow, if she is one, will be a rich woman," he went on.

"Ah!" remarked one of the company, "there's no fool like an old fool. A man of over sixty marrying a girl of two-and-twenty, with no recommendation but her beauty!"

"She's handsome enough," continued the doctor, "but handsome is as handsome does; I think if he dies, she'll soon find him a successor. The ne'er-do-weel, Simon Frazer, is always hanging about the place since he has been ill."

"Does Peters know?" asked the other.

"No! The servants all seem to me to favour their mistress," the doctor remarked. "I suppose she pays them well to keep her secrets."

All laughed, and the conversation changed.

"What might this Mr. Peters be?" asked Dick, in a careless kind of way, as if out of sheer curiosity and the love of talk.

"He's a main rich man," replied the other, glad to air his knowledge. "He used to be very generous and jolly; but some years ago an only daughter eloped with a man he did not like. He grew close and sullen, gave up all his acquaintances, and two years ago went away, to bring back a young wife, not of his own class."

"And this young spark, Simon Frazer?" continued Dick, lifting his glass and nodding to his garrulous companions.

"Nobody knows anything about him. Nobody ever saw him before Mr. Peters came back with a wife," the other responded; "he then suddenly appeared in the village, and took a small house, where people do say he receives visits from Mrs. Peters. I'm only repeating what people say."

"Yes! yes! I know," resumed Dick, and the conversation dropped—but not out of the highwayman's mind.

Somehow the story haunted him. An undefined suspicion filled his mind. He should like to know the truth about this Simon Frazer and this woman! With one of his odd ways of looking at things, he fancied something was to be made out of the affair.

When he and Tom King were alone, he told him what he thought.

"I think we might make some money out of this job," said Dick, "if we could only find out the truth."

"You're a rum un'!" laughed Tom.

"Never you mind," replied Dick; "I'm determined to sift this matter. I only ask for to-morrow evening," he added; "if I get no clue then, I will give it up."

CHAPTER LXXXIV.
THE CATASTROPHE.

Next evening, having dressed himself carefully, Dick, who had found that Elm Lodge, the residence of Mr. Peters, was not more than three miles off, started in that direction. He had easily obtained minute directions. He had to follow the main road about two miles and a half, and then a cross road led through the park to the house.

Dick was a good walker, and ere three quarters of an hour had passed was close to the house. The park was densely wooded here, and suddenly Dick halted. He heard footsteps coming behind, and at once concealed himself.

Scarcely had he done so, when he saw a tall, powerful, youngish man pass hurriedly. He waited one moment, then quickly followed. He had not far to go. About fifty yards from the house was an arbour, which the young man entered.

Dick crept stealthily up to the back, where there was a loophole, through which he could see and hear. The first thing he made out was embracing and lover-like endearments. Then the man spoke, in firm, but low and measured accents.

"How much longer is this going to last?" he asked. "I am weary and tired!"

"Donald, my husband, you cannot be more impatient than I am. All this deceit and concealment is revolting to me—but we must be rich. I can never face poverty again—he cannot last much longer."

"Cannot you end it quicker?" he asked, impatiently.

"No! The doctor has already asked me curious questions," she answered. "He looks at me with very strange eyes. When Doctor Meulbard confided this drug to me he explained that I must be careful with the doses. One every day would sap the life out of any one, without any chance of discovery—a double dose would kill—and leave traces."

"How much longer, then, am I to wait?" he asked, petulantly.

"A week, I think, will end all!"

"What time shall I come to-night?" he said, a little surlily.

"Not before twelve! I must remain with him until after eleven. But I will leave a light in my room," she replied, "and you can come when you like. The ladder is close at hand."

"I shall not be much before twelve. I hate waiting," he continued; "but still, leave the lamp."

And then, after other embraces, this guilty couple separated; he strolling away from the house, and she returning to it.

"Oh! oh!" cried Dick, in a low tone; "here's a pretty kettle of fish! But if I aint even with you two, then my name's blockhead!"

Two hours later, it was not quite eleven, he was at the back of the house under a window, in which shone a light. It was open, and close at hand against it was a ladder.

Dick at once ascended, and in two minutes was in the bed room. His first impulse was to bolt the door which led into the passage. He then looked around, and his eye fell at once on a door-closet with many shelves. On one of these was a lady's desk, which he eagerly clutched.

To put it on a table and open it was the work of less than two minutes.

It contained chiefly papers, but in the corner he saw two suspicious phials. These he secured. Glancing at the papers, he saw one packet labelled "Simon Frazer." He opened it, and scanned several. They were all addressed "My dear Wife." Then came a large document. It was the certificate of marriage between Simon Frazer, bachelor, and Ellen Monro, spinster, dated two years back.

Dick secured these also, put them in his pocket, unlocked the door, and went down the ladder. Dick was nothing if not prompt. He determined at once to go to the doctor, and tell him the facts. He could explain the burglary by what he had accidentally overheard.

He had had the doctor's house pointed out to him, and thither he took his way. It was not a mile distant, and he was there in a very brief space of time. He rang the night-bell, and soon a head was protruded from an upper window.

"Who is there?"

"Come from Mr. Peters, sir!" was the response.

"I'll be down in a minute," the other said, and with marvellous rapidity the door was opened and Dick ushered in.

Dr. Elliott looked surprised at seeing a stranger, and the other saw it.

"I am sorry to disturb you, doctor," he said, politely; "but my business is urgent, and one of

life and death! Have you ever suspected that your patient, Mr. Peters, was being poisoned?"

"Poisoned!" gasped the doctor. "Certainly I have had faint suspicions—but have rejected them. There is no motive."

"Well, sir; I shall prove to you that he is being poisoned!" was the answer; "and by his wife! Examine these!" and he produced the phials taken from the desk.

The doctor took them with trembling hands and hot, inflamed cheeks. Bidding Dick to sit down, he at once proceeded to test the contents of the bottles.

"Yes—a rare poison—very little known," the doctor remarked after a time. "Now tell me all you know?"

Of course Dick made out that it was pure accident which had made him overhear the conversation between the man and woman. He then detailed his visit to Elm Lodge, his daring invasion of its mistress' bedroom, and his capture of the phials.

"But that is not all," continued Dick. "I found that she is not Mrs. Peters, but Mrs. Simon Frazer;" and he handed him the marriage certificate.

Dr. Elliott thought deeply.

"Do you think you could put those bottles back in their place and restore all the papers but this one, so as not to rouse her suspicions?" he presently asked.

"Yes! but she will go on poisoning!" remarked Dick, rather startled.

"No!" said the doctor, drily; and, taking an empty phial, he emptied the contents of the two bottles into it. He now took down some other bottles, and made up a mixture exactly resembling the poisons.

He then returned the phials to the highwayman.

"It's now one o'clock. You had better have a shake-down here, and go over with me to the Lodge. We must consult Mr. Peters before doing anything. I shall go at seven, and take care that she is sent for. You can then enter her bedroom, and replace everything as before."

As he spoke, the doctor pointed to a kind of couch-bed, with blankets and horse-rugs.

"You must do the best you can," continued Dr. Elliott. "Here is some brandy, which will be welcome this chilly night."

Next morning, at half-past six, the doctor was on his way to Elm Lodge, in his gig, with Dick Turpin. The servants were not all up, but there was no delay in admission.

A nurse passed the night in the invalid's room. She had been sleeping, but was wide awake enough when the doctor came into the room.

"How is our patient, Mrs. Jones?" asked the doctor, in his suavest tones.

"He's been pretty quiet," she answered; "he's awake, I think."

"Well, go and get your breakfast," the doctor went on; "I'll have a chat with Mr. Peters."

"You are early!" said his patient, in a low, half-faint tone.

"Yes! I've been thinking of your case a good deal in the night," he said; "let me feel your pulse and see your tongue!"

"Ah! ah! yes!—want a tonic—brought one with me; let me give it to you myself."

His patient was quite resigned to anything his medical adviser told him to do. He drank it, and in two minutes the effect was marvellous.

His eyes grew bright, and his cheeks had a slight colour.

"Peters!" he said, "we are old friends. I have given you a powerful tonic, because I have something very serious to say to you. I feel that I have been wrong in my theory as to your illness. I know, in fact, that I have been—*for you are being slowly poisoned!*"

The man almost sat up in his bed, and then sank back nearly fainting.

"By whom?" he gasped.

"Nerve yourself, Peters, my friend ; by the woman who calls herself your wife—but who, thank heaven! is not!" continued the doctor.

Peters looked stupefied with horror, speechless, unutterable terror.

"But, are you sure?"

"Quite!" and he told him all.

"What merciful Providence brought this man here?" he asked, wildly.

"I know not; all I am sure of is—he has saved your life!" responded Dr. Elliott; "and now, what is to be done?"

"Send for the officers of justice!" he blurted.

"Had you not better hush it up, and let these two foul fiends go? They will suffer where only such wretches suffer—in their pockets."

"Yes!"—after another pause—"you are right—but do not let her know of our discovery. Say I am ill—anything you like—advise another doctor."

"Certainly. Will you ring for the nurse now—and send her for her mistress?" resumed the doctor, glad to see his patient so calm and self-controlled.

"You can prove her marriage?" he asked.

"Here is the certificate!" was the reply; "take care of it." •

"I will," answered Peters, who, thanks to his tonic, was now better than he expected. "I will now ring. You keep her in conversation. I will appear drowsy."

Twenty minutes later Mrs. Peters came in. She was rather surprised to find the doctor there so early, and had made her husband leave hurriedly. What could have happened? Could any suspicion have arisen?

But the doctor's calm manner reassured her, and she eagerly asked if anything was the matter.

"Oh, no! only, passing this way early, I thought I'd save myself a journey, as I am busy to-day. Mr. Peters is not quite so well as I could wish, and I should suggest a consultation."

Mrs. Peters bowed. What she felt it would be impossible to say, so utterly inscrutable are such women.

"Have you breakfasted?" she asked.

"No! Would you mind sending it up here? and you will find a new man of mine in the kitchen. Please send him up to me," he added, "I have some directions to give him."

Mrs. Peters gladly retired, and in a few minutes Dick Turpin came in, and was introduced as Mr. Palmer.

"I owe you my life!" said the invalid, gravely and earnestly. "But keep it secret. You are not a rich man I presume?"

"Far from it — but able to earn an honest penny," replied Dick, modestly.

"Then you'll not object to accept a couple of hundred guineas as some small mark of the service you have rendered me."

"Well, sir," continued Dick, with affected bashfulness, "if you think it worth it."

"Ten times more. But I want you to do me another service. I want you to take a letter for me, and bring back an answer. Spare no expense. Elliott, write to my daughter—say I am ill—but getting better. She is to come here at once with her children. Our friend here will take the letter and bring them back to-morrow. They are to stop here. I will have everything ready."

The doctor gladly wrote the letter which Dick Turpin was to take. By the time it was finished, breakfast appeared, and Dick went down to partake of his in the kitchen. Soon after, the two left the house, and Dr. Elliott drove Dick to his inn, where he left him.

Tom had been rather uneasy, but the moment he saw him his quick eye told him all was right.

"I've a good paying job on," said Dick, "so let us have a parting glass. I want you to wait until to-morrow here; and here's the shiners to pay," handing him a handful of guineas from a bag which the sick squire had given him.

When money was about, Tom was not curious. Enjoyment was the one thought of his life, and once he had the means of gratifying his tastes and passions he was satisfied.

Dick Turpin's letter was addressed to Mrs. Rainsford, Rose Cottage, Leeford, near Northminster. There was no difficulty in finding the place. It was a sweetly pretty cottage. It was only a simply country house, but neat, clean, and homely.

A servant ushered him into a room, where he was joined directly by a delicate-looking lady in a widow's cap, a handsome face, though rather faded, and nice manners.

"I bring a letter from Doctor Elliott," he began.

"Anything wrong? Is my father worse?" she cried, in a trembling tone, scarcely able to open the letter.

"Your father is better! I have come to take you to him," replied Dick.

She at once dropped down upon a couch and almost fainted, as a girl of fourteen and a boy of twelve came into the room, looking angrily at the intruder.

"It's all right," said Dick; "your ma's only a little agitated."

The mother bade her son read the letter out, which he did.

"We must go at once," she cried.

"I was particularly ordered to take you to-morrow. Your father wants to have everything ready for you. You will need some time to pack up, as you will stop there."

Mrs. Rainsford had all her work to do to restrain her impatience.

"I will call this evening to see what time you will be ready, ma'm," said Dick, "and will see about a post-chaise."

And before they could restrain him, he was gone.

Returning to Elm Lodge, we hasten to record what was passing there. There was only one old servant in the house of those who preceded the marriage. This was the old housekeeper, a woman of sixty, who had a niece to live with her.

For this servant Mr. Peters sent, under some pretence, when Mrs. Peters had gone for a drive.

"Martha," he said, "I have no time to explain much. But there are going to be great changes here. Open my daughter's rooms, and have them ready for to-morrow. She'll want two bed rooms, one for herself and daughter, the other for her son. Don't let anyone know about it."

Martha Bainley was too astonished at first to speak.

"Miss Leila coming home?"

"Yes! I can say no more now. Do the best you can—and keep my secret."

"I will, sir," said the delighted woman, who had been nurse to old Mrs. Peters, and been present at Leila's birth.

She lost no time; and quietly, and without exciting any suspicion, the rooms were dusted, cleaned, and got ready for the new mistress of the house.

It was eleven o'clock when the post-chaise dashed up to the door. Martha was ready to receive her darling and her children. By her directions the luggage was brought into the passage.

Then Dick Turpin entered, escorting Mrs. Rainsford and her children. At this moment Mrs. Peters came rushing in, rage and fury in her countenance.

"Who are these persons? What do they want here?" she shrieked. "Take all that luggage away!"

"This lady is Mrs. Rainsford, master's only daughter," replied Martha; "and she is here by master's orders."

The master's bell rang loudly, and one of the servants went to answer it. He came hurriedly down.

"Master says his daughter and her children are to be shown up at once," he said.

Mrs. Peters was too overwhelmed to make any resistance. What could it all mean? There could be no suspicion! The poison was safe in her desk. She had seen it that morning, and intended in half an hour to administer the usual dose.

She retired to her room, examined her desk, and found everything just as she had left it. If the worst came to the worst, it was that Dr. Elliott must have had some faint suspicion about her husband's symptoms.

Half an hour later she was summoned to her husband's room. She found his daughter seated by the bedside, the doctor standing by her.

Her husband was propped up by pillows, and looked at her with a stern and rigid expression of countenance.

"Woman!" he began; "would-be assassin! leave my house. If you are found here or anywhere near in half an hour, I shall give you into custody. Go to your worthy husband and fellow-criminal, Simon Frazer!"

She glared at him with fierce eyes—eyes with an appalled expression.

"Yes!" said Dr. Elliott, holding up a bottle; "here is the poison found in your desk. The phials you now have contain an antidote; as to your claim to be my friend's wife, here is the certificate of your marriage to Simon Frazer eight months before the false ceremony between yourself and Mr. Peters."

The woman was too utterly crushed to make any defence, or even say a word. She turned and slunk out of the room, packed up her belongings, and was driven to the residence of Simon Frazer, whose rage and fury knew no bounds.

Still, she had money and jewels, both were young, the world was all before them where to choose, and they must begin life again. At all events, they did not remain many hours in the neighbourhood, where they were never seen again.

The return of his daughter, with the society of her children, had apparently an immediate and powerful effect on Mr. Peters. He recovered completely, and lived many years to enjoy the society of his family.

———

CHAPTER LXXXV.

DICK ON THE PROWL.

Dick Turpin left Elm Lodge, a richer if not a wiser man. Mr. Peters was deeply grateful to him, imagining of course that the discovery he had made was purely accidental, and that in hastening to track the murderers to their lair, he was actuated by the most generous motives.

Such, to a certain extent, was the truth; but still Dick Turpin was not one to hide his light under a bushel, and having done a creditable and useful action, he saw no harm in being rewarded for it.

No further message had come from the Blue Dwarf, so they felt free to act wholly for themselves.

They determined to try their fortunes once more, and having effected a good haul, they would return to London and have a long spell of enjoyment—that is, at all events, while their money lasted.

The road between Northminster and Retford was much frequented by all classes of travellers, and they determined to trot along and see what turned up.

Their usual game was to attack single travellers who looked well-to-do, post-chaises, or even stages at a pinch.

The sun was going down, however, ere they encountered one single victim, and when they did, it was with poor result. One farmer they relieved had only seven and sixpence about him, which he was so loth to part with, that Dick swore at him for a cur, and then, observing his pained countenance, returned him his money, adding a guinea.

He rode off hurriedly to avoid the man's thanks—Tom King laughing.

The next man, a stout, jolly-looking fellow, tolerably well dressed, had nothing but an old watch, about the size of a moderately large turnip.

"Keep your ticker, my good fellow," said Dick, laughing; "and hark'e, my friend, don't be down-hearted—here's a guinea to drink my health."

The man glared, unable for one moment to speak. It was so unexpected.

"Well," he said presently, dashing a tear from his eye with his great rough hand. "I thank you, master, and may be I'll serve you. Ever hear tell of Lawyer Tillson?"

"No!" replied Dick.

"Well, he's a rich man; holds mortgages on most little bits of land about here," the man went on; "got one on mine for twenty guineas, which my crops can't pay. Now, he's at the 'Blue Posts' — everybody knows him about here; but you wouldn't think him worth stopping; and I'd swear my affidavy, if you did, you'd find a thousand guineas in notes and gold about him, sewn up in his great coat, or in his portmanter."

"Well, my honest friend," replied Dick, "if you'll put us up to him, I'll pay off your mortgage."

"Done!" said the other. "I'll ride back to the 'Blue Posts' with you and point him out. You'll find him a shabby sort of looking fellow —but he'll lend anything from a shilling to a thousand guineas—if you can give security."

"Trot on, my friend," continued Turpin. "We'll make something out of this," he said to King.

"It aint a do?" mused Tom.

"Oh, no!" said his friend; "we're not known about here. Besides, that man is a simple yokel if ever there was one."

Tom replied that he hoped Dick would never fall a prey to his own foolhardiness, and bade him go ahead and be hanged to him.

The "Blue Posts" was reached, and their farmer friend was invited to join them in a drink, while their supper was getting ready.

"Better have a bit of supper, too, Mr. Garrett; it will look as if we have business together."

The man nodded his head gratefully, and the three went in. Nothing was said until they were seated, and then one whispered sentence was enough.

"Him a talking to the seedy chap."

Dick never turned his head, but gravely gave orders for supper at once, and three tankards of ale while waiting.

He then, with his tankard up to his lips, eyed the two. The lawyer was a poor, mean-looking fellow enough, with a lantern-jaw and keen grey eyes, but the man speaking to him was something peculiar to look at.

He was a very tall, thin individual, whose attenuated body was clad in one of the seediest of frock coats, such as some lawyers used to wear in those days, patched and darned, and mended, to such a degree, that little of the original remained; his long thin legs, encased in an old pair of check trousers, and the said trousers being at least two or three inches too short, acquainted one with the fact, that although he was in possession of some sort of apology for boots, he was nevertheless without stockings.

His collar, whose reminiscences of the laundry were gradually fading through the lapse of time, was absolutely yellow, and he wore a cravat that a rag-picker would have disdained to cross the road for. Yet, in spite of all these disadvantages of wardrobe, he bore on his face, careworn and dissipated, and even cunning, though it was, the indelible stamp of one who had seen better days.

"Shabby, very," said Dick; "but been a gentleman once."

"You've got an eye as sharp as a needle, sir," retorted the other; "he was once Squire Denton, of Denton; ran through every penny, sold-up, ruined; Tillson got all the fat loans, mortgages, everything; and now, I'll bet, he's trying to make old skinflint lend him a trifle."

"Why," whispered Tom; "that's Joe Faker, who gets his living by writing letters for people who can't write. Does a good business at times —starves at others."

"It is no use talking, Mr. Denton," said the lawyer, raising his voice, "I owe you nothing. My accounts are all clear and correct—to the last penny. I cannot afford to give away money."

"Scoundrel!" cried Denton, rising. "I tell you that you owe me seven hundred guineas on that last mortgage. You got a receipt for a thousand when I was drunk—and only gave me three hundred. You'll swing for it yet. No highwayman is half such a rascal as you are— and you know it. Thief—robber of the widow and orphan, beware!"

And he turned towards the door. "You threaten, beggar!" spluttered John Tillson. "I've a great mind to give you in charge!"

"Give me in charge!" exclaimed Denton, with withering contempt; "why, you paltry thief, I've a great mind to thrash you within an inch of your miserable life! But everybody knows what a contemptible cur and hound you are, and a whipping would not degrade you lower than you are."

With which he walked out, slamming the door behind him. Many present would have liked to befriend him, but for reasons best known to themselves did not move.

There was one exception, and that was, Dick Turpin, who whispered to Tom.

"I won't be long. I have a good notion!" and running out he was in time to see Mr. Denton going down the steps.

"Excuse me, sir," he said respectfully, "but may I have a word with you?"

The other stared. It was a long time since he had been addressed as "sir."

"You must be mistaken!" he said, in a low voice, still trembling with passion.

"No, sir!" continued Dick. "I am not mistaken; this is not a large village; do you know any other house?"

"I know another," said the other, bitterly; "frequented by tramps and poachers—where they would not refuse to receive me, even if I had not a shilling. The landlord was a tenant of mine!"

"My object in speaking to you, sir, is a business one," continued Dick; "if we could have a private corner, I would explain. In the mean time, will you take this guinea on account. We have met in London at the 'Mews.'"

This was a rendezvous for beggars, for men who want letters written for them, for cadgers, and all the lower class of vagrants.

Denton coloured violently.

"I do not mean to pain you," quietly continued Dick. "What you did there was honestly done, and everybody knows that Joe Faker never did anything on the fly."

"Follow me," answered Denton, putting the guinea in his pocket, and leading the way to the end of the village, where up a lane was a small inn of the lower class.

Denton hurried in, followed by Dick. He nodded to the landlord, and, throwing a guinea down, said :—

"Send some cold meat and bread, with a quart of ale and half-a-pint of brandy, into the blue-room, also the change."

"Yes, Mr. Denton," replied mine host, trying not to look astonished.

And they passed into a small room where, in a very few minutes, the things ordered were brought. Mr. Denton at once attacked the viands, with the air of a man who had been some time without food. Dick filled a glass of ale and drank it in solemn silence.

"Now, Mr. Denton," he began, when the other had satisfied the rough edge of his appetite, " I will explain to you as far as I can. I am here on a secret mission—for which I am well paid, to make Mr. Tillson disgorge some of his ill-gotten gains. He has robbed a friend of mine in the same way he has robbed you."

"Scoundrel!" muttered Denton.

"Do you know a solicitor in London, a respectable and decent one?"

"Yes! almost the only friend I have," replied the other.

"Well—no matter what I am going to do—how I am going to do it. I mean to have the miserable mortgage held against my friend, which means ruin, in my possession to-night. Now, at the ' Blue Posts' you threatened Mr. Tillson, and if anything unpleasant happens to him to-night, you might be blamed."

"But you don't mean——"

"His carcass is safe—that I pledge you my word—but have that mortgage I will. That is my business."

"But what do you want me to do?" asked Richard Denton, rather anxiously.

"Go to London at once," said Dick, putting down five guineas, " the night-coach leaves in half-an-hour. You'd better go and book yourself at the office and start from the ' Blue Posts.' The moment you reach London call on your friends, the lawyers—what name did you say?"

"Newton, James & Sons."

"Best men in London; honest as the day," continued Dick ; "take care to allude to the day of the month and the hour."

"You puzzle me," said Denton with a smile, very seldom seen on his face; "but after your behaviour, I cannot refuse. We have no time to lose."

Both rose and went out, the landlord bowing as they did so.

Denton walked about twenty yards up the High-street and then stopped at a shop, asking the other to wait a moment, and shortly returned with a rough warm coat and a cheap slouched hat.

On nearing the " Blue Posts," Dick went in first, and walked up to the bar. He had not more than ordered a glass when Mr. Denton followed, and going up to a small private bar threw down a guinea.

"I wish to book for London, outside. Put down Richard Denton, and give me and Mr. Tillson a glass of brandy."

"Certainly, sir," said the landlord, civilly.

When Denton was well off he had been a splendid customer, and his old freeness had not been quite forgotten.

And there Denton stood until the coach came up. One or two old acquaintances came in and went out, but something in the ex-squire s face did not encourage familiarity.

Dick Turpin re-entered the parlour, spoke to the waiter about the beds, and then ordered three more glasses.

"But I must be going," said Farmer Garrett.

"Drink first, and then give me your address."

"With pleasure," answered the other ; "it's Stoke Farm, Hayley — not two miles from here ; any one will tell you."

"But I hate asking," continued Dick.

"Well, then ; ride a mile and a half along the road to York, till you sees a sign post, marked Hayley. Go down the lane, and the second house is mine."

"I shan't forget," remarked Dick—and he did not.

Presently, the London coach came up, and Denton, to the surprise of several lookers-on, got on the top, wrapped in his warm outer coat, which kept him from the night air, and concealed his fearful shabbiness. Two minutes later they drove off.

Tillson, the lawyer, remained up until about a quarter to eleven and then retired. Dick and Tom had pumped Garrett. As he put up almost every week and sometimes twice a week, at the " Blue Posts," he always had the same room.

The house was very seldom full and the accommodation cost the landlord very little trouble. Though he spent very little money himself, his numerous clients spent a great deal.

The house did not close until twelve, and neither Dick nor Tom felt inclined to retire until the others did.

As they entered their room, the clock struck twelve. They had secured a double-bedroom, and as luck would have it, it was next that occupied by Tillson. As soon as they had taken off their boots, Dick made use of a trick often practised by him before. There was only a wainscot between the rooms.

Producing from his never-failing portmanteau a gimlet and a bottle of oil, he lubricated that useful instrument carefully, and then began to use it. He put his lamp somewhere in the shade, and then began boring the partition.

It didn't take long, and when he withdrew it, he peered in. At a long table sat Tillson, his bag open, and on the table a number of papers, which he was keenly examining.

"Ah ! ah !" he said aloud, clutching some papers tied up with red tape ; " why be a fool, Mr. Denton ? there's the title deed and here's the mortgage, and here's a receipt for the thousand guineas. No, Mr. Dick Denton, you aint the man to fool me. Not a penny of my money—no ; all for my girl, my Clara !"

Dick smiled sardonically. This unprincipled attorney, this thief, this robber of the widow and the orphan, this callous hard man of the world had a soft place somewhere.

Still he watched.

Now he saw that Tillson was packing up his papers, which presently he thrust into a bag, and prepared for bed. After a short interval, he was in bed. Then they waited until unmistakable signs showed that he was asleep.

The house had long been silent and quiet. The highwaymen now got ready. Before, however, proceeding with our narrative, we wish to explain something which is not generally known. In the early part of the last century there was a league of bandits in Paris, whose speciality was to rob the dead and dying. Their great haul was during an epidemic of contagious diseases. It was always a wonder to the faculty that none of the gang ever seemed to fall a prey to the illness of their victims.

One day one of the gang—there were four of them,—left behind a bottle which was found to be filled by a powerful aromatic vinegar. On being analysed, it struck the doctor as worth trying. It was afterwards found that one of the gang was a clever chemist, and to this day the *vinaigre des quatre voleurs* has retained its reputation as the best safeguard against infection ever invented.

In England, burglars and others invented a soporific, which, if applied to a man in his sleep, would steep his senses in oblivion for hours, rendering him incapable of resistance, and compelling him to remain as still as a corpse for more than an hour.

Dick was in the secret and always carried a bottle of the soporific with him.

They opened their own door cautiously, closing it again behind them, and soon by the use of their perfect implements were in the room. The lamp burnt still, giving a sort of dim religious light. Dick at once went to the bedside and saw that the lawyer slept with his mouth open. Without a moment's delay or hesitation he poured the contents of a small phial down his throat.

He gave one deep sigh, and then lay like a corpse on the bed.

Dick put his hand under his pillow and found his trousers and the inevitable purse heavy with gold. Then he searched his coat and found the equally inevitable pocket book. Then he joined Tom, who was examining the contents of the table.

It was covered with papers, I.O.U.'s, title deeds, memorandums, mortgage deeds, which Tom King, who had been a lawyer's clerk, at once identified. Then Dick caught sight of one tied with red tape on which was written "Richard Denton."

"Where's your bag?" asked Dick, and when he produced it, shovelled the lot into the receptacle, closing the bag.

Dick now walked to the window and opened it. It looked out on the stable yard, and he left it open.

Both now hurried to their room, got their boots and their own portmanteaus, and hurried down stairs. They did not attempt to open the front door, which might have occasioned a noise. Dick always had a safe retreat behind him. He had carelessly examined a side entrance to the stable-yard, which was easily opened. While Tom went to the stables, Dick went for a ladder, which he placed against the open window.

Of course suspicion would fall upon them, but this would complicate matters. In five minutes Tom brought out the horses, and in ten minutes they were on the road.

They followed exactly the directions of Farmer Garrett, and before half an hour drew rein close by his cosy little farm. Dismounting, Dick rapped loudly at the front door, and soon a head peered out, and a shrill voice cried:

"Go away—what do you want?"

"We want Farmer Garrett—say his friend from the 'Blue Posts' — important business," was the reply.

Mrs. Garrett, who had not only heard of Dick's kindness, but had, with her children, experienced it in the way of food, at once went down and opened the door.

"She had awakened her husband," she said, "and would take the horses to the stable herself."

She did so, and in a few minutes the farmer himself came down. He was very much surprised, but also very glad to see them.

"We want shelter, but want half an hour's business first," said Dick.

"All right, sir," he answered; "can you eat anything?"

"No! but a drink would do no harm," laughed Dick.

Mrs. Garrett now returned.

"Let us have a jug of ale," said her husband, "and the brandy bottle, and then find a shake-down for my friends. We have half-an-hour's business."

They were in a large kitchen with a yawning fireplace.

"It's rather chilly," said Dick; "just rake up the fire."

Garrett obeyed, and threw on a faggot, which soon crackled in the fireplace.

Mrs. Garrett now returned with the drink, and then retired to get a small spare bedroom ready, her husband intimating that he would show them to their sleeping chamber when they wished to retire.

"Bolt the door," said Dick, and when Garrett had obeyed his orders, he took up his bag and poured the contents on the table before the astonished eyes of the farmer.

"Now, Tom," said his friend, "you're the scholar, so read out the names."

"That's my lease!" cried Garrett, grabbing at a parcel tied with dirty tape, and opening it, he displayed two documents, and then continued: "This is the lease, and this is the loan paper."

"They are yours; do with them as you like," said Tom, and quick as thought the loan paper and mortgage went into the flames.

"Here's a whole batch of I.O.U's," continued Tom, "about a hundred of them."

"Into the fire with them," cried Dick, laughing, "we'll have a regular bonfire."

The rest of the papers, apart from letters, which were all burned, were carefully examined by Tom King, and the names read out. They all seemed familiar to Farmer Garrett, and he volunteered to take charge of them.

"Not one will split," he said, emphatically; "the lawyer chap is hated. Everybody will scream with delight."

"All right," replied Dick; "all I want is the papers belonging to Richard Denton. I know him, and will put them in his hands. As we must be off early we must now retire."

Garrett at once rose.

"I promised," said Dick, "to pay your mortgage, you know, and here's the money. You just do as you like with it; only take my advice and don't give it to Tillson."

Garrett laughed significantly, and then escorted them to bed.

At their desire he called them early—very early; and satisfied with a stirrup cup, they rode off, determined to breakfast on the road, when at least twenty miles from Hayley.

Leaving them to get away with their plunder, which in notes and gold exceeded a thousand guineas, we will return to the "Blue Posts."

About eight o'clock everybody in the inn was more or less aroused by a violent ringing from No. 9. A waiter rushed up, to find Tillson dancing with rage on the floor in his nightshirt.

"Thieves! robbers! murder!" he shrieked; "my money's gone! all my papers are gone! I'm a ruined man! I'll hang everybody in the house. Where's the landlord?"

"I'll fetch him, sir," said the frightened domestic, glad to get out of the room.

He returned with Mr. Johnson, pale with terror, and actually shaking with trepidation.

"I am very sorry, Mr. Tillson," he began, in

a humble tone, "but I really and truly do not feel that any blame rests on me."

"No blame! I'll see if I can't fix it on you or somebody. Where's that scoundrel Denton?"

"He went to London by the night mail," said Mr. Johnson, respectfully; "a dozen people saw him start."

"And those two fellows who came in with Garrett?" he howled.

"They are asleep in the next room," replied the landlord, and rushing out he tried the door. It opened freely—the room was empty!

Tillson stormed still more; declared the "Blue Posts" was a rendezvous for highwaymen and burglars, and that he would expose the landlord. He still stuck to the assertion that Denton had committed the robbery in conjunction with his two coadjutors from London.

"Send for Malcolm!" he now yelled, "and leave me to dress." By the time he came down, the constable was there, very civil and very grave. Tillson was clerk to the magistrates, and had great power.

Having calmed his nerves with some brandy, which the landlord brought him without charge, the lawyer told Malcolm all he could, and fixed his suspicions on the two strangers and Denton. He bade the constable inquire about the two strangers, while he would direct the coach people to see if the other went to London without stoppage.

We may as well say that as far as Richard Denton was concerned there was no difficulty in proving an alibi, on the evidence of coachman, guard, or Messrs. Newton, James & Sons, the solicitors, in London. It was waste of time, therefore, to accuse him of any connection with the robbery, when he was far away from Retford, at the time.

But who were the two strangers? Garrett was interrogated, but all he knew was that, riding along the highway he met the two strangers, who asked him the way to the "Blue Posts," at Retford, and that on his offering to show them, they insisted on his coming in and having supper.

All the inquiries which were made tended to nothing else. But on market day Tillson found most of those who owed him money very complacent and not at all obsequious. A day or two later, he found that every one of the twenty-seven farmers and small tradespeople round about that district, from whom he expected money, had received their securities back. He now stormed like a madman, and insisted on their paying, under penalty of a criminal prosecution. They simply laughed in his face, and told him to produce their receipts for the money, without which they would not pay.

Tillson had no resource but to retire in confusion, vowing unheard-of vengeance against sundry persons and everybody.

––––––

CHAPTER LXXXVI.
DICK'S PLOT.

On reaching London, which they did with extraordinary rapidity, allowing no time for the grass to grow under their feet, the two at once went to one of their haunts, left their horses, and sallied forth, after resting and refreshing themselves.

Tom King resolved to go and see one of his lady friends, while Dick determined to call on Mr. Denton's solicitors. Dick could always make himself look what he called portly and respectable. He had made a neat packet of the documents abstracted from the lawyer's bag, which he directed to "Richard Denton, Esq."

The firm occupied the lower part of a respectable house in Lincoln's Inn Fields, and employed numerous clerks. Dick Turpin entered the front room and bowing, took off his hat. The firm were well known for their courtesy and urbanity, and, as a matter of course, their clerks were civil and obliging.

"What can I do for you, sir?" asked one of the clerks, descending from his seat, and approaching him politely.

"I wish to see Mr. Newton," replied Dick Turpin, equally polite.

"I am afraid, sir, unless you come by appointment, Mr. Newton will not be able to see you," remarked the other.

"I come on urgent business connected with Mr. Richard Denton," was the answer.

"I will see Mr. Newton and hear what he says," replied the clerk, and went out, returning in a moment, saying, "This way, sir."

Dick was now ushered into a neat but formal room, surrounded by shelves, on which were law books and tin cases or deed boxes. At a table sat a genial-looking, middle-aged gentleman, with gold spectacles, and a general air of solid respectability.

"Be seated. I am very busy this morning," he said; "but if you really have any business in connection with Mr. Richard Denton, I shall be most happy to hear you."

"Well, sir," replied Dick, "I, too, am engaged on urgent business, but as, under very peculiar circumstances, I have come into possession of some papers which appear to interest him, I have hastened to bring them to you—your name being mentioned in one of the documents. May I ask if you have seen Mr. Richard lately?"

"Not for some weeks," replied Mr. Newton, taking the packet from his hands.

"Please, when you see him, hand these documents to him," said Dick; "and say they are sent by his friend of the 'Blue Posts' at Retford."

And Dick sidled rapidly out of the room. Mr. Newton stared after him as if he thought he were mad, and then opened the packet. It contained the title deeds of an estate well worth two thousand guineas, and a mortgage deed, setting forth that on this estate James Tillson had advanced twelve hundred and fifty guineas.

"The scoundrel! and all Dick had was three hundred guineas!" he muttered. "At all events he's no longer a pauper, and can come to terms with Tillson."

And he put the documents in the drawer just as the door opened, and Mr. Richard Denton appeared.

"Come in," said Newton, as he saw the figure of Denton standing modestly behind. "Sit down—glad to see you."

"Well, Mr. Newton, I will not detain you long; I come on a very strange account. It almost appears to me the object is that under certain circumstances I may be able to prove an alibi. For the life of me I cannot tell why nor wherefore," continued Denton.

"Explain yourself."

Richard did clearly, briefly, and succinctly. Mr. Newton listened to the whole narrative, his interview with Tillson, the insult, the interference of a stranger in his affairs, his offer of money, and his earnest wish for him to go to London openly, and to come to him immediately on his arrival in the metropolis.

"Well, your mysterious friend was right. Your being able to prove your departure from the 'Blue Posts' at Retford, is a matter of very great importance. You really did come by that coach?"

"Yes! I travelled the whole way with an old college friend, Captain Dawson," continued Denton; "and only got off the coach for refreshments."

"Well, well! that's all right! but it's deuced lucky for you. Somebody's committed a burglary at the 'Blue Posts,' I suspect, and stole his bag. Your mysterious friend must have rode post haste to London, and beat the stage, for he's been here—just gone in fact, and left these."

And he threw the two deeds before him on the table. Richard Denton took them up and stared wildly at them.

"What does it mean?" gasped the other, in open-mouthed astonishment.

"Well," said Newton, deliberately; "it appears to me that there has been a burglary committed—that your friend is a highwayman or something of that sort. What his motive is, we cannot even suspect, but you clearly benefit by it, This man Tillson clearly robbed you of nearly a thousand guineas, and must be made to smart."

"What do you advise doing?" asked Denton, in some trepidation.

"Lying quiet for a few days. Then I will write a brief letter explaining that, under circumstances you do not understand, you have come into the titles of your Darling estate, and that, having raised three hundred guineas from him on it, you are willing to pay that!"

"How?" gasped the young man.

"I will see to that. Then on this document I will advance you all you require. You have an excellent chance, and may do something for yourself. Your friend Dacres, who lives near Retford, is willing to help you in starting afresh.

"Yes, I will go, but——" glancing at his habiliments.

"My dear sir," said Newton, taking his chequebook from a drawer, "that is easily settled. Shall I say fifty, to begin with?"

"Newton, you are my best, my only friend," cried Denton, grasping his hand.

"You forget the mysterious stranger," laughed the lawyer. "Let go, or else I cannot write."

Denton did so, and received the cheque.

"Now, if you are returning to Retford, I would not let Lawyer Tillson suspect my identity. I should fig myself up a little, a la militaire, as the mounseers say. Clap on a moustache as soon as you are ready to start. You had better draw some more money, something may turn up. Now be off and change your skin."

Richard Denton obeyed, and four hours later none would have recognised in the thin, pale, elegant officer-looking gentleman, with white teeth, short curly hair and whiskers, and a slight moustache, the quasi-beggar of a few days before.

Newton was quite astonished, wished him good luck, pressed a purse into his hand, and started him off.

Little did he imagine the consequences which were to follow from his advice.

CHAPTER LXXXVII.

THE COUNTY BALL.

Under the name of Captain Thornton, Denton reached the "Blue Posts," and took up his quarters there without being suspected. During part of his downward career he had been a strolling actor, and was an excellent mimic, could imitate any voice, and keep up any character.

Having installed himself in the country inn, he hired a horse and rode out to the bachelor residence of Mr. Arthur Dacres—a very good friend in days past, and one always ready to serve him.

He rode up to the door of the house, a very neat residence of modern erection, surrounded by a small park—Dacres' money was invested in business—and sent in written on a piece of pasteboard, "Captain Thornton, favoured by Richard Denton." He was at once admitted into the other's sanctum. Mr. Dacres was a youngish man, who took little part in business, being content to leave that to his elders. He was luxurious and indolent, but by no means extravagant.

"Welcome, sir; any friends of Dick Denton are always. Have you any message from him?" waving his new acquaintance to a seat.

"Well, Arthur," laughed his friend, "I did not think I should take you in. I thought you would see through the masquerade at once."

"Why, gracious goodness, Dick! What's up—what does it mean? Tell me at once; I'm dying to know."

"It's a long story, Arthur," was the grave reply, "and a curious one."

"Well, you're nearest the door," said Dacres; "ring the bell. Wine and cigars, James, and get ready a bed for my friend."

Cigars were just new in England, though they came in when Charles II. married an infanta of Portugal, who brought enough of India for her dower to lay the foundation of our Indian empire; and as Arthur Dacres was nothing if not luxurious, he indulged in them.

"My story is a very extraordinary one," began Denton, "and I don't quite understand it. I appear to be taking advantage of a crime—but Newton says it's all right, and that I am in no way to blame."

"Out with it; I'm dying to hear it," continued Dacres, filling up two tumblers of claret. "Now fire away."

Denton required no twice telling, but told his story in every particular exactly as it happened, his friend only interrupting with approval and laughter. When he had finished, he spoke frankly and warmly.

"I don't see how you are to blame in any way," he said. "Tillson is such a consummate rascal that whatever has happened to him serves him jolly well right. Now what do you mean to do?"

"I want you to try and get me that situation you spoke of. I want work; I want, if I can, to make money," was the reply; "and by degrees regain my inheritance."

"All right. I shall be going to London in a

week," returned Dacres. "We will go together, and by hook or by crook I will get you something."

"I am very thankful, old friend."

"In the meantime we must amuse ourselves. You will stay here. To-morrow is the county ball; we'll go. No one will know you. You look thin, pale, and interesting. Catch a heiress—harder things to do than that."

"I'm in your hands, Dacres; do with me as you will," replied Denton.

"Then we'll dine, drive over to Polworth, get a ticket, you can hire a court suit, and the thing is done," cried Dacres; "I'll find you plenty of partners."

And so it was settled.

The two friends dined, and drove into Polworth, the county town, and went to the Royal Hotel. As they went up the High Street they passed Tillson's place, a large but gloomy mansion, at which Denton scowled, but made no remark. At the drawing-room window was a very handsome girl. As he saw her, Dacres smiled. A sudden thought seemed to strike him.

They sauntered into the public room, where many acquaintances of Dacres happened to be, some who in former days had known Denton, but not one showed any sign of recognition when he was introduced as Captain Thornton.

Presently, he called to see the costumier of Polworth, and was measured for a court dress, which, as it happened, had been made for him four years before. It was ordered to be sent to the hotel.

Captain Thornton then recognised his new friends, with whom he spent a very glorious evening, wound up by a supper. Cards were introduced; but out of London few people played for high stakes, so that it was impossible to lose much. At twelve they retired to Dacres Lodge.

Next evening, at an earlier hour than is customary now-a-days, the two friends entered the really fine Assembly Rooms, which were already beginning to fill.

Dacres introduced his friend, who readily found partners. He was handsome, young, with a distinguished air about him, and he was well introduced. Dacres was not a man to be seen piloting about a nobody. An hour passed very agreeably, Denton laughing in his sleeve while conversing with old friends with whom once he had been intimate.

About ten o'clock, Dacres came up with a smile on his face.

"Thornton," he said in a low tone, "such an event! A romantic young lady has taken a fancy to you—romantic young lady—plenty of money and all that. Come along and let me introduce you. She has asked me to do it."

And he led him up to where sat a really handsome girl—pleasing, interesting, and, as far as outward appearance was any guide, very amiable and innocent.

"Miss Tillson," he began; "my friend, Captain Thornton. I think you will make a very bright and handsome couple."

And Dacres retreated, laughing, leaving his friend in a maze of astonishment. And this was the daughter of his enemy, of the man who had helped him in the downward road to ruin.

Well, it was not her fault, and he would make the best of it. He began talking, and found her, though very shy, both sensible and feeling,

but rather romantic in her notions. He became interested, he scarcely knew why.

He got hold of her tablet, and put himself down for several more dances, with the obvious approval of the lady.

After the second dance he led her to her chaperone, as he was engaged for the next dance, and then sought his friend, whom he found chatting at a kind of bar-counter with some companions. As he saw the other approach, Dacres came to meet him.

"You're a pretty fellow, Dacres, to let me in like that," he said; "do you mean to say that is Tillson's daughter?"

"Only child and heiress!" replied Dacres. "A very nice girl, well brought up by a worthy aunt. Here's a revenge for you. Tillson loves her as the apple of his eye. The man who wins her will have all his money."

"But," mused Denton; "he can easily revoke his will."

"I doubt it; but she's a fair fortune in her own right," went on the other; "enough to release all your property."

"Then, by heavens! I'll try it on! She seems all right," added Denton.

"My cousins, the Fairfields, say she is a most charming girl—unassuming and good," said Mephistopheles, fanning the flame.

Denton said no more, but marched away. All those who have studied the memoirs and fiction of the last century, must be aware that our female ancestors, however worthy and amiable in some instances, were very easily led to believe the utterances of male admirers. Denton set to work on her susceptible heart all the evening, and finally obtained a promise from her to meet him at twelve o'clock next day, in a well-known walk outside the town.

We have no excuse to make for Clara, but that she was young and inexperienced. Still, all clandestine love affairs are tarred with deceit and falsehood, no matter under what circumstances. The laws of marriage were shamefully lax in those days; in these days they are not much better. England would be a happier and a greater country, if no man were allowed to get married before twenty-five, or women before eighteen.

Ruskin is right. While we allow earlier marriages—a man has scarcely done growing before five-and-twenty—the race will continue to deteriorate. Half the sickness, misery, and vice of London is caused by too early marriages.

At twelve next day they met. Captain Thornton was pressing, warm, and ardent. He was not a poor man, he said, and not a rich man, but her father would object, would make delays, do anything to prevent her marriage with him. Doubtless he had some one in view?

Well, with a shudder, she confessed there was an impecunious old baronet, who would make her "my lady."

Captain Thornton laughed the idea to scorn, and urged her to put a complete bar to such misery by marrying him. What has Shakespeare, wisest of all cynics, said: "Frailty, thy name is woman." Clara resisted feebly, then wholly surrendered.

The gallant captain made another appointment for six o'clock, when he would have a postchaise ready, and away for Gretna Green, which was only eighty miles distant.

Thornton hurried away to his friend, who

DICK OVERHEARS THE CONVERSATION BETWEEN BRIAN SEYMOUR AND JOE ASKEW,
AT THE "HORSESHOE" INN.

No. 17.

roared with laughter at the quickness of the courtship.

"I shall start at half-past six. I hope Tillson will not discover our flight until to-morrow," said Denton; "anyway, we shall have a fair start. He will spare no expense on this occasion, I know."

"Leave all to me. There's a dinner on at the 'Royal'—magistrates' dinner," chuckled Dacres. "I'll 'ply him—don't mind drinking when it costs nothing."

And so it was agreed.

"Got enough money?" presently asked Dacres. "I've a drawer full of loose cash."

"Plenty! thanking you heartily all the same," replied Denton; and the two friends sat down to dinner.

At six o'clock, Miss Clara Tillson tripped down the steps of the lawyer's house with a small bag in her hand, which contained her jewellery—very valuable—and some money, not an inconsiderable lump. Clara had heard that very ardent lovers were often in pecuniary straits, and wished to be prepared for all contingencies.

She found the chaise waiting in a dark side alley, was handed in by Captain Thornton, who was very nervous, and then away they went.

As we have not much more time to devote to this love episode, we will briefly tell the end.

They duly reached Gretna Green about ten, were married, and had secured a small cottage on the outskirts, there to wait with tolerable equanimity the paternal fury. Interference was too late. They were bound by ties which death alone could loosen.

Meanwhile, Tillson had gone to the magistrates' dinner, which was always a grand affair in the county town. The sharp old attorney was always on these occasions at his best, affable, humble, polite, bowing and scraping to all.

He found himself next to Dacres, whom he knew, though not familiarly. Dacres was chatty, agreeable, and conversational. He took wine with Mr. Tillson several times, and towards the end of the evening he was tolerably merry, though not intoxicated quite.

At this moment, one of the attendants came to him and said a servant from his house was waiting to see him.

Tillson staggered up, struck by some warning of evil, and, aided by the man, tottered out to a waiting-room, where he found his old housekeeper in a state of frantic alarm.

"Oh, sir; Miss Clara!" she gasped.

"What of her?" he cried, in a wild tone. "Speak! or I'll strangle you."

"She's not been seen since six, when she went out. They do say," she went on, in a terrified tone, "she was seen on the road to Scotland with a gentleman."

"What are you staring at, you fool?" he cried, to the gaping attendant. "Brandy—a postchaise!"

The attendant retired and gave his orders. He presently returned with a bottle of brandy and a tumbler, which the lawyer filled to the brim and drank off. Scarcely had he done so, when he sank back on a couch helplessly intoxicated.

And there he lay until morning, when, wakening to a sense of his desolation and misery, he found the postchaise ready. He took hasty refreshment, and then, burning with hatred and revenge, he started after his erring daughter and her seducer.

On reaching Gretna Green, he found that they were duly married and residing at Woodbine Cottage, on the outskirts of the pretty little village where so much misery and wretchedness has been forged.

Burning with rage, he had himself guided to the hut-like habitation, at the door of which he knocked first, and receiving no answer, entered, to find himself face to face with Clara Tillson and Richard Denton.

He stood still, appalled, and turned as if in search of a weapon. There was a poker in the small stove; at this he flew, but Clara intervened.

"Papa, allow me to introduce you to my husband, who is all that is good and kind. I love him very much, and cannot be happy without him," she said.

"Introduce me to him! I knew him before you were born," cried the irate lawyer; "this is that unhanged thief and bankrupt, Richard Denton."

"I know it," she said, quietly; "he has told me all. We are quite willing to do without any of your money—if you will only forgive us."

"Believe me, Mr. Tillson," put in Denton, quietly; "that had I not fallen overhead and ears in love with your daughter at first sight this would not have happened. I do love your daughter, and will make her happy—of that you need have no doubt."

The lawyer reflected. James Tillson was no fool. His daughter had married well, a gentleman of ancient lineage, and capable of filling a good social position. He must make the best of it.

"What is done cannot be undone," he said, holding out his hand; "be good to my girl, and there is an end of the matter. You had better stop away a week, and then return to Denton Hall; I will have it ready for you."

And he sat down to join them at their meal. Shortly after he left, escorted to the small inn by his son-in-law.

Before ten days were over the marriage of Richard Denton and Clara Tillson was a nine days' wonder, and then the young squire resumed his right station in society, and all thanks to Dick Turpin, to whom he wrote an account of the whole affair, inviting him to come and see him whenever he was that way.

Dick did not get the letter for some time, but when he did, determined to avail himself of the invitation at an early date.

CHAPTER LXXXVIII

A PERILOUS ADVENTURE.

About the time of the elopement, Dick and Tom were jogging along the road, after a furious spell in London. They had not spent all their money, but were tired of riot and dissipation. So, leaving all but a few guineas in a safe deposit in London, they started off for a canter along the Great North-road in search of fresh air, adventure, and health.

They were in no hurry. These two were always methodical in their habits, except when actually engaged on business.

It was their second day, and they were seated at the window of a public room enjoying themselves, when a carriage drove up—a kind of open vehicle of a nondescript kind—from which alighted two well-to-do looking citizens. Dick and Tom sat unconcerned, but their eyes took in their quarry.

These two men, fat, their faces beaming over with the unction of money, with only one coachman as guard, were just the men to suit their plans.

They entered the house and at once ordered dinner, in the same room in which the highwaymen were seated. These two laid down their pipes and entered into conversation.

Presently, Dick sauntered out into the yard to look after his horses, and saw an ostler grooming those of the citizens.

"Going to make a stay?" asked the highwayman.

"No, sir! only having a rest."

"I shall want my horses in half an hour," resumed Dick, and went back to the house, which, after a while, he left in company with Tom King.

They had contrived to find out that the citizens were bound for Norwich, and trotted that way, looking out for a good place where to conceal themselves. The roadside for some way was lined by hedges, but at last they came to a spot where an old dilapidated barn stood a little way off the road.

Into this they entered, half closing the door behind them, but leaving sufficent space for them to squeeze through. Here they sat erect upon their horses, like centaurs, their ears expectant of every sound.

Half-an-hour passed, and then they distinctly heard the rumbling of wheels. They at once saw to their pistols, and put on their crape masks, which were usually turned up inside their hats.

The vehicle came along with a rumbling sound, and was soon close to the barn, the coachman driving, the citizens ensconced in the back seats. They looked fat, jolly, and complacent, as if they were at peace with all the world.

Out darted Dick and Tom, deftly knocked the coachman off his seat, and then presented their pistols to the heads of the two astonished travellers.

"Shell out, my friends," said Dick, in a hoarse, feigned voice; "no banter nor delay."

The men were pale with terror, and at once fumbled in their pockets, bringing out apparently well-lined pocket books and purses.

"Watches!" cried Dick, sententiously; "can accept anything."

They obeyed, and the two highwaymen turned and with a light laugh rode off.

They did not go far before they examined their capture. It was not so rich as they expected, but there was perhaps fifty guineas' worth in all. Still, everything was grist to their mill, and they struck off into a cross road, nor halted until they reached an alehouse, where they agreed to pass the night.

They ordered a double-bedded room as usual, thinking it safer not to be separated in case of any accident. Two such men as they were worth a dozen ordinary individuals. This done, they secured refreshments, determining to sup later on. Among the contents of the pocketbooks were some letters, which they now examined.

One was addressed to Mr. Boustead, banker, Leicester.

"Honoured friend," it said, "I shall be ready on Thursday with the two thousand guineas to lend on the mortgage. As, however, the roads are very much infested by highwaymen and footpads, I shall put on a shabby coat, and ride a scrubby horse, putting only a few bits of gold and silver in my purse, hiding the rest in my big riding boots, and I shall reach Leicester about twelve on Thursday."

"And this is Wednesday," cried Dick, after he had read the letter. "Whence comes he?" and looking, he saw it was a small town in the direction whence the citizens had come.

"It will be a rare game," smiled Tom; "how he'll stare when he finds we know. Does he sign his name?"

"Yes! Stephen Mowbray," replied Dick.

It may easily be imagined how these two gloated over this marvellous discovery. They revelled in the prospect, and ordered an extra glass on the strength of their expected windfall. Later on they supped, and retired when the house closed for the night.

After a late breakfast they started on the expedition in their usual light-hearted way, as gaily as some might have gone to a ball.

This time they selected a small but dense wood as the scene of their ambush, as they had a motive for so doing. Dick planted himself where he had a good view of the road, leaving his horse to feed on such herbage as he could find in the forest.

Presently they saw a solitary rider coming along the road. He was mounted on a kind of lean Rozinante, while he himself was not very stout. His clothes, as he approached, seemed very much like a bundle of rags, but his riding boots were unusually large.

Dick Turpin vaulted into his saddle, and the two sallied forth and went straight for the traveller, who, the moment they touched his bridle, began to speak in piteous accents.

"I'm a poor man," he muttered; "not worth a guinea."

The highwaymen made no reply, but dragged the terrified traveller into the wood, where they bid him dismount. No sooner did he do so, than Turpin knocked him down, and despite a feeble resistance, pulled off his boots. In less time than it takes to tell, they found at the bottom, under a false sole, two rolls of notes and gold.

"Have pity on a poor ruined old man!" cried the other, piteously

"Squire Mowbray," cried Tom King, "don't think to impose on me; you are as rich as Crœsus; you have mortgages all round, and this little sum won't hurt you. Thank your stars, it's not ten thousand."

The miser, for such he was, declared in tones of abject grief that he was utterly and hopelessly ruined, to which remark neither of the knights of the road paid the slightest attention.

Securing their plunder, they mounted and rode off, utterly regardless of the fearful imprecations, oaths, and ejaculations of the discomfited miser. They were, however, well aware that no sooner would the man get anywhere where he could make a declaration, than he would set the officers of justice after them, and spare no pains to capture them before they got rid of their plunder.

Where to go?

This was the important question; and, after some hesitation, they determined to retrace their steps by the cross roads, and get out of the line which connected the highway, and lie *perdu* for a day or two, when they would find an asylum in the safest place known to them in London.

Half way to the main road they sought temporary repose in an inn, where they were quite unknown, and entering the parlour determined to stay there some hours, perhaps all night. That would depend on circumstances. If they found the accommodation good, and all they could desire, they would stay.

They copiously indulged in refreshments, but always took care not to exceed the bounds of prudence. Few men were so hard headed as these comrades; but then, they were equally good trenchermen, which makes all the difference.

About six in the evening, several persons being present in the public room, the door was pushed open, and a tall, handsome-looking fellow, of about thirty, entered the room. He was evidently very much excited.

"What's the matter, Jim?" cried one of those present; "anything wrong?"

"Mowbray won't let me have the money," he cried, in anxious and excited tones; "he says he's been robbed on the king's highway—robbed and half murdered, and until he catches the criminals, will part with no more coin."

"That's bad," said his friend; and all present joined in their sympathy—one adding, "what are you going to do?"

"Give up the farm," sighed the young man; "it's terribly hard, but can't be helped. The steward would give me time if I could pay half."

Dick and Tom exchanged glances, but made no remark. They were both sorry for the young man, it is true; but what was to be done?

"May I ask who that young man is?" presently demanded Dick Turpin, of one of his companions and friends.

"Farmer James Lewis, a capital fellow," remarked the other; "but he's taken a bigger farm, a little more than he can manage. He owns a goodish bit already, but wanted to buy a vacant one which was once in his family."

"Oh, indeed," was all Dick said. A few minutes later he rose, and, leaving the room, went up to the bedroom which they had secured in case they determined to stay. Tom King followed him.

"What do you say?" asked Dick, when the two were alone. "Shall we give the poor fellow a thousand of the money?"

"This sort of thing won't do, you know," said Tom King, with a grimace. "I don't see the use of our risking our necks, and then giving up the swag like this."

"Well, we've got two thousand, and you shall have the greater part of the thousand we are going to keep," continued Dick; "let me have my way this once, and it shall not happen again."

Tom reluctantly yielded, and returned to the public room, where he found Farmer Lewis about to take his departure. Having wished his friends good bye, he went out, closely followed by Dick.

While waiting for his horse, the farmer stood cooling his heated brow in the road in front of the inn.

Dick went up and politely touched his beaver.

"A word with you, Mr. Lewis," he said;

"may I ride a short distance with you? I have something important to say."

James Lewis stared at him curiously, and then responded—

"I see no objection."

Dick had already ordered his horse, and it was brought. They rode for a few moments side by side, without speaking.

"Mr. Lewis, I understand that you expected an advance from Squire Mowbray?" asked Turpin.

"I did; but it is useless discussing the subject," retorted Lewis, wearily.

"Well; but I have something to say," continued Dick; "you said that a thousand would save you."

"Yes! because, if I paid that, I could have time for the balance," he sadly remarked.

"Well; I must ask you to demand no explanations," said Dick; "think what you please, so that you keep your own counsel. In this parcel you will find a thousand guineas in notes. I would not change them hereabout — good-bye!" and thrusting the parcel into the astonished farmer's hand, he rode off, summoned Tom, and was away before anybody could have stopped them.

That Farmer Lewis, having heard so much of the other's exploits, should suspect how the money had come into his hands, that, in fact, he should suspect him to be Dick Turpin, we believe was the case. However this may be, he acted with caution, went up to London, and changing the notes for gold at a foreign Jew money changer's, at a slight loss, returned to his native place and paid half of the purchase money of the land. Three months later he married a girl with sufficient money to enable him to pay the balance, and Squire Mowbray did not get a mortgage on that property.

———

CHAPTER LXXXIX.

A NARROW ESCAPE.

Anxious to get away from the neighbourhood of the irate money-lender, who would set the minions of the law on them without mercy, they returned to London, and took up their quarters at the "Blue Lion" in Gray's Inn Lane, a house noted for selling fine ale, and crowded every night with a motley assemblage of visitors, among whom were many thieves, sharpers, and other desperate characters, with their doxies.

Gambling with cards and dice was rampant in this place, and many a young man who came in innocently enough to see what he called life, dated his ruin from that hour.

Dick and Tom only came there for a change, it being out of their beaten track. As soon, however, as it was dark, they rose, wished such of them as they knew good-bye, and crossing Holborn, went to one of the most flash of the notorious houses frequented by the "family" as all those who belonged to the dangerous classes were called.

Here the company was a little more select, that is to say, was composed of persons who had more money than the poorer class of visitors who frequented the "Blue Lion."

Here they also met some merry lasses to whom they were well known and enjoyed themselves very much, on that and one or two other occasions.

On the fourth night, they were in one of their favourite resorts, when Tim Roach entered hurriedly, as if in search of them.

He seated himself next to Dick, and whispered, "Sapathwa wants you. I will come back in half an hour. I have another message to take."

And he went out hurriedly.

Dick and Tom now finished up what refreshment was before them, and prepared for action. They were willing to obey the Blue Dwarf, but just then were more inclined to have finished their London orgie. Still they were bound to their extraordinary employer, and never thought of deserting him.

Very shortly Tim Roach returned, and they departed with him, having already sent for their horses.

As soon as they were on the road, Tim Roach explained himself. Both Brian Seymour and Robert Woodstock had been seen on the road between Lewes and Brighton. That they were on the track of the earl's place of concealment seemed likely. But who could have betrayed them? Could Joe Askew have broken his oath? The other emissary's fatal death exonerated him.

"I fancy Joe Askew, scoundrel, thief, and tracker, as he is, would scarcely run the fearful risk of breaking that oath," observed Dick Turpin; "true he's only a flash-kiddy, and one can never know." *

"Well, at all events, they have been seen that way. I believe Teddy put them on the track," said Tim, "before he died. My lord is anxious not to move."

"I propose," retorted Dick, "we had all three better disguise ourselves and go different ways—we can meet on the road, say at Cuckfield; then we can disperse again, and make another rendezvous."

This was agreed on, and all adjourned to Dick's private apartments, where they selected some of his numerous disguises, which between them, they managed to make very complete. Dick made himself a very respectable cattle dealer, with a rather large beard on his chin; Tom made up for a city man, while Tim was turned into a very respectable jockey. He had been brought up as a groom and knew all about horses.

They kept together until out of London, and then separated. Their plan was to examine every public-house and inn on the way, these being divided between them.

Tim stopped at the first, Tom at the second, and then Dick rode on to the next, and continued in this way until he reached Cuckfield. Here he selected the "Horse Shoe," a noted house of very respectable character. He stood in the bar for some little time, and then sauntered towards the parlour.

As he did so, he passed the tap-room, the door of which was partly open. Dick started, for he at once was attracted by talking, and recognised first the voice of Brian Seymour and then that of Joe Askew.

He stood still and listened.

* Kiddy is a thief of the lower order, who, when he is oreeched by a course of successful depredations, dresses in the extreme of vulgar gentility, and affects a knowingness in his air and conversation, which renders him in reality an object of ridicule; such a one is pronounced by his associates of the same class a *flash kiddy*, or a *rolling kiddy*. *My kiddy* is a familiar term used by these gentry in addressing each other.

"I tell you, I will have no more to do with the matter. It would be certain death. Besides, I have taken a solemn oath, which I will not break," earnestly cried Joe Askew; "how you found out they are somewhere on the coast near Lewes, I cannot tell—but remember I gave no information."

"But you could," retorted Brian; "you are betraying us!"

"No, I am not! I am not against you—I cannot be for you," urged Joe.

"Well, you're a fool!" exclaimed Brian; "but mind you don't betray us, or I'll be one on your toe (be even with you some time); any way, I am going to try this new village of Brighthelmstone."

Dick waited to hear no more, but backed out, took another glass at the bar, and mounting, rode to the "White Lion," where he was to meet his companions. Going to the public room he was shortly joined by his friends. They met as strangers, but speedily contrived to make acquaintance, and sit at the same table.

They snatched a hasty meal, Dick telling them what he had heard, and as soon as that was despatched again mounted, nor barely drew rein until they reached Brighthelmstone.

The two highwaymen put up at the old farm house turned into an inn, while Tim went round to report progress.

The residence of the earl was somewhat in the character of a fortress, so well was it guarded and barred. Ever since the birth of the child, greater precautions than ever had been taken. Windows were barred, shutters securely closed at night, and no loophole left unguarded by which an entrance could be effected.

Tim Roach hurried to the house, made some signal previously agreed on, and was at once admitted to the presence of Sapathwa, to whom he reported.

"So they have tracked us again," said the Blue Dwarf, with fire-flashing eyes. "I can scarcely keep from tearing them to pieces. I will see the earl—wait here."

And he went out to where he expected to find the young nobleman alone. He did so. The countess at that hour generally visited the nursery. He told him what Tim had reported.

"What do you advise?" asked Shelton, in a dejected tone.

"Trick these rascals into some trap, and then return secretly to Elphick Castle. By using the utmost circumspection, and watching by day and night, we may defy them. Or," he continued, "go to London, and live the next seven months under an assumed name."

"Oh! here comes the colonel," said the earl, mournfully—"explain."

A long conference was held, to which Lord Jermyn was summoned, and it was resolved to wait a few hours before deciding. In the meantime Brian and Robert should be watched, and an attempt made to discover if they had tracked the fugitives to their hiding place.

Tim Roach went off to the farm-house inn and reported his instructions to Dick and Tom, who at once set their wits to work. It was decided that the two highwaymen should remain where they were while Tim Roach scouted.

He at once started, and wandered about the roads that led to the sea shore, Dick and Tom securing a room for themselves. It was small and incommodious, but it was private.

Tim, after a time, seated himself on a fallen tree and waited. Not for long. He heard the canter of horses along the road, and soon made out two horsemen, who in another moment were upon him. On seeing some one seated on a fallen tree, the riders reined in.

"Eh, my lad," said Brian, "we're strangers in these parts. Who lives about here?"

"Stranger myself—don't know," replied the other, and subsided into silence.

The men rode on.

"We're on the right track," whispered Brian, in an exulting tone; "that's Tim Roach, for a guinea; he's well made up, but I knew his voice. They're not far off."

"Let us make sure," cried Robert, "and returned at once to where the other had been sitting." But he was gone.

"You were right. Now, where can we pitch and pick up some information?"

Brian looked around.

"There appear lights in yonder farm house," he said; "we'll try."

And they rode up to the inn, where Tim Roach had preceded them. Entering, they found that it was a place where man and beast could get refreshments.

They sat down, called for what they required, and having being served, asked if a family had recently removed into the neighbourhood—a lady and several gentlemen.

The host replied that many families from Lewes lived there in the summer, but nobody in particular had come there of late.

"Could they have beds?"

"No! Their only room to spare was already let."

"Where is the nearest place we can get accommodation?" asked Brian, very much annoyed.

"'Half-way House,' on the Lewes road," was the reply.

And paying for what they had had, they went out, followed in the distance by Tim, who, seeing them safely housed at the "Half-way House," returned to report.

Nothing more could be done that night, so Tim left Dick and Tom to let the Blue Dwarf know what had happened. Again a brief conference was held, after which Dick was summoned to the house.

It was arranged that all should wait to see what was attempted on the morrow. Nothing would be done until night. This Dick returned and intimated to Tom. They presently retired to rest and lay late, knowing that Tim Roach would soon arouse them if anything should turn up.

But night came again without anything happening. Tim then came round with instructions for them to keep a sharp look out from some good vantage point, one on each side of the house.

They had not long to wait. About seven in the evening they saw Brian Seymour and Robert Woodstock, clad in rough frieze coats, come across the fields towards the house, which was enshrouded in darkness.

Dick was ensconced behind a wood pile in a stooping position. The two men approached close to where he was, and gazed up at the house.

"It looks very dark," said Brian; "but I am assured at the inn that it is inhabited, and by just the people we are looking for. That woman I got hold of has seen a spoony young couple, a nurse and a baby, while two middle-aged gentlemen often are seen out on horseback together."

"But they seem fully on their guard," replied Robert, significantly.

"Yes; and yet we might get in some night. I wish we had Jim, the Cracker, down here," Brian went on; "I have a great mind to fetch him."

"He's good at cracking cribs, I must say. The house looks pretty strong, but it has no doubt its vulnerable part," observed Robert.

"The delay is what I think of; but it would be idle for us to venture," said Brian; "we had better return and make terms with him."

"I am heartily sick of the whole business," retorted Robert; "as long as that infernal cripple exists, we shall be defeated."

"Curse him," added Brian, "his cunning has defeated us as yet, but let me but once get him in my power and I will destroy him as I would a rat. But it's no use talking; we must get back to town and hunt up Conkey Cracker, as some call him."

With which they moved away, after launching sundry warm epithets at the house and its indwellers.

Dick waited until they were out of sight, and then joined his companion. Once together, they went up to the house, and pulling a bell secreted in the ivy, were at once admitted by Tim Roach and taken to the presence of Sapathwa.

Dick without circumlocution told his story, to which the Blue Dwarf listened with the deepest attention, chuckling in his terrible way at what was said about himself.

"Forewarned, forearmed," he said; "but now as to this Conkey Cracker. Do you know him?"

"Yes, sir!" replied Turpin, "the cleverest burglar in England. He's done some fine starts, but is in hiding now, as the officers have sworn to have him dead or alive."

"Couldn't you watch and let us know when he is coming down?" asked Sapathwa; "we would then be ready for him."

"Certainly; can we take Tim with us?" asked Dick.

"If you wish. As to money?"

"We don't want any just now. We shall be happy to be paid when we have done the work; we shall be proud," answered Dick.

Sapathwa smiled his wan and almost ghastly smile, and then offering them some refreshments, they shortly after took their leave in company with Tim Roach, who thoroughly enjoyed the spirit of adventure.

Their object was to reach London in time to see Conkey Cracker before the others, and make terms with him. If he was willing to help in defeating their machinations, Sapathwa was willing to reward him most handsomely.

Both Dick and Tom knew him well and were cognisant of his different haunts, and knew where to find him.

They proceeded towards Cuckfield, where they put up about midnight, and started after breakfast for the great metropolis, which they reached by easy stages.

They used every precaution to avoid coming across Brian Seymour and Robert Woodstock, their errand to London being one that depended on these two arch conspirators being ignorant of their whereabouts.

CHAPTER XC.

THE BURGLARS' LAIR.

After putting up their horses and making arrangements for the night, they took their way towards one of the worst dens in Shoreditch, where they had heard Conkey Cracker had taken refuge. His last burglary had been of an unusually audacious character, and had brought down such animadversions on the heads of the Bow Street department, that the officers had expressed their determination to capture Conkey at any price.

He had, therefore, secluded himself for some time, begging his friends to keep his place of concealment dark.

Nobody ever for one moment would have suspected Dick and Tom of splitting, so they easily obtained a clue to his lair when they expressed a wish to see him on a matter of private business.

We will allow them to go forward while we explain a strange coincidence, which might have ended badly for our two friends and others.

Some days before, a gentleman named Whitebread, residing in Saville-place, had lost a very beautiful little King Charles spaniel. He put an advertisement in the papers offering two guineas reward for the recovery of the dog.

A man named Sargeant then called upon him and informed him that he knew where the dog was, and if he would give him something extra beyond the two guineas, he would say where it could be found, but the two guineas would have to be given to the man who had it.

Mr. Whitebread asked the man how he came to know where the dog was, and he replied : " To tell you the truth, I saw the dog stolen."

Mr. Whitebread, on hearing this, said : " You are a *particeps criminis* in the act, and, unless you produce it, I shall give you into custody." The man refused to say where it was, and Mr. Whitebread then sent for the watchmen and charged the man with the robbery.

He was taken to Marlborough-street and brought before the magistrates. He still refused to say where it was, and was then remanded for further inquiries.

After being locked up for some time he sent for the officer, and told him, if the two guineas were forthcoming, he would take the watchman to where the dog was. The magistrate directed two watchmen, named Goddard and Clements, to accompany the prisoner in a hackney coach, and he then took them to a most notorious house opposite to Shoreditch church.

The front part was a noted public-house ; but at the back of it was a large den of thieves of a most fearful description.

Here it was that Dick Turpin and Tom King had gone to seek an interview with Conkey Cracker, who received them in a private room, for which he paid a good price.

The two officers had no idea of the dangerous gang they were going among, or they would have been better prepared and gone in greater numbers. When the man Sargeant arrived with the officers at the house, he first stipulated that the two guineas should be handed to the landlord to hold while the dog was fetched.

The money was accordingly given up to him. Sargeant then sent a message to bring the dog. When it was brought, the officers requested to be informed who they had to give the money up to. There were several in the gang, and they said the money was to be left with the landlord, and they would divide it among the proper parties.

The watchmen replied : " They must take the dog, then, and the two guineas, back. The little dog in the meantime had been fondling and playing, and seemed quite delighted at seeing his master, a serving-man, there, as though glad at the prospect of getting home again.

As none in the gang would personally claim it, the landlord gave the two guineas back to the watchmen, and they at once prepared to leave with the dog.

Upon this a great row ensued between the watchmen and the thieves, and a struggle for the possession of the dog followed.

A whistle was now blown, and a door at the end of a passage was opened by some robbers concealed in a secret room. It was, in fact, a regular robber's den.

At a signal given, thirty of the most desperate cut-throats came running out, all armed with long-bladed knives, swearing with the most horrible imprecations to murder anyone that interfered with any of their body. In the terrible struggle which ensued they tried to cut off the head of the poor terrified little animal, and they declared that, unless the money was left, the dog should not go out of the place alive.

The landlord, seeing the serious nature of the conflict that was going on, at once jumped over the bar, and, opening a side door that was generally kept locked, stood between the exasperated thieves and Mr. Whitebread's servant, whom he let out with the dog under his arm.

Having got into the street safely with the dog, which was considered exceedingly valuable, he at once made his escape with it to his master's house.

The whole gang of the thieves, however, commenced to set on the watchmen in the most brutal manner. They knocked them down and trampled on them, and with the most horrid curses threatened to stab them with their knives.

The landlord now interfered, and other aid from the outside being obtained, the officers were got away from the murderous gang. Further assistance was now procured by them, and Sargeant was taken back to Marlborough-street to be charged with being an accessory after the fact, in stealing the dog, and with the assault on the watchmen.

In the meantime, Dick and Tom had introduced themselves as coming on business ; Conkey Cracker bowed, and mildly suggested that, being very short of the mopuses, he should like something to eat.

With the same frankness as he had exhibited, Dick ordered some cold meat, a jug of ale, and a pint of brandy.

A portion of this being disposed of by the accomplished burglar, with the brandy between them, Mr. Conkey Cracker politely inquired their business.

" Honour bright—no splitting."

" No faking. Whatever you trust me with— ' mum's the word,' " he said, his eyes apparently cast downwards, but ever and anon glancing up at them with a searching and curious look.

Dick now explained that two men whom he probably knew, Brian Seymour and Robert Woodstock, would, as soon as they could find him, propose a burglary to him.

"It won't be much of a 'crack' in the way of 'swag,'" said Dick; "but he wants to steal a child which stands perhaps between himself and an earldom."

"Not in my line," replied Conkey, with a virtuous shake of his head.

"Well, I think they'll make it worth your while," continued Dick; "while, if you play into our hands, we'll pay. The father of the child will pay handsomely. All we want to know is, when it's coming off. When they come, adjourn the job until a fixed day, and then tell me the date."

"No grabbing," mused Conkey.

"Under the armpits," said Dick, holding out his hand.

"Then, it's settled," replied Conkey. "Ah! what's that! Are the dabs upon us?"

And he ran out to see what was the matter, returning with rather a disturbed look.

"Some fool has let the beaks send some Charleys here for a stolen dog," he said; "but don't be uneasy; if the worst comes to the worst, I have a way out. Anyway, as this crib is blown, I shall move out to-night."

And he sat down to help finish the brandy.

The contest was not of long duration, but when the thieves and robbers returned, the noise for some time was stunning. But our friends were used to this sort of thing, and waited until it had toned down, when Dick gave Conkey Cracker an address, and retired with Tom.

On the second night after this, while Dick and Tom were enjoying their evening meal, a boy came in, and putting a bit of paper in the high-wayman's hand, retired without a word.

"The sixteenth, at midnight," was made out with some difficulty.

This gave them four clear days to work. After enjoying themselves for another hour, they rose, fetched their horses, and started for Brighthelmstone.

———

CHAPTER XCI.

THE BURGLARY.

It was a dark and gloomy night, the wind blowing fresh and the rain falling in slanting sheets, when three horsemen with heavy cloaks and slouched hats approached the mansion known as Pershene House.

It was enveloped in darkness, save that, as the house was neared, one light was to be seen from a window of the first-floor.

Dismounting near a shed, the three men put their horses under shelter, and got as near the residence as possible.

All on the ground floor was dark and gloomy, the shutters fastened on the inside, as Conkey Cracker easily made out. But the burglar was not very easily to be baulked.

The window where the light was had a balcony, and this rendered his task easy. He was always prepared for such contingencies.

Under this balcony were two pillars, up which crept some plants. Conkey removed his cloak, put it under cover, and began the ascent, which, being wiry and agile, he easily made.

In a moment more he was on the balcony and had hooked a rope ladder to it, by which Brian and Robert easily ascended.

Then they peered in and saw that the room was a bedroom, but occupied just now by a woman in an arm chair, who had fallen asleep beside a cradle containing a child.

"'Sdeath!" cried Brian; "luck is on our side—open the window!"

This Conkey Cracker did without difficulty, the iron grating usually closing the orifice having been unaccountably allowed to fall back against the wall.

Brian stepped into the room, followed by his comrades, and hurried to where the woman sat.

Without hesitation he snatched the baby from the cradle, habited in its long clothes as it was, and then, with an exasperated curse, threw it on the ground.

It was a bundle of rags dressed up to represent a baby.

"D——n!" he cried, in a tone of baffled fury, as he shook the woman violently, "What does it all mean?—hell and furies!"

The woman, like the baby, was an inanimate lay figure.

"Ha! ha! ha!" laughed a hideous voice, as a door flew open, and the Blue Dwarf entered, followed by three closely-masked men.

Conkey Cracker, with a terrified yell of fright and despair, darted for the balcony, and slipped down before anyone could stop him; but Brian and Robert were pinioned by their opponents.

"And now," said Sapathwa, in his shrillest tones, with a terrible air of menace not unmixed with dignity, "we have got you, burglars and abductors, and mean to keep you. Secure them while I send for officers."

And despite their struggles, the two were tied with ropes, which their captors were provided with in readiness.

It was Sapathwa who had arranged the ludicrous comedy to disappoint and punish these evil doers.

As soon as they were safely secured they were lifted on to the bed and left to their reflections, which we may be assured were not of the most agreeable character.

Meanwhile, Dick Turpin hurried down, and caught Conkey Cracker in the act of mounting his horse.

"One moment," he said; "here's your reward. Don't be in a hurry for a moment. Take this purse."

Conkey Cracker did what he was told without any hesitation.

"What horrible thing was that?" he then gasped; "I shall never sleep again."

"A very amiable gentleman, and a great friend of mine," replied Dick Turpin; "I must go back to him. Your friends have had a precious fright, so if you like you can release them."

"Is it gone?" asked Conkey Cracker, with an uneasy glance.

"Yes; you have nothing to fear," replied Dick; "you can go up at once and let your companions loose. Give what explanation you like, so that you allay their suspicions."

Conkey Cracker saw the necessity of this, and no longer hesitated. He secreted his money with care, and then slowly reascended the rope ladder to the balcony.

He gazed into the room, and saw the two men extended on the bed, uttering wild imprecations and curses.

He approached the bed, with a knife in his hand.

"Away! base and cowardly assassin!" yelled Brian; "back—help—murderer!"

"Hush you fool!" cried Conkey Cracker, "or I'll leave you to your fate. Do you want to bring that monster back?"

And with these words he speedily cut their bonds, and again fled to the window. Without one moment's delay they followed.

Conkey rushed for the horses, and, all three mounting, took their way over hedges and fields until they were on the main road to Lewes, and dashing up the hill for that quaint and ancient town.

So fearful were they of being pursued, that none halted until they drew rein before the "Star and Garter," where they fancied they would be tolerably safe.

They only, however, stopped for refreshments, and then made for London.

But no lesson, no punishment taught Brian Seymour anything. All he thought of was, that the time was passing fast indicated in the will, and that this once elapsed all his hopes of rank and wealth would pass away.

It was a bitter thought, and at once he began in his intriguing brain to plot something which might prove fatal to the earl.

CHAPTER XCII.

JOE ASKEW PLANS A ROBBERY.

Joe Askew, being compelled by his compact with Dick Turpin to abstain from aiding and abetting Brian Seymour, found himself at a very low ebb.

He was up to all the dodges of the metropolis, but hesitated at going in for crime on a large scale.

He had no objection to area sneaking, to joining hocussers, mobsmen, or swell mobsmen, or even sneaksmen. He had been a shofulman, a passer of bad money, a flat-catcher or ring-dropper, and at one time had aided and abetted a gang of resurrectionists.

One evening, when in the "Blue Lion," in Gray's Inn Lane, he came across some of his old friends, who, though rather short of cash, stood him a drink.

After the drink was over, the resurrectionists took Joe Askew on one side and proposed to him what might prove a very lucrative piece of fun.

The head man, whose name was Prober, told Joe Askew that they were without a body, but they knew that one Dr. Maurice was in want of a subject.

"Now," said Prober, "you're but a little fellow, and we could easily pack you in a hamper and sell you as a corpse."

"Not if I know it," cried Joe.

"But, my dear fellow, it will be the rarest fun out," urged Prober. "The doctor can do nothing. We'll see you well provided, and nothing will be easier than to escape.

Well, it is needless to enter into details. After some hesitation, Joe Askew agreed to play a corpse, for this occasion only.

Prober at once went to Dr. Maurice, and informed him that they had a fine, healthy, fresh subject, a strong muscular fellow, about five and forty, whom nobody owned.

The doctor having heard the description of him, and being in urgent need of such a subject for a lecture he was going to give in a few days, consented to purchase the body for ten guineas.

"You won't fail to bring him to-night, will you?" said the doctor, when the bargain was struck.

"No!" said the snatcher; "you shall have him here sartin, by ten o'clock to-night. Which door shall we bring him to?"

"Take him round to the back door," said the doctor, "and give him to the servant if I am out. Don't tell her what it is though, or she may be frightened, and if I am not in I will leave the money for you."

"You shall have him right enough, master," replied the snatcher; "ten o'clock, sharp."

The snatchers returned to their hovel, highly delighted with their bargain. When the time came they packed Joe Askew in a large hamper partly filled with straw, in such a position that he could be tolerably comfortable during his carriage to the anatomical school.

Joe had been provided with some bread and cheese, a flask of brandy, and a clasp knife in his pocket in case of emergency.

It was thought by the snatchers that after they had received their coin the head and body would be taken at once to the dissecting or some other room in the doctor's house, where it would be deposited for the night; and then it was arranged that as soon as Joe Askew found that the doctor and his family had gone to bed, or that he found himself in a room alone, that he should cut the string of the hamper-lid, pocket anything that he could see in the place, and then, bolting through the window, make his escape.

All parties laughed heartily at what they thought would be a fine practical joke on the doctor, and a capital sell.

When the proper time arrived the snatchers started off with Joe Askew in the hamper, and arrived at the doctor's house at the time appointed—precisely at ten o'clock. When they arrived at the house they rang the bell, and on the servant answering they inquired for the doctor and found him at home.

The doctor, to get the girl out of the room while the parcel was brought in, sent her for change, and while she was out the hamper was brought in and deposited in the servants' kitchen.

The snatchers, in order to counteract any suspicions that the doctor might have, unfastened the strings of the lid part of the way round, and, showing him the bushy hair of Joe Askew's head, assured the doctor he was one of the finest subjects he had ever seen.

The doctor, who was in a hurry to get off, as he had an engagement out, just took a hasty glance at the top of Askew's head, and the snatchers immediately sewed down the lid with packing needle and string.

Meanwhile the servant returned with the change. The doctor paid the snatchers the ten guineas, and they immediately left, leaving their confederate sewed down in the hamper, along with the servant in the kitchen.

The doctor, having told the servant to let the hamper remain there untouched for the night, then put on his hat and coat, and went hurriedly off to the engagement at which he was expected.

In this packed-up condition Joe Askew remained for a considerable period quite undisturbed, with the exception that he every now and then felt the warm breath of the doctor's huge mastiff, as it frequently put its nose to the hamper, sniffing and smelling around.

As the snatcher lay thus curled in the hamper he could plainly see through the wicker the form of the dog pacing the kitchen to and fro, and he could also see Mary, the servant, sitting on her chair, busy with her needle on a piece of embroidery.

After a little time a gentle tap was heard at the kitchen window, and the girl, rising from her seat, at once opened the kitchen door and let the visitor in.

The visitor on this occasion was one of the cupboard-loving Charleys of the day, who, instead of being out on his beat, keeping watch during the night, frequently thought it more comfortable to be sitting by the side of Mary, the doctor's maid, whom he professed to love from the bottom of his heart.

"Who's at home, Polly?" said he, in a jovial tone, as he proceeded to place his staff in one corner, and to deposit his old horn lantern in another.

"Oh, there's nobody at home to-night, Charley," said Mary, catching hold of his two hands and stretching them as far apart as she could, while she brought her lips in close proximity to his. "I'm so delighted."

"Aint there nobody at home? Oh, I'm so glad!" said he, as he began to kiss her, first on one cheek and then on the other, while he stood before her, with his watchman's rattle hanging half out of his coat-tail behind, like a great rattlesnake lubricating its prey previous to gorging it down.

"Nice occupation for a Charley," thought Joe Askew; "pretty way of spending their nights."

"What have you got in the larder, Poll, to-night?" said the Charley, after another very energetic burst of cuddling and kissing.

"Oh, I've the half of a splendid young duck and some nice cold pudding," said Mary, as she bustled about and placed the things on the table for the Charley's meal.

"Capital!" said the Charley; "them's the things—cold duck to make a feller's affections grow, and cold pudding to settle his love; that's the way to bring about the matrimonial day."

While the Charley was tucking in the duck, the cold pudding, and stout, the snatcher still lay uncomfortably tucked up in the hamper, getting considerably cramped and stiff, and anxiously wishing for some turn of events and change of circumstances which would give him a chance of escaping from his unenviable position, out of the door or out of the window, for what with the fear of detection by the doctor, and an attack on him by the dog in the night if he attempted to escape, he began to realise the danger he was in.

At length the Charley, having done ample justice to the flesh of the duck, and left nothing but the bones, got up to go, and, having again armed himself with his staff and lighted his lantern, he bestowed another battery of kisses on Mary's cheeks and lips, and then finally wished her good-night. As he took his departure he began singing, in his usual nasal twang, "Past twelve, and a starlight morning!" as if he had been assiduously on duty the whole of the evening.

Mary now quietly settled herself down again to continue the embroidery, which her love episode with the Charley had interrupted.

While she was anxiously waiting for her master and mistress to come home, the wind gradually began to rise, and the shutters outside to creak, and she fancied she heard other noises about which she hardly knew whether caused by the wind or not.

"Oh dear! I wish master and mistress would come!" said she, as she leant back in her chair and looked at the clock with a mouth wide open and a regular sleepy yawn, as she fancied she saw a table move, then a chair, and then first one thing and then another.

"Time always goes so quick when Charley's here, and I gets so frightened when he's gone. I fancies I hears all sorts of things, all sorts of noises, and sees all sorts of things move in the room. If it wasn't for poor old 'Tear-'em,' the master's mastiff, being here, I am sure I dare not stop at all—not for the world.

"Upon my word, if I don't think I've seen that hamper move two or three times to-night! But, then, I suppose it's all my foolish fancies. A hamper couldn't move, and so I must be silly to think that. I wish master and mistress would come; I've got to be up by six in the morning, and now it's nearly one o'clock.

"Upon my honour, I think I saw that hamper move again. What with the creaking noises at the windows, and my fancying I keep seeing that hamper and other things move, it's enough to make anybody believe the house is haunted. But, there, I suppose it's all my imagination." And she rubbed her eyes and gave another wide-mouthed yawn. "I'll go and stand at the front door, and run in if I see master and mistress coming."

Saying which, she opened the kitchen-door, and, calling the dog, went out.

Joe Askew breathed more freely, and, as the door closed, out with his sharp knife, and in a moment the lid of the hamper was off and Joe on his feet. He did not wait one minute, his footsteps hastened by a loud knock at the door.

Out of the door he bolted, hid in the area until the front door was shut, and darted off to the rendezvous of the body-snatchers, where he found them feasting.

They heard his story amidst roars of laughter. The girl, the dog, and the Charley were too much for them.

They congratulated him, however, on his lucky escape, and plied him with a stiff glass of spirits, after which he was comforted.

Meanwhile the girl had gone down to the kitchen with the dog, and the first thing she saw was the empty hamper and the straw all scattered about.

The dog sniffed at it and began to bark and growl, bringing the doctor down to see what was the matter.

His astonishment was too great for words.

"I thought," said the girl, "I saw the hamper move, and that made me nervous. There was a man in it. We might have been robbed, murdered, and God knows what!"

"I think there was a man in it," the doctor remarked. "A shameful trick has been played on us. But lock up now and go to bed, while I go round the house with 'Tear-'em.'"

The girl hastened to obey, and soon crept to the attic. The doctor, as we well know, found nothing, but shrewdly suspected that the body-snatchers had put a live man in the hamper, robbed him of his money, and meant to rob him of more.

He promised himself to have nothing more to do with the gang.

————

CHAPTER XCIII.

THE FIRE AT THE OLD BULL AND GATE INN.—ON THE ROAD AGAIN.

It will have been guessed by our shrewd and intelligent readers that, before the trick on Brian Seymour had been played, the fugitives had started for London, where they intended stopping for some time.

The Blue Dwarf was sure that both these relentless foes would seek them at Elphick Castle, and all determined to remain away from there yet awhile.

An agent of Sapathwa's took a house for them in Westminster, in a fashionable street, where they could have every comfort. It was in the neighbourhood of the parks, and, by dressing plainly, the countess could risk going out with the nurse and child.

As they were not known in society, they were able to take private boxes at the theatres and go about a good deal, taking care, when going to public places, to be plainly habited, as if belonging rather to the middle than the upper classes.

Dick and Tom retired to an inn in the neighbourhood, one of those old-fashioned taverns which are so fast disappearing before the relentless hand of modern improvement, which may be useful from a sanitary point of view, but is sadly detrimental from a picturesque standpoint.

This inn, known as the "Bull and Gate," was situated in a crowded thoroughfare, and was approached by a large gate under an archway.

It stood around the four sides of a court, and two of its wings were connected by a narrow wooden bridge.

This was the first floor, consisting wholly of sleeping apartments.

The lower floor was partitioned out into dining, supper, and other rooms, with a bar near the entrance. Dick and Tom, in the character of country gentlemen, had secured a private apartment, but made use of the coffee and dining rooms when it suited their purpose.

They received no visitors, as a rule, and spent the greater part of their time out of doors, as in their character of strangers to London they would naturally do.

Their principal real occupation was visiting some of their noted haunts, where they found amusement more congenial to their tastes than could be had at a place where they had to play a rather demure part.

Demure for them, as society in those days was by no means particular. Fighting, drinking, and gallantry were the principal occupations of what it was the custom to call "pretty men," while those who affected a more sedate demeanour, were regarded as milksops.

On the third evening of their sojourn at the "Bull and Gate," Dick and Tom stayed at home, having received an intimation from Sapathwa that he would pay them a visit. Though the Blue Dwarf was not very susceptible to the pleasures of the table, the two highwaymen did not neglect to order a succulent supper for three.

About nine o'clock their guest arrived in a hackney coach, wrapped in a cloak with a hood, as usual, and entered the inn unnoticed.

Before he took off his disguise the supper was ordered to be placed on the table.

"We would be private," said Dick; "if we want anything, we can ring."

The drawer retired, casting curious glances at the stranger.

Full justice was first done to the meal, and then the three associates, having sent for a bowl of punch, entered upon a full discussion of their plans.

It is unnecessary to explain these, as they will appear as we proceed with our narrative.

The conversation, however, extended so far into the night as to make it expedient that Sapathwa should remain. The two high tobies offered to see him home, but the Blue Dwarf declined. As the tavern was very full, the new guest had to content himself with a small room near that occupied by our modern Damon and Pythias.

They retired to their respective chambers somewhere about twelve, and were soon in a sound slumber.

The Blue Dwarf was ever a light sleeper, and on this occasion it was merciful that it was so. He had been in bed about two hours when he was awakened by a crackling noise, and a stifling sensation.

Leaping out of bed—he never undressed in strange places—he rushed to the window and saw at once that the opposite wing was in flames, which were making their way in his direction with fearful rapidity.

He bounded from his room and knocked at the door of that occupied by the two highwaymen, who, believing that the least thing that could have happened was their discovery by Pooly, at once secured their weapons. Then, reassured by the voice of the Blue Dwarf, they opened the door.

No sooner did they realise their position, than Tom King hurried down stairs to give the alarm.

It did not take long to rouse the terrified servants.

"Go for the watch," said Tom King to one of the ostlers; "and you other fellows rouse the lodgers."

Some obeyed, while others thought only of their own escape.

The "Bull and Gate" dates from a very early period of our history, and was built chiefly of timber, which was old, honeycombed, and subject particularly to the action of the flames.

The progress of the fire was so rapid as to threaten to consume the entire fabric.

Soon the whole building seemed to resound with cries and shrieks, made more terrible by the rushing of an excited mob into the courtyard.

The appliances for putting out conflagrations were very wretched and incompetent in those days, which some persons absurdly call the good old times.

The fire of London and that generated by the Lord George Gordon riots prove this to demonstration.

The watch came, men rushed in with ladders, men came on horseback; the ladders were short and useless; the watch waved lanterns and sprung rattles; carts were backed into the yard.

But nothing really was done.

Meanwhile, on the side where the conflagration had commenced, windows were thrown up and men and women, girls and boys, appeared, half dressed, appealing for help.

The stairs were inaccessible; they had been some time the prey of the flames, the fire having begun in the basement.

"Help! oh help!" cried twenty voices.

Dick had gone down into the yard, and at once, aided by willing hands, clambered on a cart, in the hope of reaching the windows.

Meanwhile the Blue Dwarf, closely followed by Tom King, had dashed across the wooden bridge, itself already burning, and reached the opposite side.

A very beautiful girl appeared at one of the windows, and towards her the Blue Dwarf made a rush.

Alarmed as she was by the fire, she was still more so at sight of the monster who was coming to her rescue.

She fainted, but the Blue Dwarf catching her up in his arms, rushed to where Dick Turpin stood, ready to receive her and bear her to a place of safety.

Proper ladders were now found, and after superhuman exertions the whole of the inmates of the tavern were saved.

Sapathwa and his friend now returned to their own rooms, but reflection made them feel that to remain where they were would be unwise.

The extraordinary figure of our titular hero had excited universal attention, while among the watch there might be some one who would recognise in the other two the celebrated highwaymen.

A quiet retreat was therefore decided on, and the three presently decamped without beat of drum.

Just in time.

They had not been gone ten minutes when there was a hue-and-cry, a rush up stairs, but the birds had flown.

The Blue Dwarf took them to one of his own private retreats, and there they found repose.

It was decided in the morning that a further residence in London might not be conducive to their health at present.

So they determined to go down towards Elphick Castle, as by this means they might find out if Brian and Robert were still following up their unfortunate and persecuted kinsman.

They started about mid-day, fixing their first halt at a well-known inn, where they might perhaps find some news useful in their line of business.

It was dark very early now, and they pulled up about six o'clock, at once ordering a hearty meal, and joining the guests and travellers in the public room.

They looked keenly about, as they usually did, for familiar faces, which they studiously avoided; but no one they knew rewarded their examination.

They accordingly enjoyed their meal, drank as usual, and then joined in the pipe, which every day was becoming more fashionable.

Then presently somebody proposed one of the popular round games, which proposition was agreed to.

Dick and Tom in this sort of society were always on their guard, and never attempted those tricks which, if discovered or even suspected, would have brought down a storm on their devoted heads.

While they were playing the door opened, and in came the miser, Squire Mowbray, whom they had robbed of two thousand guineas a few weeks before.

The two men exchanged meaning glances.

They knew him at once, though he was not quite so badly dressed as before. He walked in, glancing to the right and left, and occasionally exchanging a nod with one of the natives, to all of whom he seemed to be known.

He then seated himself, and called for refreshments. His chair was drawn up to the same table at which Dick and Tom were seated. As they were total strangers to him, he examined them suspiciously and closely. They stared in return in blank surprise, as if astonished at his vulgarity and impudence.

"That old gent will know us next time he sees us," muttered Tom, in an audible whisper.

Dick nodded and laughed, very much to the discomfiture of Squire Mowbray, who thought a great deal of himself, and was accustomed to be treated with great deference by his satellites and customers.

The friends took no further notice, and continued their meal; but to both of them came the same thought, "Is it worth while to rob him again?"

A man who sat next to Squire Mowbray, and who appeared to know him very well, now accosted him.

"Well, Squire Mowbray," he asked, "never got no trace of them thieves who robbed you some time ago?"

"No!" said the other, snappishly; "but it seems odd how Farmer Lewis got the money to pay for Dell's Farm. Can't make it out. The two thousand guineas were for him."

"I suppose," said a person at no great distance, "that there are other people who lend money besides you, Squire Mowbray? Farmer Lewis went to London when he found you couldn't let him have the stuff, and got it there."

"Ah!" bitterly responded Mowbray; "so he says."

"And so he did!" remarked Farmer Lewis, who had been in the room some time listening. "You'd better be careful what you say, Squire Mowbray," he added; "there's no proof you ever were robbed at all."

There was a slight titter at this, and Farmer Lewis took advantage of it to seat himself near our two friends, whom he had recognised at a glance.

"I only came in for a glass of ale," said Farmer Lewis to the waiter. "I'm off home after that."

He paid, drank his beer, and rising, went out, making a sign to the friends to follow, which they did without any apparent haste.

They found him in the portico.

"You will excuse me," he said, "if I am impertinent or mistaken, but as I came in, a man went off for the officers, saying Dick Turpin and Tom King were inside. 'I'll have the reward,' he said, as he rushed out."

"We thank you very much. Which way did he go?"

The farmer pointed with his whip.

"Ride on, we will follow," said Dick; "perhaps you may help us."

Tom and Dick hurriedly secured their horses, which in five minutes more would have been locked in the stables. As they rode out of the yard, there was a hue-and-cry from the tap room, but both Dick and his friend dashed off, their whips ominously clubbed.

MAUD'S HEART GAVE A GREAT BOUND; SHE RECOGNISED THE QUILT THAT HAD
COVERED HER UNCLE'S BED!

At the corner of the road they found Farmer Lewis waiting for them.

"We have twenty minutes," he said, gravely. "I have nothing to do with who you are, but I owe you a deep debt of gratitude, and will discharge it."

He trotted on some distance, and then turned down a narrow pathway leading into a deep wood, along which he rode until they reached a cross-road.

"My house is not far off," he said; "if you like to pass the night there, you can. I will put the horses in a shed at a distance. As we cannot know what the officers may do, I should keep good watch."

"You are very good," responded Dick, "and we are heartily thankful. Still, it may perhaps get you into trouble."

"I will risk that," said the farmer, and rode on until he came to a secluded, but neat house.

He called a man, who at once appeared to take his orders.

"Take these gentlemen's horses to the old barn," he directed; "let them be well attended to, but don't take off saddle or bridle. They may start at any time."

He then led them in, and introduced them to his wife as friends from London, who had helped him when Mowbray refused to lend him the promised money.

The good woman received them most courteously, and pressed refreshments on them. They accepted liquids, excusing themselves from eating on the ground of having just dined.

"Would they sleep there?" she asked, on hospitable thoughts intent.

Her husband explained that perhaps they might, but until their business was settled he could not say. Still, she might get a room ready.

Mrs. Lewis at once retired, and left the three men together. The children had gone to bed save one son of twelve, who came in at this moment.

"John," said his father, drawing him on one side, "these are friends of mine, as I will explain to you another time. What I want you to do is now to obey me, without asking any questions. Their business is private, and they don't want their presence known at present. I want you to go to Gable Point, and if you see any horsemen coming towards the farm, run as quickly as you can and let me know."

The boy, a shrewd, sharp lad, simply nodded, and, quite proud of his expedition, went out.

The farmer now explained that in consequence of a legacy of three thousand guineas he was quite in clover. The new farm was paid for, and he had a good balance at his banker's.

"Now I can pay you that thousand guineas in a lump," said Farmer Lewis, "if you wish it, or a hundred at a time, just as you like."

"Well," remarked Dick, "just now we are not in want of it. We are on private business, for which we are paid well, and money would embarrass us. If at any time we need cash, we will let you know."

"As you wish," continued Lewis; "whenever you want it, come, and it shall be yours."

Dick expressed his thanks, and at that moment in darted John.

"Five men, guided by Bill Hodge, are coming this way," he said, panting for breath.

"This way, gentlemen," answered his father. "Don't say a word, John, about any visitors."

And he went out at the back, where they found the man.

"Take my friends to the old barn, and show them the way to the horse ferry," whispered Lewis; "I will return to the house."

And he hurriedly re-entered the house, and, when the officers came up, they found himself, his wife, and son, sitting quietly over their supper.

"Eh, Farmer Lewis!" cried one of the officers. "Seed two men, splendidly mounted, come this way? Be quick—there's a big reward. They be Dick Turpin and Tom King."

"Well," answered Lewis, deliberately, while Mrs. Lewis and John looked astounded and horrified, "just as I reached Gable Point two smart-looking fellows did pass me, riding hard. They followed the main road."

"Thanks," cried the officer, bustling out and leaving the inhabitants of the farmhouse in a state of excitement and confusion.

"Husband!" gasped Mrs. Lewis.

"Yes, wife, and you, my son, those two men were the well-known highwaymen, Dick Turpin and his comrade, Tom King. Once they did me a great service, which I will explain to you some day, my boy. "In return for that, if ever I can be useful to them I should. To-night they were in danger. I warned them, and now have, for the time being, saved them. They are terrible men, but they did me and mine a great service once, and I have but done my duty."

"Yes, my man," replied his wife, "I know. They cannot be all bad, you know."

"You are right, Mary," he went on; "no man is all bad. We must speak of people as we find them."

"Dick Turpin!" gasped John, "and Tom King—oh!"

"Don't speak of this, John," said his father, earnestly; "if it was known I helped them ever so little, I should get into trouble."·

"I won't mention it," the boy answered, and he studiously kept his word, though very much exercised in his mind as to his father's connection with two men so universally known as Dick Turpin and Tom King.

CHAPTER XCIV.
HORSE FERRY.

Meanwhile, under the guidance of the man, the two fugitives had found their horses, and been guided through the thick and closely-grown forest towards a stream that ran through the wood. Presently it was reached, and the two highwaymen saw themselves on the border of a rather wide stream.

The man pointed out the ferry and told them the water was not two feet deep. Once over, if they followed the bank they would come to a cross-road connecting the towns of Abingdon and Earlsleigh, where there was an inn. The road was not very much frequented, except on market days.

"Thank you, my lad," said Dick Turpin, giving the fellow a guinea, which he spat upon for luck, and then the two men rode into the stream and easily got across.

They found the road-side inn open, and easily procured supper and a shake-down for the night.

The two highwaymen felt pretty safe with the

officers off the scent, but determined to be under way early in the morning, when they would ride off in a different direction from that which they had intended. They would have to be cautious for a few days, as once the hue and cry got about, there would be a general hunt, and as their description would be carefully given, they would have to exercise great caution and discretion.

It was barely daylight when they started—after swallowing a stirrup-cup—leaving their breakfast to chance.

Cutting along bye-ways and following leafy lanes, they found themselves in a small village, with a few shops, and, of course, one inn. It is to be hoped the day will never come when, as desired by fools and fanatics, a village will be without its ale house.

Temperance is good ; but a tyrannous interference with the liberty of the subject is another thing. Besides, as coercion promotes crime, so does the tyrannical closing of places of public refreshment promote drunkenness.

At the " Granby Arms," they found good plain refreshments, and decided to wait for an hour or two before starting.

They had quite made up their minds to lie quite still for a few days, but where they had not as yet determined.

About twelve o'clock, several men looked in of the small farming class. The two friends took no notice of them. Presently, however, a casual word attracted their attention.

" Squire Mowbray be a born fool," cried one, indignantly.

" Why ?" asked another Bœotian.

" To brag in a tavern about his money and diamonds," returned the other ; " he was speaking about them rascals, Dick Turpin and Tom King, and saying that he'd never be tricked again like be was by them ruffians."

" Ha ! ha ! ha !" laughed another ; " that was a bit of a lark. Should a liked to have seen the fun. The old man nearly died with rage."

" Well ! so would I," continued the first speaker ; " and now he brags that with ten thousand pounds worth of money and diamonds in his house, he defies Dick Turpin, Jack Sheppard, and Tom King, to find them, even if they broke in."

" He be a fool," the other speaker said ; " but he baint his self just now. He's taken a orphan niece to live with him."

" Ah ! but Jones," replied the other ; " she may be a orphan ; but she's got a stiff lot of money, and he's her guardian."

" Oh ! oh !" laughed the previous speaker, whose name was Morgan, " now I twigs. Now, who do you think I seed to-day ?"

" Can't say," replied Jones.

" Wilfred Mowbray, the nevvy, as he hates, 'cause he's his heir," continued Morgan. " He looked rather ill, as if he had come down for a change."

" And to see his cousin Maud," the other remarked. " I seed 'em both together in the park—wouldn't the squire be in a rage if he knew."

And all the lot laughed.

" Who is this Squire Mowbray, and where does he live ? if I may make so bold," asked Dick ; " he seems a bit of a character."

" You may well say that," put in Morgan. " The Mowbrays is a big family hereabouts ; live about a mile behind here, in the forest. The Mowbrays date as far back as history—a noble free race, until James came to be master. They do say he were jilted by a girl, which made him turn rusty they think."

" Very likely," returned Dick ; " excuse my curiosity, but we Londoners are main curious. I beg your pardon."

" No offence," hastily answered the hearty countryman, glad to be useful to strangers.

" Got any nice little farms to sell about here ?" continued Dick ; " me and my mate was thinking of settling, if we found something cheap."

All now spoke at once. The subject came home to their hearts, and ten minutes later the two highwaymen were hail-fellow-well-met with the farmers, who cordially accepted their offer to drink all round.

When the landlord announced that dinner was ready, the bucolic residents, unmindful of business, agreed to stop. Dick, who, unlike Tom, was not taciturn, had exercised a spell over them which quite entranced them.

They were easily induced to stay until evening, when the farmers promised there should be a jolly night of it.

To keep up the appearance of having business to attend to, they rode out in the afternoon to the nearest town, where they well knew resided one Manasseh, a Jew receiver of stolen goods, who also provided hiding room for men after whom justice was seeking.

Both the knights of the road knew him well, and were received with a hearty welcome. They were as usual free with their cash, and bought a fine set of instruments which had been left in the Jew's possession some months before by the notorious Blueskin.

He, however, made a bargain that they would return them when " they had no further use for them." This promise Dick Turpin very readily gave him.

A very jolly evening was enjoyed, carried on so far into the night that Dick and Tom did not rise until mid-day.

CHAPTER XCV.

THE MURDER.

The village of Hadleigh, where the highwaymen had located themselves, was a very quiet village, surrounded by extensive farms and the mansions of country gentlemen. One of these was Mowbray Hall, the residence of the squire of that ilk.

About eleven o'clock in the evening, a young girl might have been seen crossing one of these parks, coming from the village. She evidently was a comparative stranger, and was not very familiar with her way. She looked around her several times, as if anxious, but presently found herself in an avenue leading to a large mansion, which at once let her know she was on the right road.

The moon was rising, and as she walked along the winding path, she could see on either side extensive grounds, dotted with large clumps of trees ; she could hear, too, the murmur of running water, and the sighing of the wind among the naked branches.

Presently she halted, hearing footsteps, so concealed herself in one of the thickets which skirted the avenue. In another moment she rushed out and into the arms of Walter Mowbray, the squire's nephew and heir.

"Well, Maud ; what are you doing here so late ?" he cried.

"I've been to the village to post a letter to you !" she answered. "I thought you were not coming to-night."

"What was pressing ?" he asked.

"Well, this afternoon three men, one old and the other two young, called to see uncle on business," she answered. "I did not like the look of them. After dinner uncle asked them to stop."

"Very strange."

"Yes ; but Walter, not I think wilfully," she answered ; "they seemed to have some power over him—that is, he seemed afraid of them."

"Then you were quite right, my dear. Still, I know nothing in my poor uncle's past career that he could be ashamed of," continued Walter.

At this moment they heard the sounds of voices at no great distance, and then the noise of a light conveyance reached their ears. There was an opening in the thicket where a footpath had once run. They followed this and were soon beside the stream, near a small hollow, thickly set with trees, and affording a welcome place of concealment.

Here they paused and listened, neither of them able to comprehend why they were so anxious and disturbed. In after years both declared they must have been endowed for the moment with second sight.

They paused and listened, but for a few minutes they heard nothing but the soughing of the wind among the branches of the trees and the murmur of the waters. Then, as they grew calmer, they heard the sound of the vehicle hurrying forward, and then they heard it suddenly pull up.

Neither spoke.

But both strained their eyes and ears, and then distinctly heard a horse snorting and pawing the ground, as if impatient to proceed ; at the same time there was a shuffling of feet and some low-toned conversation. They had stopped—stopped near the opening through which they had passed ; and presently, there were hurried footfalls among the crisp withered leaves which strewed the narrow path leading to their retreat.

They crept further down the hollow, and crouched among the branches.

They soon found that their ears had not deceived them. Nearer and yet nearer came the sound of advancing feet ; they were evidently coming along by the hedge—in a few minutes they would be in the fir grove. They withdrew to a part of the hollow where the underwood was more dense, and concealed themselves among the bushes.

The footsteps sounded quite near by this time, and the girl thought afterwards that she must have made some slight noise, for a gruff voice asked in a tone of alarm—

"What was that ?"

"A hare among the underwood, you fool !" said another voice—a harsh voice, with a strong Yankee accent.

Then there advanced into the heart of the hollow, to within a few paces of where they lay, a party of four men carrying something rolled up in a rug, They paused, laid down their burden, and glanced furtively around. Presently the man with the gruff voice spoke again :—

"Yes ! This will do. To work !"

Two of the party stepped to a spot where the ground was spongy, covered with tangled undergrowth, and surrounded by felled trees. They carried spades, and began to dig vigorously ; and while they were so employed the other two drew aside and conversed in low tones, but not so low but that they could hear a great part of their conversation.

They still kept silent, and stood there dreading nothing, only listening, and yet both half-conscious of some impending tragedy.

They could see the faces of the men, although not very distinctly. The one who seemed to be the leader of the party had a square-shaped face, deep-set eyes, close-cut beard, and spoke with a Yankee accent. His companions were young men.

"Dig deep," said the elder man, as he stood over them, "and be quick about it."

The two men went on in silence, and then, pausing, wiped their brows, for they had worked with a feverish and desperate energy, and looked to the elder man as if for further directions.

He beckoned to them and all followed him to the cart. From this they took a rug in which a heavy burden was wrapped. There was nothing in the shape of it to suggest what it was, yet their horror-stricken senses seemed to tell them that rug contained a human body.

They seemed unable to take their eyes from it as it passed close to the spot where they lay, and they noticed that the colours of the rug were scarlet and black, and that it was fringed.

Maud's heart gave a great bound. She recognised the quilt which covered her uncle's bed.

The coarse Yankee-looking man put down a good-sized carpet bag beside the yawning grave, and helped the others. As he did so, one of the younger men let go his hold upon the rug, and the bundle dropped from their hands. As it rolled from their hands the covering fell aside, disclosing the battered, blood-smeared head of a white-haired old man.

Maud could no longer restrain herself.

"Oh, my poor uncle !" she cried ; and before Walter could restrain her, she had cast herself on her knees beside the lifeless form of her uncle.

The young man at once advanced into the open, to be felled to the ground by a blow from the brutal Yankee.

"What's to be done ?" gasped one of the young men.

"Shovel them all into the hole," cried the American, one of the early settlers expelled from New England for blackguardism, and, as it was afterwards proved, a distant relation of Squire Mowbray.

"I don't like killing her," said the young man who had first spoken ; "let us swear her to secrecy."

"Not to be thought of," answered the other, savagely ; "we can't stand here all night. Are you going to do it, or are you not ? Make up your minds and have done, else you'll find yourselves in the wrong box presently."

"Here they are, the villains !" shouted a stentorian voice close at hand ; "come up—we'll have the wretches !"

Without a word, the three assassins fled to the cart, leaving the corpse, the inanimate body of Walter, and the fainting form of Maud.

They never turned once.

But the strangest part of the whole affair was, that the owner of the voice never came forward, and the wooded glade relapsed into silence for some time, during which Maud recovered herself, and did her best to restore animation to her cousin.

While so occupied, there suddenly came upon them a posse of servants, the gardener, the house steward, a stable boy, and another, who were armed with an old gun, a pitchfork, and other such primitive weapons.

They gazed with wonder and awe at the open grave, the corpse, the lovely girl, and the young man.

"Here's a pretty to do," said the house steward, who was an old and faithful friend of the squire, "how could you do it, Mr. Walter?"

"James!" cried Maud, indignantly, "how dare you make such a charge? It's those men who came to see uncle this afternoon."

"I saw master let them out four hours ago," retorted James, sadly; "anyway, you must both come to the hall and wait until the constables come."

·They had no choice but to obey, and both walked slowly to the hall accompanied by two of the party.

Next day both were committed for trial, as at all events accomplices in the crime.

There appeared for them before the magistrates the family solicitor, Lawyer Brinsmead, who advised them both to plead not guilty.

"You'll only be in prison nine days," he said, "and meanwhile I'll find the murderers."

It was impossible to conceive a more courteous and yet more equitable man than the magistrate who heard the case, but appearances were strongly against them.

"It is by my advice, Sir Henry, that my clients," began Lawyer Brinsmead, "simply plead not guilty. I have a clue to the real murderers; but I wish the matter kept strictly private."

"I shall be most happy to aid you to the best of my ability," replied Sir Henry Howard; "but I must do my duty."

"You could do no less," observed Walter, quietly, "though how anyone could suppose a frail girl and slight delicate man like myself could murder the poor old man, carry him into the park, and dig the grave, is beyond my comprehension."

"I cannot discuss the matter," said the magistrate, mildly; "of course, the theory is that you had accomplices."

And so the prisoners were remanded and sent to the county gaol, where the governor was so satisfied of their innocence, after a brief interview with Brinsmead, that he gave them accommodation in his own house with his wife and children.

CHAPTER XCVI.

THE RESULT.

Lawyer Brinsmead's office was not a cheerful-looking place, even on a bright summer day. The little sunshine that found its way there over the surrounding dingy house-tops and smoking chimneys only showed up its cracked wainscot, finger-marked door, dirty paint, and gas-blacked ceiling.

But on a dark and gloomy morning, with the wind whistling in fitful gusts down the chimney and blowing the smoke into the room in blinding clouds, and with the rain dashing against the window, it was still more gloomy.

Here, in an old-fashioned arm-chair well worn, and covered, like the table, with morocco, sat Lawyer Brinsmead, on the morning after the murder, thinking deeply.

Suddenly a clerk entered, and told him a farmer-looking man, who gave no name, wanted to see Mr. Brinsmead at once in reference to the Mowbray case.

"Show him in," cried Brinsmead, eagerly, "at once!"

And our old friend, Dick Turpin, entered, clad in good and simple homespun, looking singularly respectable.

"Sit down, sir; and tell me at once what you have to say, Mr. ——"

"John Palmer, sir," said Dick. "Now, I wish you to understand before I speak that I do not want to appear in this matter unless absolutely required. Of course, if my evidence is positively required, I will waive my objections and appear."

"I will keep you in the background as much as possible," urged Brinsmead, "but I am on tenter hooks."

"The accused are innocent. They were in the wood sweethearting," Dick went on. "I myself was crossing the wood, and, hearing an advancing noise, did what the lovers did—concealed myself."

He now told all the reader knows, and described the murderous assassins minutely.

"Jack Mowbray!" cried Brinsmead. "Why he called on me the day before yesterday, asking for the squire's address. He said he had been to New England, and disliked the stiffness and hypocrisy of the people so much he got tired of it. Go on."

"I have little more to say, sir. When I heard that man threaten the girl with death, I roared out, as if heading a crowd, and the cowards fled to the cart and disappeared."

"That cart must be tracked," said Brinsmead; "as you saw all this, you may not object .to identify the men if caught."

"I will help to track them if needed," replied Turpin; "if you will send an officer with me, we could examine the track of the wheels. The weather was damp, and they would leave traces."

"Come to the Town Hall at once," continued Brinsmead, rising.

"One moment," answered Dick, producing a black bag of goodly size. It was open, and contained jewels, notes, and gold to a large amount.

Brinsmead stared at the other in utter amazement as he placed the bag on the leather-covered table.

"It was a great temptation," said the supposed Jack Palmer, "to a poor man; but life was at stake."

"You have acted nobly, sir," retorted the lawyer, shaking him by the hand, "and shall be well rewarded."

"I wish I could trust you fully, as you would then understand my very delicate position," said Palmer.

"I am as close as a father confessor. You can trust me as you would your priest. Nothing spoken privately within these walls ever goes beyond," returned Mr. Brinsmead.

"My name is Dick Turpin, and I was in the wood for the purpose of committing a burglary at Mowbray Hall," was the quiet reply.

"My God!" said the astounded lawyer; "you

don't say so. Dick Turpin, indeed! You are a fine fellow, anyway, if you are a damned rascal. But I'll shake your hand. You have done a noble and generous thing, and when——" here the lawyer hesitated—

"I go aloft," smiled Dick.

"Yes—I'll tell the truth about you; I will. Have no fear, but come with me."

And these two strangely-assorted beings went out, and half an hour later Dick and Thomas Rankin were riding side by side to the park. Dick took the officer—a queer-looking character, a short, thickset man, with a fiery and rugose complexion, not unlike the aspect of a mulberry, to the spot where the grave was still open, and pointed out where the cart had stood.

They, as Dick expected, saw the marks of the wheels on the avenue, and they followed them to the lodge. Here they questioned the aged woman who opened the gates, and who pointed out the direction taken by the men.

Dick and Thomas Rankin rode that way, and found traces of the cart all the way to Melrose, where the men had left it at the "Bull Inn," going off on the early morning coach to London.

It was on their way to call on Mr. Brinsmead, which they did after the magistrates' meeting. He at once bade them hurry on to London, and, if possible, secure the suspected men.

Mr. Brinsmead handed Rankin ample cash, and they at once started, Dick calling at an inn for his comrade, Tom King.

Dick had kept to himself one feature of the case. The ugly man, with the Yankee accent, might be indeed Jack Mowbray, but he was known by sight to Dick Turpin as Ramper Jack, a very low-class burglar and thief. He had only been pointed out to him once, but with his reputation he was familiar.

He was careful, however, not to betray his knowledge to Rankin.

"I believe that I know a man who has seen this fellow, Jack Mowbray, in London," he said; "but you must let me go about it my own way. You shall have all the glory of the capture," he continued, "as, if I am seen in it, I shall get into hot water."

"Mr. Brinsmead told me to trust implicitly to you," was the reply.

Dick nodded, and little more was said until they reached London, when Dick conducted his new friend to an inn in Holborn, where he bade him await his return. He then took his way by the Turnstile, and proceeded through Lincoln's-Inn Fields, at the right-hand corner of which he found, as the reader will now find, a frowsy little passage with two or three starveling shops. Here was, and is now, a slum rivalling in all detestable particulars anything to be discovered between Whitechapel and Limehouse Hole.

He went at once into the "Black Jack," the well-known haunt of Jack Sheppard, and went upstairs. He was well known to the landlord, so no obstacle was placed in his way.

The door was open, and there sat the four men carousing at a table. Dick did not go in, but entered a side room with a small table and two chairs, where a waiter soon followed him. He gave his order, and when he was served drank it off, remarked that the friend he was looking for was not there, went down stairs, and out of the house.

Half an hour later the house was invaded by a large body of Bow-street runners, who dashed upstairs, and, without resistance, captured the

whole four. All were known to the officers, Ramper Jack as a low burglar, the others as pickpockets and thieves.

They were at once taken before a magistrate, identified by Mr. John Palmer, and immediately committed to Derby gaol, with directions for them to be sent heavily ironed.

*   *   *   *   *

It was the morning of the assizes at Derby.

The trials of Maud and Walter began, and had lasted about an hour, when there was a terrific shout outside, as a post-chaise and four, guarded by six Bow-street runners, halted close to the court-house.

"What is the matter?" asked the judge.

Ere anyone could answer, those in court were themselves cheering lustily.

"What is the matter?" asked the judge, angrily. "I shall commit somebody."

"My lord," said the counsel for the defence in the case of the Mowbray murder, "the people are cheering with delight at the arrival, under heavy guard, of the real assassins of Mr. Mowbray. They are going before the magistrates."

"I shall adjourn the court for half an hour," continued the judge, amidst great excitement, and, passing through a doorway, entered the other court just as the manacled ruffians were placed in the dock.

The officer was first witness, then Brinsmead, who told the story of the six thousand guineas stolen by the assassins, and its return intact by a respectable farmer, who would identify all the prisoners.

John Palmer was called, sworn, and told his story.

"Send for Mr. Walter Mowbray," suddenly said the judge, approaching and taking his seat on the bench. Every judge is *ex officio* a magistrate.

He was obeyed without a word.

Walter entered, looking ill and half-dazed.

"Mr. Walter Mowbray," asked the judge, quickly, "do you recognise those men?"

"Yes, my lord, as the murderers of my uncle; and that man," pointing to Ramper Jack, "as the man who knocked me down."

"What do you mean to do, Sir Henry?" asked the judge.

"With your lordship's permission," replied Sir Henry Howard, "I shall commit them for immediate trial."

"Very good!" said the judge, and returned to the other court, where he at once ordered Walter Mowbray to be brought before him, with Maud, his cousin.

The crowd cheered lustily, and when silence was restored, the judge spoke—

"I have great pleasure, Mr. and Miss Mowbray, in discharging you. The real murderers have been discovered on the most undoubted evidence. I shall require, when the case comes on, which will not be until tomorrow, your presence to identify the prisoners."

Bewildered, amazed, relieved beyond description, the lovers were led out of court, where Brinsmead, with a carriage, awaited them. This took them to the "Bull" Inn, where the friendly solicitor ordered an extempore lunch, at which he introduced them to Dick Turpin.

"To Mr. John Palmer you owe all," said Brinsmead, and he told the whole story.

"And more. But for your friendly interference we should both be dead," added Walter, warmly; "dead, and buried in a nameless grave."

"How can I show my gratitude?" asked Maud, as each took a hand of his and pressed it.

John Palmer had never been so affected in his life. He drew his hands away and passed them over his eyes.

"I think I might suggest, as Mr. Palmer is not a rich man and has saved you nearly six thousand guineas, you might make him a present of a thousand, and, sure of your acquiescence, I have brought it with me in notes."

"Give them to me—at once! Mr. Palmer, this is but a slight mark of my gratitude," cried Walter, pressing the money on him. "My esteem and friendship——"

"Are not for me," said the other, humbly. "I am one hunted of men; a criminal; the notorious Dick Turpin."

"The greater the merit," gasped Walter, while Maud looked with mingled wonder and admiration on this man of many parts.

At this moment a servant entered with a note for Mr. Palmer. He opened it hastily.

"I must leave you all. My presence is suspected in the town; an officer from London has circulated a description of me. You must do without me on the trial," he urged, regretfully.

"You must go," said Walter. "Your conduct has been too noble and generous for you to risk anything. Go at once."

Again they shook hands, and Turpin hurried down stairs, accompanied by Brinsmead.

The note was from Tom King, informing him that Pooly was in the town, making inquiries in a case, and had put about some bills, offering the usual reward for Dick Turpin.

"I'm off—meet me at the 'Beehive' on the London Road," he wrote finally.

Dick pulled his hat over his eyes, hastened along the streets, secured Black Bess, and was rattling along the king's highway in less than half an hour.

His evidence was not needed, as one of the gang turned king's evidence, and the other three miscreants were duly hanged.

Before another year Walter and Maud were married, and often then and afterwards talked of what they owed to gallant Dick Turpin.

CHAPTER XCVII.

BRIAN SEYMOUR AND ROBERT WOODSTOCK VISIT ELPHICK CASTLE.—A WARM RECEPTION.

Meanwhile, Dick Turpin had rejoined his companion, who was delighted to see him. Tom was always afraid of Dick's quixotic enterprises turning out badly.

He was, of course, much rejoiced at the windfall of a thousand guineas, which, as per agreement, verbal if not written, was equally divided between the two.

They resolved to put a long distance between themselves and Pooly, whose ambition to capture Dick Turpin was well known. His patience was, apparently, nearly exhausted. The highwayman kept at a respectful distance from him, but he appeared resolved to have him at any price—red-handed or not.

It was time now they communicated with the Blue Dwarf, so they determined to get down as soon as possible to Elphick Castle, make inquiries about Brian and Robert, and return to London.

They had ample means to last them some time, so that they would be able to lie in hiding for awhile; in fact, Dick intended to spend some little time at home, putting away some of his money in the bank.

Elphick Castle was reached the second day, and quarters secured at the nearest inn. They had credentials in the shape of a letter to the steward, and they walked up in the evening.

Mr. Morris had heard nothing of the two adventurers, but he did not go out very much; and, after entertaining his visitors very freely, they returned to the "Duke of Marlborough," and settled in their quarters for the night.

Next day they rode about the neighbourhood, calling in at all the inns and taverns, but without hearing anything of Brian or Robert.

Upon this they determined to return to London and report that Elphick Castle was no longer the centre of observation.

Early next day, soon after dawn, they started, halting for breakfast at a wayside inn. They always selected a room with a good view of the road. It was a private room as it luckily happened, for they had not been seated many minutes when Brian Seymour and Robert Woodstock rode up, dressed in fashionable attire.

The friends drew back and finished their breakfast, after which they paid their score and rode off in the direction of Elphick Castle, which they reached without drawing rein. They made their presence known to the steward, who at once asked them in and housed their horses.

Dick at once explained why they had come, adding that they thought if these two fellows became disagreeable their presence might be useful.

Morris thanked them heartily, and put them in the small breakfast room, while he ordered lunch to be prepared. If there was but simple rations in the way of food, there was ample compensation in the way of brandy and wine, a bottle of the former of which the steward at once put before them.

Time passed and no sign of the adventurers. Lunch was served, and Morris himself presided at what proved a most successful little meal.

They were just proceeding to open "t'other bottle," when there was a loud knocking at the door.

"Lock yourselves in," said Morris, "and if I want you I will call."

And he hurried away to receive the visitors, whoever they might be, parleying at the gate with the sturdy boy, who with him shared the duties to be done in the deserted castle.

"Who are you, and what do you want?" asked Morris, in a stern tone.

"Visitors to see the earl," retorted Brian Seymour. "You know me very well."

"Oh yes, Mr. Brian, I know you very well," replied Morris, sardonically. "Open the door, Taffie."

The boy obeyed, and the two men were admitted. They entered in an insolent and blustering way, which made the steward feel very indignant.

"What may you please to want," asked Morris, in a stiff, cold tone.

"To see the earl; conduct me to him at once," cried Brian.

"Not only isn't the earl here at all, but I

haven't heard from him for two months. The last letter said he'd started on a continental tour and wouldn't be back until he was of age and able to make his will."

Brian swore a fearful and bitter oath, but in a muttered tone.

"I suppose you can give us some refreshments —some cold meat and wine, anything, in fact, you have in the house," continued the claimant, haughtily.

"There never was any stint in this house," replied Morris, quietly. "Please follow me," and he led them to the dining room, where he left them while giving orders for their refection.

"There does not seem to be anyone here except servants," said Brian, savagely; "but I propose stopping all night and making a search. That frightful cripple is deuced cunning," he added.

"Yes, to my sorrow, I know it. If we could rid ourselves of him, I would settle the other matter with ease."

"Ah! but he's always on his guard," said Brian; "he has the spirit of the devil in him."

At this moment Morris returned, accompanied by Taffie, who carried a tray, while a smart servant girl brought up the rear with a couple of bottles of wine.

"I presume, as we are tired and have a long return journey before us, you can accommodate us with beds to night," remarked Brian.

"You are my lord's kinsman," responded Morris, "and, of course, I have nothing to object. I will order two bed-rooms to be got ready."

And he retired, leaving the confederates to enjoy their creature comforts as best they might.

"I fear we've come on a wild goose chase," observed Brian, as he helped himself to a cut of cold roast turkey; "that scoundrel, Sapathwa, is rather too much for us. He has the cunning of Satan, and the impudence of Mephisto."

"Well, yes, and the wretched little imp is so well served," sneered Robert; "no one can move without his knowing it. His agents are everywhere. Shouldn't be a bit surprised if he knows all about our being here."

"I wish we could catch him alone," muttered Brian, in a bitter, savage tone. "I'd end his career."

"He's too infernally cunning," said Robert; "when he's about there's always somebody else about too"

When they had finished a copious lunch they rose, and, taking their hats, sallied forth for a walk in the grounds.

Both were suspicious enough to think the steward was deceiving them; but they gained nothing from their notion. Everywhere the same quiet and repose existed, and not a trace of the family was to be seen or heard.

English country houses were dull places in those days for Londoners. There were no billiard rooms, nor anything of the kind, so the two plotters were reduced to great straits.

Mr. Morris, however, at their request, found them a pack of cards, with which they proceeded to amuse themselves until dinner time.

After dinner they resumed their occupation until late—about eleven o'clock was late in those days—when they determined to go to bed.

Morris had had them shown to their bed rooms in the afternoon; they were adjacent, in a long corridor on the east side of the building.

They had both been drinking, but both pretty well knew their way.

Brian held a lamp in his hand. Now, it happened that he took a wrong turning, and went up a small flight of stairs leading to another range of rooms.

Suddenly he paused, hearing voices as he thought. He groped along cautiously until they came to an open door.

In front of them was the Blue Dwarf gesticulating as it seemed to himself.

"We've got him now," gasped Brian, mad with rage and drink, and, drawing his sword, he rushed at him, followed by Robert Woodstock. "Down, down!" he yelled, "hideous monster! to that hell from which you came."

At that moment the two enraged adventurers received each a blow on the back of his head, which knocked them forward on the floor.

When they scrambled up, with aching bones and cracked sconces, they were alone in the old picture gallery of Elphick Castle. Fortunately their light was not extinct.

"Fiend! abortion! hell-hound!" exclaimed Brian; "shall I never have revenge on this vile instrument and false pretender?"

"Never! unless we slay him!"

"Ha! ha! ha!" came from behind some hidden panel. "Beware! murderers and assassins, lest the gallows be your fate."

They waited to hear no more, but, finding their rooms with difficulty, slept soundly until morning, when, after a very hasty breakfast, they started for London, burning with hate, fear and detestation for this terrible demon of the family.

Later in the day, after a brief conference with Sapathwa, Dick and Tom also started for the metropolis.

CHAPTER XCVIII.

A STERN CHASE.

Dick and Tom took their time. They had plenty of leisure, money galore, and were temporarily free from any business confided to them by the Blue Dwarf.

They therefore determined to enjoy themselves, though, of course, if any professional business turned up, they would not neglect it. So they trotted on side by side, chatting and enjoying themselves to their heart's content.

Both were in the prime of life, with powerful constitutions, and quite able to cope with any two opponents unless they were taken by surprise. Against this they guarded by their keen sight and sharp hearing.

Though anxious to reach London, or the borders of London, at an early period, they agreed to give the scene of their late exploits a wide berth. They had a very wholesome respect for Mr. Pooly's experience. Doubtless by this time it was known or guessed at, that the man who had ferreted out the real murderers of Squire Mowbray was Dick Turpin. The moment the witness was described Pooly would recognise him as Dick Turpin, and he had no wish to be made the victim of some amateur detective, anxious to make a name, and win the much-coveted prize.

On reaching New Eltham, where the road branches off, they took the left-hand road which leads to St. Albans, and went on until about one o'clock, when they halted to bait their horses as well as to refresh themselves.

Dick and Tom could stand a good deal of refreshment in a quiet way, though they never kicked over the traces except when in the secrecy of a quiet haunt in London. They rode into the stable-yard, bade the ostler rub the horses down, wash their mouths, and give them a feed of corn, and then entered the house, going into the public room.

As luck would have it they sat in a low-windowed room which gave them a good view of the road both ways. While drinking their rummers they chatted lightly, until Dick leaped up, crying out as he did so :—

"Pooly, by the lord ! Let us be off at once."

Not one minute was to be lost. They rushed out the back way, mounted their horses, which were ready for a start, dashing through a gate which led into a back lane that did not allow of two abreast.

They had not got a hundred yards down the lane when they heard a loud voice halloo behind, and knew that they were pursued and had been recognised. Possibly the ostler had guessed at sight of Black Bess who was her rider.

At this moment they darted into a farm-yard where two men were at work, and where ducks, geese, and pigs, were feeding. The pigs began to grunt, the geese to hiss, the cocks and hens to scream, and the men to swear, but the two horsemen without a moment's delay gained a field, over which they darted in the direction of a very high five-barred gate, which was luckily open.

Through this they rode, Dick coolly stopping to close it and to fasten it securely. Then, on they went up a steep ascent which appeared to lead to a road. This was gained, and looking back they saw the runners working at the gate, which they were trying to open.

With a triumphant shout they at once put their horses to their utmost speed, their object being to put Pooly off the scent and act as circumstances directed.

Death and ignominy were behind, while liberty and life lay in front.

Where they were going to neither knew. It was an utter no-man's-land to them, but would doubtless, in time, bring them to some familiar highway. On they went, scarcely, however, using whip or spur, which were seldom needed by their noble beasts, except on especial emergencies.

They had by this time lost sight of their pursuers, and looked keenly to the right and left for some means of doubling on their adversaries. Half an hour elapsed—an hour—and then they found themselves dashing through a small town, where a market was being held.

Dire was the confusion and the hubbub, as in their reckless course they knocked down stalls and upset donkey-carts and one or two old women. With yells and imprecations they were told to stop; but Dick and Tom only shouted more lustily for them to get out of their way.

In less than five minutes they were clear of the town and bowling along a smooth way, at a rapid pace.

Ten minutes, or a little more, after the highwaymen had passed through the town, up came Pooly and his men.

They drew rein and addressed one of the excited crowd—

"Which way did they go?"

"Who go?" asked the bucolic, answering one question by another.

"Dick Turpin and Tom King!" was the savage reply of the officer.

The man pointed with his hand, and, without further ado, away went the horsemen in hot and eager pursuit of their prey.

The two fugitives kept on steadily, looking to the right and left; but, seeing no sign of any place of concealment, they hurried on. At last they came in sight of some celebrated ruins— those of Bolton Castle—which lay to the left, in some woods about half a mile distant.

Dick Turpin knew them well.

Just at this spot a stream crossed the road. It was, of course, shallow; but it afforded Dick the chance he wanted.

"Follow me !" he said, turning his horse into the river, and sending the water flying on each side as he urged him forward up stream.

Tom followed, and soon they were out of sight of the road and between two high banks, through which the small river flowed rapidly. These banks extended for about a hundred yards, and then the stream was bordered by meadow land for a short distance; then the soil grew dry and arid, extending right up to the tower and other ruins.

The ruins were considerable in extent, and parted from the stony expanse by a deep but narrow moat. The only way of crossing this was by a rude but stout plank about three feet wide. Dick bade Tom dismount, which he did himself, and then led his horse over by means of the primitive bridge.

In a moment more they were in the castle, and comparatively safe. They sat down on a stone and waited. Not for long. All of a sudden they saw Pooly and his force crossing the meadow and coming rapidly for the ruins.

"Heave away !" said Dick, and at once both applied themselves to the beam, which their united strength hurled into the moat just as Pooly came in sight close to the edge, discomfited and furious.

"Surrender !" he cried, as he and the others levelled a pistol each.

"Ha ! ha ! ha !" laughed the highwaymen, and disappeared in the ruins.

As we have said, they were extensive, and Dick, who knew them well, led his companion right through them until they reached the moat again. Here the moat was almost choked up by fallen earth and stones, across which they easily took their horses.

"Mount, and away !" cried Dick, who always assumed the command, to which Tom King's more inert nature had no objection.

Both were at once in the saddle and dashing down a narrow path bordered by high hedges, once the main entrance to the fortress. It soon brought them into an open green lane, with a church steeple in the distance.

As this indicated the habitations of men, Dick rode on until the houses became visible, and then diverged to the right over fields, leaping hedges and ditches, until they were once more on the king's highway.

They were now two miles from a quaint little village called Kingsford, near which was a place called Kingsford Chase, a large park, through which there was a road, open to the public. This road Dick intended to follow if they could do so unobserved. Both horses and men would be the better now for food and rest; but none could they allow themselves, with the Nemesis of law at their heels.

The village was passed and the gates of the chase reached. They were open, and the lodge stood back some distance, so that, confident of not being seen or heard, they trotted along congratulating themselves on their good luck.

They came at one moment in view of the house, but did not even then turn their heads, as all their thoughts were intent on escape.

Right through the park they went, nor halted until they reached a small inn on the high road, where they allowed themselves a quarter of an hour's rest.

Dick saw to the horses himself, and gave them corn and as much ale—good, old ale—as they chose to drink. He and Tom only drank a good jorum of ale. This settled, they again mounted and trotted along the road until they came to a place in the park palings where a gap had been made by the fall of a tree. The tree had just been removed, but the palings were not repaired.

"This way," cried Dick, and dashed into the park, here very thick with trees, just as the clamour of horses' feet in the rear made itself heard.

They both concealed themselves in the thickness of the wood and waited, where, however, they could see what passed along the road.

Three minutes later Pooly and his party swept by, and they knew they were temporarily saved. After a brief pause, they determined to "track back," reach the road through the park, and follow a different route to London.

They moved slowly across the turfy soil until once more they had a glimpse of the house. Dick deviated a little to the left to avoid it, and suddenly they found themselves face to face with a gentleman richly apparelled and of imposing mien, about forty years of age. By intuition, Dick knew this was Lord Kingsford.

He and his companion both took off their hats.

"Are you aware, my men," he said, in a severe tone, "that you are trespassing?"

"Yes, my lord!" replied ready-witted Dick. "But we wanted to reach the road by a short cut, as we were in a hurry."

"Oh, then, you're the two rascals, Dick Turpin and Tom King, the officers are after?" he continued, in an amazed tone.

Dick and Tom bowed.

"Be off with you," he retorted, laughing; "you never did me any harm, and I am not a thief-taker. Go away at once."

"Thanks, my lord, and may you live till I rob you on the highway," answered Dick, with unblushing effrontery. "I will endeavour, if possible, to equal your lordship's politeness."

The earl turned away to hide a smile, and the two highwaymen stole off quickly, mounting as soon as they reached the road, and riding off.

They intended to reach Barnet at nightfall, seek refuge in a house where they were well known, until late, when they would be guided by circumstances.

They passed through one village some hours later, where they took refreshments hurriedly; then they sought a deserted barn, where they lay concealed until it was dark as Erebus.

An hour later they were safely housed at the inn of Joe Barton, who in his day had been one of the fancy, and had now retired to keep a public house and live on his savings.

Here they were made welcome, and treated with that lofty consideration which their high position in the profession entitled them to. Joe Barton quite understood their desire to be incognito, and himself waited on them, bringing in a supper which made the highwaymen twice as hungry as they were to look at it.

Mine host remained with them, leaving his house to the charge of his better-half and his daughter, who were well able to attend to the wants of their customers, and to prevent any riotous proceedings when the drink was in and the wit was out.

The trio for some time talked of old times, and then Dick returned to business. He proposed to leave the horses with Joe Barton for a fortnight or more, they going up in the garb of drovers in one of the daily waggons which passed.

Joe Barton readily agreed, and after supper went out himself and got them loose smocks, boots, and slouched hats, suitable to their assumed parts.

A jovial evening was passed, and next day at ten, in their new characters, the highwaymen started by road for London, easily procuring a seat inside the waggon, with plenty of straw for them to lie on.

They happened to be the only travellers, and made themselves so jolly to the waggoner with their stories, their good cheer, meat, bread, beer, and brandy, that Tom Sutton was sorry when on the sixth day they alighted at Edgware and bade him farewell.

Here they put up at a rough inn, procured whatever they needed, and started to walk the distance that separated them from the farm. On the way they got rid of their smocks, and then were quite like superior cattle dealers or farmers, in a day when costume did indicate a man's position in life.

They were joyfully received by Mrs. Palmer and the newly-married couple,—explaining their appearance on foot by the excuse of their having left their horses at the farrier's.

They were just in time for dinner, which was of the usual hospitable and abundant character.

As he had been away so long, Dick thought he would stop at home that day, though he hinted to his son-in-law that his presence in the evening with a few merry friends would be acceptable.

Of course, all who were asked came, and a jovial evening was passed, until Dick had to be carried off to bed, and Tom ditto.

But they were up and out early, ready after breakfast for a good ride to whet their appetites, and pay some money into the bank where Jack Palmer's account was already a warm one.

CHAPTER XCIX.

DICK AT HOME.

The presence of John Palmer at the farm was a source of general satisfaction to the family and all their friends. Dick was popular everywhere, and among none more than among the poor, to whom he and his wife and daughter and son-in-law were always kind. John Palmer took an interest in his neighbours, and on many occasions was called on to decide disputed questions, and even settle family disputes.

Among Jack Palmer's most particular friends was Farmer Carlton. His history was rather mysterious. He had appeared amongst them suddenly, from whence nobody knew. He had bought the lease of Brown Beeches, but appeared after he had paid the purchase-money to have very little capital with which to work it. But Farmer Carlton had a good assistant in his young wife.

Rumour said that he was the scion of a noble house, while his wife had been a farmer's daughter, from whom he had much to learn.

But at the end of a very brief period he knew as much as she did, and with hired assistance the farm became quite a celebrated place for good management, and profit, too.

Farmer Carlton had but one child, and at the time of which we speak his only daughter was eighteen.

Hitherto Farmer John Herbert Carlton had been a prosperous man ; we say had been, for about two months before Dick Turpin returned to his home there had been a change.

Misfortune seemed to dog Carlton's footsteps ; his crops failed, and he was compelled to look around him for help. He feared a complete reversion of the good fortune which had hitherto been his, and was uneasy and alarmed.

On this point there was no secrecy between husband, wife, and daughter. The father, however, bade them be of good cheer ; he had friends in the neighbourhood of Manchester, especially the family solicitor, and he would go down there and see what he could do.

He, however, had a little business to transact before he started, and resolved to await the finishing of this before he set out.

His factotum on the farm, a man on whom he had for some time depended, was a youth named Edgar Wharton, about twenty-one, whom chance had thrown in his way, and whom he had befriended. He was clever, industrious, and good-looking—strong and capable withal.

For reasons best known to himself, he chose to lodge in the village of Finchley, in what used to be the Hog Market ; but he had the run of Brown Beeches, and was there not only in business hours, but whenever else he liked.

The elder people liked him very well, as he seemed industrious and earnest ; but Jessie Carlton in no way liked him. In fact she had a perfect antipathy to Edgar Wharton for all his politeness and winning ways, and what she called servility. It was the old story, a case of "Dr. Fell," she told her parents ; she could not tell them why she did not like him, but she did not—his eyes were too close together, and his lips were too thin.

She could give no reason for her antipathy ; the young man was always scrupulously polite to her, and gentlemanly and even refined in his manners. He never spoke of his relatives, but insinuated that they belonged to a very high family.

Mr. Carlton only smiled, but made no remark. As long as Edgar Wharton did his work he did not care. He little suspected that this young fellow was madly in love with his daughter, and was only restrained by her coldness and sternness from making a declaration. On one occasion he had ventured to touch upon the disagreeable topic ; but Jessie Carlton met his advances with simple scorn.

The generality of women are very cruel to men they do not love. Gentle as a lamb when her desires, or what is called love, is aroused, she is coldly insolent when a man arouses neither feeling in her breast.

But Edgar Wharton was one of those men who bide their time.

"Wait till I catch any of you napping," he said to himself.

About this time, Mr. Carlton announced his intention of proceeding to Manchester.

Strangely enough, it occurred to Edgar—why he could not tell—this visit to the north afforded him a chance to get his employer in his power.

Farmer Carlton started on his journey, and two days after his departure Edgar Wharton stated to the farmer's wife that he had a sudden summons to see a sick friend. He knew a man who would take his place during his absence.

Mrs. Carlton was one of the most gentle and unselfish of women, and at once allowed him to go.

She little thought that a private conversation overheard by him, between herself and her husband, had prompted this sudden journey.

Jessie Carlton was one of those sweet English girls, or, as the Scotch would say, lasses, about whom hangs a halo of beauty and love. She adored her mother, but she worshipped and looked up to her father. To her he was the perfection of manhood.

The wife, who, if the truth had been known, had cost him fortune and position, he ever treated with devotion and love. Few men, after the first magical glamour of passion is over, ever forgive the woman who has made them sacrifice worldly weal and all the possible contingencies of the future. But if this were the case with Carlton, he never showed it.

The two women were left alone. It is seldom that mother and daughter ever loved one another like these two ; but then, perhaps, this arose from the fact that Mrs. Carlton had never had any other children—Jessie no brothers or sisters.

She looked very charming in her serge dress and beaver hat as she stood before her mother on the day when her father was expected back.

"I shall go down to the cross road and see the coach come in," she said. "If pa notices me he will get out and see me home. I am sure he will bring some good luck."

"You may bring him home, my dear, but no luck, I am afraid. I fear your father is too sanguine and enthusiastic. I am almost sorry he went."

"Ma ! I believe he will have luck. We are to have luck ; don't you know what old Marian, the gipsy, said ? Didn't she bless the house and everything in it, and call down all the blessings under heaven on us, because father picked her out of a muddy ditch one night ?"

"When, my dear, she had had too much to drink," smiled Mrs. Carlton.

"Still, mother, blessings are always better than curses," replied Jessie.

The mother, who for twenty years had suffered from trouble and care, could hardly have the same faith as Jessie.

"I do not want to damp your hopes, my darling, but I have no faith in luck. You said this morning that a black cat, a strange one, came into the house ; but then, my dear, cats are very fond of cream."

Jessie laughed, put her soft arms around her mother's neck, and made her look up and smile back at her. It was a faded, wan-looking face that she kissed so lovingly. Pretty and placid it always would be, but the cares of twenty years had left their impress on it, and it was touched here and there with the lines that tell their own story. The hair that lay softly and smoothly on the fair forehead was almost white; and yet Mrs. Carlton was not quite forty.

"The lady," everybody who saw her called her instinctively, and a true lady she was in every sense of the word.

She dried the tears on her cheeks, and kissed her daughter as she stooped over her, and then as the slight form disappeared round the corner of the house, she bent her head again and shed passionate tears over the ruin she believed could not be averted. She loved her home and all in it with clinging affection. She had watched it grow from the tiny beginning that two well-nigh penniless people were able to make into a comfortable—almost luxurious—place, and it was very dear to her.

It was as dear to Jessie, whose heart was aching with a sick dread as she walked along, in spite of her brave words to her mother. She dreaded meeting her father, seeing his face, and hearing his voice. She felt sure there would be no good tidings for her.

Presently she reached the point of vantage whence she could see the coach coming.

There was a rustic bench, on which she seated herself and waited. Soon the expected stage hove in sight, drew up, and from the inside came her father with a black bag in his hand.

Jessie advanced and looked eagerly in his face. It was pale and tired-looking, and certainly there was not a trace of gladness in it, as he stooped to kiss her and return her greeting. Silently, and not daring to ask him a question, she walked by his side for a while, indeed until they were well on their way home.

"Papa," she then said, softly.

"My dear."

There was no firmness in his voice. It was like his looks, weary and trouble-laden, and her heart sank.

"Is it—have you—I mean, can anything be done?" she asked.

"About the money? Oh yes, my dear, that is all settled."

"And we shall not have to give up the Beeches?" she cried, eagerly.

"No, my child, our home is safe. Don't look at me with such very wide-open eyes. It is all right, and there will be no trouble about the money. It is mine on very easy terms. We are saved from a very great misfortune."

He said this gladly, but still he did not seem like himself. The old cheerfulness seemed to have gone out of his voice, and there was no gladness in his face as he looked at her. Mrs. Carlton was too much agitated and overcome to notice that her husband was not at all well. Their home was safe, and she could realise nothing else for the moment. Presently, however, she too noticed her husband's preoccupied manner and grave face.

"My dear, it is nothing," he said gently; "it is only reaction. No one can tell but myself what I have gone through during the last few days. I thought I had ruined you, dear one, and lost our home."

"And it's quite safe now, Carlton?" she asked.

"Quite, little wife. We are better off than ever we were—quite free from debt. I got my money on very easy terms."

"Borrowed?"

"Yes," he cried; "but my creditor will not press me. I will explain to-morrow. I am tired, and should like to have some refreshment and go to bed."

But he pulled out his pocket-book and showed her money—crisp notes of the newly-established Bank of England, and thankful tears filled her eyes and ran down her cheeks as she kissed him with heartfelt sympathy.

Jessie was satisfied to know that her father had obtained the money somehow, and was not to be pressed for immediate payment. She asked no questions about the business, but went about the house singing like a bird in the very lightness and thankfulness of her heart.

Next day Jack Palmer called. The two men were very intimate. Jack noticed that his friend looked worried.

"Still that same trouble!" said Palmer. "Why don't you let me lend you a thou'? I have plenty lying idle, and you shall pay interest for it, if you like."

"My dear fellow, I have more money than I know what to do with. My worry is over; but I have other sources of trouble," replied Carlton. "Jessie, my dear, let us have a jug of your best home-brewed."

And so the subject dropped, though Jack Palmer could hardly find a rational explanation of his looks.

In the evening Edgar Wharton returned, and was full of congratulations; but to Jessie there was a false ring in his heartiness, and a curious look in his eyes as he watched her father's face.

"You are very fortunate, Mr. Carlton," he said, as they sat in the living room after supper. "Such a large sum of money is not often easily obtainable."

"It is not," said Carlton, drily, and in a tone which intimated a desire to close the subject. "It was obtained under very exceptional circumstances."

After some further talk, the two men smoking, and sipping nut-brown ale, while the women plied their needles, Edgar Wharton again spoke.

"Do you know Messrs. Wilcox and Heavyside, of Manchester?" he asked.

"Intimately! They are related to my agent in Manchester," replied Carlton. "What of them?"

Wharton pulled out a broadside—one of those sheets published at uncertain intervals, which then served the purpose of second editions and evening papers.

"Great robbery at Manchester!" it was headed.

Carlton read down the sheet, which gave full details of the crime, saying that a great robbery had been very cleverly perpetrated at the place of business of a private banker. A large quantity of local and Bank of England notes had been abstracted; but they were all marked, and could only be got rid of abroad. The thieves had also stolen a very rare ring, of great value, antiquity, and rarity. It was a large cat's-eye stone, set round with coloured gems, and having an Arab inscription at the back.

A hundred guinea note had stamped on the back, "Keziah Hardwicke."

"A very odd affair," said Edgar, when Carlton laid down the paper.

"Yes," was the quiet answer; "and I am very sorry for Wilcox and Heavyside. The

BRIAN SEYMOUR'S DARING ABDUCTION OF LADY MILICENT GRAFTON FROM SION HOUSE.

No. 19.

thieves will never let that ring or note out of their hands, I should think."

"I should think not," answered Edgar.

Next day he went to work as usual. His business lay out of doors, principally; but he had the run of the house, often writing letters in Mr. Carlton's room. This man had made up his mind to make Jessie his wife, exactly how he could not say, as she ever repelled him, sternly and coldly.

He met her next day in the grounds near the farm, and tried to resume the subject; but she repulsed him with such indignant scorn that he hastily retired, resolved to gain her somehow, and have revenge besides.

The very next day Farmer Carlton harnessed his stout cob, put it in his gig, and started off to London with his wife. Jessie went into her father's room to put it to rights, singing merrily all the time. While dusting his desk she noticed a very unusual thing—that the keys were hanging in it. She tried it and found it open, looking as if some papers had been disturbed and hastily thrust back.

She went to put them to rights, and as she did so, something fell on the ground—a heavy substance folded in paper.

She was about to stoop to pick it up, when Edgar Wharton, who had come into the room, forestalled her.

"Allow me!" he said, and clutched what was indeed a prize to him, for opening the parcel he held before her the note on which was stamped "Keziah Hardwicke," and the Arab ring.

Jessie gave one faint cry and swooned. When she came to, she found herself on a couch, with Edgar Wharton beside her. He had called no one, but had simply bathed her face and forced some brandy down her throat.

───

CHAPTER C.

THE EXPOSURE.

Jessie gazed wildly around. He still held the note and the ring in his hand.

"Give them back to me!" she said, in a husky, choked voice. "They belong to my father. You had no business to come prying here."

"I had no idea of prying," he replied, still holding up the ring, and gloating over it, with a kind of a dazed, surprised look; "but how came it here?"

"What?" she said, faintly.

"The note and the ring. You know them as well as I do. You heard me read that account of the robbery at Manchester. A large reward is offered for their discovery. It is odd they should be found here."

"My father will explain, of course," Jessie said, her breath coming in gasps, and her whole frame trembling. She was beginning to understand what the finding of these two articles must mean.

"Give them back!" she cried, passionately. "I had no business to touch the drawer. Oh! if they would only come home!"

"It is quite as well he should not come home and see these things in our hands," was the quiet response. "Don't look so frightened, Jessie, my darling. Ah! forgive me! I did not mean to let the word slip out. But you

know what I feel—what I shall feel to my dying day—for you will always be my darling, treat me as you will. I will not talk of that now, only of what we have discovered. Why did you not destroy them? But even now we need never know anything about it."

He spoke half to himself, looking gravely at the ring he held, and Jessie staring blankly at him, the whole meaning of the discovery beginning to break upon her.

The money which her father had procured from somewhere—neither she nor her mother knew where—his evident low spirits and preoccupation when he came back from that journey to Manchester, and a certain nervousness that seemed to have been upon him ever since—all came before her with terrible suggestiveness, and seemed to chill her to the heart.

Ah! if she had only left the desk alone and never opened it, or if she alone had seen what was hidden there! Half of the horror of the dreadful discovery would have been taken away if it had been hers alone; but Edgar Wharton had seen what she had found.

Edgar Wharton was poor, and to him the big reward that was offered would, indeed, be an object. What would he do? Would he denounce her father? Much as she disliked him, she could scarcely believe this. Her loved and honoured father, to whom the very thought of dishonour was as impossible as to an innocent child to whom the meaning of the word was unknown, he would explain.

"Give me the note and ring," she said, holding out her hand. "I will put them back back before my father comes home. He will tell us then what he is going to do with them. Of course, he found them."

"Of course!" replied Edgar, in a sneering tone. "Mr. Carlton will know what to do with these little articles. I wonder a man of his common sense should have put them where his daughter could find them."

"Mr. Wharton, what do you mean?" gasped Jessie Carlton, wildly.

"I mean that your father's good name—even his very life—are in our hands. It is for us to decide what is best to be done."

"Surely you would not betray him?" gasped the unfortunate girl.

"'Betray' is an ugly word, Jessie," he said, with the utmost effrontery. "But I will keep the secret on one condition."

"And what may that be?"

"You have it in your power to save your father. His life and honour are in your hands."

"What do you mean?" she cried, in an angry tone.

"I mean that I will be silent on one condition. I will swear to any oath you like that not a breath of what we two have seen shall ever pass my lips if——"

He drew her close to him as he spoke, and whispered the remainder of his words in her ear. She looked at him one moment in undisguised amazement, and then recoiled, with fear and aversion in her eyes.

"Never!" she gasped, in a faint and trembling voice. "I would gladly die first."

"Do not say your 'no' too hastily," he continued, quietly enough. "Think over what I have said to you. Your father's life and honour are wholly in your hands. If you refuse me——"

"Well," she asked, trying to speak calmly, with a calm she did not feel; "if I do?"

"Then I go to Manchester with this ring in my hand and claim the reward offered from the magistrates. I have the bill here," and he displayed it. It was headed—

"FIVE HUNDRED GUINEAS REWARD."

"Yes, I know, Mr. Wharton," she said, with a wild and choked gasp. "Edgar, have mercy! Whatever have I done to you that you should ask such a price at my hand for one little favour?"

"*Little!*" he cried, with a hoarse laugh. "You have curious notions of the value of things, Miss Carlton. Most daughters would think nothing too much to give for the service I will undertake to render you for that little word 'yes.' The price is not at all a heavy one. What I should get from the government would be of far more money value to me."

"Perhaps," she said, bitterly; "you would like the money better," she added, with utter scorn. "You had better go and earn it, Edgar Wharton. It is some horrible lie; my father is as innocent of what you fancy as I am. It can and will be explained."

"Not easily, I believe. There are already ugly rumours afloat about the money which he found just at the right and convenient time. I have only to open my mouth, and that which is mysterious will at once be clear to all. Now then, decide at once whether I shall speak or not."

"No! no! no!" she faltered, bursting into passionate tears, her self-control now a thing of the past. "I cannot—I will not."

"Very well," he said, coldly; "you have chosen, so do not blame me;" and he moved as if to go.

"Stop!" she exclaimed. "Give me time to think. It is too, too horrible. I must have time to think and understand; it can all be explained. My father will——"

"Your father will not thank his daughter," sneered the other, "for condemning him to the consequences of his crimes. Oh, you begin to wince at that word. It is a plain one to use, but it is right, is it not? Mr. Carlton in prison will have plenty of time to reflect on the humanity and generosity of his child, who could have saved him, and who wouldn't."

"Cruel monster! You would have the child stoop to hopeless degradation to save her beloved father," she half shrieked.

"If you consider it as hopeless degradation to marry me," he said, sternly and coldly, "I will go."

"No—no—but do wait until to-morrow," she urged. "Give me time to think."

"No. A good smith strikes while the iron is hot. Decide at once, and leave me to do my best and worst. You can have five minutes to decide. Is not that enough to decide whether your father shall hang or not? Will you decide at once?"

"You leave me no choice," she answered, in choked accents; "but if I agree, I must make my conditions."

"Anything in reason."

"In the first place you swear solemnly to keep this secret," she began.

"I will swear any oath however solemn, any oath you may impose," he said, earnestly, "and I will swear to keep it."

"Will you swear to let me alone; never to approach me until I give you leave, never to allude to the compact between us, nor betray me to anyone?"

"I will swear it with the greatest of pleasure," he said, smiling; "for I know the day will come when you will remove the veto you have placed upon my actions—when we shall be as if this miserable secret had never entered into our lives. Give me your hand upon it."

With a look of unutterable loathing, but with a gesture as if she were forced to the action against her will, she slowly held out her hand and laid it in his. He grasped it warmly, and carried it to his lips.

"Don't," she said, with a cold shiver; "I have already promised too much. Let me alone, or I shall go mad."

"I will not trouble you," he replied. "Give me the note back."

"What are you going to do with it?"

"Put it back exactly where we, that is, you found it. Mr. Carlton must never know it is discovered. I will find a way to give him a hint to get rid of it. I believe I can do it without his knowing it has been discovered. Darling! well then, Jessie, if you insist—Miss Carlton, if you will."

"I think that will be best," she answered curtly.

"Then be it so, Miss Carlton. Do not look so disconsolate and miserable. If you allow yourself to be so unnerved by me alone, when your parents return your face will inevitably betray your feelings."

"No," she answered, "I am hardened for ever now. Nothing will move me. I can play the hypocrite, too. Go!"

Edgar Wharton saw that he was going too far, and taking his hat off a chair prepared to withdraw, not, however, before Jessie had replaced the note and the ring in the desk and locked it carefully.

"Now be careful to excite no suspicion. This robbery is no great secret," he continued, "and people are already talking of the strange way in which your father was assisted, and some clue may have been given. Don't look so terrified. I say may have been. It will be well for us always to be on our guard; scared faces and trembling lips have taught shrewd people before now where to look for a great criminal."

"They shall track nothing here," Jessie said, resolutely, stilling her trembling by a mighty effort, and forcing her pale lips into a smile, as if she feared that even then, as they stood talking, there might be listening ears and watchful eyes.

Had she but guessed the truth.

She watched him in absolute silence as he went out.

Mr. and Mrs. Carlton did not return until five o'clock, she bright and cheerful and invigorated by her little outing, he grave and silent as he had been of late, with a look in his face as if some secret care were weighing him down.

Jessie understood all now. She knew the secret which seemed to be crushing out her father's life, and she longed to tell him that she did so. She longed to throw her arms around his neck, as she would have done before that fatal journey, and whisper that she knew all, and would help him to keep the terrible thing from the knowledge of anyone else. But a bar seemed to have arisen between John Herbert Carlton and his household. He had a concealed care that was pressing him down and crushing out the spirit that had been such a charm in his every-day life.

At six Edgar Wharton came in, cheerful and sprightly, upon which supper was placed upon the table, and it was partially consumed, when John Palmer entered hurriedly, with two constables behind him.

Jessie's eyes were a sight to see in their fixed glare of horror and despair.

"Don't be alarmed, neighbour," said Jack, heartily; "these gentlemen only want me to ask you a question or two. They have discovered a clue to the Manchester robbery."

Emily seemed turned to stone.

"Without your knowing it, the clue is in this house. Don't be alarmed, Miss Carlton," added John Palmer; "be calm, and all will be well."

"What do you mean, Palmer?" asked Carlton, in a surprised tone, while Edgar Wharton looked white and red.

"Go and fetch your private desk, but don't open it until you come back."

Carlton, though very much puzzled, rose and went out. Edgar made a move, but Palmer requested him to remain where he was.

"No one may leave this room until the mystery is explained," he said.

Edgar sullenly acquiesced, while a faint suspicion of the truth began to expand the soul of Jessie, and fill her with joy.

Carlton soon returned with the desk and the key; placing the former on the table he opened it, and Palmer at once spotting the criminal evidence, caught up the ring wrapped in the note.

He placed the ring on the table and spread out the note.

"Did you ever see these before, Carlton?" asked Palmer, earnestly.

"Never," replied Carlton, his face wearing an appalled expression.

"Of course not. They were placed there by this unhung scoundrel," continued Palmer, clutching Edgar Wharton by the throat. "He put them there yesterday morning, and contrived that your daughter should find them."

"What for?" gasped Carlton.

"To force her into a hated marriage by inducing her to believe you the criminal. Yes; he asked her to be his wife, the alternative being that he would earn the great reward offered for the discovery of the burglar."

"Jessie," said Carlton, in a deeply reproachful tone, "how could you?"

"Father, forgive me; but he wove his plot so cunningly, and your sadness seemed so strange," she gasped.

"All this is very fine, Mr. Palmer," began Edgar, in a blustering tone, he having recovered himself; "but all this means nothing. How could I have put the note and the ring in the desk? Search further, and perhaps you may find the rest of the swag."

"I have it here, found at your lodgings, Mr. Edgar Wharton," cried John Palmer, in an exultant tone. "I was coming into my friend's room, the door of which was open, when I saw the little episode of the ring and note. I at once drew back and listened. My suspicions were quickly aroused, and going away I applied to Sir George Gregory for a search warrant, and accompanied by our two friends here went to your house and found these."

"Heaven bless you!" cried Jessie, as she cast herself, sobbing, on her father's breast. "And may heaven forgive you, Wharton, for rousing this wicked suspicion in a daughter's bosom, and causing the misery you have to me."

"You've not done with me yet?" sneered Edgar; "you've got to prove your father innocent yet?"

"Remove the scoundrel," said John Palmer. "We will appear at eleven before the magistrates."

The prisoner, despite his bluster, was completely cowed, and being well secured, was taken to a cart which awaited him outside.

Palmer would now have taken his leave.

"No!" said Carlton, "not yet; let us have the best the house affords—mother, put a bottle of brandy on the table. I have an explanation to give; but for your interference, Palmer, I might have gone to a dishonoured grave. What a scoundrel!"

The brandy was brought and uncorked, with a bottle of wine for the women.

"I have a confession," began Carlton; "my father is Sir John Hunter Carlton, and I was the second son. My brother Philip was the heir, and when I married my wife here my father forbade me his house."

"Poor father!" said Jessie.

"When I went to Manchester awhile ago, I found that my brother and both his sons were dead, and I was heir both to the title and estates—which were strictly entailed. Thus it was I was enabled not to borrow money, but to obtain a liberal advance on my own future property. But my father, old and sick almost unto death, refused to see me. Hence the sadness which seemed so unaccountable."

Both wife and daughter pressed each a hand of the husband.

"I am in hourly expectation of learning that I am Sir John Carlton, and my wife Lady Carlton," he added; "but it grieves me to know that my father will pass away without our being reconciled."

All were glad, however, that the mystery was cleared up, and a quiet but happy day was spent by them.

Next day, previous to going before the magistrates, a messenger came post haste from Manchester to announce that John Herbert Carlton was a baronet—his father being dead. His presence was at once requested by the executors.

Carlton, in order to obtain permission to absent himself, was compelled to reveal his secret when put into the witness-box before a crowded court and sworn.

"As I have to ask permission of the court to absent myself for a time to attend my father's funeral, I must be sworn as Sir John Herbert Carlton, baronet, of Eccles Hall, near Manchester. I only heard the sad news this morning—but of course, felt it my duty to attend and give my evidence," he said.

The sensation in court was most intense. Sir George Gregory congratulated him, and then he gave his evidence, followed by Jessie, whose deposition excited a murmur of disgust in the audience.

John Palmer followed, proving the discovery of the stolen notes during a search of the prisoner's room in the presence of the two constables.

"Those who hide can find," muttered Edgar. "The whole thing is a scheme to ruin me!"

"Silence!" said Sir George Gregory, severely; "such assertions will only aggravate your case. Our worthy neighbour——"

"Oh! he's Sir John now," sneered Edgar

Wharton; "of course everybody will side with him now."

Nobody took any notice of the baulked villain. He was down, and despite his crimes, it is not usual for an English crowd to trample on the fallen.

We have little more to say, except that some months later Edgar Wharton was tried and condemned to death. But, by the exertions of the man he had tried to ruin, his sentence was commuted into twenty-one years in Newgate.

CHAPTER CI.

ON THE PROWL.

As soon as Edgar Wharton was committed for trial, John Palmer intimated to the family that Tom and himself must start on business once more. The family objected; but Jack Palmer on this point was utterly inexorable.

He however yielded so far as to stop four more days, which they spent in their usual way, alternately at the farm and the inn, where in the evening the presence of this jovial couple was always welcome.

Palmer's son-in-law was too recently married to join his father-in-law and his friends, at which Jack laughed.

"Let the boy alone," he said, "they're all like that—but a year's dose of matrimony soon knocks all that nonsense out of them. He'll be glad of a little change soon."

On the second evening after the committal of Edgar Wharton (a circumstance which, with the discovery that their neighbour and friend was a baronet, had created intense excitement all about) Palmer and his friend Mr. Robson, as Tom King called himself, were making the frequenters of the inn laugh over one of Jack's stories, when a stranger entered the public room.

He was of the pedlar persuasion, though his pack was but small, consisting of such jewellery as he sold to the farmers' wives and servants. He wore spectacles and a sort of gaberdine; but the two highwaymen at once penetrated the disguise, and knew him to be Joe Askew.

It was with some feeling of discomfort that they made this discovery, but both relied on the oath, as Joe Askew knew that, did he break its terms, not all the power of the law could save him from being put to death by a tribunal as unerring as the secret societies of the middle ages.

The pedlar took a modest place and ordered supper, after which he indulged in a pipe and tobacco, with some rum-and-water—this liquor having recently come into vogue from the West Indies.

He was seated near enough to the two friends to hear all they said, and on one or two occasions ventured to put in his word. Finding himself not snubbed, he presently launched out and told some stories which the friends believed were illustrative of his own life.

They were tales about the mazes and man-traps of London, warning all who went from the country to beware of strangers and their ways and wiles. As they were told with dry and infinite humour, the farmers all laughed, and none more than the two high tobies.

Presently, with a shrewd look at the friends, he began:

"I'll tell you a capital story about Dick Turpin, if you like."

"D—— his impudence!" muttered the supposed Mr. Palmer, who, however, could make no objection.

"Some two years ago there was a big ball at St. James's Palace; it was to be what is called a masked ball, where everybody dressed up as somebody else. As it was a big, nobby affair, it was not easy to get admission.

"I had a friend, and wishing to see a little bit of high life, I got him to get me taken on as one of the waiters. At all events I should get my pay, a jolly good feed, and perhaps some pickings."

"D——l doubt you!" muttered Dick, under his teeth.

"Well, it appears that Dick Turpin, for some purpose best known to himself, determined to go to the ball, but as one of the guests. He got a fine court dress, hired a sedan-chair, and was set down in the midst of the genteel crowd which thronged the doors," continued Joe Askew, who had picked up somehow a very nice way of speaking, "and you will not be surprised when I tell you what he did.

"Nobody was admitted unless he produced what they called a voucher. He took care to have one, and was in the hall safe enough, when there came a great cry at the door. Somebody was being refused admission because he could produce no ticket.

"He insisted that he had one—that he was Lord John Thornton, and that he must have had his pocket picked. He was recognised by several present, and, of course, admitted. A royal personage also interfered in his favour.

"Nothing more was thought of it at the time; but, as the evening went on, there came to be a loud outcry about snuff-boxes of great value, bracelets, and other jewellery being missed; and the rumour was raised that the man who had stolen Lord John Thornton's ticket was a pickpocket. The rumour spread fast, though not until some had prepared to leave.

"Among these was the Archbishop of Canterbury, who was very much annoyed at the loss of a small collar he wore round his neck, with a diamond cross suspended from it.

"As he approached the door he was followed by a very polite gentleman in court costume. He, bowing, showed him the collar and diamond cross.

"'Did your grace drop this?' he asked, with great suavity. 'I picked it up just now, and then rumour reached my ear that you, sir, had lost something of the kind.'

"'It is mine—I value it very much,' retorted the archbishop. 'Which way are you going?'

"'Towards Lambeth,' ventured the stranger.

"'Then let me offer you a seat in my carriage,' replied the prelate.

"The stranger accepted, offering his arm to the archbishop, who was very feeble; and so it happened that the Archbishop of Canterbury went out of St. James's Palace leaning on the arm of Dick Turpin, the highwayman."

"But how did it become known?" asked one of the company, when the laugh was over.

"Impudent fellow! D——d impudent!" said Joe Askew, with a fearful wink at Palmer. "Told the archbishop himself as he got out of the carriage; the archbishop was thanking him.

"'Don't mention it,' said Dick. 'It is I who

have to thank you. Couldn't have got out safe but for you. Thought it worth while restoring your cross to be sheltered by your august protection. I'm Dick Turpin,' he added, and vanished."

Again the company laughed, glasses were filled, and conversation became general.

"Would you like," presently asked Joe Askew, who was in a jolly humour, "to hear how George Barrington became a thief and a pickpocket? It's the story of his first adventure."

All joined in chorus in asking to hear the story, which Joe Askew told very well, but not exactly correct. We prefer to tell it ourselves, with the needful corrections :—

George Barrington, when young, about nineteen, was at school in a very high-class school, where young men were educated for the different professions. Barrington was vicious, extravagant, and, though well provided by his parents with money, pilfered from his master, his comrades—anybody.

He was finally found out by the confession of a penitent accomplice of the name of O'Neil, whom he stabbed with a knife, and, in the confusion, escaped.

He leaped over the playground palings, and, reaching the main road, ran at a rapid rate for three miles; then, feeling himself exhausted, he sat down by the roadside to consider his future plans.

The remembrance of his crime tortured him greatly, and he felt helplessly miserable. Summoning, however, all his fortitude, he determined to obey the dictates of his enterprising nature, and gather courage from despair. Unfortunately his exchequer was at a very low ebb, his pockets yielding exactly fourpence.

After walking for about a quarter of a mile, he entered a roadside public-house, and took his seat in the taproom, where some labouring men were regaling themselves. All eyes were fixed on Barrington, whose appearance surprised them. Barrington felt very embarrassed; after ordering a pint of beer he broke silence by informing the company that he had committed some trifling offence at school, and had run away to avoid the consequence of a severe flagellation. He represented his master to be a very stern man, who had severely treated many of the boys; he also explained the state of his coffers, and so eloquent an appeal did he make, that the company clubbed together and raised him a shilling.

On the landlord coming into the room, the situation of our hero was explained to him, upon which that worthy person provided him some refreshment free of expense, and, as night was approaching, and Barrington had told him he was very far from home, offered him a bed for the night. Barrington thanked his benefactor, and accepted his generous offer. In the evening he was introduced to the family, who greatly sympathised with his situation; indeed, so artfully and ingeniously did he manage his address, that in a few hours he had established himself a great favourite in the house.

After our hero had sipped a little warm rum and water out of the ample beaker of the landlord of the hostelry, he was invited to his couch, which was placed in a snug little room, replete with comfort. Barrington locked the door and threw himself on the bed; remorse and compunction took possession of his breast. The past was clothed in terror, the future was involved in dread uncertainty.

These terrible and conflicting feelings so harassed his mind, that he resolved on suicide.

Leaving his bed, he opened the drawer of a deal table in the hope of finding a razor; the drawer contained nothing, however, but an old toothbrush and a rusty nail.

He threw his eyes wildly round the room. His attention was drawn to an old bureau in the corner of the room. His evil genius suggested to him that it might contain money. His resolution of suicide was broken by a determination to investigate the drawers of the ancient piece of furniture.

How was it to be accomplished, for the drawers were locked? He bethought himself of the rusty nail as a fit instrument for his purpose, and which he immediately bent. Fearing the noise of his experiment might disturb the family, he tore off a portion of his handkerchief, which he bound round the nail, secured by some thread which he drew from the bed curtains, The locks being of the simplest construction, yielded at once to his ingenuity; he found the drawers stored with wearing apparel, among which was a quantity of lavender; the perfume was so powerful that his guilt suggested that *that* simple circumstance might expose his crime.

For some minutes he remained in a state of uncertainty as to whether he should rob his benefactor or leave the property untouched. The glimmerings of virtue were, however, soon extinguished, and he at once proceeded to a nearer investigation of the articles. After overhauling them for some time, he found the foot of an old stocking that weighed tolerably heavy.

"Ah, ah!" he exclaimed, "I'm a lucky dog. This contains money."

Taking out his knife he cut it open, and counted out upon the bed twenty-three guineas; this money he resolved on appropriating to his own use, and therefore stowed away about his person with considerable judgment. Having carefully relocked the drawers, he laid himself upon the bed, but he could not sleep. At daybreak he rose and determined to pursue his journey without delay. Hearing footsteps about the house, he resolved to make his appearance, and on proceeding downstairs he found the worthy landlord busily employed in opening the house.

"Well, my young fellow," said mine host, "so you're up, are you? How did you sleep?"

"Very well, I thank you, sir," said Barrington; "but I'm going now, sir, as I wish to get home as fast as I can."

"Nonsense!" said the landlord; "you must have some breakfast first; it will be ready in half an hour."

"I'm greatly obliged to you," said Barrington, "but I must be going, sir. I shall never be able to repay your kindness."

"Nonsense, nonsense!" said the landlord. "I'm glad to have been the means of serving you. Pray, how far are you going, my lad?"

"To Wakefield, sir," said Barrington, mentioning the opposite of the place he intended to go to.

"Ah, well, you haven't far to go then. But, I say, my lad, you must have those dirty shoes cleaned. Here, boy," calling to a boy in the yard, "take this young gentleman's shoes and clean them."

Barrington was for a moment in a dreadful perplexity, for some of the money was stowed away in his shoes.

"I beg, sir," said Barrington, "that you will not trouble yourself, and so needlessly occupy the boy's time. The roads are very dirty, and I shall have to cross some rough places."

"Well, well," said the landlord, "just as you like."

After Barrington had shaken the rough hand of his benefactor, and expressed his gratitude in glowing terms, he turned from the house into the high road. When out of sight of the house he determined on taking any road but the main one; he feared pursuit. After walking some considerable distance he took some refreshment and asked the way. He found he was about eight miles from Warrington. In the dark of the evening he entered an obscure inn in that place.

"This way in," said a facetious-looking personage in a fustian jacket.

Barrington paused, for his guilty fears suggested that perchance his crime was discovered.

"Walk in, sir; walk in, sir." continued the facetious-looking personage. "There's the room, sir."

"What room?" asked Barrington.

"The gentlemen are all here, sir," said the other.

Before Barrington had time to pause, he found himself in a room full of tobacco smoke, and at a long deal table were seated numerous gentlemen, the majority of whom were buttoned up to the chin; their habiliments were of a decidedly shabby character; yet in some of their faces was the stamp of gentility.

At the end of the table sat a coarse-featured man, with a red face, attired in rusty black; a large ring sparkled on his finger. As Barrington entered this personage made a low bow, the meaning of which Barrington could not understand; he, however, bowed in return, and took a seat.

"What are you disposed to drink, sir?" said this personage to Barrington.

"Me, sir," said Barrington; "I must take something, of course, but not, sir, at your expense."

"Shall I drink, then, at yours, sir?" said the stranger.

"Really, sir," said Barrington, "I do not understand the meaning of your observations; you are quite a stranger to me. I would much rather drink by myself, as I am unknown to any gentleman here."

"We none of us, sir, can drink here without money; money's the great thing, sir," replied the stranger.

These observations were made with so much emphasis, and accompanied with a look so searching, that Barrington wished himself a thousand miles from the place; his suspicions were aroused, and remained unallayed the rest of the evening.

Another circumstance greatly affected our hero; it was this, that after ordering his drink it was necessary he should pay down on the nail, for he had observed a very scrupulous regard exhibited by the facetious attendant in obtaining the money for the liquors supplied; indeed, in one or two instances he had noticed that a sort of guarantee was insisted upon, by the exhibition of coins antecedent to the trouble of the attendant in furnishing liquors.

His presence of mind, however, never deserted him; so he resolved, as his money was hidden about his body, to draw a cheque upon his boots. To this end he talked of the misery of corns, and forthwith proceeded to rifle his pedal coverings.

"You don't appear very thirsty, sir," said a small man with a Bardolphian figure-head, and his hat resting on the bridge of his nose.

"No, not very, sir," said Barrington, as he searched for a guinea.

"You've dropped something," said a weasel-faced looking man, the entire faculty of whose head appeared to be all ear.

"I've picked it up," said Barrington. "Curse the fellow!" he remarked to himself; "he heard the guinea rattle in my boot. It fell from my waistcoat," he added, aloud.

Barrington then ordered his drink and placed the gold piece on the table. All eyes glistened at sight of the coin.

"Will you join us, sir, in a bowl of punch this cold evening?" said the low-featured man in the shabby black.

"No, sir," said Barrington.

"You can't do less, sir," replied the other.

"Oh, yes, I can," said Barrington; "I can do more—I'll pay for a bowl myself."

"'Angels and ministers of grace defend us!'" said the stranger.

"The largeness of your bounty, my lord, doth outshine the sun itself," said the man with the hat on his nose.

"Now blow, ye winds, and crack your cheeks; fleet messenger of air, make known the bounty of the prince," exclaimed the personage with the weasel face.

"If 'twere done when 'tis done, then 'twere well it were done quickly," said a pale youth, with the voice of a penny trumpet. "Here, waiter, bring the bowl; that gentleman will pay."

"You're very complimentary, gentlemen," said Barrington. "I never heard until now of so complimentary a method of expressing the familiar English word 'thank 'e.'"

"Now, gentlemen, for a toast," said the chairman of the assembly. "I'll give you, sirs, 'The Immortal Bard of Avon, Billy Shakespeare.'"

"I don't know him," said Barrington.

"He's a silversmith of Sheffield," said the articulator in the penny trumpet voice.

"Sheffield!" said Barrington, affecting to understand. "Well, I'll drink to him, live where he may."

"And now, sir," said the chairman, addressing Barrington; "but I have not the happiness of knowing your name, sir."

"Jones is my name, sir—Jones, Jones," replied Barrington.

"The highly respected name of a somewhat numerous family," said the chairman, now thoroughly warmed by the liberal potation of strong waters he had imbibed; and then relapsing again into his Shaksperian vein, he exclaimed, "What's in a name; the thing we call a rose, by any other name would smell as sweet."

"Billy Shakespeare again," said the weasel-faced man.

"Now, then, Mr. Jones, I'll sing you a song, for your punch deserves a return of some sort, and mine's but a poor sort, for I manufactured it myself," said the chairman.

That worthy, having filled up a tumbler of punch and swallowed it, then sang the following song :—

"We *gaggers* have a jolly life,
As jovial as can be ;
Apart from care, away from strife,
We chaunt right merrily.
If the *rum culi* of our boozing *ken*
Should stop our drinking score,
We'll *fake* his *cly*,* my merry men
For the *raps* to pay for more.

Then here's success to the strolling *gaff*,
And the lads who so jolly *hump* it ;
If we find a cove with a flowing *kick*,
We're the boys to ramp it.

Then drink until the break of day,
No princes live more jolly ;
We care not how the score we pay
To banish melancholy.
We're kings sometimes and sometimes thieves,
Our life is gay and free,
Though the fatal branch that bears no leaves
May be our trysting tree.

Then here's success to the strolling *gaff*,
And the lads who so jolly *hump* it ;
If we find a cove with a flowing *kick*,
We're the boys to ramp it.

Fill high the cup, ye *mummers* all,
And blow your *blazes* rare ;
If you swing, your saucy velvet pall
Shall be borne by maidens fair.
Young Gilderoy, the toby cove,
Like us was a *gagger* brave ;
And six fair damsels, deep in love,
Did bear him to the grave.

Then here's success to the strolling *gaff*,
And the lads who so jolly *hump* it ;
If we find a cove with a flowing *kick*,
We're the boys to ramp it."

The most rapturous applause followed this song, the language of which everyone appeared to understand except Mr. Jones.

"Do you sing, Mr. Jones?" said the chairman.

"I do not, sir," said Barrington ; "I know not a single song, indeed not a verse of one."

"That's sufficient, Mr. Jones," said the other.

The company now began to drop off, and finally the chairman and Barrington were left together.

"You're a very young man, Mr. Jones," said the stranger.

"Yes, I am, sir," said Barrington ; "just nineteen."

"Your figure is good, Mr. Jones ; very good."

"I'm rather tall," replied Barrington.

"You may trust me, Mr. Jones ; pray do you reside here at Warrington?" said the other.

"No, sir, no, I do not," said Barrington.

"Would you like to accept an engagement, sir," he continued.

"At what, sir?" said Barrington.

"An engagement, sir," said the other. "To be frank with you, my name is *Price*, sir, *John Price*. I'm manager of a theatre in this town; I travel through the country. Everybody knows John Price in these parts."

"Indeed, sir," said Barrington.

Barrington paused for a few moments ; and, believing the man to be frank, open, and generous, he determined to open his mind to him. His future prospects were undefined, vague, and uncertain ; he, therefore, risked all

* Pick his pocket

hazards, and communicated to the stranger, in the most undisguised manner, all that had taken place, not excepting the stabbing of his school-fellow ; he, moreover, informed the worthy itinerant lessee that his real name was Waldren, but that he had assumed the name of Barrington.

"Give me your hand, Barrington," said the familiar personage ; "I'll protect you, be a father to you, and soon teach you how to affect an audience, sir ; for know it, young man, that John Price never tarnished his honour, sir."

Price then rose, and emphatically shook the table, and exclaimed, putting his hand on his heart—

"So help me ——, I'm all right here."

This was accomplished in a most superlatively theatrical manner.

"Yes," observed John Palmer, noticing that Joe Askew paused ; "I understand he proved it by corrupting young Barrington, and inducing him to become a thief and a pickpocket."

"I believe there is some truth in that, sir," replied Joe Askew, and the subject dropped.

"I was thinking of having supper, presently," remarked Joe Askew to Dick ; "will you and your friend join me?"

"With pleasure," smiled Dick ; "it is quite a pleasure to be in your company."

So supper was set on ; and then a jolly late evening followed, as was always the case when Jack Palmer was at home.

Next evening he bade farewell to his family, and started in search of their horses.

CHAPTER CII.

LADY MILICENT GRAFTON.

We return for awhile to Brian Seymour and his friend, Robert Woodstock. After their last failure to find out anything with regard to Elphick Castle, they returned to London and mixed in good society.

A man who is not only the relative of an earl, but also his heir presumptive, is always admitted everywhere, no matter what his character may be.

To be a *roué*, a seducer, a blackleg, is not of the slightest consequence as long as you belong to an aristocratic family ; you may commit follies, crimes, be addicted to every vice that is unpleasant or otherwise, as long as you belong to a good old county family.

One day he met a friend, Lord Vincent by name, a man he principally knew as a frequenter of some of the low hells of London.

"Ah, Brian, how are you?" he said. "Where have you been all this time? I'm going to that new sensation, the Duchess de Longueville's, to-night. Will you come?"

"If you can get me an invite—yes. But I've been away so long," replied Brian, "I don't know how to manage it."

"I'll send my man with a card," remarked Lord Vincent. "Give me your name and address ; and then at dawn we'll adjourn to the 'Junior Cocoa-nut.'" said Brian Seymour.

"All serene!" said Brian Seymour.

Going two hours later to a small and quiet hotel, he found an invitation from the rich young English widow of the French nobleman. He dressed himself in the most fashionable style and started.

The Duchess de Longueville did everything in the most magnificent style. She had secured the finest vacant residence in St. James's, just then what vulgar Americans now call the "hub" of the metropolis.

The reception was grand.

Once introduced, Brian Seymour was left to his own resources, and wandered hither and thither at the direction of his own sweet will.

Not meeting for sometime anyone he knew, he presently seated himself on a couch in a corner. Near to this was the entrance to a conservatory. Beside the door stood two ladies, talking.

One of these fixed Brian's attention. He was an admirer of the beautiful, and never before had he seen anyone to equal her.

Her face, as she spoke, was turned full towards him. Never had he seen anything so lovely. She was apparently about twenty, her hair was of the richest chestnut, and a golden light played through its darkness, as if a sunbeam had been caught in those luxuriant tresses, and was striving in vain to escape.

Her eyes were of light hazel, large, deep and shaded into softness by long and very dark lashes. Her complexion alone would have rendered her beautiful, it was so clear, so pure.

Her nose was of that fine and accurate mould that one so seldom sees, except in the Grecian statues, which unites the clearest and most decided outline with the utmost feminine delicacy and softness; and the short, curved arch which descended from thence to her mouth was so fine —so airily and exquisitely formed, that it seemed as if love himself had modelled the bridge. On the right side of the mouth was one dimple, which corresponded so exactly with every smile and movement of those rosy lips, that you might have sworn the shadow of each passed there; it was like the rapid changes of an April heaven reflected upon a valley. She was somewhat, but not much, taller than the ordinary height, and her figure, which united all the freshness and youth of the girl with the more luxurious graces of the woman, was rounded and finished so justly, that the eye could glance over the whole without discovering the least harshness or unevenness, an item to be added or subtracted.

But over all these there was a light, a glow, a pervading spirit, of which it is impossible to convey the faintest idea.

Brian Seymour said afterwards, "You should have seen her by the side of a shaded fountain on a summer's day; you should have watched her amidst music and flowers, and she might have seemed to you like the fairy that presided over both."

Presently he caught sight of Lord Vincent, and, crossing the room, indicated the girl.

"Who is that beautiful girl?" he asked.

Lord Vincent smiled rather sardonically.

" O Dea certe !" said that jocose individual ; "you have spotted Helen of Troy, the most beautiful girl of the season, and the richest heiress. That is Lady Milicent Grafton, only child of the duke. His nephew takes the title and some of the estates ; but Lady Milicent inherits a vast fortune."

"Hem !" remarked Brian ; "she is one of those few women one would take without a fortune."

" Struck !" said Lord Vincent, with a laugh. "You are like a good many others. But she is not for us. She is affianced to her cousin Reginald, the future duke."

" Oh !" remarked Brian Seymour, and dropped the subject.

A wonderful change had come over him. This man of violent passions, and strange, unprincipled character, was carried away for once in his life by real feeling.

He loved the Lady Milicent Grafton with one of those wild and stormy passions which take hold of a man but once in a lifetime.

"Beauty and money !" he muttered to himself. "My name is not Brian Seymour if I do not win her."

" Who had thought this clime had held
    A deity so unparalleled,"

laughed Lord Vincent, watching him keenly.

Brian Seymour was not disposed to prolong the discussion, but a word from Lord Vincent stopped him as he was about to move away.

"Lady Milicent is very gentle and sweet-tempered," said Lord Vincent. "If you like, I will introduce you."

"I shall feel deeply grateful ; " and the two approached the spot where Lady Milicent stood in conversation with her chaperon.

"Lady Grafton," remarked Lord Vincent, with a very low bow, " my friend, Mr. Seymour, wishes the honour of an introduction to yourself and Lady Milicent."

Luckily for Brian, Lady Grafton had not heard the scandals about him, and was very gracious, as was the younger woman, who vouchsafed him one dance ; more she could not, as her card was extra full.

The dance vacant happened to be the next, and Brian became even more infatuated with the lovely being than before.

Brian was wildly impulsive, which explained many of his evil deeds, and he was now utterly conquered.

When the dance was over, a tall, handsome man of about six-and-twenty, aristocratic to the fingers' ends, approached, and with a stiff nod to Brian, took Milicent away without the least ceremony.

Brian knew him, and bit his lip. He knew, too, what the young heir to the dukedom would say about him to Lady Milicent. He was not mistaken.

"Milicent," he said, kindly but firmly, " you must never be seen speaking to that man again. He is the most noted roué in society, and suspected of even greater crimes."

"Why did Lord Vincent introduce him to Lady Grafton and myself ? " observed the girl.

"Lord Vincent is a feather-headed fool," resumed Lord Reginald Somerset ; " he means no harm, but he never thinks."

Lady Milicent laughed, promised not to encourage him, and determined to repel his advances gently but firmly.

Perfectly satisfied, Lord Reginald claimed the next dance, while Brian sat down, deeply mortified at the revelation which he knew would be made. The cool way the young lord looked at him as he passed, with Milicent on his arm, satisfied him that he had spoken, and served both to inflame his passion and excite bitter anger against one whom he, in his own mind, called the calumniator.

He would be revenged.

But how ? An outrage upon a woman of such high rank and fortune was a thing to be carefully weighed before it was undertaken. There must be a place to take her to, a willing priest discovered who would tie the knot indissolubly, despite any outcry she might make.

Of the after consequences he was reckless. The haughty pride of the family would repel the idea of an open scandal, though he much feared that a deadly encounter with Lord Reginald would ensue.

But Brian was physically brave, and was utterly careless what followed if once he was master of this peerless creature.

He never in his impetuous passion reflected that the duke would probably revoke his will. He knew, however, from Lord Vincent, that she had a considerable fortune in her own right. He was moreover blinded by this sudden and wild passion.

Never was more restless spirit known than Brian Seymour. He could never bear solitude. A very great philosopher has said : All evil arises from the fact that few men can live alone ; hence gambling, luxury, extravagance, dissipation, wine, women, grievance, calumny, envy, and utter forgetfulness of self and heaven. Certainly Brian Seymour could not live alone.

He retired early from the ball to think. His plans were as yet vague and in the clouds ; but he was resolved to mature them, for which purpose he sought a brief solitude.

It was perhaps the most difficult enterprise in which he had ever engaged, in fact the most perilous. So dangerous was it, that if he tried and failed society would see him no more, until he blossomed into a full-blown earl. Then and then only would much be forgiven him.

Though Brian desired to be where he could think quietly, he could think of no better place than the coffee-room of the Junior Cocoa-nut, where he found his friend Robert Woodstock.

Him he would not trust, unless compelled. He therefore simply nodded, and seated himself in a corner, where the other at once joined him.

"Aint you going to play to-night?" asked Robert.

"I wanted to be quiet," responded Brian. "I don't feel very well."

"They've got young Stammers in there, the millionaire's son," continued Brian ; "he's very well plumed, and there will be some very good plucking."

Brian rose. After all his master passion was gambling. It over-rode everything, and while under its influence he forget everything, even love, ambition, and avarice.

They entered the card-room and found young Stammers, a blonde youth, with a fat face, eyes bleared by dissipation, and countenance flushed by wine, just in the act of putting down heavy stakes.

With rare exceptions the frequenters of the Junior Cocoa-nut, generally known as the Rookery, were sharpers, who lived on pigeons and flats.

There was an understanding between this nefarious gang which was, that when there was a fat pigeon to be plucked, all should share and share alike, no matter what their stakes.

Young Stammers played high, and not being under the influence of sense, lost heavily. His pretended guide, philosopher, and friend, Major Rintoul, encouraged him to drink, and told him when to play, so that at the early dawn, when the play ceased for him, he was dead drunk—he had lost over ten thousand guineas.

A few hundred guineas which remained in his pockets Major Rintoul contrived to ease him of on the way home in a hackney coach.

After the division of the plunder, Brian Seymour and Robert Woodstock retired to the rooms of the latter to seek repose.

It was late when both sat down to breakfast, and then, after some reflection, Brian spoke.

"You don't know of some comfortable furnished little crib near London, where I can take a golden canary bird," observed Brian ; "she's rather a skittish creature, and the place would have to be retired."

Robert Woodstock stared as if rather surprised at Brian.

"I know a fellow," he answered presently, "who has a sweet cottage at Twickenham. He lets it for the fishing season at times, but has no objection to make money at any time. He's a little daft, but very fond of money."

"Ah ! secure it for me ; pay in advance for a month," added Brian, "and let it be at my orders at a moment's notice."

"It's done," said Robert.

"Next, I want a parson, a real parson, who will not scruple to tie the knot, whether the bride be willing or no," continued Brian, with a laugh.

"What's up ?" asked Robert.

"Money and beauty !" was the answer, "I can explain no more. Have the parson ready and willing."

"Jack Stainforth's the man," said Robert ; "he's a full 'canonical', but so long as he gets drink and coin, does not care what he does."

"'Tis well. I will now go forth and discover the movements of my Helen for the next few days," cried Brian, rising. "We'll meet at the 'Cocoa-nut' to-night."

Brian went home, and after a stormy explanation with the lady of his love, dressed himself in the costume of a gentleman's gentleman, and strolled out in the direction of St. James' Square, where his beauty resided.

It was the custom of an afternoon of this class of personages, perhaps the most insufferable and conceited class in the world, to meet at a tavern down a mews, where good liquor was provided.

These apes of fashion, accustomed to every luxury at the expense of lavish, careless and extravagant masters, knew good liquor when they tasted it, and Joe Standish stood in too great awe of the mighty flunkies not to provide them with the best of everything—even to the exclusive possession of a parlour of their own.

How Brian Seymour knew of this it is best not to say, but know it he did. Many a time in his chequered career he had indulged in low intrigues and schemes, which required many and strange refuges, and this had been one of them.

He entered with all the air of an *habitué*, and took the first vacant seat, next to a gloriously-clad footman in gorgeous livery.

"Gentlemen," he said, as soon as he was seated, speaking in a humble and diffident tone, "I am almost a stranger here. May I be allowed, by way of paying my footing, to order in a bowl of the best punch ?"

The domestics present looked at him with a peculiarly critical air, and then the senior, or chairman as he was called, a bloated butler, as the landlord called him in private, signified in a dignified way their acceptance of the peace offering.

The bowl was brought, and harmony prevailed. After the first tumbler had been ladled out and partially consumed, conversation became general.

Constant allusions were made in the most familiar style to the families with which those present were living, and whom they condescended to honour by their services, so that it soon came out that Yellow Plush, Brian's neighbour, was head footman in the service of the Duke of Grafton, while Brian declared himself to be in the service of the Earl of Elphick.

Then the important flunkey unbosomed himself.

"Hour people is going to Sion House, the 'ouse of the Dook of Northumberland. It's 'orrid bad form going hout of town this time ov 'ear, when hall the fashion and beauty his in town. What possesses Lady Milicent to go, I can't tell."

"Is Lord Reginald going with them?" asked Brian.

"Yaas!" drawled the gorgeous one with a sigh; "though, what she can see in 'im, I can't make hout."

"Wonderful, when you're by," remarked an older domestic, sardonically; "but some people think him the finest man in London."

"'Orrid taste," again drawled the footman.

"Quite horrid," put in Brian. "I've only seen him once, and can say there's no comparison between you."

"Your 'ealth," responded the gratified servant, with a glow of pleased vanity, as he filled his glass and drank it off.

The others now clubbed round, and another bowl was filled, to the great delight of the meeting which got particularly harmonious.

Having after awhile heard all he wanted to know, Brian Seymour retired, after promising to make one of them whenever his duties to society allowed him.

──────

CHAPTER CIII.

THE PLOT.

Brian happened next day to meet a friend and missed Robert Woodstock, who, however, came to him in the evening to a late dinner, at which the supposed Mrs. Brian Seymour presided.

The lady was getting weary and sick with hopes deferred. He had taken her from a happy, if comparatively humble home, in the pride of her beauty and womanhood. He had seduced her away from her family by false and lying promises.

He had told her that, being dependent on an uncle, he dare not marry without his consent, that it would be ruin to him, and the usual false and lying hypocrisies with which silly women are too often artfully deceived.

But all belief in him had long vanished. She knew him for what he was—a villain.

She had two children. Nothing that could happen could put them in the position they ought to occupy. She was therefore careless and ruthless. But this she was decided on—no other woman should call him husband—that is, if woman's wit were of any avail.

After dinner, Brian requested to be left alone with his friend on business of an important nature.

"Let us have a bowl of punch, some real Virginia, and a pack of cards."

Mrs. Seymour rose with a smile, but with doubt and hatred in her heart.

She always suspected these secret meetings, and believed that if there were anything to conceal there must be some plot against herself.

Aided by her own domestic, Mrs. Seymour brought in all that was required, and then, with a sneering "good night," retired.

"Hem!" observed Robert Woodstock, "aint you afraid she may turn rusty some day?"

"No. And if she did, what good can she do herself?" he answered, in an angry tone. "Besides, if this affair come all right, I shall give her the slip altogether. Of course, I shall make her an allowance, but I am determined to end it all. A grumbling woman is not to my fancy. Now to business. Is the cottage at Twickenham ready?"

"Yes. I have paid a month in advance," answered Robert Woodstock.

"And the parson?"

"Is ready and willing!" answered the other. "I have tipped him, and he's all right. But as it is a real buckle-to this time, he'll want a big fee."

"He shall have it."

"Now, about the girl!"

"Yes. There's the rub! She's neither ready nor willing," replied Brian, gravely, "and she has powerful friends; but I am not going to be baulked—*I love her—yes, I love her!* and will not be baulked of her possession by man or devil."

"Really in love!" sneered Robert.

"Yes—no pretence this time. It means riches, glory, rank," cried Brian; "but on my soul I love her. *Never* before did I know what the sensation meant, and now I do—I am as a child. She must be mine, if I perish body and soul."

"A pretty speech," went on Robert, laughing; "I should have expected a boy to make one so foolish."

"Never mind that," said Brian, drily; "you will be well paid for what you do. Now, finish up the bowl, and away for the Cocoa-nut. I'm told Stammers will be there to-night again."

They finished the drink, and, rising, went out, without any attempt to bid a farewell to Mrs. Seymour.

The door had not been closed a moment when Mrs. Seymour was in the room, not by the door they had used, but by a sliding panel, which connected her bedroom with the sitting-room.

She was pale with rage.

"Ah!" she cried, "he wants to get rid of me—does he? But I'll baulk him in this villainy. This girl, whoever she may be, shall be torn from his grasp. Let the memory of my own wrongs rouse me."

And in a moment more she called her attendant, bade her help her to dress, and went out.

Brian Seymour little suspected that the Blue Dwarf knew all about his home and supposed wife. With a view to keeping a strict watch on the deadly foe of the house of Elphick, Sapathwa had sent Tim Roach under some pretence to make inquiries of Mrs. Seymour.

She happened to be in trouble when he called. Brian was away, and she was summoned to pay a large debt of his to a man who had a lien on his furniture.

Tim Roach reported this to his employer, who

paid the money, sent to say that *in secret* he was a friend of the family, and begging her to apply to him in any future difficulty.

Tim Roach left an address.

To this Mrs. Seymour went that night, and fortunately found the young man alone.

She told her story minutely, concealing as much as possible her feelings of deadly hate and vengeance, while laying great stress on her desire to save the girl.

Roach knew where to find Sapathwa that evening, and at once on her leaving went and told him the story.

He at once resolved to baulk the villain and ruffian, and sent Roach to look for Dick Turpin.

He happened just to have reached London after his journey home, and was with Tom King about to start in search of the horses.

He obeyed the behest, however, of Sapathwa, and went to his head-quarters.

As they knew nothing of the individuality of the girl, the only plan was to watch Twickenham, discover the retreat to which she was to be taken, and rescue her after the abduction.

This became the duty of Dick Turpin, though Sapathwa was at no great distance, in a secluded lodging.

It was a small, neatly-furnished house, at no great distance from the cottage which Brian had hired for the purpose of concealing Lady Milicent. This had been easily discovered. It was temporarily occupied by a noted angler named Atherton, a simple, half-witted fellow, devoted to the rod and line.

In his days of peace and quietness at home, Dick Turpin had sometimes indulged in the mild, unexciting sport.

Dick easily made friends with the quiet, good-natured Jacob Atherton, and on the morning after his arrival in Twickenham was seated quietly in a punt with him. For a whole hour they sat without a nibble.

Even the ardent fisherman found it rather trying to his patience and temper.

Dick thought it an intolerable bore. He was the first to speak.

"I say, Mr. Atherton," he said, "don't you think this is very slow work? What can have taken all the fish?"

The old man pondered a little, and then answered, slowly and deliberately—

"Perhaps this is fast day with them, you know. I have some slight sort of impression that fishes are more particular in their religious duties than we are," and the simple old man heaved a deep sigh, expressive of extreme contrition on this point as far as he was personally concerned.

Dick at first thought that this was a joke on the old man's part, and was just preparing to laugh at it, when he caught sight of the awe-struck face, and then understood what he had heard from the people of the neighbourhood about Jacob Atherton being slightly demented.

"Ah, well, Jacob," he said, willing to humour him, "perhaps you are right, and we had better let them alone, as the beggars will not be enticed. I see a respectable alehouse on the bank. Let us go ashore and have some refreshments."

"Well, yes. The servants of the people who have hired my house have taken possession," replied Jacob, "so I cannot offer to take you there."

CHAPTER CIV.

SION HOUSE.

Sion House, the residence of the Duke of Northumberland, is a great oblong, ugly building on the banks of the river Thames. It is never used now, from a singular peculiarity in its building. It has a vast number of bedrooms, but most of them only to be reached one through the other. In the last century this was not objected to, but now-a-days it is considered improper, and the huge palatial mansion is not used.

On the present occasion, on the evening of the day just recorded, it was one blaze of light. A large party was assembled.

The evening was fine, and the grounds towards the river were illumined by a variety of lamps, giving it a very Vauxhall-garden look. As the weather was hot, very many of the guests were in the grounds.

At the foot of the water-steps were several boats, in one of which were Brian Seymour and Robert Woodstock, with two watermen. They had just come, and prepared to go on shore. Brian carried a heavy cloak.

The grounds were extensive, and in some parts had shady walks, which by some, lovers, of course, were preferred to the brilliantly lighted ones.

Brian and Robert made their way to the vicinity of one of these, and then concealed themselves behind a thicket of trees, which was called in the quaint fashion of those days a quincunx. It gave a very extensive view of the grounds.

Of course, Brian Seymour was well aware that accident alone could serve him; but, like most bad men, he had great belief in his star.

He and his companion took care to keep close, listening to the music, the hum of voices, and the clear, shrill laugh of happy girlhood as they flitted about in the dance, or strolled along the alleys in the gardens of Sion House.

Presently a stately figure, that of a woman, entered the alley, with a glance over her shoulder, as if expecting to be followed.

It was Lady Milicent.

Brian Seymour knew her at once, and glanced eagerly over the grounds to see if Lord Reginald was about; but he could not make him out.

Lady Milicent approached still nearer, and Brian rushing out cast the heavy cloak over her head, and catching her up in his arms, fled to the river. Unfortunately, everybody was too much occupied with their own affairs to notice what happened.

The two men reached the boat, put off from the stairs, and began at once pulling up the river.

For a moment we will return to Sion House. Lord Reginald, as soon as he could rid himself of a garrulous friend, hastened to join Lady Milicent in what was called the Orange Walk, where she had agreed to meet him.

Hurrying down the path, which was roofed by overhanging trees, he looked in every direction for the young lady, and not seeing her, ventured to call her name, thinking perhaps that she might be playing hide-and-seek with him in a frolic.

"Milicent!" he cried, in earnest accents; "don't play with me, but come out and show yourself."

No answer. Lord Reginald now grew alarmed, and called her in such a loud tone that others were attracted.

A scene of great confusion ensued, and after

DICK TURPIN'S CLEVER ESCAPE FROM THE MAIL COACH, WITH MOSES LARKIN'S BAG OF GOLD.

No. 20.

a brief wild search, Lord Reginald returned to the house in order to summon the servants, who might have seen her. But no one had seen her.

What could have happened?

She could not have hidden herself voluntarily.

He rushed to the water-side, a fearful and horrid dread upon his soul. Could she have fallen from the terrace while looking over? He reached the head of the embankment which skirted the shore, and peered out into the night.

"Looking for anything, sir?" asked a waterman's apprentice.

"Well!" said Lord Reginald, in a low tone; "there is a lady missing."

"Ah!" the other continued; "well, a boat put off half an hour ago, with a waterman and two gents—one of these carried something wrapped in a cloak."

"Great heavens!" cried Lord Reginald, "what can this outrage mean? Surely that scoundrel Brian Seymour has not carried her off? I saw he was struck. Quick, my men!" he exclaimed to the crew of a boat which was rowed by six men in Northumberland liveries—row for your lives. Which way my lad?" he asked, as he got into the boat.

"Up river, my lord," replied the youth, who now recognised him.

He hastily gave the lad a guinea, and seating himself, proceeded to steer the boat up the reaches of the river, with which he was well acquainted. But the pursuit was vain; he soon met a boat returning, and found that going up some distance the men had landed with their burden.

"I'll have you hanged as an accomplice," said Lord Reginald, sternly, "if any harm come of this."

"The gent said as how it was a runaway match—only the lady wanted to be taken away, as if by force," the other urged, apologetically.

Lord Reginald made no reply, and returning to the house, made further inquiries, and found that no trace of Lady Milicent had been found. He spoke to no one of the supposed outrage but to her father and his uncle, and then retired to send messengers to Bow-street and Richmond, with full particulars of the outrage.

He then himself mounted his horse and rode into London to await news. He was wild with rage and mortification, and vowed that if Brian Seymour had anything to do with this outrage, his life should pay the forfeit.

The messengers returned, but without bringing one atom of news.

Lord Reginald was furious. Sleep he would have none that night. He walked the dining-room in a frenzy of rage and despair. Day-break came—still he walked from side to side of the room.

Suddenly he heard horse's hoofs coming down the street, and a farmer-looking man halting before the door, alighted.

Lord Reginald rushed down stairs three and fours steps at a time, and opened the door.

"Lord Reginald?" said Dick Turpin, in his suavest tones.

"Yes. You have news for me—good news, I think," exclaimed the other.

"Yes, my lord; but Lady Milicent has had a great shock," responded Dick, "but I left her with a good nurse and doctor."

"Come in, my man," said the young lord, "and tell me all about it."

We will, however, do so in our own words:

As soon as the boat was quite out of sight of Sion House, the two abductors told the boatmen to pull in to a waterside inn where they had ordered a chariot to await them. With this, they started for the furnished cottage.

They had removed the cloak from around the girl's head, but in answer to her remonstrances and threats, they said nothing. It was useless for her to resist, in the hands as she was, of two powerful men.

She recognised Brian Seymour at once, and having been enlightened as to his character, feared the worse.

"Villainous coward! I know you, and you shall be punished for this outrage," she cried.

But he made no reply.

They soon reached the cottage by the river, into which Lady Milicent, scorning to be carried, entered with a haughty step.

To her surprise, it was lighted up as for some festive occasion, while a middle-aged man in the garb of a clergyman, stood beside an improvised altar, a woman standing in the rear.

The middle-aged man, whose face was that of a soaker, bowed respectfully, and produced the book of common prayer.

"What wicked mockery and cruel farce is this?" she asked, proudly. "Why am I brought here?"

"Lady Milicent," said Brian Seymour, in a most humble tone, "all is fair in love and war. When I saw you the other night your beauty overshadowed my soul, and I swore you should be mine!"

"Wretched cur, as if my father's daughter would descend so low as you—never! If you would not be scourged at cart's tail, let me go."

"You will never leave this place except as my wife," was the cold reply; "here is a clergyman ready to perform the ceremony. You have no chance of escape—none!"

"Nothing will ever induce me to ally myself to one so vile."

"Mr. Preston," said Brian, coldly, "read the marriage service. We will contrive to reduce my lady to submission once the ceremony is over. Proceed."

"At your peril!" said Lady Milicent, firmly. "You know who I am?"

Mr. Preston bowed.

"And you will risk the displeasure of such a family as ours?" she asked, in utter amazement.

"When the marriage is once solemnised, their interest will be to keep the secret," responded Mr. Preston, in a thick, hasty voice. "I will read the service."

"Are you mad?" asked Lady Milicent; "you will get no responses from me."

"The ceremony can easily be repeated," said the hedge parson, one of what were called the Fleet bucklers, "when you wish it. For the present, I shall presume your consent."

At this the wretched victim of vice and drink opened his prayer book.

"At your peril!" she began, and turned to seat herself.

"Go on!" said Brian Seymour, cynically, "I will hold you harmless."

"Scoundrel! villain! rascal!" cried a terrible voice, and the door was burst in. Dick Turpin, Tom King, and Tim Roach, dashed into the room, armed to the teeth, and confronted the astounded abductors.

Lady Milicent gave a great cry of joy, as she

stared at these extraordinary-looking champions of virtue in distress.

The parson was the first to escape, which he did with a readiness and agility which did great credit to his acuteness.

Brian Seymour and Robert Woodstock were too astonished to speak ; but after a moment's reflection, followed the hedge-priest's example.

"My lady," said Dick Turpin, "your pardon for interfering in your affairs. By the rarest accident in the world, I and my friends heard of this intended outrage. We did not know your name, only that you were to be brought to this place."

"No matter," replied Lady Milicent, in her sweet, but noble, aristocratic voice, "how you heard of this crime ; you and your friends have done me a great service, one I shall never forget."

"You must leave this place, lady," continued Dick Turpin ; "that bad man is in league with many others. It is too late, I fear, for you to return to town to-night ; but my patron and friend has one close by, where you will be treated with all honour and respect."

"Lead me where you will," replied Lady Milicent ; "I trust you thoroughly. I think I know an honest face when I see one."

Dick Turpin and Tom King had both the grace to blush. The former was utterly over-whelmed. Never in the course of his life had he seen anything so sweet, gentle, and beautiful. The rough highwayman felt as if he could have fallen down and worshipped her.

Telling her she would not have to go far, he offered his arm, as he saw she was overcome and faint. As she walked along, she told him her name, and recommended him, as soon as it was time enough in the morning, to go to the residence of the Duke of Grafton, in St. James' Square, and see Lord Reginald.

Dick promised ; and, in a few minutes more, they reached Woodbine cottage, which Sapathwa had secured, and she was glad to find a respectable woman there awaiting her with a cup of tea, which she much needed.

But she had scarcely sank in a seat, when she broke down in a kind of hysterical fit. It was the reaction of the terrible adventure she had passed through. The woman at once took her to a bedroom, while Tim Roach went for a doctor who lived close at hand.

He found the young lady suffering from a severe attack of hysteria, with some fever, for which he prescribed a draught and rest. As soon as the doctor was gone, the Blue Dwarf emerged from his place of concealment, and complimented Dick and the others on the marvellous way in which they had frustrated one of the most impudent cases of abduction he had ever heard of.

The Blue Dwarf took one glance at the girl as she lay on the couch, and he stood amazed at her marvellous beauty. Never before had he seen anything to equal it. The unfortunate man sighed deeply, as he reflected, that never for him could there be the joys of love and paternity ; and, leaving the chamber, shut himself in his own room, where he wept bitterly.

As soon as the report of the doctor was made, Dick Turpin mounted his horse and rode off, as we know, to advise Lord Reginald of what had happened. We know with what result.

Lord Reginald was appalled when he heard the narrative.

"But for you, where would my affianced wife have been ?" he said, wringing the other's hand with the utmost enthusiasm ; "what a consummate scoundrel that Brian Seymour is !"

"Yes, my lord, I know it," replied Dick Turpin. "I am watching him for another purpose. Hence my discovery of this wicked plot."

"It was indeed a mercy," the other went on, "that threw you in the way of these vile conspirators. If you have rested enough, we will start for Twickenham. But you have had a cold ride—help yourself to some refreshment," pointing to a spirit-stand on the sideboard.

Dick Turpin never required to be very much pressed on this point, and taking a stiff glass, declared himself quite ready.

When they reached Twickenham, the girl was found to be in a heavy sleep, from which, by the doctor's orders, she was not to be awakened.

Lord Reginald was, however, allowed to see her, and gazed with deep love and reverence on the countenance of the girl he loved, and who had escaped from so foul a fate as that of being mated to a roué and gambler like Brian Seymour.

To say that he was amazed at the sight of Sapathwa, whom he insisted on thanking in person, would be to say little, but like a courteous man and high-minded gentleman, he concealed his feelings, and thanked him with a warmth and heartiness that brought tears into his eyes.

"You have little reason for thanking me, my lord," he said quietly ; "my mission in life is to thwart Brian Seymour."

And he told him the story of the Earl of Elphick, and the persecutions he had to endure from this wicked, grasping, and covetous cousin, to which Lord Reginald listened with disgust and amazement.

"But why does not the Earl of Elphick invoke the law, and punish this unmitigated scoundrel for his many villainies?" asked Lord Reginald.

"There are family reasons which forbid it," replied Sapathwa, gravely ; "but the time will— yes, the time will come, and then——"

He did not finish his sentence.

Soon after, the doctor came, and after a careful examination of Lady Milicent, declared that she must not be moved for a few days, as the least exertion might bring on serious fever.

Sapathwa at once placed the cottage at the disposal of Lord Reginald and his friends, until the young lady was able to be moved.

But Lord Reginald declined to turn them out.

"It is to your generosity and self-sacrifice," said the young nobleman, "that I owe her safety. Remain all of you, and guard her. I will return to London and see her father, who already knows of her safety."

Half an hour later, Lord Reginald was on his way to London, and after satisfying the duke of his daughter's safety, held a long conference with him as to what should be done about Brian Seymour.

The Duke of Grafton had a sensitive dread of scandal, and he resolved to give him warning to keep out of the reach of any of the family, as they would resort to the final arbitration of the law to rid themselves of this atrocious persecution, and punish the offender.

A mysterious paragraph, which was not mysterious to any who had been at Sion House, appeared in one of the flying sheets, alluding to the abduction, and giving broad hints as to the perpetrators of the outrage being known, and warning them to keep out of the way, lest punishment should follow.

The next day Lady Milicent was able to get up and sit in an arm chair for an hour, during which time she insisted on seeing those who had saved her from dishonour worse than death. Sapathwa hesitated at first, but when Lady Milicent insisted, yielded, and came into her presence with all the shamefacedness of a blushing boy.

This the girl at once realised, and a great pity filled her heart. She saw only the sad side of the case, and not the hideous and ludicrous. She spoke to him with the deep affection and gratitude of a daughter.

Wild and strange mystery of the human heart! Never before had the Blue Dwarf been so affected by the sight of a woman. The impression was such as never left him to his dying day, and added one more to the anguishes which tormented the soul of this singular man.

Yes! strange as it may appear, both Sapathwa and Dick Turpin fell in love with this incomparable girl, loving her too with a self-sacrificing devotion, which sought only the happiness of the object of its love.

Such things have been, and simply proved that though both were seared—one by sorrow, the other by crime—yet, there was at bottom, in the secret depths of their souls, a sense of chivalry not surpassed by that of any real knight of the middle or any other age.

Four days later Lady Milicent left 'for London, all the sunshine, these two strange beings thought, going out with her departure.

Sapathwa, for his comrades and himself, refused any pecuniary reward. He sternly, but resolutely, declined any allusion to the subject. Money was no object to him, or to his friends. They wished to remember having done an act useful to their fellow-creatures without any sordid motive being ascribed to it.

The duke and Lord Reginald appreciated their feelings, and promised themselves to find some way of showing their deep and lasting gratitude.

"We are going into Devonshire," said Lord Reginald, "in a week, to Landsdale Hall. We should be glad to know if you are that way."

"Landsdale!" cried Sapathwa; "Brian Seymour has a small estate near there. Be on your guard. Perhaps we may be useful as a bodyguard. We shall very likely come down, in which case you shall know."

And thus they parted, to meet again under peculiar and even tragical circumstances.

CHAPTER CV.

DEAD OR ALIVE.

A couple of days passed, and then Sapathwa was determined to return to the home occupied by the Earl of Elphick and his friends, while Dick Turpin and Tom King decided to indulge in some private business of their own.

Tom had for some time felt a little home-sick. He belonged to a very decent and respectable family, living a long way from London, and who had not the faintest suspicion of his true vocation. They thought he was doing well in a lawyer's office in the great metropolis, which

surmise was encouraged by the fact of his always bringing home money presents for the old people, and knick-knacks for the young ones.

Dick was thus left to his own devices. He longed for adventure. Never was he so happy as when on the road riding over moor and heath, cantering beneath the light of Sir Oliver, and saying, "Stand and deliver," to a fat citizen or rich gentleman as the case might be.

Fortune favoured him in a way he little expected. Sauntering through the streets of the city trying to hit upon some means of replenishing his coffers, he recognised the form of one Moses Larkin, a diamond merchant, who was hurrying along the streets in the direction of the great stage-coach office, attended by a stout youth carrying a kind of carpet-bag, which Dick Turpin shrewdly suspected was worth his attention.

He followed in the trac of Moses Larkin until he saw him enter the office. When in the city Dick Turpin was always disguised and prepared for action. He followed the Hebrew citizen into the office. He booked one inside for Manchester. Dick at once did the same, and the coach at this moment appearing, the two got inside, the citizen rather in an ill-humour at being forced to travel with a total stranger, and Dick complaisant as usual.

The coachman clambered up to his seat, the guard examined his waybill, and they were about to make a start when the door opened, and the guard bundled another passenger inside with but scant courtesy.

Then he slammed the door, the horn sounded, and they were off.

The Hebrew diamond merchant seemed relieved by the presence of a third party, though, to judge by Dick's grimace, he was not. His plans for robbing the other had not been at all decided; but now the presence of a stranger hampered his movements.

Still he was hopeful; it was part of his character never to allow himself to be cast down by any difficulty great as it might be.

When they had gone a few miles Dick began to be chatty, to talk of incidents of travel in his life as a bagman, and told some stories, which made even the diamond merchant smile.

The third party merely nodded his head occasionally, eyeing Dick admiringly with two ferrety orbs that seemed to read your very soul.

"Know this road well, sir?" asked Dick presently, of Moses Larkin.

"Yes! I've travelled it pretty often," replied the other, in a half-surly, half-jovial tone. "I have business in Manchester four times every year with my people."

"I go there about twice a year," continued Dick; "remember the case of Wilcox and Heavyside? That was a smart rogue, but he got found out."

"Oh, yes! I know Wilcox and Heavyside," the other answered; "very warm people. I do business with them sometimes. Shall give them a call this journey."

"You mean the great burglary?" asked the stranger in the corner.

"Yes, sir! very remarkable affair," responded Dick; "found out in a curious way, too—lucky—or the other fellow might have been hanged."

"Yes!" observed the other, "it was a rare stroke of luck—could never make out how it happened."

"Well," said Dick, modestly, "I had a hand in it;" and he told what he thought proper of the discovery he had made, and the way the tables had been turned on Edgar Wharton.

"Very smart, very clever," remarked the stranger; "seen some life in your time—eh?"

"Yes!" continued Dick, with one of his fat chuckles. "I have seen a little of life—more than most men."

"Very likely—very likely," the man remarked, nodding his head. "Ever been stopped by highwaymen—eh?"

"Yes! once or twice," returned Dick; "but didn't get much out of me. Only carry samples—got one in the boot now."

The stranger nodded.

Dick now launched out into some absurd narrative of adventure, full of exaggeration and fun, as to one or two of his apocryphal adventures with highwaymen, which seemed to alarm Moses Larkin very much, but which made the other laugh in a half-sniggering, sneering, sort of way.

"That's a very good story," he said, presently, "a very good story, but I can tell you a better, Dick," and he presented a pistol right at his breast. "I've got a warrant in my pocket, and my instructions is to take you back to London, *dead or alive!* them was the very words, and what's more, you will find them written in my pocket-book, which you very cleverly took out of my pocket when you were telling that wonderful story, Dick."

The highwayman stared, and looked perceptibly paler, as he gazed down the barrel of his adversary's pistol.

"What do you want, and who are you?" asked Dick, recovering himself.

"Well! I'm Tom Carroll, my boy, and mean to take you back to London by the return coach."

"Well, I suppose it's all up!" observed Dick Turpin, with a sigh.

"Yes, Dick, it's all up! You can make a row, or you can go quietly—just as you like. It makes no difference to me; dead or alive, them's the instructions. Now, stand up, and catch hold of them two straps. Now Dick, I've got my eyes on you. Let go those straps, and you are a dead man. Now, Mr. Larkin, search his pockets, and hand me out his pistols."

"You'd do it better," grimly remarked Dick, as he saw Moses Larkin hesitate.

"Right you are," replied the officer, still covering the highwayman with his pistol, which he held in his left hand, while he went over his clothes with his right.

"Now, Dick," he went on, when he had secured the other's pistols, "just put back that gentleman's purse and watch; remember, my eye is on you; no tricks, Dick; dead or alive, that's my motto."

"What's it all mean?" asked the amazed and trembling Jew.

"Only that I've captured Dick Turpin!" answered Tom Carroll.

The watch and purse were handed back, and then Dick sat down.

"I must put on the irons you know," continued Tom Carroll.

"Anything for peace," replied Dick.

The bracelets as they are now facetiously called, were put on. While so doing the officer put his pistol in his pocket.

As soon as Dick had been handcuffed behind his back, this being done at his own request, the two sat down, Dick beside his captor.

They were within a mile of the end of the stage.

"Been long in the service?" asked Dick, in a low, miserable tone.

"Yes! some time—long enough to catch the cleverest high toby in London."

"Ah!" quietly remarked Dick, "that is because dead or alive is your motto!"

"Dead or alive, Dick—dead or alive! and I've got it in writing, too."

With that, Dick jumped up, and placed at the head of the astonished officer, his own pistol. The handcuffs lay on the seat beside him.

"Officer!" said he; "when you've had a little more experience, you won't be taken in by a pair of artificially-swelled wrists. Don't let the next man, officer, clench his fists when you are putting on the bracelets; don't let your pistol out of your hands while your motto is dead or alive!"

He now secured his own pistols, and made a sign to Moses Larkin.

"I'll thank you for that purse and watch again," he said.

Moses, trembling with fear, handed them up. Dick Turpin then whipped his carpet bag off the seat, and opening the door, sprang out, despite the shouts and yells of the other passengers.

He darted for a narrow lane.

Tom Carroll was out in a moment, but knew it was of no use to follow. The highwayman was armed. He was without a weapon of any kind.

He got surlily back into the coach, and at the next stage returned defeated and disconsolate to London. This defeat was not all. The story leaked out, and from that day he was known as Dead or Alive Carroll.

Dick returned by devious ways to London, disposed of his plunder, and then started for the neighbourhood of Landsdale, to await orders from his chief, not, however, before leaving a significant message for Sapathwa.

Dick had time to visit one of his haunts, to leave a message for Tom King, and here he heard the story of Dead or Alive Carroll.

CHAPTER CVI.

LANDSDALE.

Landsdale Hall was full for the shooting. Every sleeping-room was occupied, even to the haunted-room, where no one ever saw a ghost, and which was now tenanted by a strong-minded Oxonian who kept a bull dog.

The big drawing-rooms were brilliant with wax lights, the sparkling eyes of high-born women, and the family jewels of noble houses. Rich dresses and choice flowers added colour to the scene, and furnished the room as mere upholstery cannot do.

It was a hot evening, hot as July, though at the end of September, and though it was the harvest moon that shone through the great windows as if with a contempt of the paltry lights within. More than one couple had found the heat of the drawing-room oppressive, and were pacing up and down the broad terrace on which the room opened. Below the terrace stretched the rose garden, and beyond that a triumph of landscape-gardening—miniature water-falls, bridges, arbours, and the cone walks, a series of grassy paths bordered by every species of pine and cedar and fir, for which the duke had a sort of collector's mania.

Up and down the remotest part of "The Cones," walked a man and a woman on this last night of September.

These were Lord Reginald and Lady Milicent, who had come out as a relief from the heated drawing-room, and perhaps to avoid the other guests who were laughing and jesting in the usual light and after-dinner vein.

Lady Milicent had wrapped a long white lace scarf round her head and shoulders. The moonlight touched her golden rippling hair, and silvered it as completely as time itself could ever do. She looked very lovely, and Lord Reginald looked as if he thought so.

And so did another, who had been watching her from a secure place of concealment.

He suddenly, however, appeared before them.

"Don't be alarmed, my lady, and you, Lord Reginald," he said; "I am Jack Palmer, from Twickenham."

"Glad to see you; but why do you come thus secretly?" asked Lord Reginald, laughingly.

"I come to warn you, my lord!" he responded. "Brian Seymour and his accomplice, Robert Woodstock, are down here, hiding, I know not where, but I have seen them. We are on the watch—but be careful, my lord. You know the villains, but not as we do."

"Brian Seymour and Robert Woodstock near Londsdale! What can they be doing?" cried Lord Reginald.

"No good," said Dick Turpin, "rely upon it. I thought it wise to warn your lordship, as well as to let you know that I am here and shall be on the watch."

"I thank you heartily," replied Lord Reginald, "for myself and Lady Milicent."

"I have but done my duty as one man to another," continued Dick Turpin, gravely.

"You are not a rich man," observed Lord Reginald, musingly.

"I am not," responded Dick; "but I do not do this thing for gain."

"Still you must let me be of use to you," continued Lord Reginald. "Would my influence be of any use to you?"

"No, my lord, not at present," he said, gravely. "I am engaged in an important and mysterious business in connection with this Brian Seymour, for which I am well paid."

"Still I cannot remain your debtor," urged the young nobleman.

"We will talk about that matter another time, my lord," was the response. "When you are out to-morrow I should advise you to keep near your friends and not leave your party. Brian Seymour is capable of any villainy."

"From what I have seen I should say so," resumed Lord Reginald; "and now we must return to our guests. Will you sup with us to-night, Mr. ——?"

"John Palmer," was what Dick Turpin responded. "I must decline your kind invitation; another time, perhaps," with a glance at his riding-coat and boots.

"Don't let that consideration upset you," laughed Lord Reginald. "We are all in disguise to-night. You might have assumed the disguise of a highwayman. With a mask you might make up very well for Dick Turpin."

The other slipped a mask from out his pocket and put it over his face, hiding all but his mouth.

"Supposing," he said, gravely and yet humbly, "I were Dick Turpin himself?"

"Great heavens! Mr. Palmer, why this joke?" asked Lady Milicent.

Lord Reginald looked keenly at him, without speaking.

"It is no joke, my lady. *I am Dick Turpin!*" he went on. "Hence my desire to do a good action without fee or reward. Circumstances have thrown me into a wild and adventurous career, but when I can serve one so beautiful as you, my lady," with a sigh, "one so immeasurably above me, I feel myself not all bad."

"You are right," said Lord Reginald. "You have bright, brave, and noble principles. It is never too late to mend," he added. "I could get you a commission in the army, when all might be forgiven and forgotten."

"You are very kind, my lord," said Dick Turpin, almost sadly; "but I fear I cannot change my nature and submit to discipline and command. It is not in me. I cannot conceive why I told you; it was a sudden impulse."

"We shall think none the worse of you," said Lord Reginald, taking his hand. "The service you rendered us was inestimable, never could be repaid; our debt of gratitude is deep and eternal. Hark, the bell sounds for supper. All will unmask now, and you must join us."

Milicent joining in the request, this strange man yielded, and half-an-hour later was seated in the splendid banqueting hall, amidst the noblest in the land.

Introduced by Lord Reginald, and in friendly intercourse with Lady Milicent, no one presumed to ask any questions.

He stopped all night, and went out shooting with the others. He kept near to Lord Reginald, shooting side by side, and meeting with tolerable success.

It was getting near lunch time.

"There's only one more covert to be shot before lunch," said Lord Reginald. "Come along."

When they were about half-way through, Lord Reginald, who was not unnaturally impatient to return to the ladies, entered a path through the wood. When they were about half way through the wood, Lord Reginald said:

"We shall never get there at this rate. The wood is not so thick here. Let us take a short cut."

He pushed through the wall of green to the left, and Palmer followed him.

"There's no path that way," cried one of the keepers, but Lord Reginald and John Palmer were already hidden by the hazels and beeches, the rest of the party passing on along the grassy green ride.

Lord Reginald's strength and breadth—he was, though well-proportioned, a young Hercules in make—pushed aside the brambles and young oaks with ease, and he went crashing through the wood like a powerful animal. Dick kept level with him.

But they found, as many do in so many walks of life, that the shortest cut was the longest way. They made but slow progress, for the wood was dense just there, and so the trees slapped their faces and the brambles twisted themselves round them.

"I think, my lord, we had much better have stuck to the path," said Dick Turpin.

"I begin to think so, too," responded Lord Reginald.

Still they went on through the sunlit woods, still thick with green and gold, for not many leaves had yet fallen, though it was the 1st of October. Presently they came to a dip in the ground, and Lord Reginald dashed forward at a quicker pace. Dick followed closely, anxious to keep up with the other. And so they went on over the rough ground.

A stubborn oak suddenly checked Lord Reginald's progress.

At this moment there was a loud report, and Lord Reginald crashed headlong down, breaking through the young oaks and hazels, and falling on his side in a clump of brown bracken.

Dick rushed to his aid and knelt beside the fallen man, who seemed but an inert mass of convulsively-quivering flesh. The leaves and brambles were splashed and streaked with blood.

"Murder! help!" bellowed Dick, at the top of his voice.

He heard voices at no great distance as he reached the edge of the wood, and burst into a smooth, thyme-grown ridge, where sportsmen and keepers were standing watching.

Dick's face was white, set, and resolute—his lips drawn back.

"What's the matter, Palmer?" asked one.

"Lord Reginald has been shot, and I fear not by accident," replied Palmer. "Is there a doctor here?"

"I am a doctor," answered an active middle-aged man.

"Then follow all, in G—'s name," continued John Palmer.

All obeyed, though they were too stunned to speak, and soon reached the spot, guided by Dick Turpin.

Dr. Barham hurriedly examined the prostrate nobleman, and at once decided that the wounds were not very serious, though the loss of blood had been very great.

He always carried, on shooting days, a few bandages and some lint, with which he at once staunched the wound.

Dick stood aloof with lowering brow. He had not not seen the man who had fired that shot, but he was as certain of his personality as if he had. Much as he was occupied, he could not repress a smile when he saw one of the keepers examine the two guns, that of Lord Reginald and his own. When he found them both loaded he quietly put them down.

"How did it happen?" asked one of the men, presently.

"The shot was fired from yonder thicket," replied John Palmer; "but I saw no one. Whoever did it fled at once. I was too anxious about my lord to pursue."

"Quite right," said the doctor; "your promptitude probably saved his life. We must get him to the house. I think a rough litter might be made."

One of the keepers, expecting this, had gone in search of a hatchet and cords, with which he soon returned.

Saplings were cut, cross branches tied, and then leafy boughs, over which was placed a blanket.

He was then placed gently on the improvised litter; and, following a winding path, they made for the open.

To reach the house in a direct line it was now necessary to pass a clump of trees, where lunch awaited them, and where they were to be met by the ladies.

The doctor suggested that this spot should be avoided; but several ladies were there already, and some had seen the mournful procession.

Of these one was Lady Milicent, who at once, with a wild, strange foreboding, rushed towards the group.

"Keep back, my lady," said Dick Turpin, hurrying forward; "he's only wounded—faint from loss of blood. The doctor says it will be all right."

But Milicent would approach.

"What is it?" she gasped, her face white as her cashmere morning gown.

"He will live," said the doctor, cheerfully; "don't delay us. All depends on care and quiet. Forward!"

Lady Milicent stood as if turned to stone; but, leaning on a gentleman's arm, she walked beside him.

As soon as the house was reached, the wounded nobleman was taken to his room, and at once put to bed. The astonishment and horror of all were general.

The head gamekeeper at once reported the news to the duke himself, adding that the guns of both Lord Reginald and his friend Mr. Palmer were loaded. He repeated also what Mr. Palmer had said.

"What do you think yourself, Morris?" asked the duke.

"I can't make it out, my lord," said the head keeper. "There ain't been many poachers about lately. It may have been an accident, and the awkward person may have run away."

"It's a most unfortunate affair," continued the duke. "I wish you would ask Mr. Palmer to step into the library. I will await him here."

So Dick Turpin was shortly after ushered into the presence of the courteous duke, who received him most cordially.

"I am sorry to trouble you, Mr. Palmer," said my lord, "but I should like to hear your version of this sad affair."

"Certainly, my lord," answered Dick, and told what the reader knows, leaving out, however, his suspicions of Brian Seymour.

"It's a very sad affair," continued the Duke of Grafton; "and, I presume, an accident, only the perpetrator is too cowardly to come forward and explain."

"I can offer no clue," resumed John Palmer, "and regret that I must leave. I came to see Lord Reginald yesterday on a small matter of business, and he forced me to remain. I shall be in the neighbourhood for some little time, though, and should like permission to call and make inquiries."

"Most certainly," said the affable nobleman; "now we must to lunch with what appetite we may. If I hear a good account after the meal, I shall request my guests to remain. We will keep the house very quiet."

Mr. John Palmer retired, took his lunch, and then finding the report about Lord Reginald very favourable, took his departure.

Lady Milicent was said to be quite calm, and would be allowed to see her future lord and master in the evening.

When Dick called again two days later, he found that Lord Reginald was convalescent, but doomed to inaction for some considerable time.

He insisted on a private interview with Mr. John Palmer, and asked eagerly if he had any clue, or supposed clue, to the man whom they both suspected.

Dick Turpin said "yes, he had been at an inn the night of the accident, with his companion, Robert Woodstock. But they went away early the next morning, and all trace of them was lost."

"Well, my good friend," said Lord Reginald, "you have done me a service such as I never shall forget. You saved her whom I love far more than life, and then you warned me against these foul schemers; probably, but for your presence with me I should have perished. Now, Mr. Palmer, you must not refuse. Money is no object to me; if you do not use it now, you can put it away for a rainy day. I understand and admire your scruples; but neither I nor Lady Milicent will forgive you if you refuse."

"You are very kind, my lord," said our hero, with a flushed face, "and I presume I must yield to your wishes."

Lord Reginald smiled as he put a pocket-book in the other's hand, and then cordially dismissed him.

When Dick examined the pocket-book he found that it contained notes for a thousand guineas. He smiled as he put it away, thinking that had he but saved all the money that had passed through his hands, what a rich man he might have been!

CHAPTER CVII.

HIDE AND SEEK.

When Brian Seymour found that his attempted assassination of Lord Reginald was known, at all events, to Dick Turpin, it struck him that the better part of valour was discretion, and he determined to keep away from the society of his fellows for some time.

He allowed Robert Woodstock to go to London, and thus keep him well informed of what was going on, while he himself took up his abode in a small out-of-the-way inn in the centre of the forest.

Here he remained a fortnight, going out, however, every day, seeking some means of amusing himself.

Brian Seymour at five and thirty was still a very handsome man, and his favourite source of enjoyment was looking after the fair ones of the other sex.

Brian believed himself to be almost irresistible in this line, though he had met with rebuffs in his time. The dwellers at the inn were his landlord, a comely landlady, and their daughter Phœbe, a young lady by no means devoid of good looks, but shockingly affected and empty-headed.

Though she served Brian's turn very well for a mild flirtation, yet she was not one likely to create a *furore* in his *blasé* bosom. He was too much used up for that, and sought not ripe charms, ready to fall beneath his amorous sway, but those which were of difficult attainment, and to win which required a spice of excitement, with perhaps a little modicum of danger.

That he found this will be seen. He had been sleeping at the "Silver Cup" about ten days.

It was growing dark in the woods; the sun had sunk long since behind the proud crowns of innumerable trees, and the stars had not yet begun to appear. There was scarcely a sound to be heard; the pigeons had ceased their cooing; the chirp of the grasshopper grew fainter, and the brown, bright nightingale as yet was silent.

Under the shadow of the chestnuts stood a girl waiting and watching. She made a bold dash of colour in the sombre scene, and could not have failed to attract and hold the attention of the most casual passer-by. Tall, with a beautifully-proportioned figure, the little delicate hands, slender arched feet, and small aquiline features, of the pure gipsy type, even in her strange garb made her lovely to look on.

The rich bloom of health shone through her olive skin; her large dark eyes, soft now as a gazelle's, gleamed duskily under her black brows and long lashes, and the scarlet lips, parted slightly, revealed the prettiest, whitest teeth.

The short red skirt she wore was admirably calculated to display her pretty ankles and small feet, and about her head, with its masses of raven hair, she had tied a bright orange handkerchief.

"He will not come to-night," she whispered, again and again. "Ah! 'tis foolish to wait here longer;" but she sighed as she spoke, and did not evince any inclination to return to her people. "He is doubtless taking his pleasure whilst I stay here, hungering to see him. Oh! but what a fool I am. Why could I not love one of my tribe? Why can't I listen to Zohrab, who loves me, I know?"

'Tis ever thus with woman, never content to have what they could command, always hankering after the impossible.

The girl locked her hands together, and stood a moment with her face upturned to the clear evening sky. Such love, such longing in her starry eyes, such pain about the exquisite mouth, that even the man who watched her could not but feel some compunction.

"Zelah!" he said; "I am here."

She started, and the hot blood rushed tumultuously over throat and brow, as she cried, "Oh, Philip, I thought you were never coming."

He had an arm around her now, and was gazing down into her eloquent eyes.

"I could not come earlier," he said, "without exciting suspicion. I fear always my evening walks may be noticed, and, besides, I am daily expecting news from London."

"I must not remain long; if I am missed I shall be hunted for."

"By that precious cousin of yours, as you call him," remarked the other, rather contemptuously; "of course he is full of animosity to me."

"He is. Am I not his affianced wife? Is it not arranged that I am to wed him in little more than a week? The tribe has so decided it."

"But you will not do this thing?" asked the pretended Philip Danebury, with specious anxiety in his tone.

"How can I help it?" she asked, with downcast eyes and burning cheeks.

He seemed to reflect deeply for a moment, and then he spoke vehemently.

"My beautiful queen, I cannot give you up. You are too good for such as he," he said, "and I cannot see you thus sacrificed."

"It is my fate," she answered.

"No; you must be mine. You must leave the forests and the woods, and come to my home," he cried.

"You think you love me now," she answered, in a sad tone; "but I am told the Georgios are all false. Besides, you will be sure to love in your own sphere, and, were I to believe you, would soon repent."

"Never!" he went on passionately. He was an accomplished hand at blinding women's good inspirations. "I cannot give you up. No; I leave for London soon, and you must come with me. I cannot let you slip out of my life."

"But it is impossible," she answered, trying to be cold and stern. "A Georgio cannot marry a poor gipsy girl. Besides, I am not fit to associate with your fine friends."

"Don't talk nonsense, Zelah," he went on; "you are now the equal of anyone. When we are married you will soon fall into the ways of my people. It is only to listen."

"You will be ashamed of me."

"Never!" he continued. "Now, listen to me, Zelah. I am going away in a few days to London. It is the safest place to which we can go. I know many who will marry us without difficulty."

Zelah listened, but she did not seem convinced. Still, the girl was ambitious. If the truth were told, though she had been won over a good deal by the insidious speeches of this man, it was the prospect of grand dress and rich finery which tempted her most.

"Will you consent to be my wife?" he went on, in his most insidious tones.

She listened in a dazed kind of way, scarcely comprehending all his words implied. Still, to a certain extent, she was proud and happy; and yet, so powerful is instinct, she hesitated. Suddenly she fell on her knees, clasping his hand in hers.

"Are you in earnest—will you never repent? I have nothing good enough to give you for your love. I will be your slave—your happy slave."

The man, despite his seared heart and utter selfishness, was moved. But his iron purpose never swerved. He was determined to win this forest flower, regardless of the pain, misery, and probable death to follow.

With rare exceptions the gipsies never forgive the females who leave the tribe for the Georgios, while the latter themselves, if discovered, run a great risk.

But Brian trusted a good deal to his ubiquity and cunning.

To his knowledge, this girl's cousin had never seen him, and he depended a great deal on the confusion that would ensue when it was learned she had eloped with Philip Danebury. What consequences ensued to the popular young squire he cared not; so long as he escaped all responsibility he did not mind.

He raised her up, and then began to unfold his plans. She interrupted him.

"But I cannot marry you without the chief's consent—without Balthazar agrees," she said, plaintively.

Brian's lip curled.

"We will ask no one's consent," he answered; "of course he would refuse. I know the hatred your people have for the Georgios, and have no wish to place my life in his hands. You must meet me here to-morrow night at eight o'clock. I will be ready. We can post to London, and then, heigho for happiness!"

Zelah still hesitated a little; but love and ambition prevailed, and she gave the desired promise. Brian at once left her in order to make his preparations. He expected Robert Woodstock that night with news from London.

He found his comrade as he expected, who informed him that nothing had been seen or heard of the earl or any of his friends. Their foes appeared to have vanished into thin air.

After a good supper a bowl of punch was ordered, and then Brian revealed his scheme against the beautiful gipsy girl.

Robert heard him with impatience and disgust.

"You will bring ruin on yourself," he said, "especially if you play with gipsies. They are vindictive in the extreme, and, even if they have to wait years, will have their revenge. I would rather have a sleuth hound after me than a gipsy. I could not sleep in my bed."

"I shall never show my nose in this part of the world again," laughed Brian.

"I should have thought you had trouble enough on your hands already, what with the Blue Dwarf, Dick Turpin, and Tom King, to say nothing of their employers," continued Robert Woodstock, irately.

"Well, if you are going to give me up, do," said Brian, coolly. "I can find other men to serve my purpose."

"Can you!" sneered Robert. "I think not. You would find me a dangerous enemy. If you are bent on this mad project, I am at your service."

"Is the Red House on Hounslow Heath to be had?" asked Brian, filling their glasses.

"I believe so," replied Robert.

"Well, here's cash," handing some notes. "You ride forward to-morrow morning, and secure it; I'll follow with the divinity."

Robert Woodstock made no reply. The subject was changed, and when they had finished another bowl, they retired to bed, after giving directions to be called to breakfast early.

They were obeyed, and after the meal was over, Robert Woodstock mounted his horse and rode for London. Brian Seymour remained behind until mid-day, when he rode into a neighbouring town and ordered a post-chaise and four.

CHAPTER CVIII.

A DARK FLIGHT.

Meanwhile, what had happened? Zelah stole on the previous evening through the wood until she came to an open space, where tents were pitched and camp fires burning brightly. She leaned against a tree, and looked upon the picturesque scene with melancholy eyes.

To-morrow she was leaving all this behind. To-morrow she was going to begin a new, strange, and untried life.

A few men and women were smoking and talking at intervals; but the girls and youths were dancing to the sound of a cracked fiddle, and their gay voices came towards Zelah, softened by the distance, and thrilled her soul with indescribable pain. One woman was cooking some birds, which most certainly had never been purchased; but Zelah would not think them less savoury because of that, her ideas of *meum* and *tuum* being extremely shadowy.

At some distance from the others stood a young man, lithe as an antelope, with a handsome but sullen face. This was Zorab Smith,

Zelah's cousin, and the husband her tribe had chosen for her. He refused to join in the sports, and from time to time cast furtive glances around, as if seeking for the girl; and at last a brighter flame flickering in her direction revealed her to him. He hastened to her side, and muttered something in their own *patois*, to which she listened disdainfully.

"Where have you been?" he demanded. "Is it really to meet this lover of whom I have heard, who talks to you so softly and swears he loves you? Idiot! Ask him if he will marry you. Are you caught by his fine white hands, by the glitter of his gold?"

He paused, as if waiting for her to speak, but she maintained a rigid silence.

"Tell me truly; do you meet him?"

She nodded.

"Then it's time I made you hear sense; you've got to listen to *me* now. To-night I spoke to the chief, and we are to be married in a week; then let this Georgio cast his eyes on you *if he dare!* Are you deaf and dumb, that you treat me like a dog! My girl, I'll change all that soon, when I'm your *master!* Do you hear? A week from now you will be my own to do with as I like."

"Very well; it's no use to fight against the chief's orders," she answered, quietly; but there was a very dangerous gleam in her dark eyes; "and if I am to be free only seven days, I must make the most of my time;" and, quitting his side, she ran towards the dancers, and was soon whirling round with the gayest of them. Zorab swore a very ugly oath, and went to his tent, nor did he appear again that night.

Any one who had studied Zelah closely the following day would have noticed a nervousness in her manner totally new to it; a restlessness never observable before. She was particularly amiable to Zorab, apparently forgetful of his words and manner the previous night; she gave him her brightest smile and kindest speeches, charming the frown from his brow, and the sullen look from his eyes.

Had he known much of women, his suspicions would have been aroused.

But she was evidently thankful when towards evening several of the men started from the camp on some mysterious errand, the success of which must be known at supper time, and, retiring to her tent, she proceeded to set her small affairs in order.

Her heart was very heavy, for, rough as her people were, they had been kind to her, and she was breaking away from all old habits; she knew nothing of the life to which she was going, and if Philip failed her she would henceforth be alone in the world. She knew, too, that according to Romany ideas she would be for ever disgraced by her marriage, and he who followed and took her life would be honoured by every member of her tribe.*

She stole out at last into the gathering dusk, and went swiftly and safely by all the tents until she came to the chief's. He was standing outside, a tall, muscular figure, with a weird dignity about it, and he called her by name; she obeyed the call with fast-beating heart.

"Where are you going?" he asked, gruffly, and regarding her with stern eyes.

She hesitated, being all unused to lying, and he repeated his enquiry.

"I am tired of the camp," she said, slowly, all the lovely colour leaving her exquisite face.

He stepped to her side, and laid his heavy hand upon her shoulder.

"Don't lie to me," he said, fiercely; "you are going to meet the white-handed Georgio."

She was silent, knowing it was a grave misdemeanour to rebel against his authority or answer insolently; and he went on, impressively, "Seven days from now you will marry your cousin. It is my will, and you know what they get who go against me. What would you have? He is of your people, he is handsome, quick with the snare, ready to join in all our foraging parties, and it is not well that you, the most beautiful of our maids, should be the plaything of a stranger."

The hot blood flushed into her face, but she said, quietly, "You speak without cause. I am willing to marry Zorab if he wants me to, and I am going to look out for him and tell him so."

The chief gazed into the deep, dark eyes searchingly, and seeing they did not waver, said, "If you are lying you will suffer for this;" and he swore a terrible oath. "Well, go and meet him;" and he pushed her away.

Glad enough to be released, she sped towards the thickest growth of trees, and presently came to the trysting place where Philip Danebury, as she thought, was waiting for her.

"Quick! quick!" she said, breathlessly; "in a little while they'll be back, and Zorab will guess all. Then they will track us down, and the dogs are keen of scent. Give me the cloak."

He gave her a cloak and hat as well, which she put on with a coquetry which was part of her nature. He folded the first round her, and then would have clasped her in his arms.

"No, no, not yet; we are not safe. Let us away," she cried, in a tone of genuine nervous apprehension.

He was quiet in a moment, and catching her hand he hurried her through the bracken and bushes, out towards the open ground. Here a post-chaise and four awaited them.

Brian hurried her in, and away they went, stopping only for needful refreshment, all that night and all the next day until evening, when they drew up at a lonely house on Hounslow Heath. This did not in the least alarm the unsuspicious gipsy girl, whose ideas of London were peculiarly vague and unreal.

The post-chaise drew up in a kind of courtyard, and Brian knocking, the door was opened by a respectable-looking woman, who ushered them into a comfortable sitting-room, where a pleasant and grateful meal was provided.

Brian was all smiles, and behaved in such a respectful way as to prevent Zelah from experiencing any feeling of fear or doubt.

After a short but pleasant evening, Zelah complained of being tired. A journey of four-and-twenty hours in a post-chaise was a novelty to her, and had fatigued her more than a long walk would have done.

It was her first experience of a bed, and she slept soundly, to awake long after sunrise, a very unusual event with her.

When she rose and looked around her, she found herself in a very large old-fashioned chamber, with one solitary casement looking upon a deserted road, stretching for miles over a barren

---

* To such an extent is this true, that when, some years ago, a young squire in the neighbourhood of London desired to openly wed a gipsy maiden, it was only after unheard-of difficulties that the tribe consented. They are not even now comforted with the knowledge that the descendants of the gipsy lass are now lords of the manor of F——.

heath ; in the distance could be discerned some hills, but there was not a vestige of a house anywhere to be seen.

The furniture was scanty and old, consisting of a huge press, two chairs, and a large four-post bedstead.

But this did not in any way strike Zelah with any emotion. He had told her this was only a temporary sojourn while preparations were made for their marriage. The casement was barred with iron, and even this in such a wild district was quite natural.

On one of the chairs were placed some clothes more suited to civilisation than those usually worn by gipsies. Zelah looked at them with a smile, but put them on. Clothes come natural to a woman, no matter what be their kind or character.

While she was dressing, a knock came to the door, and the woman intimated that breakfast was ready.

Zelah tripped downstairs and found Brian awaiting her. He was pleasing and affable, but there was a rather triumphant look on his face that gave the girl some matter for thought.

The room in which they breakfasted was quite as much a prison as the bedroom, and this Zelah could not help remarking.

"This is not half so pleasant as the forest," remarked Zelah, as she joined in the morning meal. "It is dull and heavy, just like my idea of a prison."

"Well, it's not so pleasant as it might be," said Brian Seymour ; "but wait until we get into London. I will find you a gilded cage there."

"I would submit to no cages, gilded or other," she answered. "I must be free as air ; the forest bird brooks no restraint such as the wicked Georgio imposes on the feathered race."

We may as well mention here that Zelah had been taken when young from her tribe, educated by a zealous, perhaps fanatical, lady, from whose custody she had escaped after a reluctant residence of four years. This accounted for her language and partial cultivation.

"Now, Zelah, you must not talk such nonsense," he said, with an unpleasant tone. "Birds are very much like women ; so they are well treated, it matters not whether it be in cages or not."

"I shall never agree with you," remarked Zelah. "But what of our marriage ? I dread pursuit above all things."

"While we are here we are safe," he answered, evasively.

"But of our marriage ?"

"Well, now, Zelah, you must listen to reason," began Brian, not without some trepidation of manner. "Our marriage cannot take place just yet. There are formalities in civilised life, especially in aristocratic life. I am the cousin of a peer, and heir to the peerage. My marriage will require great caution."

"Then let me be free at once," Zelah cried, rising —she began to suspect the trap she had fallen into—"let me return to the forest. I must be married this day, or go back to my woodland home."

"Sit down and listen to reason. Return to your tribe you cannot, after what has happened," he urged. "I will make inquiries, Zelah, my darling girl, as to how soon the ceremony can be performed. After breakfast I will seek a friend in holy orders, and ask him to perform the ceremony."

"No hedge thief priests for me," cried Zelah, whose passion was overflowing. "I must be married openly, with witnesses, and not in secret. Truly was I told never to trust a Georgio."

"Really, Zelah, you are very clever," said Brian Seymour, boldly ; "but if I do not intend to marry you at all, but only to keep you with me—to adorn my house, as my queen bird——"

Zelah turned and snatched a knife off the table. At this moment there came a furious tugging at the door bell, accompanied by loud shouts.

Brian at once darted out of the door of the apartment, locked it behind him, and descended to the hall, where he found the old woman approaching the door.

"Stop until I see who it is," cried Brian Seymour, and approached the thick oaken door.

Peering through a small loophole or judas, he saw to his horror and astonishment not only Zorab, the gipsy, and several of his gang or tribe, but Dick Turpin, mounted on his bonnie Black Bess, directing their movements.

With a fearful curse he retreated from the door. He knew the game was up ; but how had he been tracked ?

He never knew. It was, however, the jealousy of a woman. Phœbe Miller had been eaves-dropping, and overheard enough to know that they were going to abduct someone. When the gipsies, in their wild chase after Zelah, came to the "Silver Cup," where Dick Turpin had been just inquiring for information in connection with Brian Seymour, whom he had tracked to the spot, she at once mentioned about the Hounslow lone house.

Without the slightest hesitation, Dick Turpin offered to guide them to the spot, which he knew well.

The gipsies were tolerably well mounted, and so it happened that they reached the lone house just in time.

They soon broke down the door, and forced their way in, to find no one in the house but a woman crying for help.

Dick Turpin had sufficiently described Brian Seymour's real character, and prepared Zorab for his infernal seductions for that worthy to be prepared to listen to reason. Zelah, when the room in which she was confined was forced open, took the most effectual means she could of satisfying the gipsy's scruples.

When the door was broken open, she rushed into his arms, crying, "Thank the stars I am saved," and fainted, or pretended to do so—which, after all, is much about the same thing.

At all events Zorab was satisfied, and a week later they were wed.

CHAPTER CIX.
A SURPRISE AND A RIDE.

Two or three days after these occurrences, which are narrated with a view to show the character of Brian Seymour, Dick Turpin and Tom King took their way along the north road to a well-known hostel known as the "Cat and Bagpipes," where every year there was held a meeting of the high tobies.

The spot was tenanted only by this ancient hostel and one farmhouse. The inn was a substantial-looking tenement of the good old stamp, with great bay windows, and a balcony in front, and shaded by a spreading elm. A circular bench embraced the aged trunk of the tree, sufficiently tempting, no doubt, to incline the wanderers in those lonesome parts and dusty ways to rest and be thankful, and to cry encore to frothing tankards of the best ale to be obtained for miles around.

In the parlour was a table laid out for a jollification, covers being laid for twelve, which was exactly the number who had announced their intention to attend.

By twos and threes they came up to the inn; and, giving their horses to the ostler, gave him strict injunctions as to the treatment of these precious animals.

On their condition often depended life itself.

By two, all the party were collected, and seated at such a spread as would make some of our mouths water even now-a-days.

The guests were all well known to one another. In addition to Dick Turpin and Tom King, there were some less well-known to fame, such as Jerry Juniper and others.

The dinner consumed, the table was covered by bowls of punch, pipes and tobacco. The conviviality was great; songs, stories, and, we are sorry to say, oaths, were heard on all sides.

But a little after dusk Dick Turpin saw Tim Roach appear at the door of the room, and make a mystic sign, which meant there was danger.

"I shall be off," said Dick, rising and whispering to Tom "danger," after which he added aloud, "I think we had all better be on the fly."

And, rising, followed by Tom King, he went out by the window on to the bowling-green.

It was a delicious evening. The sun was slowly declining and glowed like a ball of fire amid the foliage around them. They hastened to the stableyard, and, as they did so, Dick made out a post-chaise dash up to the door furiously, escorted by several riders.

"I think we'll mizzle as quick as need be," said Dick, and dashed into the yard.

The ostlers had rushed out to see to the newcomers, and Dick and Tom at once proceeded to mount their horses, they being already saddled.

They quietly approached the entrance to the stableyard leading into the road, when they caught a glimpse of three Bow-street runners in conversation with the landlord, who was complacently rubbing his hands.

"Wouldn't I like to slit his nose," whispered Dick; "he's betrayed us, and that post-chaise was for us. One moment—they are going into the house. Wait till the coast is clear."

It soon was, and then, without making any noise, the ostlers being too busy to notice them, they trotted to some little distance.

Perhaps they were half a mile from the "Cat and Bagpipes," on the top of a slope. Arrived at the brow of the hill they looked back and saw that their flight had been discovered, by the fact of the runners rushing out and mounting.

They took one look at their pursuers, and then started down a steep decline skirted by thick trees. There was a glorious prospect in front, lit up by a glowing sunset.

Their horses were fresh, properly fed, and thoroughly up to their work, as they well knew. But the runners knew this quite as well as themselves.

That treachery had been at work they were aware, as some one must have betrayed their presence. On they went, swerving to the right, and, just as they reached the bottom, were joined by Tim Roach, who had started before them.

"Many thanks," said Dick; "what put you up to their dodge."

"I heard the landlord say that he believed you and Tom King had had your last ride," replied Tim; "the man was speaking to his wife. 'I'm sorry to lose such high fugle men,' he said, 'but, after all, number one goes first.'"

"I'll slit his nose for him before I'm done," said Dick.

And then they continued on their way, as yet uncertain whether to try the mettle of their steeds or attempt one of their common tricks.

They at all events entered a narrow lane, with various twistings and twinings, which they passed through without other adventures than scaring one or two farmers and farm labourers, and upsetting the equanimity of a few broods of ducks. They began the ascent of another hill, which two of them knew led to a gorsy heath.

They did not inconvenience their horses at this stage of the ride, being rather anxious to reserve their mettle for the moment when they were pressed.

Dipping into a pleasing valley, they ascended another hill, which brought them to the heath, which they skirted by a path that led to the furze-crowned summit. But they avoided the path when it began to ascend, and kept lower ground. They now distinctly heard the clatter of the pursuing horses.

"Now, put your tits to it, my boys," said Turpin. "Perhaps they may lose sight of us."

And he led the way down a narrow sandy lane that deadened the sound of their horses' hoofs.

Dick was, we have said, in front, and soon brought them to a broad expanse of water, nearly half a mile across.

"Single file," said Dick, entering the water, "and don't tarry. They won't dare to follow."

They had not gone two hundred yards, moving cautiously through the water, which was only up to a little over the horses' knees, when the pursuers came in view.

They shouted to the fugitives to stop, to which appeal Dick's answer was only a ringing laugh.

"Catch 'em who can!" he roared, in his most stentorian voice.

The runners appeared angry at this and attempted to follow, but not knowing the ford, slipped and fell into the water.

Again the three fugitives laughed loud and long, reached the opposite bank, and dashed into a wood which lay before them.

"But," observed Dick, "we must not remain here long. They will not be easily put off the scent, and in their rage will raise a general hue-and-cry. Where can we go?"

"Let us to Dun's Hole," said Tom; "I have not been there for some time."

"Lead on, my friend."

The weather had changed now. The night was wild and stormy, which was in their favour, as their inveterate foes might give up the chase on this one occasion to renew it on the morrow.

As they advanced they saw that a storm was brewing, one of a very serious character. The kine that herded on the margin of the water

DICK TURPIN AND TOM KING INTERRUPTED WHEN RECOVERING THE HIDDEN DOCUMENTS AT
CURZON CASTLE.

wended stallwards undriven, and deeply lowing. The deer, that had herded too, trooped thither for refreshment, suddenly, with "expanded nostrils, sniffed the air," and bounded off to their coverts amidst the sheltering fern brake. The rooks, "obstreperous of wing in crowds combined," cawed in a way that, as plainly as words could have done, bespoke their apprehension; and were seen, some hovering and beating the air with flapping pinions, others shooting up in mid-space, as if to reconnoitre the weather; while others again were croaking to their mates, in loud discordant tone, from the highest branches of the lime trees; all seemingly as anxious and as busy as mariners before a gale of wind.

The highwaymen and their companion skirted the water as if returning on their way until they came to another path, which led downwards into a quarry.

This was Dun's Hole. It was honeycombed by time and afforded an excellent shelter for pursued and benighted travellers.

They rode down the narrow pathway to it, a cutting, and were under shelter just as the clouds turned to an inky blackness. A single sharp, intensely vivid flash, shot from the bosom of the rock, sheer downwards, and struck the earth with a report like that of a piece of ordnance.

"Just in time!" said Dick, as they dismounted, and secured their horses.

"It is," replied Tom, drily; "but as the sailor says, 'any port in a storm.'"

"Our horses are safe, but must want refreshment. We've done more than twenty miles, and may have to start at any moment. Let's see if the Dun's Hole is clear."

"Isn't this the Dun's Hole?" asked Tim Roach.

"Oh, no; that's an inn inside," laughed Dick. "We'll leave the horses, and try our luck."

They now entered a kind of vaulted tunnel through the granite formation, which brought them after some minutes to another long-disused quarry, which had been utilised as the site of a house and garden.

It was well lit up.

"Follow this path to the left," said Dick, "and when you reach the front of Dun's Hole, that's the inn's name, enter and see if the coast is clear. It may be empty such a night as this, and it may be full. The landlord is a short, stumpy fellow. If there are any suspicious characters about, say 'Toby,' and ask for a bottle of bingo."

Tim Roach nodded. He was getting quite knowing in his secretiveness and cunning.

The front of the inn was soon reached, and Tim entered, going straight up to the bar, from which he had a sight of the parlour.

There sat Pooly and his two followers drowning their sorrows in good liquor.

Behind the bar, and out of sight of the people in the parlour, stood a jolly-looking fellow of rather stout dimensions, who was serving.

Tim went up to him, winked, and whispered as he put down a guinea—bingo.

The landlord also winked, and put his thumb over his shoulder, and jerked it in that direction.

Tim nodded.

The bingo was served, with a glass and a corkscrew, and then Tim departed.

"I will bring the change," said mine host.

Away went Tim without a word, and reported that their pursuers had taken up their quarters at the same inn.

They were surprised, but not alarmed. The bottle was uncorked, and its contents being handed round, were thankfully swallowed. Nothing came amiss to these wanderers.

As Tim finished, the landlord appeared with a dark lantern, with which he threw a light on the subject.

"Why don't you come in?" he asked. "The coast is clear."

"No! They do not wear their livery; but you have three redbreasts in the house," replied Dick, "Pooly and two others."

"Oh my ——" said the other, scratching his head; "then I suppose you must stop out here till they go. Their horses are only under a shed."

"Good," continued Dick; "but send Jack with some forage."

"Serene," said Joe.

He then left, and soon the ostler came with hay, corn, and water for the horses.

The storm now gave signs of clearing, and when Joe returned to his quarters he found the officers taking their departure.

Dick and his party were sent for into the house. The officers had gone away to make inquiries in the neighbourhood.

The three men determined to pass the night at the "Dun's Hole," leaving early, so as to avoid all chance of meeting those who were in search of them with such pertinacity.

Dick felt nervous. At bottom, there was a dash of superstition in his nature, and somehow he had a presentiment that this expedition would end badly.

"I feel," he said, in confidence to Tom King, "a presentiment—that is 'crawley,' as if some one was walking over my grave."

Tom King laughed heartily. He was somewhat of a cynic, and during his short stay at college had learned to be sceptical.

"Where shall we go?" he said.

"Anywhere! Let us ride away north, and seek our fortunes," continued Turpin; "we must keep quiet in this neighbourhood."

And so away they trotted at early dawn, along the highway, by winding lanes and through some of the many beautiful woods which have disappeared before the rapid advance of population.

Towards night they entered one of these forests—one more thick and gloomy than any they had yet passed through.

They followed a winding-path. The place was new to them, but, according to the proverb which says that all roads lead to Rome, they presumed it must lead somewhere.

After a ramble of an hour, however, they began to get tired, while even their horses manifested signs of fatigue.

"I hope we shan't have to camp out all night," growled Dick Turpin, "without anything to eat or drink!"

"I hope not!" responded Tom King, in anything but a cheerful tone.

"Eh! what's that?" suddenly exclaimed the first speaker—"a light?"

"Yes! let us see what it is!" responded Tom, and both hurried along the path in the direction of the twinkling illumination.

Two minutes later, they saw that it came from the upper window of a large and gloomy-looking house.

It had a wall all round, but the gates were open.

"I wonder if we could shelter for the night!" said Dick Turpin.

"There's no harm in trying!" replied Tom.

CHAPTER CX.

BURNHAM BEECHES.

They went up to the door, and, lifting the heavy knocker, gave a loud appeal to whoever might be inside. Then they waited, for some two or three minutes in vain; then they heard bolts withdrawn, and the door was partially opened, the chain being still retained.

"What want you at this hour?" asked a cracked, thin voice.

"We are travellers, who have lost our way!" put in Dick; "we are utter strangers, and can go no further. All we ask is shelter for a few hours, and any refreshment you have will be gratefully paid for."

"I will ask;" was the reply, and the man went away, leaving the door still chained.

He returned in a few moments, removed the impediment, and the door opened.

"Master aint fond of strangers," said the servant, an old man of thin and wizened appearance; "but he said as how you could come into supper, and then go early."

"Many thanks," replied Dick; "we are deeply grateful, even for small mercies," he added, in a lower tone.

They were now ushered into a moderate-sized room, well lighted and furnished, where stood a gentleman of about forty, well dressed, but with a severe, or rather saturnine, expression.

"I am not much accustomed to receive guests," he said, with an odd, surly politeness; "there are reasons for it into which it is unnecessary to go. You are strangers to this neighbourhood, my servant said."

"Quite so, sir!" replied Dick.

"Then, of course, you know nothing about our family matters, and there is no reason you should," replied the other. "James, let us have supper at once."

The domestic retired without a word to obey his master's orders. Mr. Devereux then invited the strangers to be seated, and placed a spirit-stand before them.

"If you are tired, you may as well refresh yourselves," said the master of the house.

Dick thanked him, and they at once proceeded to avail themselves of his invitation.

Later on, a very substantial supper was placed before them, to which they did ample justice. They found their host very affable. Though living in seclusion, it was clear that it must be forced, for he was evidently quite fond of company.

After supper ample refreshments in the shape of drink were placed on the table.

"I suppose you gentlemen can shake the ivories?" the host said, apologetically.

"We are rather fond of it in a moderate way," replied Dick, who was quite delighted at the proposal, as he had expected a dull evening.

Both Dick and Tom were well provided with money, and the game commenced.

It was rather late when the party broke up. It might not have broken up even so early as one, had not Mr. Devereux shown signs of sleepiness. Morris, the servant, acted in rather a strange way. He was constantly in and out of the room, saw to the fire, poured out the punch, and made himself as useful and officious as possible.

When at last Mr. Devereux succumbed in a strange way to slumber, Morris chuckled.

"Drugged!" he said, with a horrible laugh. "I've been and done it."

"Scoundrel!" cried Dick, "what do you mean?"

"He's the scoundrel," replied Morris, "and going to let his brother be hung this morning for a murder he never committed."

"How's that?" asked Dick Turpin, who at once became interested.

"'Cause Mr. Devereux he keeps the murdered man locked up here till after the execution is over," continued Morris. "Will you help me to save my master, Sir Melville Devereux?"

"How can we do it?"

"He's—that is Mr. Granville—the man for whose murder Sir Melville is to be hanged—in a room up stairs, locked in. I am too old and feeble to break open the door."

"Lead the way," said Dick.

The man hastened to obey, and holding a lamp in his hand, advanced rapidly before them.

Up a flight of stairs, to a floor above, where was a stout door.

Dick tried to push it open, but it was far too heavy and strong.

But Dick never was without his instruments, and gliding his hand into one of his pockets, he produced a small instrument which the anxious domestic did not notice, and speedily opened the door.

It was that of a large bedroom, in which was a pallid, rather sickly-looking man of about forty, who rose from an arm-chair and stared at the intruders.

"Oh, Mr. Granville," cried Morris, with clasped hands; "do you know my good master is to be hanged this morning for your murder?"

"Great heavens!" gasped the other, "that explains all. Where is Philip Devereux?"

"He entertained these two gentlemen, strange travellers, to-night, and being unusually jolly, I drugged his punch; and this gentleman contrived to open the door."

"Be quick, my faithful Morris—while I dress get me brandy. Semi-starvation has made me weak. The execution would be at Worcester?"

"Yes, sir!" the man replied, as he hurried away.

"You two gentlemen, to whom I owe so much," asked Granville courteously, "are perhaps too tired to ride with me?"

"Oh, no!" said Dick; "there is too large a spice of romance in the adventure not to see it to an end."

"Many thanks. We have ample time to reach Worcester before eight, if we start in an hour," remarked Granville. "During the time I shall devote to refreshing myself, and getting ready for a start—I will explain matters."

Dick nodded, but his mental reflection was of a philosophical nature.

"Mighty cool! If he were going to be hung himself he would not be so tranquil."

* * * *

As Sidney Granville had no time to tell the whole story, only to give an outline, we shall narrate the tale in our own words.

Sir John Melville Devereux and Philip Devereux were two brothers, the elder not only the possessor of a title but of fine estates, and money in the funds ; the younger inheriting only Burnham Beeches, and a very small income to keep it up.

Philip had mortally offended his father in many ways, first by his extravagance and debauchery ; next by marrying an actress of questionable character.

His will had rendered Philip furious. The estates were strictly entailed, but it was usual to settle a very handsome income on the younger son, but in Philip's case he inherited nothing but his mother's small fortune, which his father could not alienate.

In the will his name was never once mentioned, but it contained a clause which everybody understood. It was enacted that should John Melville Devereux marry an actress, or any body connected with an actress, he was to lose all the personalty, with three hundred thousand pounds, the said sum to go to hospitals and kindred institutions.

The new baronet had been married to a very charming young lady, of good birth and family. Unfortunately there were no children, and her death preceded that of Sir George, his father, by two years.

During that interval, the old baronet, eager that neither title nor estates should ever go to Philip or any of his children, had urged John to marry again, and had even found him a suitable mate in the person of Lady Grace Mackintosh, a Scotch lassie of good family and excellent prospects.

But John's heart was in the grave, and though he promised to do all in his power to fulfil his father's wishes in the future, he would not make any exact promise.

Lady Grace was a most charming personage, he owned, but he was not prepared to place her on the same pedestal, as yet, as his "dear departed."

Then came his father's death, which scattered all such thoughts to the winds.

Still, during his last moments, Sir George extracted from his elder son a promise to give Grace a fair chance.

After the funeral, Sir John went abroad, and on his return he went to Bath, where he found his brother and his family, whom he personally treated with kindness and cordiality. He also found Sidney Granville, an old college friend, in whom he had great confidence. He was a man of noble and elevated character, who, when Sir John was young, had been of great use to him.

Sir John, when at college, had plenty of money, and, being of an easy-going nature, was easily tempted, and was on several occasions led into mixing with a class who were not really in accordance with his real character—men who drank too much, and wasted their time in frivolous amusements. He became, as himself described it afterwards, "a contemptible lounger and idler, letting all the good that was in me run to waste."

From this life Sidney Granville by practice and precept saved him.

No wonder they became fast friends.

Sir John spent a few days at Bath, and then returned to his ancestral home, Devereux Hall. He was not indisposed to society, but he was lonely at the Hall, and very often made excursions into Worcester. Here, by accident, he got introduced behind the scenes at the theatre, and made the acquaintance of several of the company.

Among others, of a Mistress Mortimer, who, by her quiet manners and gentleness won his sympathy.

Urged on by what she called an irresistible influence, she told her story to him one evening. Of a good family, she married a gentleman well connected, but without fortune. Still, while he lived, she was tolerably comfortable and happy. At his death, left without means and an only daughter, chance enabled her to get an engagement on the stage.

"I accepted it gladly," she said, "and have had no cause to repent. I make a very decent living, and am able to give my daughter a good education."

"You have been a good mother," remarked Sir John ; "are you bringing up your daughter for the stage ?"

"No," she said, with a deep sigh. "I wish you could see her."

"I should like to," replied Sir John.

"To-morrow is Sunday," she remarked. "Will you look in and drink a dish of tea with us, if you don't object to that new-fangled beverage ?"

"I rather like it in moderation," laughed Sir John ; and, taking down the address, wished Mrs. Mortimer "Good evening" and departed.

Next day he rode over to a small street in the outskirts, where Rose Cottage was located, and was introduced to Miss Corinne Mortimer.

She was resplendently beautiful, with soft grey eyes, a fair complexion, a rich crop of glorious sunny hair, and an expression of half modest, half voluptuous attraction, which amazed Sir John.

He fell there and then over head and ears in love with her. He never had seen anyone so lovely, while the charm of her manner was something new to him, and fresh.

He went away ; and, on reaching the hall, sat down to reflect deeply.

He was a free man, he had never compromised himself with Lady Grace Mackintosh, and could do as he liked.

Then came the thought of his father's will. But Corinne Mortimer was not an actress. That she was the daughter of one it was true ; but sophistry is the revenge of love.

He could easily induce her mother to leave the stage, and thus cut off all connection with the profession his father so much disliked.

Time passed, and every day while the company remained at Worcester his horse stood at the cottage door, until people began to talk.

Still Sir John hesitated to make the plunge and propose. Something, he knew not what, restrained him.

Then Sidney Granville came to Devereux Hall on a visit. Sir John thought him rather more stiff than usual. He seemed changed in some way ; there was the usual familiar, serene look on his pale face, but something of anxiety was mixed up in it.

He, however, greeted Sir John heartily. In the evening they went out in the park for a walk together. They selected the riverside. When speaking of it afterwards Sir John would say—

"The whole scene is before me now—the low tufted bank, the red swirling river, and the clouds crimson in the west with the sun's red glow."

As they walked along in silence for some time, Sir John felt puzzled. What ailed his friend?

"Sir John," suddenly asked Sidney, "are we the same friends we used to be at college?"

"Yes. Why?"

"May I speak plainly to you?" continued Sidney Granville.

"Yes," continued Sir John, rather stiffly, as he feared the topic that was coming.

"Is it true you have taken to go behind the scenes, frequenting the green room of a third-rate theatre?" he asked, gently but resolutely.

"Yes; but what of that?"

"Is it true that you are going to marry the daughter of that painted Jezebel, Isabel Mortimer?" asked Sidney Granville.

Sir John, like many another outwardly calm and serene-tempered man, was volcanic when roused. His pride was hurt.

"Granville," he said, "I cannot allow you to interfere with my private affairs. You have gone too far."

"I have not gone far enough," was the calm answer. "It is my duty to warn you against this woman and her daughter."

"What know you of them—you who pretend to lead such a sainted life?" cried the angry baronet. "Why have you dogged me, spied on me, hounded me down?"

"I feel devoted and earnest friendship for you, and I have made it my business to find out the character of this dancing woman, Corinne Mortimer," continued Sidney.

Sir John made some furious reply, accused Sidney Granville of meanness and half-a-dozen other things, accusing him also of descending in the scale of human nature to a degraded level.

"The level we sink to," said Sidney, "is the level we must live on ; and you may only marry her if you are satisfied to abide by a standard as base as her own."

Then with a wild cry Sir John flew at him and struck him in the face. He staggered, and fell back into the river.

At this moment two men came up. They had seen and heard all the latter part of the scene, but at the time said nothing.

Sir John fled towards the house, and speaking of what had happened as an accident, ordered men to take boats and to drag the river in every direction.

But nothing was found. Next day Sir John was arrested, and committed for trial for wilful murder on the evidence of the two passers-by.

The case was clear, and admitted of no defence. Sir John could say nothing but that the blow was given in a passion, and he had no thought of killing his friend ; but the jury brought in a verdict of guilty, and he was sentenced to be hanged.

What had happened?

Philip, who was staying in the house, guessing the motive of Granville's visit, had followed them, and heard the conversation and quarrel. When his brother fled, he went to the river bank, where he had seen Granville fall, stunned, in shallow water. By superhuman exertions he got the half-drowned man out, carried him to a boat, and by degrees got him to his house, where he meant to keep him in strict seclusion until the execution was over.

His brother, Sir John, once out of the way,

Philip vainly reasoned that the splendid inheritance would become his.

But that day Morris had discovered the truth. He meant to have given information, and the arrival of Turpin and King seemed to him providential.

It was three o'clock when the three men mounted, and rode off in the direction of Worcester. They reached it at a little past seven.

Already there were crowds in the street, and the gallows was being erected. Dick and Tom went to an hotel, while Sidney Granville, who was a magistrate for the county, went at once to the prison, where already the sheriff and other officials were collected.

His appearance among them caused no little surprise and delight. Of course, the high officials took upon themselves to adjourn the execution. No one but the authorities in London could free him. Still a messenger was sent off express to inform the government that, the supposed murdered man being alive, they had stayed the execution.

Then Sidney asked leave to see the prisoner, and a magistrate, a mutual friend, at once offered to lead him to the condemned cell, where they found him praying with the chaplain.

The meeting was most deeply affecting. Sir John actually wept from excess of emotion.

"Where have you been hidden all this time, my friend?" asked Sir John, presently.

"I have been kept in 'durance vile' ever since the accident," replied Sidney. "I will explain when we are alone."

The news spread like wildfire that there would be no execution that day, the supposed murdered man having turned up.

Except in the case of the roughs and some outsiders, there was great rejoicing, the two men being loved and respected.

An hour later they had a room to themselves in the governor's house.

"Can you ever forgive me, Sidney?" asked Sir John, gently.

"Yes, my dear fellow," replied his friend ; "you were mad. I should have been a little more cautious. But I saw through the whole plot at once. Philip was at the bottom of it. Corinne, or the Zephyr, was a ballet girl at a low theatre, and a tool of his ; his object was to make you forfeit the personalty by getting you to marry an actress."

"But where have you been all this time?" asked Sir John.

"Confined in your brother's house at Burnham Beeches, where he intended me to remain until after to-day."

"Most consummate villain!" said Sir John, "he is a disgrace to humanity. He shall be punished."

"He is. The discovery of my escape, and the knowledge that I can expose him is enough. He will not trouble us much for a time."

And so it proved ; for when Sir John was free they found Burnham Beeches deserted, Morris having migrated to Devereux Hall, where he was warmly received by Sir John.

To finish with this episode, we have only to say that Sir John married Lady Grace Mackintosh, and effectually cut off the hopes of Philip Devereux by having a large family of children.

CHAPTER CXI.

A NIGHT CELLAR.

By devious and roundabout ways Dick Turpin and Tom King returned to London, hoping to put the officers off the scent by keeping quiet for some time.

All their ordinary haunts were so open, that should the officers finally determine to take them and prove former crimes against them, they could easily do so.

So they determined in the first place to live in private lodgings for awhile, frequenting places of amusement, and confining themselves to the picking up unconsidered trifles, and going to such gaming houses as were open to men of all sorts.

When in London, on the apparently respectable dodge, Tom King set up for a man of fashion. He wore a light summer riding-dress, fashionable according to the taste of the time, of plain and unpretending material, and rather under than over-dressed, and therefore was very often taken for a gentleman. There was altogether an absence of pretension about him, which, combined with great apparent self-possession, contrasted with the vulgar assurance of most of his fellow high tobies.

Dick Turpin assumed the garb of a bluff country gentleman.

Thus accoutred, they found no difficulty in gaining an entrance to any of the ordinary gaming houses, which were not clubs, and on the first night of their arrival in town, after putting their horses in safe custody, they sauntered into a well-known hell in a court out of St. Martin's Lane.

They found it tolerably crowded, but at once noticed that the rook element predominated. Still, there were enough genuine players—men led on by hope to risk their money—to make it worth while for them to stake something.

Still, for an hour or two they amused themselves, and went away clearly satisfied with their bargain.

But it was a little too slow for them, and they started off for some place where they could have a little more excitement.

"Where shall we go?" asked Tom.

"Do you think Jack would let us into the 'Wrekin'?" asked Dick.

"Oh yes!"

The "Wrekin" was a very well-known tavern in those days, where men of real fashion collected to gamble, drink, and enjoy themselves after the fashion of the day.

Jack was a kind of door-keeper, and supposed to know most of the *habitués*, or regular frequenters, of the place; but of course, by introduction, others could be admitted, and when once in no questions were asked. The object of making it select was to prevent professional gamblers and rooks from making it a centre of operations.

They sauntered into the hall, after seeing that Jack was there, and asked him if there were many upstairs.

"A goodish few!" said Jack, as he secreted a guinea put in his palm by Dick; "and some fine country samples. You'll not be noticed in the crowd."

They nodded, went to a little private bar, where they "wetted," and then went upstairs.

The "Wrekin" first floor consisted of three rooms, devoted to Bacchus, Ceres, and Mercury. Eating, drinking, and gambling were thus exemplified; but Venus was excluded, as too disturbing an element when men were on business or pleasure bent.

The two "sparks" strolled into the rooms, first into that devoted to eating, where they despatched a hasty snack, and then entered the gambling department. This was crowded. A very strong detachment of country cousins were present, and all busily engaged in getting rid of the rolls of notes and rouleaus of gold which they had brought with them to London.

It was difficult to get to the table where play was going on; but Dick and Tom had patience, and gradually edged their way up. The chairs were all taken, but the game was one in which those behind could join who were standing up.

Dick cast his hawk-like eye around, and noticed that one man close to the chair behind which he stood was raking in a lot of money.

He at once backed him by putting a stake close to his. The stranger nodded his head without turning, just to let him understand that he knew, and the game went on.

The cards were turned, and again the man won, Dick sharing his luck. Turpin left a portion of his winnings on the table and then again won.

Well satisfied, he took up the whole of his stakes this time and looked around. The place was truly filled by people from the country, noblemen, baronets, and landlords, who for some special occasion had been summoned from their hearths.

Some of them, indeed, looked like substantial members of society, and both Dick and Tom surmised that many of them might be worth interviewing.

But how was it to be done?

Dick pushed back, making way for others, but not going far enough to lose sight of the table.

"That chap you played with and backed," said Tom, "has made a haul. I watched him; he must have a few thou' on him. I know the fellow. How he got in here I don't know.

"Just as we did, I suppose."

"Perhaps so; but he's just lost. See if he don't move soon," continued Tom.

"Shall we wait for him outside?" asked Dick, who at once "tumbled" to what the other meant.

"Yes."

And slowly both of them went out, crossed the road, and stood in a doorway.

Soon the man came out, and looked up and down the street. As he did so an oil lamp over the door revealed the face of a man still young, but thin, pale, and cadaverous. There was no excitement or elation in his looks. What he did seemed to be serious business.

He walked away rapidly.

Not a soul was in sight, and the two men followed him as noiselessly as they could.

Not many yards, however, for suddenly they seized him, one on each side, and, clapping a pistol to his head, whispered—

"Give up your money, quietly!"

The man turned his wan face upon Dick and stared, as if in wonder.

"What money?" he asked.

"The money you won in the 'Wrekin,'" was the quiet and terse reply.

He sighed, put his hands in his pocket and pulled out a bag and a pocket-book.

"You do not look cruel or hard-hearted," he said, "and will surely spare me a little. I am not a gambler for the love of gambling. In the first place I have a wife and two children, and in the next I need money to enable me to play for very high stakes,—rank, and immense wealth."

They looked at him.

He was, as we have said, still young; but his face had a pinched, drawn appearance, which indicated a not over-free indulgence in the good things of this life. His clothes, too, though without tear, bore evidence of long wear and constant renovation. His hat at a distance might seem glossy, but on close inspection it was evident that the glossiness was due to grease rather than to the hatter's iron.

He wore a long brown overcoat, of the genus known in those days as wrap-rascal, reaching almost to his heels; but as it was buttoned close up to the chin, and as he shivered constantly, it was not unreasonable to suppose that the overcoat did duty for undercoat and vest, and perhaps even for shirt.

"Well, we have no wish to be hard," said Dick Turpin. "Here is the 'Jolly Anglers.' We can go in there and have a talk."

The man did not hesitate, and they were soon in a room, which they requested should be considered private. Dick ordered drink, and food in the shape of cold meat, and all three settled down to enjoy a hearty meal.

"To save money to go to that infernal den," said the stranger, "I have starved myself. You will understand presently."

The meal having been concluded, pipes and grog were introduced, after which the supposed gambler told his story.

He was the elder, and only legitimate son of the Earl of Lisle, and was, in fact, the Lord Henry Curzon, heir to the title and strictly-entailed estates.

His father had married when young, in Italy, a chaplain's daughter. They were married in a Protestant church, but under a false name, and he was christened in the same way.

His mother had lived until he was ten, and then died, leaving him to the charge of some humble friends, who gave him a good education.

His mother had, after her husband left her, which he did in the first year of his married life, changed her name to Harding. The unprincipled young nobleman had persuaded her that the marriage was illegal. When he, however, came of age, his friends had got him into a lawyer's office, and he laid his case before a barrister, who assured him the marriage was quite legal.

Going down in the country to the neighbourhood of Castle Curzon, the seat of the Earl of Lisle, he had gone over the castle one day and been shown the picture-gallery. There he saw the portrait of a gentleman so like himself that he stood amazed; so did the housekeeper, Dame Atkinson, who invited him to take lunch in her sanctum.

She then asked him for his story, which he told without hesitation or reticence.

"You are the rightful heir," she said, without hesitation. "When did your mother die?"

He told her.

"Then milady was never a wife!" she cried, "and the young viscount is a bastard."

Dame Atkinson now explained that not two years after his marriage in Italy he had married Lady Grace Twyford, by whom he had a son and two daughters.

Then came a severe illness, during which the earl confessed his previous marriage, the birth of a son, and the consequent fact that his acknowledged son was not his heir.

He told Dame Atkinson where the documents to prove all this were, with a will providing for the false wife and her children.

But ere revealing the hiding-place of these valuable documents, he had made her solemnly swear never to reveal the secret while he lived.

"I was, as a young girl, his nurse," she continued, "and I dearly loved him. I swore. All I can tell you is that the packet containing the whole explanation is in the house. I can say no more. Find it if you can."

Mr. Bernard Blair, as he called himself, explained that on his return to town he fell ill. He had married a fellow-lodger, a young lady of excellent family, but only a poor governess. His illness was serious, and his convalescence long deferred.

Ever since that day there had been one long struggle for existence. He got a precarious living by law-copying, while his wife, through privation and sickness, had to give up her work.

Then he hit on the desperate idea of raising money to go down to Devonshire and search for the documents, which would give him a position and a name.

"Well, my hearty," said Dick Turpin, "consider the thing done. There's your money back. Get a good horse and good togs by to-morrow night. We'll arrange a meeting-place. When I say that I'm Dick Turpin, and undertake the job, consider it done."

Bernard Blair stared in wild astonishment at the speaker.

"Yes; I'm Dick Turpin," said that worthy, rather proudly; "but that, as I suppose, you want to get home to your wife and kids, I could tell you some cases in which I have been trusted by men of quite as high rank as yourself."

"You amaze me. True, I do wish to get home and take my poor girl some delicacies she has long wanted," the other went on; "but I would gladly have a long talk after."

"Do you live far off?" asked Dick.

"Not a hundred yards away," was the answer. "I will just tell my wife that I have met a friend who is willing to help me in getting my rights, and that he has advanced me money, which you have," with a grim smile, "and then I will return and talk over our plans."

They started, and soon were in a poor, miserable-looking street, filled with wretched shops, evidently the residence of the most indigent classes.

"You must remove your wife and family from here," said Dick Turpin. "Take a furnished cottage at Hampstead or Highgate. If it delays a day—what matter?"

The man could not speak. The very idea seemed paradise to him.

He rushed away to a better-looking street at the end of the one they were in, and soon returned with a basket containing wine, bread, and cold fowl and cakes. He then dived into a passage next to a coal shop, and remained about a quarter of an hour, when he came dashing out ready to accompany them.

It was late when they parted, after agreeing to meet on the next day but one at a place indicated by Dick.

Next day Bernard Blair was up early and off to Hampstead in a cab. He had taken Dick's advice and purchased some new clothes, so that he found no difficulty in securing a neat little cottage and a respectable handmaiden ere he returned to London.

Then that afternoon Edith Blair took her last look of Cremer-street, which was a long one, and, as we have said, with a row of shabby-genteel, narrow houses on each side—houses, on the dirty steps of which children of all ages and sizes played, talked, laughed, and called to each other from across the road in no very select language; children with saucy, bold-looking faces, and still more saucy tongues; girls with tawdry finery on them, and boys with hats at the back of their heads or cocked on one side, and bad cigarettes in their mouths; children crying, children fighting, children rolling in the dust, or sloshing through the mud, made up a complete Babel from sunrise to sunset, and even later.

It was a street full of dust and mud, according to the weather; and the vestry seemed to consider it was not worth while to clear it more than once a year.

A cab pulling up at the door of one of these houses created quite a sensation, which was redoubled when Mr. Blair was seen in excellent clothes, spick and span new, handing in his well-dressed wife and children.

There was quite a crowd of boys and girls around, and Bernard Blair felt so happy that just before they started he threw a handful of coppers and small silver to the amazed and delighted children.

CHAPTER CXII.

THE CASTLE.

About a fortnight later three well-dressed men, mounted on noble steeds, rode up to the "Sceptre and Crown," in Crewhall, a village situated about a couple of miles from the residence of the Earl of Lisle.

From the front steps of the inn an extensive view was visible. The eye of the traveller could gaze up the road to where it had been made to take a turn in order to avoid the brow of the hill, and then the eye turned downward to the place where the highway opened into the country beyond, after passing over a small bright stream by a brick bridge of ancient date.

Looking onward, the centre of the picture presented a fine view over a bright and smiling country, with large masses of woodland, sloping up in blue lines to some tall brown hills at the distance of ten or twelve miles. A peep of the gleaming river was caught in the foreground, with a sandy bank covered with old trees; and above the trees again appeared the high slated roofs of a mansion, whose strong walls, formed of large flints cemented together, might also here and there be seen looking forth, grey and heavy, through the green, light foliage.

Three or four casements, too, were apparent, but not enough of the house was visible to afford any sure indication of its extent, though the massiveness of the walls, the width of the spaces between the windows, the size of the roofs, and the multitude of the chimneys, instantly made one say mentally—the Manor House.

On the rising ground, on the opposite side of the picture, seen above bridge and trees and the first slopes of the offscape, appeared at the distance of three miles or thereabouts a large, irregular mass of building, apparently constructed of grey stone, and in some places covered with ivy—at least, if one might so interpret the dark stains apparent, even at that distance, upon various parts of its face. There was a deep wood behind it, from which it stood out conspicuously, as the morning sun poured clear upon it; and in front appeared what might be a deer park filled with stunted hawthorn and low chestnut trees.

The three horsemen ordered breakfast, secured two bed rooms, and then began planning their arrangements.

After the morning meal they decided to visit the castle, that is to say, to enter the grounds for Bernard Blair to point out the different entrances to the castle, so that when they made their night experiment they might know how to begin.

They did not hurry themselves, eating their meal with hearty zest. A fortnight's journey on horseback, with few rests between, was enough to rouse an appetite in any man.

Besides, the rest also enabled them to discuss their plans.

Mounting their gallant steeds somewhere about eleven o'clock, they rode to a little roadside beer-shop near the park gates, where they put up their steeds.

They heard at the "Bagpipes" that the earl was away from home, but was hourly expected. Mrs. Atkinson still ruled the roast. He knew she would readily allow himself and his friends to see the house, picture gallery, and so on.

He was right. Mrs. Atkinson was proud of the castle and its contents, and at once offered to let them see all the show rooms.

When Mrs. Atkinson came into the library, where they waited, she started. In the tall young man, whom a fortnight of exercise and cheerful sensations had restored to his normal appearance, she at once recognised the youth who had come to her years before.

She made no remark at the moment, but determined to have a conference with him before he left.

She was very polite, and led the way herself. After she had shown them the picture gallery, and the room which contained the old armour, she casually mentioned that there was one room which, though not usually a show room, was still well worth seeing.

Bernard Blair thought that she said this with a very peculiar look on her face, which he interpreted to convey to him that that apartment was in some way connected with his fortunes.

The room itself was a cheerful and pleasant one, with a vaulted ceiling richly ornamented; while the thick walls of the tower in which the room was situated were lined with oak, very deep in hue, and finely carved with Gothic tracery.

The form of the chamber was perfectly square, and its extent might be four-and-twenty feet each way. The furniture, too, was good, though ancient, and of the same carved oak as the panelling. It consisted of a large table and a smaller one, eight or nine large high-backed chairs, and several curious carved cabinets.

But the objects which most attracted the attention of Bernard Blair were two small panels, distinct from the rest of the wainscoting, and ornamented in such a way as to show that they were not at all intended to be concealed, with a small pointed ogee canopy above each, similar to that which surmounted the door by which they had entered, only smaller in size.

In each of these panels was a key-hole, surmounted by an intricate steel guard ; and it was evident that each covered the entrance of one of those cupboards in the wall in which our remote ancestors took so much delight.

Bernard Blair felt convinced that in one of these secret recesses was hidden the secret of his life.

Presently he and his companions went down stairs, Dick and Tom going off to the inn, while Bernard went to the housekeeper's room, where she had cake and wine awaiting him.

"So," she said, after the first greeting, "you have come again. I wish you luck."

"Many thanks," he replied, warmly. "I hope this time to be successful."

He did not, however, offer any explanation, as he desired in no way to compromise his new friends, and accordingly soon took his leave.

Bernard, more and more hopeful, went out into the porch, which was one of the finest in the county.

He had reached a rather wild and yet picturesque spot beneath the trees, when he heard footsteps, and, turning, found himself face to face with a tall, handsome, powerful man, wide chested, broad shouldered, and still very muscular, without being at all corpulent.

He might have been about sixty, and his hair was snowy white. His eyebrows, however, and his eyelashes, both of which were long and full, were as black as night. There was many a long, deep furrow on his brow, and a sort of scornful and habitual wrinkle between the nostrils of the strong aquiline nose and the corner of his mouth.

On his right cheek appeared a deep scar, round, and about the size of a pistol ball ; and on the chin was a long scar, cutting nearly from the lip down into the throat and neck.

He was dressed in a suit of plain black velvet, with the large riding boots and heavy sword which were common about fifteen or sixteen years before the period of which we now speak, but which were beginning by this time to go out of fashion.

Bernard Blair knew that this man was his father ; but, conquering his emotion, he spoke :—

"I presume I am trespassing," he said, politely doffing his hat, "and if I am addressing, as I believe, the Earl of Lisle, I have to apologise."

But the nobleman did not reply. He was looking hard at the young man, while he raised his hand towards his head, passing it twice before his eyes, as if he fancied some delusion had affected his mind.

"There is no trespass, young sir ; but may I ask who you are?" asked the earl, with some hesitation. "Your face seems familiar."

"I am a very humble individual, my lord," was the quiet response ; "but happening to be in this part of the country on business, I took the liberty of going over the castle, of which I have heard many times."

"Is your stay likely to be long ? " asked the nobleman.

"I cannot say, my lord," observed Bernard. "I must be governed by circumstances," and with a low bow he moved away, leaving Lord Lisle astounded.

That face! it was so like her, and then so like himself.

Why had this man come—did he possess any clue? The thought was excruciating to him after all that had passed, the more that he was deeply attached to Lord Harold Curzon.

Should his suspicions prove correct, what would be his fate?

But the earl, as he walked back towards the castle, registered a solemn vow that this man should never carry out his designs, at all events while his acknowledged son lived.

On reaching the castle he at once sent for Mrs. Atkinson, and asked her what sort of people had been to visit the show rooms of the castle.

"Two were strangers to me, but the other I strongly suspect to be one who has a right to be here," was her dogged answer.

"Woman! what do you mean?" he gasped.

"You know, my lord," she answered ; "you know, as well as I do, what I mean."

"Would you betray me?" he cried.

"No! but I hope the young man will be successful," was her cold reply. "It will be but justice."

"Beware how you anger me," he said, his teeth hard set together, his thick eyebrows meeting, and his whole air fierce and agitated.

He then bade her return to her own apartments and keep a still tongue in her head.

"Oh! he's a hard man," she said, when alone, "but let the heir once discover the proofs, and he will be able to command and not sue."

Meanwhile Bernard had rejoined his companions who were enjoying themselves after their usual fashion.

As soon as he reappeared, they all three returned to the "Crown and Sceptre," now their head-quarters.

Dick and Tom, leaving Bernard at the inn, were to feign a long business journey, which would enable them to reach the park, hide their horses, and enter the castle.

Both these men carried on all occasions housebreaking tools with them.

It was always wise to be prepared for any emergency, however sudden and unexpected.

It was midnight and somewhat more when they reached the castle. All the place was wrapped in profound darkness.

Passing through the dense woods, they found themselves in the midst of the park, where, backed by the thick wood, stood the house or castle, and the name was not ill-deserved. It was an irregular pile of buildings, erected in different ages by successive lords, and showing the tastes of the various individuals who had possessed it, as well as of the several ages in which it had been constructed.

On the left was an unornamented tower in the simplest style of the old Norman architecture. It was like the square towers of some of the old Kentish churches, with square-cut windows, or rather loopholes, under a semicircular arch, which denoted the original form. It was crowned by a plain parapet with a high conical roof.

The two men crept round to where a narrow window opened into the kitchen, and this they had no great difficulty in opening.

Once inside their work was easy. They knew the exact position of the room they had to search, and the stairs that led to it.

They soon reached the landing of the floor on which the room opened, and found the heavy door locked. But this was not a difficulty which they feared to encounter. Bolts, bars, and locks, were as nothing to them. They were soon in the room, and the door closed and fastened behind them.

They had a dark lantern, and this they placed on the table, while they attacked the two panels which Bernard Blair had previously pointed out to them. A couple of sharp and well-tempered chisels were produced, and with these the two panels were easily prised open.

From one of them Dick took a parcel tied with string, which was all that was concealed in the hiding places.

"That's the ticket, no doubt," said Dick; "eh, what's that? We have startled some one."

But Bernard had pointed out to them that to leave that room they would not have to go out by the door they had entered by. The young man had indicated one which led to a staircase in one of the buttresses. Hastening to this door they opened it and found that it led them down a spiral way, which they at once decided to follow.

At the bottom was a heavy door with strong bars which defended it from the outside, this was easily forced, and in another moment they were in the open, speeding away across the park. Scattered here and there were groups of old hawthorns contorted into many a strange and rugged form; while on either hand there appeared clumps of fine old trees, the chestnut, the beech, and the oak.

The latter were seen gradually deepening and clustering together to the right and left of the house, till they joined a thick wood, through which, here and there, stood forth dark and defined, amid the tender green of the other plants, the sombre masses of the pine and fir, like some of those stern memories of sorrow, of sin, or of privation, which are to be found in almost every human heart, and which still make themselves known in gloomy distinctness amidst the freshest scenes and brightest occupations of life.

The two men saw lights moving in the castle, and lost no time in getting to a safe distance from the scene of their audacious violation of the rights of property. As soon as their horses were found, they mounted, and soon put a considerable distance between themselves and any chance of pursuit.

Bernard Blair was waiting up for them, and when they joined him in a private sitting-room which they had engaged, received the package taken from the castle with a wildly-beating heart.

He opened it hurriedly, and a mere cursory examination showed him that he had found all he wanted.

There was every legal document to prove that he was the elder and only legal son of Geoffery, Earl of Lisle, with a full statement in his father's handwriting of the deception which had been practised upon his mother.

It prayed his son to soften the blow as much as possible to his illegitimate brother and sisters.

Bernard Blair, or as we must call him now, Viscount Curzon, smiled bitterly. After what he had suffered he was not much inclined to listen to this prayer. At all events, he determined to think the matter over, and make sure of his inheritance ere he determined on any course of action. The first thing to be done was to get away from that neighbourhood before the details of the audacious burglary were known.

There was no saying what the enraged earl might do in the first exuberance of his passion.

He was known to be a most vindictive man, and capable of anything when his evil feelings were aroused.

It was determined to snatch a few hours of repose, and then start at early dawn for London, where they would be comparatively free.

Accordingly, having paid their bill, they decamped in the morning without beat of drum, and were speedily out of the county, of which the earl was lord-lieutenant.

They rode by easy stages to the metropolis, which they reached one evening, and were glad to seek the refuge of the first inn they could find.

The young man expressed his deep gratitude to the two high tobies for what they had done, and intimated that the moment he had money in his possession he would make their reward substantial to the last degree.

"I will take the advice of my solicitors to-morrow, Messrs. Godfrey and Lawson, my late employers; they have had the management of the Curzon estates for years," he continued, "and see what they say."

"The wisest thing you could do, my lord," said Dick, with a smile.

Bernard started; but the unfamiliar sound seemed pleasant to his ears, so strange and novel did it seem.

"We shall soon see how the earl takes it," answered Bernard. "If he purpose showing fight, I should like you to come down with me again, and watch. In his desperation he may, for the sake of the son he loves, take some means of putting me out of the way."

"Understand, my lord, that when we undertake a job, we are in earnest," said Dick, "and until you are formally recognised we shall be at your beck and call."

Shortly after they retired, after refreshing the inner man, and at an early hour were up again. Bernard engaged a trusty messenger, whom he sent with a letter to his wife. Dick and Tom went to see if there were any orders from their master, the Blue Dwarf.

After breakfast Bernard, having put all his papers in a portfolio, took a hackney coach across to Bedford Row, the residence of Messrs. Godfrey and Lawson. He had written his name, Bernard Blair, on a card, with "important business" in the corner.

After a delay of ten minutes the young gentleman was ushered into the sanctum of the head partner, who stared in rather a surprised way at the fashionably-dressed visitor.

"Well, Mr. Blair," said the stout old gentleman, "and what may your business be?"

"Very important business," replied the claimant. "When I was in your office I learned that you had charge of the affairs of the Curzon family."

"But in what way can that concern you, Mr. Bernard Blair?" was the bland inquiry.

"In that I am not Bernard Blair, but Henry Viscount Curzon, only son and heir of the Earl of Lisle," replied the young man, quietly.

"Viscount Curzon!—God bless my soul—is it possible? Sit down, my lord," cried John Godfrey. "Have you any papers?"

"Yes, Mr. Godfrey," said Bernard, opening his portfolio and placing them on the desk. "Will you just look over them, and I will return early to-morrow."

"Certainly; but take a receipt," said formal Mr. Godfrey. "Remember that I am solicitor to the earl, and you might have done unwisely in coming to me."

"Mr. Godfrey, I know you to be a gentleman and a man of honour," replied Bernard, very warmly..

"You are very good, my lord; but wait a few minutes," continued the gratified lawyer, as he rang a bell.

A junior clerk came.

"Tell Mrs. Hutchinson to bring wine and biscuits, and ask Mr. Higgins to step this way," was the dual order given by the head of the office.

It was obeyed rapidly. Higgins came first, and was told to make a list of the documents on the desk, labled already—"Statement of the Earl of Lisle; marriage certificate; birth and death certificates," and prepare a receipt form.

Higgins went to another table and did as he was told, casting curious glances at his old fellow-clerk while he hobnobbed with the governor.

He was certainly lost in astonishment. He had known Bernard Blair when living on a guinea or little more a week, when he considered a pint of porter and a biscuit quite a treat.

But the list was made out and handed to the principal, after which Higgins retired to tell his fellow-clerks what had happened.

Presently the well-dressed ex-clerk came out and offered his hand to Higgins, who accepted it with perfect awe.

"You can come out for half an hour," said Bernard. "Mr. Godfrey gives leave, and I thought you'd like a little lunch."

Quite in a dream, Philip Higgins put on his hat and went out. Bernard took his old friend to a well-known coffee house of a very "tip top" character, and ordered a lunch which opened Higgins's eyes.

They had a table to themselves.

"Well, I see you haven't forgotten me, Higgins—bottle of port, waiter—best," said Bernard.

"Come into a good thing, I suppose?" Higgins ventured to ask.

"Well, yes, Philip—I believe I am the heir to a title and very extensive estates," was the quiet reply.

Higgins, as he afterwards remarked, was far too "flabbergasted" to make a reply. He swallowed his wine in silence, and looked at the other with perfect amazement.

"You see, I don't forget old friends," the young man went on. "You always were civil to me, and when I have got into my property I will stand something handsome for the sake of old times."

Higgins was really much moved. He was a simple-hearted fellow, and it seemed astounding to him that a nobleman should condescend to speak to—even shake hands with him. As to the lunch, it was long to be remembered. It was an era in the law clerk's history.

"When I lunched with Viscount Curzon," was a remark he was fond of making to his friends.

Bernard was rather anxious to get to Hampstead, and so, directly lunch was over, he paid for the luxurious meal and dashed away as fast as a pair of hackney coach horses could take him.

He found Edith his wife, and the two children, waiting for him in the little garden—but oh, how changed! Health was clearly visible—what explanations!

The poor governess of three weeks ago was now the wife of the heir to an earldom. We cast a veil over the rapturous happiness which had turned them from starving paupers into rich and titled people, who would know no more the cares of poverty and starvation.

"And you won't be ashamed of your little Edith?" said his wife, in a coaxing way.

"Never! You were faithful and true in adversity!" he responded, "and I shall ever be proud of you in my prosperity."

CHAPTER CXIII.

A FIGHT FOR LIBERTY.

Having a couple of days before them and ample funds at their disposal, they determined to put on their most fashionable dresses, and, favoured by a friend, to visit the "Young Cocoa Nut" on one of its grand nights when ladies were admitted.

Whatever the rank of the persons attending this club, they were men of tainted character, and some of them as anxious to avoid the ken of the runners as Dick and Tom.

Several of those frequenting the place were under obligations to the high tobies, who had often assisted them liberally with cash, to get the unquestioned *entree* of places frequented by themselves.

It was a lady's night—when a queen of the then *demi-monde* would be present; flaunting molls, Dick called them. But Dick and Tom were both partial to female society.

For a family man, Dick was particularly lax in his observances.

But then he was away from home, and playing the bachelor.

The club was elegantly furnished, and in every way made attractive. There was a well-fitted up ante-chamber, looking out on one of the parks, with pictures, counter for refreshments, and every convenience.

Beyond this was a very well appointed supper room, where every delicacy of the season was provided gratis.

Wine was choice, varied, and served without stint.

They went straight to the supper room, and, sitting down, had themselves served speedily. The waiters knew them, and knew them to be liberal. They got the best of everything, and wines in abundance.

As soon as they were satisfied, they rose and went into *the* room, where they found everybody either hard at work or looking on.

Dick and Tom picked out a couple of flaunting molls, all furbelows and laces, and began a regular flirtation with them.

In this way and in playing, a very jolly evening was spent; then they rose, in company with their inamoratas, and with several other persons of both sexes prepared to retire.

In the front, or floral hall, was an ancient French cook with a paper cap, dispensing delicacies.

Suddenly a bell rang, and it was known that there was a raid on the part of a large body of officers on the club. They at the first rush nearly broke open the doors, but were now being forced back by the liveried servants.

The gentlemen had their swords ready, while to give them courage the women began fainting in their arms.

One gentleman, who had strong reasons for not coming in contact with the police, made for the window, and forced his way through.

Dick and Tom, supporting their several ladies, threw their arms round their waists most gallantly, and put their right hands to their sword hilts.

Then some of the strongest men and attendants made a dash, and the door was closed.

But the officers, once they had started on the job, were not to be baulked. They would soon have the door open. Dick and Tom, dragging their molls with them, darted back and ascended to the second floor, where they passed through a window on to some tiles, entered another house, and walked quietly down stairs.

In a moment more they were in the street, and, finding a hackney coach, drove with their charmers to a fashionable rendezvous, where they ordered a sumptuous and copious breakfast, which did not end until long after sundown.

Then the pair took horse and rode out of town some distance to refresh themselves, after which they once more returned to London.

No more visits to the "Young Cocoa Nut," when it brought them into such dangerous company as it had on the previous night.

When they reached the vicinity of Hampstead Heath they were attracted by the hospitable look of the historic "Bull and Bush," and went in to refresh themselves.

Their horses they left in charge of a youthful ostler.

"He must be a bit of a nob," said one, "but what does he want to live *there* for?"

Dick and Tom listened, and soon found out that the gossiping idlers were referring to the fact of "the house that would not let" having at last found a tenant.

They knew it well.

It lay at some distance back, in a sort of sleepy hollow, the hill side sloping behind, crowned with dark woods, shut in by four grim wooden walls, two tall, twisted chimneys, like scowling eyes, to be seen from the path.

It was an ugly place, a ramshackle place, the most lonesome place you could imagine.

And now it was let!

Yes, and as the two professionals heard, it had been furnished well, as if for a family, and, strangest fact of all, they were coming in that night after all were in bed.

"Strange," thought Dick, who never threw a chance away; "Why this secrecy?"

And he finally determined to be there, as probably it was some craft, some sequestration of a rival heir, or an inconvenient relative.

He strolled into the coffee room, almost deserted now, and ordered some cold meat and a tankard for himself and Tom.

As soon as they were alone Dick expressed his motive for delay.

Tom laughed, and told him he was quite a knight errant, a paragon of chivalry, and what not, but agreed that it was worth while stopping to find out what might be a profitable secret.

They remained until the house was about to be closed, eleven o'clock, and then, taking their horses, rode off.

They knew the house well. It was only pulled down for modern improvements at the beginning of the present century.

They soon reached the spot, and drawing into the shadow of some trees, waited, where they had a full view of the house and the house gates.

Grey, lonely, weather-beaten it looked, with the mysterious shadow of desolation brooding over it, those two upper windows frowning down—sullen eyes set in its silent face.

But the highwaymen had seen it before, and their minds were set on the events about to occur, which interested them in a way that, at all events, Dick could not understand.

It was a cold night, and a freezing blast swept over the heath, and over the black treeless road by which the strangers must come.

Once alone they had seen a flicker of light, as if some one were descending from the second to the first floor.

And now they heard the sound of horses and wheels.

Oh, then, they were right! It was an abduction at which they were about to "assist," as the Frenchman says.

But they would have a finger in the pie, and know what was what before any possible victim was immured in that house.

Both were of course well armed; swords by their sides and pistols in their holsters.

These they now removed to their belts.

The lumbering vehicle was within a hundred yards. It had been coming down hill, but now it had to ascend a steep incline.

At this moment the clouds broke asunder and a ray of moonlight illumined the scene.

There was the postchaise and pair, with a postillion riding the near horse, and in front were two mounted men.

Dick Turpin, with his usual perspicacity, had guessed why "the house that wouldn't let" had been taken, the house that seemed struggling out of sight, and trying to hide itself among the dwarf cedars and spruces.

Nearer! and nearer!

Heavens! what does it mean? They have, under the pale, silvery moon, recognised Brian Seymour and Robert Woodstock!

Who, then, is inside?

They do not wait a moment to answer any mere questions, but, rushing out, fired their pistols at the pair of scoundrels, and then made towards the vehicle with their drawn swords in their hands.

Startled and terror-stricken the ruffians fled, and the highwaymen, rushing to the door of the coach, threw it open.

There, gagged and wrapped in a cloak, was the Blue Dwarf.

How Dick Turpin thanked the flash of forethought which had sent them to mount guard over the old house!

They speedily released him from his bonds, and when he saw who were his champions, he was utterly amazed and expressed his feelings.

"Explain presently," said Dick; "and now, you fellow, back to London as fast as you may."

They knew not what number of men were in the house.

The postillion, who had been shivering with terror, hesitated not a moment, but, turning round, at once started for Hampstead under that formidable escort.

When they were near the well-known Chalk Farm, the Blue Dwarf bade Dick take him to a house near Drury Lane, where he had apartments, and to which he could get admission by

GREY RUSHED FRANTICALLY IN CRYING "TRAITRESS!" LEVELLED A PISTOL AT HIS
DAUGHTER AND FIRED!

means of a key that he always carried about him.

They obeyed. The vehicle was quickly in London itself, and within an hour Sapathwa and his friends were in the lodgings situate in Drury Lane.

The Blue Dwarf struck a light and then set fire to sticks and coal that were always ready in the grate, and put on a kettle.

He then explained that having occasion to go out that evening for some purpose, he had been suddenly assailed by five men, gagged, and thrust into the post chaise, which was in waiting.

"But for you, my friends," he said, fervently, "I might have been slain—killed before my mission was accomplished. Death I fear not, but I could not sleep happy in my grave knowing these incarnate fiends were alive to persecute my friend.'"

He paused.

"By what marvellous run of luck," he presently asked, "were you able to trace me?"

Dick Turpin explained. The Blue Dwarf listened in amazed surprise.

"Marvellous are thy ways, oh! Providence," he said; "but this must cease. Take the spirit flask from the cupboard, and give us a steaming hot jorum," he added after a pause.

Dick obeyed, and then he and Tom helped themselves freely.

"But this must end! Presently you shall escort me to another retreat, whence I can communicate with Colonel Grant. Hold yourselves in readiness within ten days to leave the country. We must go, no matter where, so we be out of their reach—Scotland, Ireland, even America, if need be," said Sapathwa excitedly.

"We are at your orders, sir," said Dick, little dreaming to what he pledged himself.

Ten minutes later they issued from that secret haunt—never more to be visited—and went to one in quite another quarter, where they left him.

"Of our next flight we will speak another time," he said, slipping a heavy purse into their hands.

"By Jove!" cried Dick, "that was a piece of luck."

"Which it was," replied Tom; and away they went to spend a few of their guineas in some of the wild dens of this ever-seething metropolis. Next day they placed themselves at the disposal of their new employer.

CHAPTER CXIV.

IN DEVONSHIRE.

Next day, when Bernard called, Mr. Godfrey and his partner awaited him. They first began by shaking him heartily by the hand.

"A clear case, my lord," said the principal; "the earl has not a leg to stand on. What are your immediate instructions?"

"Write and state the facts!" was the answer, "and tell my father that if matters are settled amicably I will consent to something being done for my brother, in fact, will agree to keep his illegitimacy secret. Let him know I have already a son, so that he has a grandson to love."

"Very good!" continued Mr. Godfrey; "and now, as to money. I have opened an account at my bankers' for a thousand guineas in your name—you can have as much more as you like."

"Well, I won't refuse," said Bernard; "I am under deep obligations to friends who procured me these papers. They were written when he thought himself dying. When he recovered he did not like to destroy them. Will you write to-day? I shall start for Exeter to-morrow, and there wait his pleasure."

"Very good! very good!" cried Mr. Godfrey. "I should be cautious. My lord is a very hard man. When he was a young man he was very wild," added the lawyer, in a low tone; "when he came into the inheritance, was hard to be found. Came from the Spanish Main."

Bernard was thankful for this warning, as it put him on his guard. There had been a hard look in his father's face which rendered him uneasy.

Shaking hands heartily with the partners, he went out, and was driven to the bank, where he was received with a deference quite new to him. He got a cheque book, drew some money for himself, and then drove to the rendezvous where he was to meet Dick and Tom. He found them waiting, and perfectly free, as the Blue Dwarf had not communicated with them as to his contemplated need for their services abroad.

After lunch, Bernard drew a cheque for a couple of hundred guineas, which he handed to Dick.

"Something on account," said the young nobleman, heartily. "And now will you engage a post-chaise for me? My wife and children, with a lady's maid, will occupy that. We shall make up a goodly escort."

"Pretty formidable," replied Dick, laughing, and the young man again returned to Hampstead to bring his wife and children to the hotel, and there succeeded in getting a lady's maid.

Next day the whole party started for Exeter.

We will precede the travellers.

When the earl got the letter from his London solicitors his rage was fearful. He had, of course, found out that the documents involving the proofs of his son's legitimacy had disappeared, and Mrs. Atkinson had to bear all the full brunt of his rage and fury. He freely accused her of breaking her oath, and betraying him to ruin and disgrace.

"I did nothing of the kind, my lord," replied the housekeeper; "but I'm very glad, if right is to be done. Why should not the rightful son inherit?"

"And Lord Harold?" he gasped.

"Must suffer for the sins of others, as many have done before," the old woman cried. "I knew Lord Henry the instant I saw him—that was six years ago—when he came down here alone. He saw and recognised your portrait."

"Treacherous woman! Then it's all your doing! But I'll have him taken up for housebreaking," cried the earl, passionately.

"He only took his own, my lord," was the cool reply.

And the earl left her.

What was to be done? Resist the weight of evidence he could not.

His own solicitors had practically thrown up the case. They recognised the proofs which had been produced, and there was nothing to contest.

Still, it was deeply humiliating to be found out, and to have to accept a stranger as heir, when he had the son of whom he was proud, and whom he loved in his hard way.

After his first marriage, rendered desperate

by heavy losses, he had fled to the West Indies and served under Morgan for awhile, being one of the most ruthless of all the pirate crew.

In good society even it was hard to tone himself down, and he never was popular. Haughty, overbearing in the extreme, it was only his wealth made him tolerated, as is the case with many very better personages than he.

But what was to be done?

In the first fury of his wild passion the earl made up his mind to make away with the rightful heir at any price. He would not allow his son and daughters to be bastardised. He would find someone to do his dirty work for him. He had not far to seek.

The woods between Exeter and Plymouth and around Castle Curzon were very dense and thick, and infested by gangs of robbers, which, if not very numerous, were as daring and unscrupulous as Robin Hood, to whom all came alike—friar, monk, fat citizen, or town clerk.

The chief of the crew who held high revel in the wood was a certain Laurence Grey, an ex-lieutenant of the earl, and one who knew his secrets.

It was this man the nobleman had resolved to interview and induce to join him in his conspiracy against his own son.

Laurence Grey commonly used one little inn, and there a messenger would always find him. So the earl sent him a message to meet him the next night at a certain spot.

The moon had not risen; the sun had gone down; the sky, which for nearly a month had been as calm and serene as a good mind, was covered over with long lines of dark grey clouds, heavy and near the earth, when a solitary horseman took his station under a broad old tree upon the wide waste known as Uppington Moor, and gazed forth as well as the gathering darkness would let him.

It was a dim and sombre scene, unsatisfactory to the eye, but exciting to the imagination. Everything was vague and undefined in the shadows of that hour, and the long streaks of deeper and fainter brown which varied the surface of the moor spoke merely of undulations in the ground, marking the great extent of the plain towards the horizon.

A tall, solitary, mournful tree might be seen here and there, adding to the feeling of vastness and solitude; and about the middle of the moor, as one looked towards the west, was a small detached grove, or rather tall clump of large beeches, presenting a black, irregular mass, at the side of which the lingering gleam of the north-western sky was reflected in some silvery lines upon what seemed a considerable piece of water.

This was the only light the landscape contained, and it would have cut hard with the gloomy and ominous view around had not a thin mist, rising over the whole, softened the features of the scene, and left them still more indistinct and melancholy.

The hour and the place favoured sad thoughts and dark forebodings, and the horseman sat upon his tall, powerful gelding in the attitude of one full of meditation. He had suffered the bridle to drop, his head was slightly bent forward and his eye strained upon the scene before him; while his mind seemed to drink in from its solemn and cheerless aspect feelings as dark and dismal as itself.

He sat there about a quarter of an hour, and not a sound had been heard upon the moor but the deep sort of sobbing creaking of a neighbouring marsh, or the shrill cry of some bird of night as it skimmed by with downy and noiseless wings.

There was not a breath of air stirring; there was no change taking place in the aspect of the sky or the earth; it was as if nature were dead; and the feeling seemed to become oppressive, for the horseman gently touched his beast with his heel and made him move slowly out from under the branches.

Scarcely had he done so, however, when the distant sound of a horse's feet was heard, as if coming at a very tardy and heavy pace from the west. The sound, indeed, would not have been perceptible at that distance but for the excessive stillness of all around, and the eagerness with which the traveller listened.

His eye was now bent anxiously, too, upon the western gleam in the water, and in a few minutes the dark figure of another man on horseback was seen against the brighter background thus afforded, riding slowly on, as the road he followed wound round the moor.

The first horseman waited until the other man came close up.

"Who goes there?" cried the man under the tree, coming into greater prominence.

"Spanish Main!" was the answer, and the last arrival rode up close to the first speaker.

"Will you follow me?" he said.

The other nodded; and then Laurence Grey—that was the speaker's name—led the way over the moor to one of those old towers which so often rose alone in solitary places, when every man's hand was against every other man.

It was ivy-clad and solitary.

The man who took the lead, on reaching the spot, whistled, and a kind of dwarf came from an outhouse and took their horses.

Laurence Grey took a key from his pocket and opened the door, admitting his guest to a small round apartment, with a table, a couple of chairs, and a warm and comfortable fire.

There was a lamp on the table, which only wanted a little trimming to make the place as cheerful as it ever could be made.

"'Tis not much of a place for the likes of you, my lord," said Laurence Grey, the outlaw.

"We have seen worse quarters on the Spanish Main," said the earl, "especially in the underground cells of Vera Cruz."

"Well, yes; that was a narrow squeak; but what is your business with me to-night?"

The earl put his hand out, clutched a bottle of brandy; and, filling a tumber full, drained it to the dregs.

"Grey," he said, "I am threatened with ruin and destruction. A claimant has arisen to my title and estates."

"A rash man," if he knows you as well as I do," said his old lieutenant, Laurence Grey, coldly.

"He knows little or nothing of me," was the curt answer; "though he claims to be my son. I cannot and will not admit his claim, which means ruin to my recognised heir."

"Oh—then that is it—the son of the first has turned up after all," said Laurence, with a sneering laugh.

"So he says," was the cold reply.

"What do you want me to do?" asked the robber, for he was nothing else.

"I cannot and will not yield a point," said the earl. "This man must be removed out of my path. You have places where you could keep him until he promised to withdraw his claim."

"I have; but I should want good pay to suppress so important an individual as your son," the other retorted.

"Money is no object," was the response; and on this a bargain was struck.

The chamber under the tower was usually in these old feudal buildings a place which could either serve the purpose of hiding yourself or somebody else.

Laurence Grey agreed in all things to carry out the desires of the earl; and so it was arranged that the young man should be waylaid and carried to this loathsome dungeon, there to be detained until such time as he withdrew all claim to the title and estates.

The earl knew Laurence Grey too well not to be aware that nothing but a pecuniary reward would tempt him to do anything for the advantage of anyone else.

His fee was therefore a large one, a considerable portion of it being paid down.

Then these two men parted. Many an evil deed had they done before, but this was, perhaps, the most nefarious they had undertaken.

The earl had no thought but of Lord Harold and his sisters, Clarissa and Florence, while the other was influenced by no considerations but money—the love of gold.

The earl would have looked with terror at the suggestion even of personal violence to the man who claimed to be his son, but if he could immure him where his claims could never be made known, he believed himself perfectly justified in doing all he could.

With this sinister project in their heads the two rank conspirators parted.

CHAPTER CXV.

FATHER AND SON.

Viscount and Viscountess Henry Curzon, as they openly called themselves, reached Exeter in safety, under charge of their redoubtable bodyguard. Dick Turpin and Tom King were a legion in themselves.

Of course, with a post-chaise they followed the king's highway, stopping at first-class hotels, and resting at night under the doughty championship of their strong guards.

Dick and his friend knew all the best houses, and were in this way invaluable, as they thus secured excellent accommodation and good treatment; that, however, never fails to those who have plenty of money, and show no disinclination to spend a fair ration of it.

Bernard had suffered too much from poverty to be wasteful of his money; but he was free and liberal in his expenditure, enough to satisfy those whom he mixed with.

Landlords, waiters, and chambermaids were quite satisfied, and the young nobleman and his wife were quite pleased with their treatment. And thus they reached Exeter after a long and very pleasant journey, through some of the pleasantest parts of England.

They put up at a first-class tavern; hotels had no meaning in those days, though the grand tour was common enough with our young sparks of nobility, who must see the Tuileries and waddle through the Louvre.

As soon as they had enjoyed a day's rest, Bernard made up his mind to ride over to Curzon Castle and see his father.

The surprise of the people at the "Royal George" when the young couple gave the name of Viscount and Viscountess Henry Curzon may be imagined. Lord Harold, who claimed to be the only son and heir, was well known in Exeter, and the assumption of the title by these distinguished strangers surprised a great many.

On the morning of the second day after their arrival in Exeter, Bernard decided to make a personal attempt to persuade his father to see and recognise him.

He trusted a good deal to natural affection, backed up with such undoubted proofs as he was able to show as to his identity.

He little understood the nature of the man he had to deal with, selfish and opinionated to the last degree.

Bernard rode on horseback from Exeter to the castle, the two inseparables following him at a distance. They kept him in sight without appearing to be connected with him in any way. On reaching the castle Bernard sent in his card, and desired to see the earl in private.

He was admitted to the library, where, cold, stern, and implacable, Lord Lisle awaited him.

He stood with his back to the fire, an Englishman's favourite attitude.

"Well, sir," he began, coldly, "to what do I owe this intrusion? I am not in the habit of seeing strangers."

"A son can be no stranger to his father."

"Son!" cried the earl, in choked accents; "what do you mean? My son is absent in London, attending the court."

"And yet you know that I am your son—your legitimate son and heir," Bernard went on, calmly. "But I came not to ask affection alone. I want but my rights, and I wish to avoid the scandal and publicity of a trial, which can only end in disgrace."

"Disgrace, sir?"

"Yes. There is much in the past which you would wish to conceal," said Bernard, calmly. "My desire, therefore, is that you should acknowledge me openly, and then we can arrange the provision to be made for my brother and his two sisters."

"You are very kind," said the earl, a bitter smile on his cruel face; "but I believe their future is pretty well provided for."

"Then you seek war," he responded sadly. "Well, I have done my best to avoid it. I must now seek the protection of the law."

And he turned towards the door.

"Stop, sir," cried the earl, to whom the hint about secrets in his life had caused much alarm. "Be seated, and perhaps we may come to an understanding."

Bernard bowed and took a chair.

"Admitting that your assertion be true," the other went on, savagely, "how did you obtain your information? By stealing it like a thief in the night!"

"I did nothing of the kind. Someone who takes an interest in me did that, and the act was perfectly justifiable," continued Bernard, gravely. "I was refused my rights—I took them where I found them."

"Well, if ever you are able to prove your

assertions, which I do not for a moment allow," continued the earl, "will you be content to accept five thousand a year, and leave your claim in abeyance while I live?"

"No, sir—you dead, I should be looked on with great suspicion," was the answer. "Why did I not make the claim in your lifetime?".

"Then, sir, do your worst," the earl cried rising. "I will resist your claim with all the power of my wealth and the prestige of my name. Our interview need not be any further prolonged."

Bernard rose, bowed, and went out, bitterly disappointed with the result of his interview. He had hoped in some way to move the man of blood and iron, but he had failed.

He had, however, done his duty, and he must now turn to the law to assert his just rights.

At the door he found his horse awaiting him, and, mounting it, he turned away from what should have been his home, and, not following the beaten road, turned down one of the winding paths that led through the magnificent park to another and smaller exit.

And thus it happened he was turned away from what he knew to be his rightful home, the inheritance of his forefathers.

The afternoon had gone by, and the brightness of the day had become obscured, not only by the sinking of the sun, but by some large heavy clouds which had rolled up, and seemed to portend a thunder storm.

Bernard Blair looked up towards the sky, not with any immediate purpose of returning home, for the rain he feared not, and in witnessing the grand contortion of the elements he had always felt an excitement and an elevation from his boyhood.

His mind, too, was in an uproar, suited to the stormy sky above.

Suddenly, however, he recollected his sturdy friends, and judged it might be wise to rejoin them, as they probably would be uneasy at his absence. Riding forward, therefore, he soon reached a small gate, which opened from the park into a rural lane, which was but a belt of planting cut off from the enclosed ground.

Just as Bernard entered this secluded way, he heard a shriek proceeding from the lane to his right, and somewhat ahead. It was the shriek of a woman.

He paused for no other indication, but, vaulting at a bound over the paling, he stood on one of those little greens to be found in this secluded part, an unexpected intruder upon a party engaged in no very legitimate occupation.

On the sandy path which marked the passage of the lane across the green stood a young lady, with a tall, powerful man grasping her tightly by the right shoulder, and keeping the muzzle of a pistol to her temple, in order apparently to keep her from screaming, while another was basely engaged in rifling her person of anything valuable she had about her.

So prompt and rapid had been the approach of Bernard, that the two gentlemen of the road were quite taken unawares; and the one who held her was in the very act of vowing that he would blow her brains out if she uttered a word, when the muzzle of the pistol he held to her head was suddenly knocked up in the air by a blow from the unexpected intruder. The first impulse of the robber was to pull the trigger, and the pistol went off, carrying the ball a foot or a foot and a half above the head of the young lady.

Instantly letting go his grasp of the terrified girl, the man who had held her threw down the pistol and drew his sword upon his assailant. But Bernard's blade was already in his hand, and his skill in the use of the weapon was remarkable, so that in less than three passes, which took place with the speed of lightning, the robber's sword was wrenched from his grasp and flying amongst the boughs of the trees, while he himself, brought upon his knees, received a severe wound in his neck as he fell.

At that moment, however, another terrified scream from the young lady called her defender's attention, and, turning eagerly towards her, Bernard saw that it was for him she was now alarmed. The robber whom he had seen engaged in rifling her of any little trinkets she bore about her had instantly abandoned the occupation on the sudden and unexpected attack upon his comrade, and was now advancing towards Bernard, better prepared than the other had been, with his drawn sword in one hand and a pistol in the other.

The moment which Bernard had lost in hurrying towards the girl had been enough to enable the man whom he had disarmed to start upon his feet again, and to run to the spot where his sword fell; and the young man found that in another instant he should be opposed single handed, and with nothing but his sword, to two strong and well-armed men. He did not easily, however, lose his presence of mind, and, seizing the girl's arm with his left hand, he gently drew her behind, saying, "Crouch down low, miss, that you may not be hurt when they fire. I will defend you with my life."

Scarcely had he spoken when the second ruffian deliberately presented the pistol at him and fired. Bernard felt that he was wounded in the left shoulder and the blow of the bullet made him stagger. It was not very much, but still it was a wound.

The two assailants, however, were rushing fiercely upon him, and the odds seemed strongly against him.

At that moment a shout was heard, and a strong arm came in—a rough peasant-looking man, who had heard the shots, had rushed in and taken the weaker side.

At this moment the gallop of horses was heard, and the ruffians turned, hoping it was some of their robber crew. To their amazement the two new arrivals were strangers to them —no other than Dick Turpin and Tom King, followed on foot by one or two yokels.

Just in time, for what with loss of blood and pain, Bernard had fainted.

The lady, whom the peasants recognised as Lady Florence Curzon, at once directed that her wounded preserver should be carried to the Castle.

Knowing what they knew, and the mansion being the nearest place at hand, the high tobies made no objection, and so Henry, Viscount Curzon, was taken back to the home of his fathers an honoured guest.

When the earl heard how his son had rescued Lady Florence Curzon from the ruffianly robbers, and been severely wounded in the scuffle, something like repentance came over his soul.

Why should he not acknowledge one so noble, brave, and unselfish?

He must think.

CHAPTER CXVI.

LORD HAROLD CURZON.

MEANWHILE we must revert to a character whose name has been mentioned, but who has not appeared bodily in this narrative.

We have said that Lord Harold was in London; so his father had given out, but it was not true.

Lord Harold was only one-and-twenty, but was a *roué* and a gambler. With regard to women, he was ruthless. All who came in his way and who believed his honeyed words were sure to repent it.

He was that worst of human characters—a male flirt.

On the borders of the forest at no great distance from the highway, was a delightful residence known as the Rosary.

It was the home of a couple who, though not well assorted by age or character, seemed to be tolerably happy.

The husband was about forty, the wife not much more than twenty.

He was what we call a commercial traveller, what they called at that time a bagman; was a good jolly round-faced fellow, fond of his glass and a good story and not averse to a pipe. But above all was he deeply attached to his wife.

He had taken her from a humble sphere and married her without much delay.

Daisy, as he called her, was very grateful; but she had no love to give him.

Only gratitude—affection, such as she might have felt or shown to her father.

She was well known in the neighbourhood as a beauty, and had been the toast of the beer shops and public houses. There were very many present to whom her marriage was a bitter disappointment.

Among others who had seen and admired her was Lord Harold, and at one time her silly little heart fluttered with the pleasurable excitement of hoping to be my lady.

But she soon saw her mistake. Lord Harold bluntly told her she might come to London with him, but held out no prospect of marriage.

It was the usual excuse of aristocratic profligates, that his father would never forgive him.

But the girl had a spirit, and Mr. Robert Crackem, a smart bagman who frequented the house where she was chambermaid, made her a serious offer, which, in a fit of pique, she accepted.

And now she was Mistress Robert Crackem, and the head of a charming little house on the borders of the forest, with everything that her heart could wish. She had servants to wait on her, and yet the wilful heart of the girl-wife was not satisfied.

Lord Harold had found out what she had done, and one day when he knew her husband had started on one of his long journeys, had called to congratulate her.

Jenny Crackem's heart beat pit-a-pat. There is something in the very smell of a lord's name which is dear to the English heart, especially that of a vain and foolish girl.

Jenny was overwhelmed; and when Harold condescended to stay and take some of the wedding cake and wine, her satisfaction was unbounded.

"Ah!" said my lord, with a deep and artful sigh; "but for cruel fate this might have been our wedding cake."

"Law!" cried the pretty little hypocrite; "don't you talk such rubbish."

"It isn't rubbish," he said with a woful look. "I almost wish now I had defied my father."

"It's no use crying over spilt milk," was the chambermaid's suggestion.

"I suppose not," was the reply, given in a sorrowful and lachrymose tone.

But there was something of an air of triumph too. He knew the weakness of this silly and foolish girl, who, led by a glib and lying tongue, would believe him and forget everything else.

Harold did not go away until late that evening, and his visits were renewed almost every day.

Bernard had been a week at the Castle, and learned to love his gentle and beautiful half-sister. He had been nursed carefully by her and was rapidly approaching convalescence.

One evening he received a message from Dick, asking him to meet them at the "Pig and Whistle," as they desired to be on the move so as to make arrangements as to future proceedings. The rendezvous was appointed at no great distance from the residence of Jenny Crackem.

The distance was so trifling that Bernard never thought of taking a horse. A walk through the wood would do him good.

The "Pig and Whistle" was a large roadside inn, where Bernard found his friends. They had been summoned to London, but would, if he desired it, be back in a week.

Bernard thankfully agreed, and, after a short jollification, shook hands and started on his return journey to the castle.

He had not gone quite a hundred yards, when he heard a pistol fired, and hastened to the spot whence the sound proceeded just in time to see a figure dart away into the forest, while a body lay upon the sward.

This is what had happened.

The visits of Lord Harold to the house of the bagman's pretty wife had excited comment. In a foolish and unguarded moment someone had spoken of them to the husband.

That very evening, on his arrival at the "Pig and Whistle," someone a little advanced in his cups had jeered him about the folly of marrying a skittish young wife.

When told angrily to mind his own business, the malicious talebearer blurted out all the local gossip about Jenny.

Robert Crackem's fury knew no bounds.

Going to the stables, he had taken a pistol from his holsters. Then he had secreted himself within view of the doorway of his own house and watched.

It was eleven o'clock when the door opened, and Lord Harold came out, exchanged a warm embrace with Jenny, and left.

He took his way towards the forest, followed by the husband. Just as he entered beneath the trees, Robert came up and clutched him by the shoulder.

"What is it?" asked Harold, turning.

"Death, scoundrel!" said the husband, and fired.

Then, hearing footsteps, he fled, leaving his pistol on the ground.

Stooping, Bernard saw that he had a dead or dying man on his hands.

What was to be done?

His first thought was to return to the inn; but, before he could do so, two other men appeared on the scene. They had heard the shot without seeing who fired it.

And now they found a body on the ground and a stranger standing over it.

"Lord Harold!" cried one, as he gazed at the upturned face on the ground.

His brother! Bernard was horrified.

"Where can we take him?" asked the young man; "he may not be dead."

The men eyed him askance. There could be no doubt that they suspected him.

"The 'Magpie and Stump' is the nearest house," growled one, and to this place he was carried and placed in bed, one messenger being sent for a doctor, and the other to the castle.

When the former arrived he pronounced the case hopeless, and when the frantic earl came, it was to find one son dead, with the other watching beside him, charged with his murder.

They were alone.

"And you have done this deed, fiend incarnate!" said the nobleman, with horror and hatred in his tones.

"My lord, you misjudge me," said Bernard, in earnest tones. "I know nothing of this man —your son, if son he be. I will tell you all I know."

"Lies! falsehoods!" cried the earl. "You have slain him. But, old as I am, I will take your heart's blood, and you shall find that this arm has lost nothing of its skill and but little of its strength. You shall learn what a father's arm can do when heavy with the sword of the avenger."

"Once more, my lord," replied Bernard, "I assure you that I am perfectly innocent. I assure you that neither fairly nor openly, covertly nor treacherously, have I had ought to do with your son's death. The sole ground for suspicion against me is having been found near him."

He then told him the truth, but the bereaved parent was too wild with grief to heed his words.

He ordered the body to be at once conveyed to the castle, whither he had insisted on Bernard also returning.

"I am no cowardly assassin," said Bernard, "and have no fear of the result."

So again a mournful procession was organised. A cart conveyed the body, and the earl and Bernard walked beside it. The two men who had found Bernard near the body volunteered to attend next day at the inquest.

It was held at midday in the library of the castle, two magistrates being present. The earl took no part in the proceedings.

All the servants were there, while Bernard stood apart at no great distance. His arms were folded, and he leaned against a bookcase.

The earl was seated in an arm chair, his face in his hands.

The first witnesses called were the two men who had come upon Bernard standing over the prostrate body of the young nobleman.

When they had spoken, Bernard volunteered an explanation, which he was allowed to give.

It was to the effect that, having been at the "Pig and Whistle" on important business, he had heard a shot fired, seen a man fly into the forest, and then had discovered the body, with a pistol lying by his side.

The pistol was on the magistrate's table; the body, with a sheet over it, was on trestles in an adjoining room.

"That I am accused is fearful, and that the earl believes it is worse," said Bernard, in a firm voice. "As the earl will not speak, I must.

The murdered man was my brother, for I am Viscount Henry Curzon, heir to the earldom of the very man who allows me to be accused."

"'Tis a lie!" shouted the earl, rising and confronting Bernard.

"'Tis truth!" replied Bernard, "and will be fully known in a few days."

At this moment there was a scuffle at the door; a man in dishevelled dress, without a hat, forced his way in, despite the efforts of the servants.

"I will come in! I will let no man suffer for my crime!" he shouted, as he struggled.

"Admit the man," said one of the magistrates, Sir Michael Scrope.

He was admitted, and the two men who had witnessed against Bernard at once guessed the terrible truth.

"Where is the body?" he asked, in wild accents; "where does he lie?"

"Be calm, and tell us what you have to tell," said the magistrate.

"I killed him, and would do it again! Why could he not leave my pet lamb alone? I am Robert Crackem, who married Jenny Hargraves. When I was away this foul snake crept into my Eden. I only found out his knavery last night," the man continued. "I was told of it at the 'Pig and Whistle.' It was the talk and jeer of all around. I went to the stable, secured this pistol," taking it up, "and waited until he came out. Then I shot him. I would do it again, had I but the chance."

The earl was too crushed to speak. He sank into his armchair, overwhelmed with shame at the fearful exposure.

The son of whom he was proud, and for whom he had sinned, had died in his sin.

It was a terrible and awful humiliation.

And the other son had probably saved his daughter's life.

Constables took charge of Robert the bagman, and then another witness presented himself.

It was the exciseman, who, in a sheepish kind of way, explained how when Robert Crackem came into the parlour the night before he had foolishly repeated the village gossip about Lord Harold and Jenny.

"Not but what it was gospel truth," said the exciseman; "only I'm sorry I spoke."

The magistrates put their heads together, the clerk whispered to them, and in a minute more Robert Crackem was committed for the wilful murder of Lord Harold Curzon.

"Which, of course," said Sir Michael Scrope, "is equivalent to a withdrawal of the charge against anyone else, Mr. ——"

"Henry, Viscount Curzon," interrupted the earl, in a choked voice, rising as he spoke; "who will do the honours for me until I have recovered."

And he went out, glad to get that heavy sin-shadow off his shoulders.

The prisoner was given into safe custody, and then the court was cleared.

As soon as they were alone with Lord Henry, the magistrates congratulated him on his acquittal and recognition by his father.

Very delicately they asked for no explanations, which was fortunate, as they would have obtained none.

He then rang the bell, and summoned Mrs. Atkinson, who hurried in, pale and ghastly.

"Get us a quiet lunch, Mrs. Atkinson," he said; "and let it be known that my father has recognised me as his son and heir."

And by his proper name and title only shall we in future speak of Henry, Viscount Curzon.

"I knew he must," cried Mrs. Atkinson, warmly. "I have known it twenty years."

"Hush, Mrs. Atkinson," said Henry, gently; "not a word about my father. He has suffered enough already. We will follow to the dining-room. Send a groom to me."

How proudly he said "my father!"

"And have rooms prepared for my wife and children," he went on; and Mrs. Atkinson, big with her own importance, retired.

At last the boy, whom she had loved from the first, had come to his own.

The lunch was a very quiet affair, and the magistrates left early.

Overwhelmed with grief as they were, Lady Clarissa and Lady Florence found great comfort in the society of their handsome brother.

"You will be kind to my wife and children," said Henry, when the explanation had concluded.

"Wife! children! are we really aunts?" cried Lady Florence, his first friend, the one he had saved from violence.

In the meantime Henry had sent off a missive to his wife at the "Royal George," Exeter, explaining the terrible trials he had passed through, and bidding her come at once.

"I cannot come myself. My father clings to me, and will not let me leave. He is terribly crushed. Let us heartily forgive him all our troubles in the happiness of reunion."

And starting this off, he went to join his father, who was very ill, and really needed his presence.

In fact, crushed and humiliated as he had been by the wretched death of the son he had so much loved, the earl fell back helplessly on his stronger-minded heir.

Lord Henry was tender in the extreme, and did more to soothe his parent's sorrow than anyone else could have done.

Some slight allusion was made to the girls, and the earl regretted to leave them with nothing but their mother's small fortune and dowry.

"Father," said Henry, "make your will leaving them just what you would have done had Harold lived, and it shall be carried out. I have taken a great liking to them. I hope to see you walking proudly through the park with my children."

"Do not deceive yourself," said the earl; "do not deceive yourself, my son. From this bed I shall never rise again. The day is past, the night is coming. The fire is burnt out, and there lingers but a spark behind; the oil in the lamp is exhausted, and though the flame may flicker up once or twice, it soon must pass away and be extinguished. Henry, I am dying!"

But the son would not agree to this. Indeed he had great faith that his father would still live and bless his children.

But he knew that the earl, like all others in his position, would not be contradicted.

"'Tis close to-night," he said, presently.

"Yes; I never felt it more so except in the Gulf of Florida," was the musing answer. "Ah!"

And, as he spoke, the storm which had long been coming up burst forth with a bright flash, which blazed with a blue and ghastly light round the dark wainscotted chamber in which they sat, lighting up every cornice and ornament in the carved oak, and seeming to play amidst the papers on the table.

At this moment, after a discreet knock, a domestic entered with a note, a rude kind of scrawl, which the man said had been left by one who would take no denial.

The earl took it impatiently; but when his eyes fell upon it he could not read it.

"Read it," he said to his son.

Lord Henry took it up, and in some surprise read out the contents:—

"The person we waited for interfered with my men in the execution of their legitimate business, wounded two, and carried off a squalling wench. What does it mean? I want an explanation."

The earl almost leaped from his bed, and shook his fist in the air.

"The scoundrel! It was his minions who insulted my daughter, and from whom you rescued them. I wish you had killed them. Again I must blush before my son!"

"Father!"

"Do not interrupt me, son. That man was once my friend, my lieutenant and companion," said his father. "That man, by his few words, has laid before me," he added, "the picture of my life." Here the earl paused.

"It was only two years ago," he went on, "that I heard from this Laurence Grey, and knew that he was possessed of knowledge regarding the darker part of my history, which I believed buried in eternal oblivion."

He then explained that this man had, on their first meeting, mentioned the name under which he was known years ago; and he, the earl, had casually asked him if he knew him well?

"Yes; oh, yes. I know his whole history well. He was an English gentleman of a brave, daring, and enterprising disposition, who, having been driven from his country and deprived for the time of his possessions, pursued a wild and fitful course of life—now serving with gallant distinction in the armies of foreign countries, now becoming a rover on the high seas, and acquiring for himself a fearful and redoubtable fame, till the restoration of the king suddenly recalled him to fortune and honour in his own land."

The earl owned that he was stunned, and asked the audacious intruder if he knew the name of the rover?

"Yes, my lord," was his answer; "and his whole history from that time to the present hour."

The earl owned that this assertion was a great blow to him.

For more than twenty years he had heard no allusion to those days of wild and roving adventure, when, driven forth as he fancied for ever from his native land, stripped of his rank and possessions, he had given way to the impulses of a rash, daring, and fierce spirit, and piled upon his own head many a heavy remorse, and seared his own heart with many a deed of evil.

"And this man, one of my crew, had recognised me," the earl groaned; "and I feared him. I thought all who knew of those days to be far removed, plunged beneath the rolling waves of the ocean, buried upon the sandy beaches of distant lands, or with their bones whitening—a public spectacle—in the sun.

"I gave this man money. I had little to fear from him—he was an outlaw. But I gave him money, and there I thought the matter ended.

"Then came your threat to expose me, and I thought of this man," the earl went on. "I met him and asked him to secure your person, and keep you immured in his tower on Uppington Moor until we could come to terms.

"What followed? My daughter's terrible adventure and your severe wound.

"Besides, there is now no Harold. Can you wish me to live?"

"Yes, father," said Lord Henry, almost gaily; "to live long and die at a good old age, surrounded by your proud heir and successor."

"Well, boy, I will rest now," the other said; "but the man must be got rid of. He is a thorn in my side."

"What can he do?"

"Let the world know that the proud, cold, and wealthy Earl of Lisle, the domineering spirit of the country round, is identical with the wild rover of the western seas, whose deeds of daring and of blood are still remembered with awe and fear in a land fertile with strong passions and great crimes."

"None would believe him," said Lord Henry; "but if you wish me to see him I will."

"You will do me a favour," the old man returned. "Pay him for the crime he has committed, and then bid him do his worst. I am dying, and he will not be able to hurt me soon."

"I will do what you please, father, so that you do not worry."

Lord Henry was now called to dinner, and the earl sent for Mrs. Atkinson to keep him company.

After dinner, Lady Henry Curzon and family arrived, and were received warmly by the girls.

In the evening, later on, they were taken to the room occupied by the earl, and had no reason to complain of their reception by the father-in-law and grandfather.

He took particular notice of the grandson, the future wearer of the family honours.

He declared him a true Curzon.

But his son would not allow them to tire the old man, who had passed that day and the previous night through trials enough to have killed the strongest.

Once more the father and son were left alone.

"Now I can die in peace," said the earl.

"Don't talk to me of dying, father," replied Bernard. "I'll take the trouble off your hand about this man Laurence Grey. I'm afraid, though, father, that lawlessness runs in the family."

"What do you mean?" asked the earl, looking rather annoyed and vexed.

"I must tell you my story;" and he did, explaining his connection with Dick Turpin and Tom King truthfully and frankly.

A dark frown was instantly visible on the countenance of the earl.

"These men hold my secret."

"My lord," the young man went on, "Dick Turpin has been trusted by men of all ranks. The Earl of Mountjoye trusts him wholly. He is specially employed by his friend to guard against the machinations of Brian Seymour, the expectant earl, who is believed to have tried on more than one occasion by himself and emissaries to kill him."

"I have heard something of this," said the earl, "and know Brian Seymour to be an unmitigated scoundrel. I can't understand why he and his associates have not been put on their trial for the murder of his aunts."

"How bravely Dick Turpin behaved then," added Lord Henry, "and now, with your permission, I will to my wife and sisters."

He left his father more happy and contented than he had been since the discovery of his elder son.

Lord Henry spent a calmly pleasant hour or two with his wife and sisters, their feelings tempered, of course, by the reflection of what lay in that not far distant room, and then preparations were made for repose.

First, however, he went to the library, and stood in the presence of the dead.

> He who hath bent him o'er the dead
> Ere the first day of death is fled;
> Ere yet Decay's effacing fingers
> Have swept the lines where beauty lingers,

will understand his feelings.

Stranger though he was, still he was his brother, and there is a mysterious affinity in this relationship which never fails. Men seldom love anyone so much as a brother, while, once this feeling change the other way, the hate is baleful.

He then covered up the still form once more and left.

CHAPTER CXVII.

THE OUTLAWS.

A very quiet day was passed. Cards were left, but no visitors attempted to enter the house except the clergyman, who was seen only by Lord Henry. He was a good and worthy man, warmly congratulated the other on his good fortune, and then discreetly retired.

During the day Lord Henry intimated to the earl that Dick and his comrade might call to claim the balance of the reward, during his absence. He was not bound to see them. The man would give the name of John Palmer.

"I will see Mr. Palmer whenever he calls," the earl replied; "except Laurence Grey, I have seen no one of the class for some years."

His son made no reply. He knew the feelings which prompted this remark, and then prepared for his adventure.

The earl had sent word by a trusty messenger that, though from illness he could not go himself, he would send an accredited messenger, who would meet Grey on Uppingham Moor under the old tree, to confer on business.

"For the nefarious deed I prompted him to do," said the earl, "I promised him two hundred guineas. Take that sum with you, and tell him that is the last he will ever receive from me. Tell him that I am sick unto death, and that I defy him."

And so Lord Henry started, on a stout horse, and, by his father's express desire, well armed.

He easily found the tree, but instead of the stalwart horseman he expected to see he found a smart youth.

"Be you he as wants Mr. Grey?" he asked, touching his cap.

"Yes; why is he not here?"

"He aint far off, and told me to say there was hawks abroad. Would you come to his house?"

"Lead on," replied the viscount, who was one who knew no fear.

The boy trotted on before him half a mile further till, amid a clump of tall trees, at the very edge of the moor, where some unproductive fields connected it with the cultivated country, they perceived a light shining from a small window in a tall building before them.

As we have already observed, there still remained scattered over the face of England a number of those edifices which, fortified to a certain degree, combined the modern house, to some extent, with the ancient feudal hold, and had been rendered very serviceable to both parties in the progress of the great rebellion.

These fortified houses were of every size, from that which really well merited the name of castle to that which was no more than a mere tower, and many of them, either from being injured by the chances of war, or from having lost a great part of their utility when the scourge of evil contention was removed from the country, had gone to decay, or had been applied to the calmer and more homely uses of the barn, the granary, or the farmhouse.

Such was the house which Lord Henry and the boy approached, and as far as the darkness of the house suffered its outline to appear, it seemed to the former to be a tall, heavy tower of stonework, with four small windows on the side next to them.

Beneath its protection, and attached to it on one side, with the gable end turned towards the road, was a lower building with a high peaked roof of slates, and close by another mass of masonry, apparently the ruins of a church or chapel.

The light that the horseman had seen came from one of the upper windows of the tower, but there were lights also in the less elevated building by its side.

A low wall stood before the whole, enclosing a little neglected garden, and through a gate which stood open in this wall the boy led his companion in, and up to the door of the house.

There, beside the door, stood the ancient steps, which many a burly cavalier in the cavalier days, and in days long before that, had employed to mount his horse's back ; and there, too, on either side of the entrance, was many a ring, staple and hook, for the purpose of fastening up the troopers' horses, while their masters rested and caroused in the hall hard by.

The boy attached Lord Henry's bridle to one of these, and, opening the door, led the young man into the house, and finally into a large room, where awaiting him stood a man of saturnine appearance, stout, powerful, and about fifty years of age.

"My lord's eldest son, I presume !" he said, presently.

"His only son ; but I am anxious to return—my father is very ill—as he thinks, sick unto death," replied Viscount Curzon, "let us to business at once."

"Father," said a sweet and fascinating voice, "supper is ready. Will the gentleman join us?"

Lord Henry now beheld as lovely a creature as the eye of man ever rested upon. She was a young girl of about seventeen ; her eyes—her large, full, liquid eyes—were as black as jet, and the long, dark fringe that edged both the upper and the under lid, left but little of the white visible.

The glossy black hair, divided on the forehead, was tied in a large wavy knot behind, without any ornament whatsoever ; but along the whole line might be traced a strong undulation, which told that, if free, it would have fallen in ringlets round her face, and even as it was, two or three thick curls escaped from the

knot behind, and hung in glossy masses on her neck.

"You must ask the gentleman himself, Alice," replied Laurence Grey.

Then, bowing her head gracefully, she asked him to accept her father's hospitality.

"I am rather pressed for time," said Henry, courteously ; "but I cannot refuse."

His eyes plainly told the admiration he could not conceal, a result on which the cunning outlaw had calculated.

The girl went out, and soon returned with a lad and a girl, who in a few minutes had an excellent supper laid, which the trio enjoyed.

The conversation was almost wholly confined to the men. Lord Henry found Grey a highly-intelligent man, one who had travelled and seen the world, and mastered some of its accomplishments. The viscount had read much, and spoke more from what he had learned in books than from observation ; but his was a poetical and imaginative mind, and the girl listened to him with entranced ears.

Jocelyn, the boy, who knew who he was, had already inflamed her mind, by recording, in his uncouth way, something of his romantic career.

But at last the supper was over, and Grey bade her clear away and take herself off, leaving him to talk business with the gentleman.

She reluctantly complied, and soon the two men were alone, with grog, pipes, and tobacco, which Lord Henry had found a great comfort in his days of adversity.

"And now, my lord, to business," said Grey. "I presume the earl has no secrets from you."

"None."

"What is your errand, may I ask ?"

"I bring you two hundred guineas," replied Henry. "His message is this, that after that he repudiates all connection with you—he will be preyed upon no longer."

"And," the outlaw said, in a tone of anger and disgust, "If I refuse this paltry sum as final —what then ?"

"He defies you to do your worst," was the calm reply.

"He threatens me, does he ! Harkee, Lord Henry Curzon——," began the other, rising.

*   *   *   *   *

Midnight had come, but not Viscount Curzon. None had gone to bed.

The doctor had not left. The earl had had a relapse, and bitterly reproached himself with having sent his son on a dangerous errand. The doctor had sent home for a drug, which he purposed administering to give him that sleep without which he must die.

The anodyne was administered at last, and the old earl slept. In such cases sleeping potions are admissible ; but their frequent use is sure to end in death, as the sleep they induce is false and unnatural.

The viscountess was in agonies, and could not be consoled. She knew enough of her husband's errand to be aware that it was a dangerous one, and her mind was on the rack.

The sisters would not leave her. Towards morning she cried herself to sleep.

Then they also got a little rest.

Morning came, and with it no news. The earl was half frantic, and yet in his inmost heart he had no fear for his son's life ; but the uncertainty was terrible.

About mid-day a message came to the earl,

asking if he knew when the viscount would return, as a gentleman named Palmer, and a friend, were waiting to see him.

"Bring them up here," said the earl, eagerly, "and put the bottle-case on the table by the bed."

The domestic went out, and in a few minutes returned, ushering in two smart-looking gentlemen wearing swords and riding-dresses.

"Be seated," began the earl, when they were alone. "My son, before going out, commissioned me to see you, should he be absent. I know all; and as I am in great trouble about him, you may serve me. Fill your glasses, and listen."

They obeyed at once, and the earl told all that concerned the disappearance of his son since the previous night.

"And the man he went to see is Laurence Grey!" said Dick Turpin, in a musing way.

"You know him!"

"By reputation," replied Dick; "once a sea-scourge, now a land-shark; very much suspected of villainous crimes for which better men have suffered."

"That is the man," continued the earl, whose cheeks were tinged with crimson.

But the two men were too busy drinking and listening to observe this.

"In your case, my lord, he will be cautious. Doubtless, he has detained your son in the hope of ransom," said Dick; "what do you wish us to do?"

"Track him, and if the worst comes to the worst, treat with the scoundrel for a ransom," cried the earl. "I will give a thousand guineas rather than harm shall come to him."

"When shall we start, my lord?"

"'Tis best at night," said the nobleman; "you can lunch with Mr. Jacobs, my steward. Shall you want any assistance?"

"We should like a sharp youth to send to you in case we have a message," replied Dick.

The earl rang the steward's bell, and he at once presented himself.

No one ever kept the earl waiting.

"Jacobs," said the earl, "these gentlemen desire to see my son on business. As he is absent they will wait. Take them to lunch with you, as I am not up."

"Yes, my lord," said the obsequious steward, bowing, and leading the way.

The two highwaymen followed, leaving the earl very much more confident and hopeful.

All he said to the ladies was, that these two friends of Lord Henry were going in search of him. They seemed to guess at some reason which would detain him.

"But he would write," urged his anxious and pallid wife; "I know Henry."

"We must be hopeful, my dear," said the earl, kindly.

As soon as darkness set in, Dick and Tom, guided by a smart youth named Alison, who had his instructions from the earl, took them direct to the residence of Laurence Grey.

As soon as they were in sight of the tower they left their horses with the lad in a thicket, and moved slowly towards the house.

There were lights in the lower story, but none in the upper.

From the silence which prevailed the two friends came to the conclusion that the bandit was alone.

Could they only get in, they would be able to overcome the robber, against whom these high tobies had a professional grievance.

A man they knew to be innocent, but in whose favour they dared not appear, had been hanged for a crime committed by Grey.

They crept cautiously up, but not so cautiously as not to be seen, as in the neglected garden they found a woman with a shawl over her head.

"Are you friends of the young lord?" she whispered, in a low, terrified tone.

"Yes!" cried Dick.

"Hush! father has been drinking very hard; and if he hears us he will be terrible," she said, in trembling tones.

"We will not speak a word," was the answer.

The poor girl, who had fallen head over ears in love with the first gentleman she had ever seen, led them to the door, which she had left ajar. In the passage was a small oil lamp, which Dick took in his hand and led the way to the other end.

Alice pointed to a heavy stone trap in the floor, with an iron ring in the centre.

Dick stooped and began to lift it.

Herculean in his proportions, and strong as he was, it resisted him a moment; but in an instant or two more it yielded, and, aided by Tom King, he lifted it off the hole.

Looking down, it was dark as Erebus.

"What cheer, messmate?" said Dick, putting his mouth to the orifice.

"All the better for light and air," was the reply.

"Be cautious and silent. Help is at hand," replied the highwayman; and he turned to find Alice beside him with a rope, at one end of which was a loop.

Dick took it with an approving nod, and lowered it.

"Fasten that under your armpits, and pull when ready," said the highwayman.

The other simply made a monosyllabic answer, and next moment the rope was pulled, and in less time than it takes to tell, the captive's head was seen peering out of the trap orifice.

The two men helped him to his feet.

At that very instant the door of the front room was thrown open, and a bright light was seen within.

It was Grey, a lamp in one hand, and a pistol in the other.

"Traitress!" he cried, in a thick voice—that of an infuriated drunkard—as he levelled a pistol at his daughter's breast, and fired.

Then he darted back into the room, fastened the door, and began ringing a bell.

The viscount stooped towards Alice and caught her hand.

"I have saved you!" she faltered, "and I care not—fly—that bell!"

Then there was a slight gasp and a shudder, but neither groan nor cry, and the breath stopped for ever.

"Accursed fiend!" cried Henry, paralysed with horror; "but she shall be avenged."

"Come! we shall have more of the gang on us," said Dick, and at once, aided by Tom, dragged the young man away from the scene of this awful tragedy.

In the outer yard they found Jocelyn, and by putting a pistol to his head, Dick made him show him the stables.

He at once selected the best horses of the lot, and started for the thicket, where Alison awaited them.

All mounted, and bidding the boy make his way home, rode off.

The bell still sounded, and they distinctly heard horsemen coming in their direction.

But they were well mounted, and were soon in the park, and in half an hour they were in the castle, where all were delighted. After a hurried interview with the ladies, Lord Henry went to his father's room.

The interview was of too sacred a character to be more than mentioned.

After a time, the son told his father all that had passed.

"That man must die!" said the earl, "I will rouse the county. You and your friends shall join in the chase."

"That I will do cheerfully," replied Lord Henry; "that poor girl's death shall be avenged!"

CHAPTER CXVIII.

THE PURSUIT.

Next day, the earl sent for Sir Michael Scrope, to whom the viscount told the story of the murder, and intimated that he and two friends were ready to start in pursuit; but as the band was numerous and well armed, they would need all the support they could obtain.

"And you shall have it," was the frank response; "the miscreant is not worthy to live. I will at once rouse the *posse comitatus*. In two hours will your lordship be at my house with your friends? We will then ride for the tower, which I think we shall find deserted."

"Doubtless——"

"But some of the country folks will see them," observed Sir Michael; "when they learn the horrible tidings they will be furious. The poor girl was much beloved by the poor. Hitherto, the villain has never committed himself so near at hand—and so carefully were his plans laid, we could never prove anything against him. Commend me to his lordship?"

"I will;" and so for the moment they parted.

Lord Henry having informed his father of his plans, went to join the two visitors at lunch—the ladies remained in their private apartments—and informed them of his plans.

Both were delighted. In actual self-defence, both had killed their man—but never in cold blood. Dick Turpin was never what some had represented him to be—a ruffian. Of course, he was guilty of some terribly evil acts, but cruelty was not one of his crimes.

After a very hasty lunch, the viscount went to bid adieu to the ladies, assuring them that in their present enterprise there was little danger, as they would have the aid of experienced thief-takers and runners.

"Nice job this," said Dick, when alone, with a grin; "set a thief to catch a thief, eh?"

"Yes! but this bloodthirsty scoundrel is no ordinary thief!" remarked tender-hearted Tom.

"But to be acting with runners and so on!" went on Dick; "luckily, no one knows us down here—and police portraits don't favour us much."

"No!" continued Tom, laughing, as he remembered one particular "ugly mug" professing to represent his counterfeit presentment.

Both were silent as they heard footsteps approaching, and next moment they were joined by their host.

Ten minutes later they left the castle on their way to the house of Sir Michael Scrope. They were accompanied by a stout groom who knew the way well, and was well up in the topography of the forest. The worthy magistrate's residence was near the little town of Ealing-cum-Shove, much approved of by bucolics.

The residence of the knight was a fine one, with a small park and huge gardens. He had been mayor of Exeter once, and a tanner by trade, but retired, keeping a large interest in the business. But his blushing honours made him aspire to be country gentleman.

He found Moulscombe in the market. It was not very large—but it was large enough for himself, Lady Scrope, and her family.

His elder son was four-and-twenty, and remained in the business, but nothing was said of this at home. He had a very liberal share in the receipts, and cultivated the officers, so that when he came home he was able to bring a captain, or if not, a lieutenant with him.

He was very free with his cash, and never asked for money back!

He had, as all may well imagine, no end of friends.

In front of the house were some dozen or more mounted men—stout fellows who seemed ready for action. Three were evidently official thief-takers, but the others were mostly farmers, all tenants of the earl.

When they recognised the Curzon livery, they set up a loud cheer.

A servant requested the gentlemen to walk in. They assented.

The young viscount had heard of the harmless vanity of the retired tanner. He wanted to be thought one of the upper classes, and a visit from the earl's son and heir, the observed of all observers, would be something to talk about.

As he expected, he found the whole family collected. Sir Michael, who had solid common sense, and had forbidden all display of finery, had placed wine and cake ready, of which of course, all partook.

Mr. John Palmer and Tom King took Lady Scrope in tow, and began to tell her of fashionable life in London, while Henry, Viscount Curzon, was very attentive to Maud Scrope, the eldest daughter, a very pretty girl, who listened, was delighted, and answered in monosyllables.

But suddenly the viscount looked at his watch, and Sir Michael took the hint.

"We must not lose a moment of daylight, my lord—I dare say you will honour us by making a longer stay on some future occasion?" said the knight, rising.

"Certainly!" replied the young lord, "and when our house is quieter, and we are a little over our troubles, I will name a day for you all to come to the castle."

The knight spoke not. His surprise and delight were too great for utterance, while the wife and the girls were utterly overwhelmed.

Then the males disappeared, and the women were left to discuss their visitors.

Lady Scrope declared Dick and Tom to be true gentlemen, and men of court manners; but the viscount was a paragon, a word one of the girls had learned at school.

Everyone was ready, and Sir Michael, placing himself beside his lordship, the two led the way.

The viscount found the knight shrewd and very capable of leading such a party. It was at first determined, as soon as they reached the top

"NOW, JOE SIMON, I ARREST YOU FOR THE MURDER OF COLONEL PICKARD—AND TWENTY
OTHER CRIMES!"

of the hill they were ascending, at the point where they could first see the house, that the party should divide, and one body, under the direction of the magistrate, should sweep through the hollow in the hills, while the other, under the viscount, should pursue the road by which the three had escaped.

They would thus approach Laurence Grey's abode both ways at once.

By this means no one could quit the house without being seen by one or other of the parties, and the possibility of the robbers making their escape by one side of the building while their assailants forced their way on the other was guarded against.

A very shrewd farmer, one who well knew the country, accompanied the viscount, and soon they emerged from the woods, lanes, and cultivated ground between the villages, and began to take their way over the soft turf, which was only varied by the innumerable scattered stems that covered the higher ground on that side.

This man rode between the viscount and the magistrate, who suddenly saw that his hawk eyes were fixed upon a particular spot on the hills, over whose soft green bosom the sunshine and the shade were chasing each other quietly. The knight saw it too.

"Yes, yes, I saw it move!" he cried. "Didn't you, my lord? Look ye there, upon that hollow space the shadow is just leaving. I have been for the last ten minutes trying to determine whether that is a man on horseback or a hawthorn tree. It's a man, I'm sure! I saw it move this minute, a bit to the left, so as to get a better sight of us."

"There's a hawthorn there," said the farmer. "I know it of old. But you're right, sir, you're right. There is something moving from behind it. It's a horseman, I believe, watching us. See, he's cantering up the hill."

"I think this bodes disappointment," observed the viscount. "The house will be empty."

"There's another on the top of the highest mound," cried the magistrate. "They have a terrible start of us. But let us away—we must not be afraid of breaking our horses' wind."

"Onward!" cried Curzon, and at once all set their spurs to their horses' sides, and were soon in sight of the house.

It was empty of all save the body of the unfortunate girl, beside which sat the maid who waited on Alice Grey.

Lord Henry bade them take care of her until they returned, and away went the whole party. The farmer, named Simmons, believed they would seek shelter in an old house in the hills, where they could defend themselves.

The farmer went straight ahead, and soon they saw a body of horsemen passing over the slope beyond, and then giving rein to their horses and galloping away as hard as they could over the open downs beyond.

Man is certainly a beast of prey. There is an instinct about him which prompts him to run after everything that runs away. It may be partly the dastardly tyranny of cowardice which gains courage to pursue and worry by the sight of an advantageous flight; but it is chiefly, in all probability, upon the same principle whereon a fierce dog chases and slaughters a sheep, which is solely because the sheep runs away, and the dog, thinking the sheep knows its own business and his better than himself, judges that it is both right and pleasant to run after and verify to the utmost the victim's estimation of his powers and his purposes.

Yes! man is undoubtedly a beast of prey; and in this instance no sooner did the posse who followed the magistrate, the young nobleman, and others, see a body in flight, than those who had been most timid and fearful of leading the way, were all setting off at full gallop in pursuit of fugitives whom they had little chance of overtaking.

Farmer Simmons, however, confidentially assured the magistrate that he would take them to the bandits' lair.

It was with the utmost difficulty that the fat but powerful voice of Sir Michael Scrope and the stern, commanding tones of the viscount, each exerted with considerable force, could induce these hot pursuers to halt and receive orders ere they separated.

When they were at length brought to pull up their horses, however, a few words between the leaders seemed to settle their arrangements. After a brief conference with the farmer the magistrate spoke:—

"All of you know of the 'Withered Oak'—make haste every man there his own way, and rouse the country everywhere you go. Keep them in sight as far as possible; but at all events keep above them on the hills, and drive them into the populous country. There you may follow them by the tongue as well as the eye. Now, off with ye, quick!"

CHAPTER CXIX.

THE ROBBERS' LAST STAND.

The escape of the viscount had thrown Grey into a fury of passion, only equalled by his consternation and terror. The little band who had come at his call were equally terrified.

The death of Alice was regretted by all. She had been kind to them in sickness, and generous to their wives and little ones.

None dared speak to Laurence Grey. His mood was a dangerous one indeed.

That which he had done in a moment of passionate fury he deeply repented. Alice had been all he had ever loved since her mother's death, and now he was alone, left to brood over sorrows none could share.

It was arranged that the tower should be abandoned in the morning, when the party would scatter around and collect their forces.

The old house at the peak was not known much. The region was too wild and desolate for the people in general to visit it. Here they might lie perdu until arrangements could be made to leave that part of the country, or defend themselves if tracked.

The old house had secret ways known only to the chiefs of the band.

Grey little suspected that Farmer Simmons who was hotly guiding them was Tim Allport, one of his most trusted lieutenants twenty years before, but who had mysteriously disappeared during one of their raids—it was supposed killed.

But Tim Allport had fallen unexpectedly into an inheritance and gone to London, whence returning two years later he took possession of his farm, married, and cut all his old associates.

He was too well acquainted with their haunts, public houses, &c., to fear meeting them. He had but to exercise his discretion to avoid them.

Wishing utterly to cease his guilty connection with the bandits — he was only a hotheaded young man, fond of wild sports and forest life, when he became a follower of Grey —he made up a good story :—

He had once been held at ransom in the old house of the peak, and, after an imprisonment, had escaped with the connivance of a wench.

"But from her I learned all the fox-holes—we'll stop 'em up, and catch 'em like a rat in a trap !"

But to return to Grey.

He left the tower before dawn and joined his people, who were, however, so scattered, that it was late in the afternoon before they began to move in small bands towards the house.

Then they knew that the hue and cry was out, and hastened to gain their most secret retreat.

When they saw the force behind them, they knew the country was astir, and bitterly did the men anathematise the folly of their chief in giving way to passion.

The murder of Alice Grey would rouse the passions of the whole country. Every man, woman, and child, would be against them.

"If we find the country too hot to hold us," said Grey to Hardtop, one of his leaders, "I know where to find safety for the band. I know of a ship that sails for St. Malo in four days."

He spoke calmly ; there was no heat, nor haste, nor agitation in his tone. On the contrary, it was unusually slow and distinct ; but there was a knitting of the dark heavy brow, a setting together of the white teeth between every two or three words, which made Hardtop, bold man and daring as he was, shrink within himself, at signs of deep and terrible passions, the effects of which he knew too well.

"Had I but that traitor lord by the throat !" he continued, talking more to himself than to the other, " I would make him pay for all. But for his base treachery, I should not have been—pshaw ! am I a woman to repent. Forward !"

Spies and scouts had let him know that he was hotly pursued. It was clearly their endeavour to keep them in sight.

This put him on his mettle.

"Away ! meet me at the Withered Oak !" was his cry ; " every man for himself."

Still the pursuers kept them pretty well in view, and not until they had plunged into a narrow gorge in the hills did they feel that they had lost the track. It was a little way round, but his object was to put them off the scent.

It was sundown when all met at the rendezvous—some came straggling up at the last minute, others had been there several minutes.

Not a moment was lost, and entering the wood, they reached a narrow path in the forest which led upward to the peak.

Here was situated the old house which Grey looked upon as a safe place of concealment.

It was an old-fashioned fortified farm-house, with moat and drawbridge, but still very ruinous. Here, a brave band of men could make a stout defence.

The postern-gate had a narrow bridge, and over this the whole party rode in single file, the keeper, an old man with an old wife, opening at a given signal.

Meanwhile, about half an hour later, the whole force of the pursuers, much augmented by volunteers, met at the Withered Oak.

Most knew the spot, but none save poachers and desperadoes had ever ventured into the hills.

A council was held, and after some earnest debate, it was resolved to attack at once.

It was dark, but there was something to be said in favour of surprise.

There were over thirty men present, all stalwart men, and though some were not much used to fighting, the presence of brave and professional men roused them to courage.

Example is the best teacher.

But they had not calculated on one thing. One of the laggers had come up in the darkness and heard the decision.

This man was a robber, and believed himself to be in the company of his fellows. He was, however, speedily undeceived, and getting out of the crowd slipped into the forest, and very soon was making the best of his way for the general rendezvous.

He was followed at a more leisurely pace by the avengers, who little suspected the reception that awaited them.

They were not at the small bit of table-land without a tiresome climb, which fatigued them.

Once they were in sight all dismounted, and prepared for the attack.

Farmer Simmons, who knew the ground so well, went forward to reconnoitre.

He returned at the end of a quarter of an hour looking anxious.

"They are on their guard," he said. "Heavens ! what a fool ! I saw a fellow edge out of our party into the wood—he was a robber, and has warned them."

"Let us not lose our heads !" said the magistrate, " but consult."

"Come on one side," put in the viscount to the magistrate, James Morris, and the chief of the police.

They moved aside out of the crowd, and seated themselves under the shelter of a tree.

"They are in a fortified house," the viscount began, " and hold us at a disadvantage."

"Well, my lord," said Sir Michael Scrope, " if you will allow me to advise, I would say let us repose. Most of my men are raw, very raw, and won't do much in a night fight. They want to see their enemies, and will fancy all sorts of things."

"I agree, with your permission," the head constable added, " that fighting at night won't suit our fellows. They'll see ghosts in every bush. I told them all that we might pass a night in the woods, and I dare say they're well provided with bed and grub."

"We are," said Dick, calling attention to a couple of rather heavy wallets hanging one on each side of his horse—Tom had done the same —" and I highly approve of rest."

"So be it, my friends," cried the viscount, " but the outlets must be guarded."

"Certainly, my lord," said Farmer Simmons, " I'll take Byles with me, and watch in turns."

And so it was settled.

*   *   *   *   *

What was going on inside meanwhile ?

Grey was in a large old-fashioned kitchen, where in that old residence, with its thick walls, a fire was ever agreeable, surrounded by his men.

They had finished their suppers, and were playing dice and cards, while he sat smoking in moody silence, when two men who were on the look out entered with Bob Harvey, the man who had overheard the plans of what might be called the Government forces.

"Well!" asked Grey, with a dark and gloomy frown, "what is the matter?"

"The enemy's close behind," the man replied, "they'll attack us in less than an hour."

With an awful imprecation Grey rose to his feet, foaming with rage.

"We've been betrayed again!" he shrieked. "Whoever did it, I'll have his blood!"

"Well," said the other, "he's an old traitor, then. You mind Tim Allport, many years ago?"

"Tim Allport! Yes, yes. What of him? He's dead long ago," cried Laurence.

"I see him to-night. He's guiding the enemy. I heard him say as he knew every secret of the place," the other observed.

It would be painful to record the foul language that burst from the lips of the baffled robber.

He went to the table and drank a whole tumbler of brandy.

He then bade his men keep a good look out, to man the fore court overlooking the moat, and to fire on any one who approached.

"Rowland," he said to one of his best-trusted men, "there are plenty of stones outside the secret passage. Take two or three sturdy fellows and choke up the entrance. Be quick about it. Call me if I'm wanted."

And going into a side room he lay down and slept soundly.

He was not called that night, as no attack was made; but at daybreak he was awakened by the sound of firing.

Starting to his feet, he hurried out, and found his men occupying every possible point of vantage.

The enemy in the night had cut down trees, bushes, and boughs, which they had carried to within a reasonable distance of the old farm, which they were by this means enabled to command.

Not a soul could show himself within the works without being shot at.

The back of the farm was without windows, and the walls here were on the edge of the moat.

Neither attack nor defence were of any use on that side.

All was concentrated on the front.

The attackers, having examined the place with keen eyes, came to the conclusion that an attack on the postern gate would be the most practicable.

Six men were to be selected for the assault; the others would take steady aim at the garrison until the postern-gate was won, when all would rush in.

Meanwhile, Farmer Simmons and three others were guarding the secret passage, and clearing it of the stones that choked its entrance.

Farmer Simmons was a long-headed fellow, and as soon as the vaulted passage was clear, piled against it a huge stack of dry wood and boughs. These could easily be removed if they wished to enter that way, or set fire to if that would prove useful.

No sooner was attack on the postern gate decided on, than it was commenced. Sir Michael Scrope selected Dick Turpin, Tom King, two constables, and two stalwart farmers to lead the attack.

Lord Henry would have led, but the magistrate earnestly requested him not to risk his life.

"You are not used to this rough work, my lord," he said. "Besides, think of your father."

He had done so, sending back the youth Alison with a leaf torn from a notebook, to say what they were doing.

He yielded on the strength of this argument to the wish of the magistrate.

When the rush was made the attackers left their guns behind them, carrying only their pistols and heavy axes, which had been brought with them at the suggestion of Farmer Simmons.

A loud yell greeted their advance, and a dozen robbers rushed to meet them; but these were at once driven back by a withering fire.

The postern-gate was old and rotten. Its ironwork had long since fallen away.

In five minutes it was broken open, and the whole tide of the assailants poured in like an avalanche.

The defenders either fled or threw down their arms, the orders being to give quarter to all who surrendered.

The viscount, accompanied by Dick and Tom, rushed into the house, seeking everywhere for Laurence Grey; but he was nowhere to be found.

All who were questioned declared that when the rush took place he turned and fled.

"He has gone by the secret passage," said one of the robbers, "and left us to our fate. Follow me."

And he turned down a small flight of steps, revealing the opening of a narrow passage, over which was suspended a lamp. Another hung on a hook, and this Dick secured.

He led the way, followed by Lord Curzon and Tom. The way was winding, but soon they came in sight of a man walking along the passage. He too carried a light.

But his ears were keen, and, turning, he saw that he was betrayed—pursued.

He bounded towards the entrance, to be cast back by a volume of flame and smoke.

With the furious cry of a maddened dog, he turned at bay to face Dick, who was close to him, with Lord Henry not far behind.

The robber fired wildly in his desperation, and missed. Dick rushed on, and, taking aim, blew his brains out.

He fell without a murmur.

The others at once retreated, leaving the body of the murderer to the smoke and flames.

The robbers made no resistance whatever. They were utterly cowed.

Then began another search—that for plunder —but the results were small.

The treasure of the band was never found; but shortly after Farmer Simmons bought a large quantity of land, and became the equal of many of the squires.

Whatever may have been suspected, nothing was said. John Simmons got to be a magistrate, and gave his daughters extensive dowries.

With the dead robbers' money he founded a family, which still exists in those parts.

The band on their trial were sentenced to be transported. No actual overt acts of robbery could be proved against them.

The next day Dick and Tom left the castle, after receiving hearty thanks from father and son, and an ample reward.

All we need say in regard to this episode is that the earl lived a few years, and then died deeply regretted, his son, however, being infinitely more popular than ever he had been.

Soon after they went away the viscount told his wife who his singular friends were, to her great surprise.

But for them, where would she have been? Probably in a pauper's grave.

CHAPTER CXX.

LITTLE ISAAC STREET.

On reaching London, the two adventurers reported themselves to the Blue Dwarf and took up their quarters in their old haunts.

For a day or two nothing was thought of but pleasure, dissipation, and amusement.

When the modern Damon and Pythias had money they found plenty of friends, male and female, quite delighted to be their panderers, flatterers, and courtiers.

They held quite a levee of a morning in their dingy chambers, and, like many more important individuals, scattered their favours very recklessly.

The usual plan was then to make appointments for the evening, and thus the days passed.

One afternoon the two friends were sauntering along in the neighbourhood of Holborn, when they were recognised by a man in a humbler way of business than themselves, whom they spoke to when they met him.

He now came up, and in a timid kind of way asked to be allowed to say a word.

"Know'd old Captain Pickard?" he said, in a deferential tone.

"Yes, I mind him," replied Dick.

"Well, the old boy's sprung—hard up—got a little ben on," continued the other. "If you'd come it 'ud be the making on him."

"Where?"

"'Two Spies,' Little Isaac Street," was the answer.

The two highwaymen made a grimace. It was an ill-favoured locality, but their good nature got the better of their repulsion, and, handing the requisitionist a crown, they promised to go.

It was a rough and rude place, but both these men had been glad to harbour in worse dens, and after all it was not an unpleasant change.

Variety was the delight of these men, and here was an occasion to enjoy a little change.

Both assumed a garb more suitable to the locale they were about to visit than that they wore in the flash crib, and were driven in a hackney coach to within half a mile of the place indicated.

They then alighted, and, walking, soon reached the locality they were in search of.

There was not a narrower nor a more crooked street in all London at the time of which we write than Little Isaac Street, and there was not a more old-fashioned house in the great city than the "Two Spies," kept by Mrs. Smithers.

The street was as crooked as the letter S, and the house lurched forward like a drunken man in the last stage of intoxication, and threatened to tumble down every moment.

In all probability it would long ago have collapsed and fallen to the roadway had not two stout beams been fixed against the opposite house, making a kind of wooden bridge over the thoroughfare.

Very much like an old cripple was the ancient thoroughfare, and, like a cripple, it needed support in the shape of a stout pair of crutches.

Many persons had told the landlady of the "Two Spies" that the place would have to be pulled down; but she shook her head, and was heard to declare that it would last her time.

"Let us hope that it will, and that your time will be a long one indeed," said one of her customers, a small, broken-down poet, who from uncontrollable circumstances had had to migrate from west to east.

Mrs. Smithers was a very popular landlady, fat, fair, and over forty—as a landlady should be.

If the appearance of the place was peculiar without, it was much more so within. The door was very low, so that even a man of middle height would have to stoop if he did not wish to get a knock on the head, and if he were not very careful would moreover fall down three steps, for the passage was by no means light.

It was already dark, and the murky old inn was unusually full. The bar was crowded, and many were moving up-stairs, when Dick and Tom entered, and going into a semi-private bar, ordered drink and exchanged a password with Mrs. Smithers.

"Glad to stick eyes on your slashing peepers," she said, proudly; "aint seen yer mengo mugs for a long time."

Dick answered in some similar silly slang, which he never used except on such occasions, drank his glass and went upstairs, followed by Tom.

The room was crowded. No sooner were they recognised than the excitement was great, and all began to "patter flash;" but as our readers would not understand it, we shall decline to record it.

We introduce our readers to this scene merely to explain how the two men got mixed up in a very extraordinary series of events.

The crowd consisted of the lower order of the criminal classes, ordinary pickpockets, confidence-trick men, and the like; but the hero of the evening was a character.

He had once been a trooper in the army in the Low Countries, a soldier of fortune, if ever there was one.

He dubbed himself "captain," and called himself Pickard, showing his commission in proof of this; but there were many who doubted his right to the title and name.

He had, however, tried ever since to wear a military suit, tarnished, it is true, but still, renewed whenever he had luck.

In fact he kept two suits, one to wear when he was in luck. When the run was against him, this went to his uncle, and he appeared in his old clothes.

As his runs of luck were very rare, his fine uniform lasted him an indefinite period.

He was a man of nearly fifty, with hair once black, but now grizzled; while his uniform, once drab and orange, was of no particular colour at all. The drab was nearly whitey-brown, and the orange, from exposure to sun and rain, was simply indescribable.

He, however, wore a sword of such portentous length as to be jeeringly spoken of as a roasting-spit.

He was usually a braggadocio, that is, when there were any friends about.

To-night he was very humble, and bowed and spoke gently to all who entered.

When Dick and his friend came in he rose, bowed, and was most effusive in his thanks. He was well aware that it would bring him a bumper.

Dick pooh-poohed his gratitude, and ordered, amid loud applause, drinks all round, after which he slipped five guineas into the tattered captain's hand, who coloured with pleasure and satisfaction.

Then came toasts and songs, always the staple of such proceedings.

They were of the usual slangy character, and even worse—coarse beyond anything we can conceive, but all the more enjoyed in such a company.

What wonder, when in society they were as bad, though the words used were not so rough and crude.

There was much smoking and drinking, and the atmosphere began to be simply dreadful. Dick whispered to Tom that it was almost time to go; but Tom had to give his donation, and give a song.

Tom was a wag always. Brought up at college he retained many of the traits which he learned there, and there was a certain amount of refinement under the roughness which his profession necessarily engendered.

He determined on a topical song, but one which he firmly believed not one of the company would understand.

When it came to his turn he began in a rich voice as follows :—

THE WATERY MOON.

The wat'ry moon is in the sky,
Looking all dim and pale on high;
And the traveller gazes with anxious eye,
 And thinks it will rain full soon ;
And he draws his cloak around him tight,
But if I be not mistaken quite,
He will open that cloak again to-night
 Beneath the wat'ry moon.

The wat'ry moon is sinking low,
The traveller's beast is dull and slow,
And neither word, nor spur, nor blow
 Will bring him sooner boon.
But the saddle-bags are heavy and full,
And all too much for a beast so dull,
Up this steep shady hill to pull,
 Beneath the wat'ry moon.

The wat'ry moon is gone to bed;
The traveller on his way has sped ;
The horse seems lighter the road to tread,
 And he'll be home very soon :
But with a young man he met on the hill,
Who lighten'd his load with right good will,
Hoping often to show the same kindness still,
 Beneath the wat'ry moon.

Before he had finished there was almost dead silence in the room.

These wild, rude east-enders were utterly overwhelmed. There were perhaps half a dozen in the room who understood, but to the others it was utter Hebrew.

Dick laughed silently until the tears ran down his cheeks, while the others looked on dumbfounded.

But the convivial spirit prevailed, and slight applause arose. Dick, to put them in good humour, started with one of his hottest ditties, after which Tom rose and added his contribution to Captain Pickard, and with Dick slipped out of the room.

"That was rough on the rum uns," said Dick, when they were at the bottom of the stairs, laughing heartily ; "I never saw such mugs in my life."

"Did it for pure fun !" remarked Tom.

"Of course, but they mostly thought it was Hebrew," continued Dick.

And after that they went to a den where the smoke was less dense, the atmosphere not quite so thick, the drink better, but the company after all not much better.

Meanwhile, how had Captain Pickard fared out of that night's entertainment ?

He had got twenty guineas. What for? To aid him in carrying out one of the most cruel and remorseless schemes ever concocted, a scheme which could only be carried out by means of murder.

CHAPTER CXXI.

IS HE THE MAN ?

Sometimes when the captain had a few shillings to spare, he would visit one of those recently-introduced dining places, where boiled beef and carrots were disposed of with suet dumplings and beer.

It was a filling dinner at the price. He knew several dens where, in the evening, he could come upon drinks, on the strength of past geniality, but none where a dinner could be procured on credit.

The captain had exhausted his credit years before. He took it good humouredly, and when he had money spent it freely in his old haunts, but could not restore confidence in the landlord class.

About a week previous to the convivial meeting at the "Two Spies," he was in one of these places called the "Mustard Pot," from its using this recently-introduced condiment.

He had a small table to himself and sat next to two young gentlemen of that class yclept lawyer's clerks.

They were talking, as is common with such juveniles, of business, relating the secrets of the office.

"Rum thing about the Pickard case," began one ; "queerest thing out."

"What's up ?"

The tattered captain pricked up his ears.

"Well ! Pickard, who came into some coin unexpectedly, about fifteen years back, died suddenly a month ago—no will and that sort of thing. But nobody cared."

"What's the upshot ?"

"Ten days after, an heir-at-law turns up, Samuel Pickard's elder brother, thought to be dead long ago, writes to say, knowing of the fortune—land and money—that being tired of the Low Countries, he is about to return to England."

"Ah ! quite startling !"

"Says he'll be here three weeks after the letter," the other continued, "coming along the Dover Road. Hopes to reach London next Saturday. This is Monday. But time's up."

The two talkative young fellows rose and went out, leaving the captain dumbfounded.

His cunning and tortuous brain at once conceived a cold-blooded and nefarious design.

Already he had in his possession some papers belonging to this man, his commission, private letters, and diary, in which were entered the dates of the births of several members of the family, and all concerned.

What foul thought is this which falls from some infernal cloud on his black soul ?

To waylay, murder, and personate this man!

To this end it is that he goes east, hunts up his friends, and gets up the friendly lead—a subscription—to facilitate murder!

The day after the meeting he borrowed a horse and rode along the direct road to Dover.

In those days there was but one, and there could be no mistake about it.

The captain knew that almost every traveller stopped at one particular house—the " Blue Boar." It was one easy stage to London.

The battered captain took a modest room, paid for it in advance, and lived soberly and quietly, thus earning a favourable name in the house.

He took his horse out for exercise every day, took his meals in the taproom, and behaved with such modesty that he was very well thought of. He was not penurious or mean, and even invited some of the visitors to join him in a modest drink.

It was Friday, about four o'clock, when a man about the captain's size and build came up to the door of the tavern, and alighted. He was well though plainly dressed, and had a small portmanteau strapped behind.

Though his dress was not actually military, it was impossible to mistake him for anything else but a soldier.

He was pleasant, full of life and energy, and told capital stories.

He spoke like a foreigner; but this he explained by saying that he had been out of England in a Walloon regiment for years, and was now come to England to seek his relatives, and to spend on them his savings and his half-pay.

All had congratulated him on his good fortune. The traveller invited them all to drink his health, and a very pleasant evening was spent.

It was late when they retired, but the traveller said it mattered not, as he had now only an easy stage to London, and should start very early.

It was late when he resumed his journey; in fact, four hours after the stranger from London had taken his departure.

He had paid up scrupulously, thanked everybody, behaved fairly liberal to the servants, and then departed.

That evening, in a copse by the roadside, on the skirt of the wood, some poor women who were collecting sticks found the body of a man and the body of a horse.

Both were quite dead.

The news spread like wildfire, and the occurrence having taken place within a mile of the inn, many visited the scene of the tragedy. Amongst others was the landlord of the " Blue Boar."

He at once recognised the inoffensive if impecunious lodger, who had only left his tavern that morning.

He knew him by his clothes, his general appearance, and other signs; but his face was so gashed that it was undistinguishable.

Still, everyone who had seen him would swear to his identity.

By one of those extraordinary coincidences which do happen sometimes in life, Dick Turpin and Tom King, rather wearied with dissipation, had started for a long ride that day, and, going rather farther than they expected, determined to rest that night at the " Blue Boar."

The first thing they heard of in the coffee room was the cruel murder.

They paid little attention until a description of the clothes caused them to exchange glances and start.

" Can I see the body? I seem to recognise the description," said Dick.

" Certainly, sir," said the coroner's officer, rising and preparing to lead the way to the out-house, whither the two strangers at once followed him.

A light was held up, and the travellers gazed fixedly on the body.

" Very like," said Dick, " but not the man I thought."

And the disappointed officer turned away, but was soon recompensed by a crown piece.

" Sorry to have troubled you," Dick said.

" 'Taint no trouble at all," the other replied.

In the course of the evening they heard about the traveller who had returned from the Low Countries in search of his relations, and to enjoy his money.

Dick could not help it; couldn't tell why, but the matter puzzled him.

" Who could want to kill old Pickard?" remarked Dick. " It seems strange to me. He always said he was in a Walloon regiment. It's queer altogether to me. Hanged if I don't look the thing up."

And when Dick made a promise he generally carried it out.

CHAPTER CXXII.

ON THE TRACK OF BLOOD.

Dick and Tom went to London and made inquiries; but of course, having no clue, made no progress.

They went here, there, and everywhere in search of the other traveller. They had gathered that he was of the same size and build as the poor traveller, only he was so well dressed.

The rich man appeared younger than the poor man, though bronzed and tanned.

A vague suspicion of an awful crime entered into the mind of Dick.

But days passed and no clue came.

Then one night he and Tom strolled into a semi-fashionable gaming house, where there was no restriction except good dress and readiness to spend money.

The tables were pretty full, and several persons were crowded round one particular player. He was well dressed in foreign uniform, and playing with marvellous recklessness.

Dick placed himself in a position where he could see without being seen.

He started and drew back

" If that aint Jack Pickard, then I'm a Dutchman," whispered Dick to Tom.

He now went to an *habitué* of the establishment and asked for information as to the incautious player.

" Oh, he's new in town. He's Colonel John Pickard, who has just retired from a Walloon regiment on half pay. He had come home to enjoy his savings, which are said to be large. While looking for the address of his relations he found himself heir to considerable property, to the great grief of a widow and an orphan son."

" Very hard!" said Dick.

" He was the elder son, you see, and the property was willed to him, and in default to his younger brother."

"Thanks," said Dick, and he went out with Tom.

Dick saw it all at once.

The dead man was the real John Pickard, whose name this swaggering captain had assumed for so many years. He must have heard of the officer's good fortune in some mysterious way, and laid an infernal plan to supplant him.

Dick had met many men who asserted that the sham captain was really a certain Joe Simon; but if he chose to swagger about as a captain, it was no business of theirs to interfere, they remarked.

Dick determined to watch. He had got a task after his own heart to do.

About two the Walloon officer came out. If this man were indeed playing a part, he was playing it well.

He had taken enough to enjoy himself, but not to lose command over himself. If Dick's surmise proved right, he knew too well the value of the stakes he was playing for to run any risk.

He turned to the right and went up the street—one of respectable appearance in a good neighbourhood. Before he had gone a hundred yards he entered a well known hotel, and disappeared.

Dick made up his mind. As he had seen the other leave the hall he entered, and went up to the night porter.

"Rather late to-night," he said, "and a long way from home. Can you manage me a bed?" and he put a guinea in the other's hand.

"Yessah!" and the obliging Cerberus rang a bell, when a sleepy-looking night chambermaid appeared.

In those days of rollicking Mohawkism, hotels that wanted to make money had to be up to all these things.

"Bed for a gen'lm," said the porter.

"This way, sir," said the woman, and, taking up a candle, she led direct to a room, where she left him.

"Call me at nine," he said, putting half a crown into her hand.

Precisely at nine he was called, and as soon as he was dressed said he should take a stroll before breakfast, and went out.

His first visit was to a friendly costumier, where he changed himself from the smart swaggerer about town to a respectable city scrivener, with a scratch wig and spectacles.

He then went and breakfasted elsewhere.

This ceremony over, he returned to the neighbourhood of the hotel, where there was a smoking den, in which a man could lounge, gossip, smoke, and sip liqueurs.

Dick had a hackney coach waiting, and as long as he paid, no questions were asked.

His patience was rewarded, for precisely at twelve he saw a coach drive up into which Colonel Pickard entered and drove off.

"Follow at a distance," said Dick, entering his coach.

"Right, you are," replied the other.

The colonel drove to the City, followed by the sleuth hound. Dick was nothing else when once he set upon anyone's track.

The first cab halted in Fleet-street, near the end of Chancery Lane, before the house of a well-known firm of solicitors, Bagshaw and Lyons, who bore a high character, as Dick had often heard.

Dick drove past a little way.

Then, as now, there were taverns in Chancery Lane, and there happened to be one of some note, though grim and small, near at hand—near enough to observe the house.

We will follow Colonel Pickard in his interview with Mr. Bagshaw.

This gentleman had been a personal friend of the late Samuel Pickard, and had acted as his solicitor ever since he had come into his property.

He was a friend, too, of the widow and orphan.

The appearance of this claimant was a terrible blow to the man of law. In strict legality, the estate was liable for all arrears, but if this man proved himself the rightful heir, there would not be a penny left for Mrs. Pickard and for her only son Joseph, a fine youth of sixteen, who was at school when his father died.

But the documents produced by the Walloon officer were unimpeachable, and his account of himself in accordance with family tradition.

Mrs. Pickard, who had been married twenty two years, remembered well the restless scapegrace uncle going away after a quarrel with his father. As a young man, he had been rather wild, and given his father a great deal of trouble

He wound up by decamping with a considerable amount in cash, and from that day until his return, nothing had been heard of him.

But his papers were all right, and the little book in which were the names and dates of the family, with their births, on being compared with the family bible, was found to be correct.

Mr. Bagshaw had seen the disconsolate widow, and she had reluctantly owned that, as far as she was able to judge, everything was correct and proper.

The lawyer could not deny that his brevet papers were all that could be desired, and his testimonials of the highest character.

He was at his wits' end.

It was useless going to law. There was no money to speak of, and the poor disinherited family wanted all that was left.

When Colonel Pickard entered the lawyer's room, it was with an air of easy swagger, not uncommon on the part of a soldier of fortune.

"Well, Mr. Bagshaw," he said, "I suppose all the proofs have been looked into, and everything is quite clear and shipshape?"

"Yes!" replied the lawyer, reluctantly. "I think we may say, yes—but of course, there are the law's delays. Meantime, wouldn't you like to see your property? Young Joe, your nephew, is a fine fellow, and, I presume, you will do something for them, as you take all!"

"Well!" after reflection, "I will go down this very day—it isn't far?"

"Only at Chiselhurst; it's a very pretty place. No children?"

"No."

"Then you may make young Joe your heir?" insinuated the lawyer.

"S'death—not a bad notion!" responded the Walloon officer, with a few choice oaths.

Swift was right. They did swear a little in Flanders in those days.

A brief conference followed, after which Colonel John Pickard left to lunch and ride down to his little place in Kent, as he already called it.

He had not been gone ten minutes when a clerk entered with a roughly-folded note fastened with a wafer.

The lawyer tore it open impatiently.

"Matter of life and death *in re* Pickard!" a

lawyer's clerk had written this; "Must see you. A friend of the widow and the orphan !"

"Show him up," exclaimed William Bagshaw, with a great bound at his heart—though a lawyer, he had a good deal of heart.

Dick entered demurely, and took a proferred seat.

"Well, sir ?" cried Bagshaw.

"One moment, sir," said Dick, "I have my reasons for not appearing publicly in this matter. My name is John Palmer, but if my information proves valuable, you will need no more. I ask no reward, but to expose a most nefarious transaction."

"No reward—that be——! but I give you a promise never to reveal anything you tell me, as from you," cried Bagshaw.

"Then, sir, that fellow who has just gone out is no more *the* John Pickard than I am. The real John Pickard lies buried in a pauper's grave, murdered by that unhanged scoundrel, Joe Simon, *alias* Captain John Pickard. The scoundrel robbed him of his name and other things twenty years ago—and I can prove it !"

"God bless my soul, sir !" gasped the lawyer, very red in the face. "That cupboard—brandy !"

Dick in a moment had the spirit-stand and glasses on the table. He helped the lawyer first, and then himself. In his absence of mind he took two.

Mr. Bagshaw soon recovered himself, rang the bell, and when the clerk appeared, told him that he would see nobody until further orders.

Then Dick told pretty well all the reader knows, and what he suspected.

"If this body is exhumed, you can bring witnesses to identify it ?" asked Mr. Bagshaw.

"Yes ! but, Mr. Bagshaw, this man is a lawless ruffian of the lowest kind, the companion of the worst criminals, a footpad, and now an assassin. Those who identify him must not be troubled."

"I will contrive all this !" said Bagshaw; "anything to save the widow of my old friend. But now, Mr. Palmer, can't you help me in this matter ?"

"Privately !" the other answered, hesitatingly.

"It is a terrible crime, and I would do much to have it laid bare and the man punished—but, I myself—if I could only trust you !"

"Sir," said Bagshaw, taking his hand, "anything you tell me, shall, on my honour as a man, be held as sacred secrets of my office."

"Then, sir, I am Dick Turpin !" was the quiet answer,—"the highwayman !"

Mr. Bagshaw let go his hand and stared at him in utter astonishment.

"It is true, sir. My life has brought me acquainted with many rare and extraordinary secrets. Many noblemen have trusted me. When I tell you that I am confidentially employed to frustrate the machinations of Brian Seymour against the Earl of Elphick, Baron Mountjoye, you will understand."

"I don't, upon my soul ! But I know what you mean," said the amazed lawyer; "all I do know is, I want you to help me to unmask this villain."

"I will, sir," was the fervent reply.

And a long and confidential interview followed.

CHAPTER CXXIII.

DOWN AT CHERRY FARM.

The late Samuel Pickard when he succeeded to a snug City business and a compact little estate in Kent, well worth eight hundred a year, conceived the idea of sending his son to school, with a view of bringing him up to one of the professions.

So Joseph Pickard went on until at fifteen he was in the sixth form of an excellent school. He was a tall, handsome fellow, brave as a lion, no bully, and the protector of the weak.

From the moment he was promoted to the position he now occupied, he was looked upon with awe by those below.

To appreciate this, the reader must understand that the highest form in the school—the sixth—were regarded by the fags and other subordinate classes, with an inexpressible reverence and terror.

They were considered as exempt from the frailties of schoolboy nature ; no one ventured to affix a limit to their power. Like the gods of the lotus eater, they lay beside their nectar, rarely communing with ordinary mortals, except to give an order, and set a punishment. On the form immediately below them part of their glory was reflected ; these were a sort of demigods awaiting their translation into a higher Olympus of perfect omnipotence.

In this intermediate space flourished, at that time, one Teddy Bowles, a fat, small-eyed youth, with immense pendent, pallid cheeks, rejoicing in the name of "Buttons," his father being eminent in that line in the midland metropolis. The son was Brummagem to the back bone. He was intensely stupid ; but having been a fixture in the school beyond the memory of the oldest inhabitant, he had slowly gravitated on into his present position, on the old ring principle—"weight must tell." He had been bullied continuously for many years, and now, with a dull pertinacious malignity, was biding his time, intending, on his accession to power, to inflict reprisals on those below him ; or, in his own expressive language, to "take it out of 'em, like smoke." He was keeping his hand in by the perpetration of small tyrannies on all whom he was not afraid to meddle with.

But hitherto, from a lingering suspicion, perhaps, that it was not quite safe, he had never annoyed Joe Pickard.

It was on a Saturday, the hebdomadal saturnalia, when the week's work was over, and no one had anything to do. The heart of Teddy was jocund with pork chops and mulled beer, and, his evil genius tempting him, he proposed to three of his intimates "to go and give the Count a turn."

Nearly everyone had a nickname, and this had been given to Joe, partly from some dormant idea that his standoffishness and dignified manner were due to aristocratic origin.

When the quartette entered the room, Joe knew perfectly well what they came for ; but he sat quite still and silent, while two of them held him down by the arms in his chair.

"I think you'd look very well with a cross on, Count," Buttons said ; "so keep steady while we decorate you."

As he spoke he was mixing up a paste with tallow and candle snuff, and when it was ready came nearer to daub the cross on Pickard's forehead.

The two who held him were quite deceived by Joe's unexpected tranquility, and had somewhat relaxed their grasp as they leant forward to witness the operation; but the fourth, standing idle, saw all at once the pupils of his eyes contract, and his lips set so ominously, that the words were in his mouth, "hold him fast," when Joe, exerting the full force of his arms, shook himself clear; and, grasping a brass candlestick within his reach, struck the executioner straight between the eyes.

The effect of freeing himself to some extent broke the force of the blow, or the great Bowles dynasty might have ended there and then; as it was, Buttons fell like a log, and, rolling once over on his face, lay there bleeding and motionless.

While the assistants were too much astonished to detain him, Joe walked out without a glance at his prostrate enemy; and, going straight to the head of the school, told him what had happened.

The character of the aggressor was so well known, that when they found he was not seriously hurt, they let Pickard off easy with two books of the *Iliad* to write out in Greek.

Buttons kept the sick room for ten days, and came out looking more pasty than ever, with his pleasant propensities decidedly checked for the time.

In his parish church at Birmingham—two tons of marble weighing him down—the old button-maker sleeps with his fathers, and Joseph II. some time reigned in his stead, and exercised while he lived, over his factory people, the same ingenuity of torture which in old times nearly drove the fags to rebellion.

But though he rose to the distinction of alderman, and was a Demosthenes in the town council and a Draco in the board of guardians, in the centre of his broad face, marring the placidity of its smooth-shaven respectability, still burned angrily a dark red scar—Joe's sign manual—which he carried to his grave.

Such was the youth who was suddenly summoned to his sick father, at Cherry Farm, as the estate was called, to find him dead.

The citizen had been a good parent and an excellent husband, and was mourned accordingly.

The funeral was over, and Joe Pickard was discussing his future career with his mother. He had quietly determined to buy a commission, the business being carried on by his worthy trustees, when the awful news came that uncle John was coming home.

The long-lost elder brother had turned up at last.

It was an awful blow. It meant almost ruin.

The business was the outcome of the money, and a strict inheritor could claim that instead of ten years' income illegally spent.

At all events, there would be a ruinous lawsuit.

Mrs. Pickard had her jewels—not many—and some fifty guineas, and that was all with which to begin the world anew, if this terrible news proved to be true.

On the day before the appearance of Dick Turpin on the scene, the lawyer had seen them both, and told Joe that he was afraid he was solely dependent on his uncle's bounty.

Joe was for a moment struck down.

"Mr. Bagshaw," he then said, "you must find me work."

"Well, now, Joe, your uncle doesn't seem such a bad fellow. He only takes what the law allows him. You are his sole heir, and I should do nothing until I saw him. No doubt he will be delighted to let Mrs. Pickard remain here, and let you finish your education."

"He is a stranger, and never bore the best of characters," insisted Mrs. Pickard.

"Young men will be young men. The colonel has changed much. His letter from abroad, written to me, which proves his identity more than anything else, or how could he have recollected my name, expressly says that he is coming here in the hope of making his relatives happy with his savings and his pay."

"It speaks well for his kindness," said the widow, in a musing way; "Joe, I think we'd better wait and see what he is like."

And they did wait, and when they did see him some instinctive monitor bade them dislike him.

He was pompously generous, told them to consider themselves at home, and later on they would discuss the future.

Then he asked for strong waters, and having satisfied himself, walked out to a hostelrie called the "Wheatsheaf" to introduce himself as the new owner of Cherry Farm and all its belongings.

That evening the widow and orphan received a visit from a Mr. Foster, a gentleman dressed in quiet civilian garb, who brought a strong letter of introduction from Mr. Bagshaw:—

"Trust him and be careful. He brings you good news."

They were together in a small cozy parlour.

"What can he mean?" asked Mrs. Pickard.

"Be calm, my friends, and learn to conceal your feelings. If you betray the least sign of what I am about to tell you all may yet be lost. That man who came to-day is an impostor. Mr. Bagshaw has sent me to give you hope. Only wait, and I promise you justice will be done."

It would be idle to attempt to depict the astonishment of the widow and the orphan.

When they recovered themselves they asked for an explanation.

"You would never be able to conceal your abhorrence of this man if I told you all," he retorted.

"I hope he will go away," said Widow Pickard.

And he did. Next morning after breakfast he declared that it would take time to get used to country life after the existence in courts, camps, and towns, and he should go up to London, make it his headquarters, and only come down occasionally.

In the meantime all was to go on as usual, he said, magnificently.

"It shall, sir," said Joe, with an emphasis which rather startled the colonel.

He, however, made no remark, and bolted off to the metropolis, never to return.

As soon as he was gone, Mr. Foster, otherwise Dick Turpin, told them the whole awful story, to which they listened with mingled awe, horror, semi-incredulity, and relief.

"That is not uncle!" said Joe.

"It is not," replied Dick.

"Thank heaven!" was his genuine cry, and soon after the visitor took his departure.

Meantime the order for exhumation of the body had been obtained, and about midnight, in an outhouse of the churchyard, the ghastly object was exposed to view.

There were present tavern-keepers, women of low stamp, and others, who declared they had known Joe Simon, alias Captain John Pickard, for years, and that was not his body.

Mr. John Palmer, who had had business with the rowdy captain, swore solemnly that not only was this not the body of the pseudo-Captain Pickard, but also swore solemnly that he had seen him alive there, within forty-eight hours, in the disguise of the Walloon Colonel Pickard.

Dick did not add, though everyone understood it, "and that is the body of the colonel."

The officials, Mr. Bagshaw, and Dick returned to town at early morn, and went to the private house of Sir John Fielding, the magistrate, and laid the case before him.

There was the affidavit of Mr. Bagshaw, of John Palmer, and a statement signed by several others.

But one piece of evidence was even more conclusive.

Mr. John Palmer had on several occasions seen in the possession of the battered captain of the stews that very stolen commission on which for twenty years he had founded his claim to brevet rank.

Sir John Fielding at once signed the warrant for his apprehension.

The supposed Walloon colonel had not returned to London in such high spirits as he had left it.

That morning the manner of the widow and orphan had changed. There was a stiffness and coldness about them he could not make out.

Did they suspect him?

No—it was only his fancy. Everything was all right. Even the lawyer had confessed that his proofs of identity were complete.

But the colonel longed above everything for his old life. He dared not, however, go to any of the haunts which had recently been his for years.

He knew, however, of others of a superior kind which he had not visited for years. He knew, too, where to find some of the *habitués*, and in the afternoon sauntered into one of them, made himself agreeable, and when he expressed a desire to see life, several eagerly offered to take him to some famous places.

"Been a soldier, you know—dice and cards, you know!" he said, laughing.

He was supping with three rollicking blades whom he knew by sight, but who never suspected in this resplendent new arrival from the Continent battered old Jack Pickard.

After a copious and jovial supper they rose and started, arm in arm, for the Rum-Pum-Pah Club, as it was called in the slang of the day.

It was particularly flash, but attended by all sorts of men—highwaymen, broken *roués* with some means left, gamesters, and the like.

Some called it the Gleaners' Club, because it was frequented by men who had once been rich, but had been brought to ruin by women, dice, and cards.

These men would sneak in and sit down, on the strength of old membership, waiting for something to turn up. It generally did in the shape of a chop, a bottle, and perhaps a guinea, from a chum in luck.

The sham colonel knew it well, but was careful not to reveal his knowledge. He listened, and was soon hard at some game with his new friends.

They at once saw that he was not a man to be cheated, but ready to win or lose as fortune decided.

It happened on this occasion that he was losing, and he never moved a muscle.

The fact was, having plenty of money at his disposal, he wanted to establish a good reputation at first, let what might come afterwards.

They played and drank, and some sang, in glorious thought only of to-day. To-morrow was an unknown quantity.

Several persons came in and out as lookers-on or to drink and exchange words with friends. All were not necessarily gamblers there. Some were artists, poets, and *petit maitres* of the second or third-rate class.

There were tables for eating and drinking, and a bar, round which lounged several of the usual customers.

They chatted, laughed, and made jokes as if there were no care nor trouble in the world.

Presently in lounged Dick Turpin in his usual town costume, with Tom King behind. There was, moreover, another—a quiet, seedy-looking man.

To him Dick whispered, and the other immediately went out.

Dick and Tom went up to the bar and ordered brandy, keeping their eyes on the wretched assassin.

Presently four men, known as Bow Street runners, entered, causing a great flutter. But they took notice of one man only.

Upon him they soon had a powerful grip.

"Hands off!—what does it mean?" that man gasped.

Now—Joe Simon—*alias* Jack Pickard—I arrest you for the murder of Colonel John Pickard—and twenty other crimes!"

The scene may, as it is commonly expressed, be more easily imagined than described.

All rose in confusion, and stared wildly at the Bow Street runners and their struggling victim.

He was instantly overcome and handcuffed, and marched out amidst murmurs of abhorrence and detestation.

The evidence was too clear to be resisted, and ere a fortnight was over, the bragging captain suffered the just penalty of his crime.

The widow and her boy came into their inheritance; their gratitude to Dick Turpin being great indeed.

Mr. Bagshaw, the lawyer, insisted on his taking a hundred guineas, which, after some hesitation, he accepted.

CHAPTER CXXIV.

A STARTLING RESOLVE.

Two days later, Dick Turpin had an interview with the Blue Dwarf, at his own residence.

He little expected the startling nature of the announcement that was about to be made to him.

"Would you like to go to America?" said Sapathwa, with a grin.

"America!" gasped Dick.

"Yes!" replied the other. "The fact is, my Lord and my Lady Mountjoye are weary of the persecutions they are enduring. To lead the life they do is simply beyond their power. Lady

Laura is in delicate health—so is the child. A month hence we shall start for America. I go with them. We intend to travel, to penetrate into the Indian territory. Now, we shall want some brave friends. I have thought of you and Tom King; what say you?"

"Done!" replied Dick.

"Well, be ready in three weeks. During that time you can amuse yourself in the best way you like. Don't take much luggage. You will get a rough outfit when over there."

"All right, sir," replied Dick, rising.

"You will find a goodly sum in this pocket-book."

"About Black Bess?"

"You must put her out to grass for awhile," laughed Sapathwa; "she will be all the better for it."

Dick after this retired, and went to announce the amazing intelligence to Tom. It almost took his breath away.

After some little discussion, it was decided to take a week or ten days' jaunt into the country, and then to pass a week with Dick's friends.

Where should they go?

Well! they would start in the direction of York, and let chance decide the rest.

A very jolly evening followed, spent in one of their favourite haunts, where wine and wassail ruled the roast.

It was noon the next day before they were ready to start, which they did at a trot. Their first stage was Hounslow Heath, to visit the renowned "Cat and Bagpipes," which hostelry was a favourite rendezvous of theirs.

Mine host was fat and jolly, with a greasy chuckle of the most unctuous kind. He was on excellently good terms with himself and all the world, excepting the poorer portion of it.

Tramps, beggars, and such like he detested. Paying poor rates, he washed his hands of the poor; they were to him as noxious vermin in the land.

Josiah Myrtle was at his door when the two friends rode up.

He laughed with delight. He knew them of old, and knew that after a ride they would want copious refreshment.

He hurried in, gave hasty orders, and then returned to receive them.

They had already alighted and were ascending the steps. Myrtle preceded them into the parlour, where they shook hands heartily.

"I've ordered dinner in the bar parlour," he then said; "but here comes Joe with the tankards."

And so he did come, with shining goblets filled with foaming old ale.

'Tis marvellous how much beer drinking has to do with the prosperity of a nation. England and Germany prove this.

The Puritans were good soldiers and pious men, but they would not have fought so well had they not lived on rounds of beef and quarts of strong ale.

Temperance is good in many ways, but the cant of abstinence is wearisome and nauseous.

The tankards were soon put away, and then the friends talked.

Myrtle found business pretty "fairish," he said, but it might be better.

And so the hours passed until it was time for dinner, which turned out to be a most recherché little affair.

None of your kickshaws, French and Italian messes, for them, but solid English fare of the cut-and-come-again sort.

After dinner Dick and Tom announced their intention of passing the evening there and making a night of it. Both Dick and Tom had friends in the neighbourhood, and expressed a wish to see them.

So about an hour later they determined to stretch their horses' legs, each going to invite his friend to the festive board that night.

Dick's friend, Farmer Jenkins, lived about five miles off in a pretty rural village on the borders of the heath.

He was at home, and gladly accepted the invitation, of course with the inevitable condition of Dick's coming in and taking something.

Taking something was Dick's weakness, and a very jolly hour was spent before he mounted Black Bess to return.

His way lay along a green lane. He had not gone far before he came to a place where one large tree overshadowed a dark and gloomy pool.

Here he was met by a man who was what was then called half-saved. He was perfectly harmless, though often very annoying, and the malady of the brain under which he was suffering was rather an aberration of intellect than the complete loss of judgment.

He approached Dick with a quick step, waving a stick. Dick had befriended him on more than one occasion. He was dressed in an old white coat, now of very indifferent colour, with a steeple-crowned hat which had seen the wars of the Great Rebellion, rusty and battered, but still whole, and decorated with two cock's feathers which he had torn himself from the tail of some luckless chanticleer.

His grey worsted hose were darned with many a colour, and in his lean but muscular hand he carried a cudgel, which usually steadied his steps, he being slightly lame in the right leg.

"Ware-hawks!" he said, pointing to the heath; "just seen the fox and the dog. The dog was telling the fox that he had seen you; and the fox had a red coat on, and has gone to fetch his fellows."

"Thanks, John," exclaimed Dick, throwing him half-a-crown; "many thanks. If you find anything fresh, come to the "Cat and Bagpipes.""

And Dick rode off to the end of the lane, where the heath began, and peered out. About a mile off he made out one of the Bow Street runners riding off. He was waving his whip as if for a signal, and Dick knew there was not a moment to be lost.

About a mile off was a deep pond, in the edge of which was a gallows, with some notorious criminal hanging in chains.

When he reached this, Dick could make by a roundabout way for the "Cat and Bagpipes," which he did not intend to visit, however, until after dusk.

He made for the gallows; but just as he reached it he saw Pooly emerge from some bushes not far in front of him, while on the other side were four other officers.

He clenched his teeth, saw that his pistols were prepared for service, and rode for the head officer. He had his heavy riding-whip ready.

The officer awaited him calmly, calling to his men to join him.

"THEY HEARD A SHOT FIRED, AND NEXT MOMENT SAW THE YOUNG SQUIRE
RUNNING AWAY!"

Dick never swerved to the right or the left; but, when within twenty yards of the runner, levelled quickly and fired.

The runner's horse swerved and threw him. Dick urged his horse to its utmost speed, and soon found he was leaving his pursuers far behind. Besides, they had seen the accident, and could not leave their chief.

Dick continued on his way, and, going a long way round, returned to the inn, where he was anxiously awaited.

He had a brief conversation with the landlord, who agreed to keep a sharp look-out for dangerous characters.

With this assurance Dick went in and joined his friends, who were delighted to see him.

They spent a most jovial evening, and did not break up until the early hours of the morning.

Soon after breakfast our adventurers again started on their way, reaching St. Albans in the afternoon. Here they determined to pass the night, there being another hostelrie where they were well known.

Here they were quiet, as the guests in the coffee-room were strangers, and our friends on the look out to pick up something that might lead to trade.

But they were not in luck that night, so went to bed a little dissatisfied with their day's work.

Up early. All work and no play might make Dick a dull boy; but all money going out and none coming in was eminently unsatisfactory.

They were on foot early next day, and rode along quietly. Their way now was along a long and rather unfrequented road which passed through an extensive wood of a very pleasing and picturesque character.

At length a pleasant open glade was reached, where they agreed to pause and refresh, they being always provided with everything needful in case of accident.

A meat-pie and a hunk of bacon were, with bread, the solids provided, and, as a matter of course, there was no lack of drinkables.

They consumed a hearty meal, and then sat down to smoke and drink.

After that they indulged in a nap, leaving themselves to be protected by their horses, who would be certain to warn them in case of danger.

They slept a couple of hours, and then rousing up continued their journey.

They had gone about a hundred yards, and were still in the thick of the wood, when they heard a shot fired, and next moment saw a young man come running away.

He crossed the path which they were following and dashed into the wood upon the other side.

Guided by groans, they went to the spot whence the man had emerged, and found a rough-looking, tolerably-well-dressed man lying on the ground in the agonies of death.

"What has happened?"

"Shot—by him!"

And the man leaned back and died.

Dick and Tom returned to where their horses stood, and, remounting, rode off to the nearest village.

Finding a constable, they gave information, agreeing to wait at an inn until the return of the men with the body.

They were an hour gone, and when they came back the body was recognised as that of a small farmer of not too good a reputation.

When Dick described the appearance of the man who had fled after committing the crime, all exchanged glances.

"It was young Squire Stuart, surely," said one, "he who was knocked down by Jackson at Sandy Fair."

"How was that?" asked Dick.

"He insulted a girl, and the squire took her part, and Jackson, who was a big brute, knocked him down, and then bashed him about the head with a stick and ran away," said the other. "Then the squire swore that he would shoot the scoundrel whenever he found him."

"Looks bad!" said Dick.

"Main bad!" the other answered.

While they were speaking the constable had slipped out, going direct to a magistrate to give information.

Before two hours had elapsed it was known that young Squire Henry Stuart had been arrested for the murder of Jacob Jackson.

The squire was universally beloved and respected. It was true his temper was hot, but his feelings were always on the right side.

The fatal incident had been preceded by an event which made some give credence to the report.

It was Sandy Fair, at which it was the custom for all classes to show themselves, if even only for a quarter of an hour.

It was a fair for fun and frolicsome enjoyment as well as for business.

One of its principal features was a great booth, which combined a ball room and a drinking bar.

Here the lads and lasses disported themselves on the light fantastic toe, while the elders drank, smoked, and looked on.

Squire Henry Stuart and a friend, Harold Glenmore, were passing, when they were attracted by a singularly sweet voice, that of a woman, who between the dances was singing for the delectation of the crowd.

"Let us go in," said the squire, laughing, "and hear this siren."

And he led the way, followed by his friend.

The singer was a dark and very handsome girl of about nineteen, beside whom stood a tall, thin man, rather the worse for wear.

They were both gipsies, but he had been pulled down by a long illness, and was glad to seek a living by the exhibition of his daughter's and his own accomplishments on the zither, then a favourite gipsy instrument.

The girl having finished her song took off her little velvet cap and came round in search of her reward, which consisted of coppers as a rule. But as she passed Stuart and Glenmore they gave her silver.

She smiled and curtsied in a most bewitching manner, and turned to continue her round.

The next application was to a rude, rough farmer named Jacob Jackson—a coarse, ugly, and herculean brute.

"Money for that squeaking! Not I. But here's sixpence for a kiss from them red lips."

Several laughed, and the girl was about to pass on, when, before she was aware, he had thrown his strong arm round her slender waist and drawn her close to him. Uttering a cry of terror, she pressed him back with her hands, exclaiming—

"Father! help!" adding something in the Romany dialect.

Like a flash the old gipsy, feeble as he was, his eyes glittering with passion, darted across the floor, and sprang at Jacob Jackson with a scream of fury.

"Coward! brute!" he said frantically.

The fellow held the girl back with one arm. With the other grasping the old man, he hurled him back as if he had been a child.

All had occurred in a few seconds.

"Let the girl go!" said the squire, quietly, with a look in his eyes there was no mistaking.

A gleam of hate shone in the rascal's eye.

"Aint no business of yours," he said.

The squire advanced quietly.

Rapidly releasing the girl, who fled instantly to her father, before his opponent could suspect his intent, Jacob Jackson dealt him a fierce and savage blow, straight from the shoulder, that might have felled an ox.

Stuart reeled back. He must have been a stone wall not to have done so; but he would have recovered himself had he not tripped over a low seat, which sent him heavily to the ground.

Before he could recover himself, Jacob gave the squire a kick and fled, amid universal hootings and yells.

Glenmore helped his friend up.

"It was a cowardly, base thing," he said.

"Yes; but rest assured of this," replied Stuart, as he quitted the place, "in the end it is the coward who pays for it."

These words were remembered.

CHAPTER CXXV.

A DISCOVERY.

Dick Turpin was determined to see a little more of this affair.

Knowing the gipsies as he did, he thought that perhaps the old gipsy might explain the matter.

He was now very sorry for having made any allusion to the person whom he had seen flying from where the body was found.

He had heard the whole story, and heartily sympathised with the squire.

He invited Tom to take a stroll with him, to talk the matter over.

"I think the young squire might have trounced the vagabond," said Dick; "but I don't believe he shot him in cold blood."

"That's my idea, too," replied Tom; "at the same time I say, Served him right!"

Tom, however, agreed that it was just possible that if the gipsies could be found it might put another complexion on the matter.

Talking thus they had got into the very depths of the forest.

"Hist!" suddenly whispered Dick.

At no great distance they heard voices speaking in the Romany language.

They listened.

"I tell you, father, the brave young man shall not die," said a female voice. "He was injured in trying to save me from insult, and I will say I did it rather than harm befall him."

"You are very tender to the Georgios all of a sudden!" sneered the old gipsy; "what matters one more or less?"

"He shall not die! You shot the evil man who would have insulted me, and did right; but you must let them know."

"Go to prison! be shut out from the sun, the forest, and the light?" shrieked the man, whose name was Malachi; "be stuck between four

walls—never! I would rather kill you, Zarah, and fly."

"No—you stumpy Romany! you will do neither," said Turpin, stepping in and securing one arm, while Tom seized the other. "You must come before the magistrates."

Malachi struggled, but in vain. The girl did nothing, but looked inexpressibly pained.

Resistance she knew was useless, and when the two men carried off the furious, but sullen gipsy, she followed in their wake.

When they reached the village, they found it in an uproar. A great crowd was collected round the inn where the magistrates were sitting.

All withdrew to let the little procession pass. It was like a revelation.

There were several constables present, who at once made way, and when spoken to by Dick, secured the person of the gipsy.

Dick then passed on to the justice-room, where his presence excited some attention.

"That's him who saw the squire running away," said the constable who had given information of the murder.

"Well, sir, and why have you absented yourself, when your evidence was wanted here?" asked a fussy little magistrate.

"Because, sir, I was better employed!" was the cool, collected answer.

"Better employed!" cried the other; "take care; or I'll commit you for contempt. How could you be better employed than furthering the ends of justice?"

"But justice is sometimes blind, sir!" was the demure reply. "I have been looking for the real murderer!"

"And you have found him?" gasped several of those present.

"Yes! your worship!" continued Dick.

"Bring him in!" was the cry.

Dick made a sign; and, to the astonishment of Henry Stuart and Harold, the old gipsy was ushered in.

"How do you know this is the man?" asked a magistrate, in reality very much relieved.

"By his own confession!" and he told what he had heard.

The gipsy was now asked what he had to say. But he refused to answer.

The girl was asked if she could explain anything, and she made a passionate appeal for mercy.

When calmer, she volunteered an explanation.

After the scene in the booth, she and her father left the fair and went to one of their retreats in the forest. Her father was much put out and very angry with the Georgio. On her persuasion he, however, agreed to go away.

Next day they had started for another county. When passing through the forest they met Jacob Jackson. He felled her father to the ground, and seized her to carry her off.

But her father had recovered himself, and rose with a pistol in his hand. Jacob Jackson laughed him to scorn when he told him to put her down. Then the gipsy fired and the Georgio fell dead.

Hearing footsteps, they hid in the bushes in time to see Squire Stuart come up, gun in hand.

He stared wildly at the corpse, leaning on his gun, and then hurried away.

"I was so dazed and stunned," said the squire, "that I acted like a coward. Remembering what I had said at the fair, I thought if found standing over the body I should be accused of the murder. To avoid unpleasantness I hastened away. That is my explanation."

"I don't think anyone can blame you, Stuart," said the senior magistrate. "Such a charge is very unpleasant. Of course you are discharged, and the gipsy is remanded in custody."

Stuart moved away bowing.

"We are very much indebted to you, sir," addressing Dick Turpin, "for your prompt discovery of the real murderer. You have done a great kindness and service to a neighbour, for which we heartily thank you."

"And so do I," said the squire, shaking the highwayman heartily by the hand. "What put it in your head, if I may ask?"

"I know the gipsies well, even to speaking their lingo," replied Dick, "and when I heard the rights of the story I quickly came to the conclusion that you were wrongly accused of the old man's crime, so I set off at once to find the fellow, and by accident found him."

"Will you come and dine with me, Mr. ——"

"Palmer," was the reply. "Well, sir, I have a friend with me. We are only two London men about town taking a holiday."

"I don't care what you are," exclaimed Henry Stuart. "I know this, that under Providence you have saved my life."

By this time they had reached the coffee rooms, where their appearance was greeted with loud and tumultuous applause. Squire Stuart was a general favourite, and Dick had won all hearts by the service he had rendered to their friend.

A glass or two were taken in all goodfellowship, and then the squire, accompanied by Dick, Tom, and three other friends, started for Stavely Hall, owned by the squire.

It was a snug and comfortable place—a complete liberty hall—where good real old English hospitality was always to be found in copious abundance.

There was substantial fare and plenty of liquid to wash it down.

After this came a mighty bowl of punch, and cards.

It was a genuine case of won't go home till morning.

Dick Turpin and Tom King knew they were wasting their time very foolishly, but even great men must unbend sometimes, and they determined to see this case through.

Next morning was Tuesday, and the remand would be for Thursday, at the "Royal George," where the race balls took place, and quarter-sessions were held.

For in that time it was a very grand place. It was situated in the centre of the town, which was quite a rural place, with a river running through its midst.

The inn was close on the banks, and the magisterial inquiry was held in a large room with a balcony overlooking the stream.

The day was hot, and the windows were open.

There were three magistrates, a few of the upper ten, and a small muster of the popular class, so as to make it an open court.

A couple of constables stood, one on each side of the gipsy, whose daughter was allowed a seat on a bench.

She was quite overcome, and trembling.

The meeting was only a formal one. The only evidence to be given was that of Mr. John Palmer, of London, and Mr. Henry Markham, of the same place, as to the confession they had overheard.

They gave it as briefly as possible, signed their recognizances to appear at the trial, and stood down.

The senior magistrate turned to the gipsy and told him that he would be committed to prison to take his trial.

"Prison!" cried the gipsy, in a wild, raspy voice: "why should I go to prison? A vile Georgio insults my daughter, tries to steal her from me, and because I use the privilege of a man to chastise him, I shall be shut out from the light of day, taken away from the forest green and the bright sun. Never!" and with a wild bound, he rushed to the balcony, and before any one could interfere, had plunged into the river below.

It was too suddenly done for any to interfere. All stood spellbound, and with open mouths.

When the constables rushed to the balcony after him, not even a ripple was to be seen on the waters, which sped on quietly on their way to the ocean.

"I am not surprised," said Dick Turpin, quietly; "a gipsy would always rather die than suffer imprisonment."

The magistrates shrugged their shoulders. It was not their fault. Everybody to their taste. If a man preferred suicide to being shut up in a comfortable cell—well, it was his look-out.

Of course, there was a hurrying here and there on the banks of the stream, a search in all possible and impossible places, but nothing was found.

Only, that evening, after dark, a gipsy about fifty years of age, with a zither on his arm and a girl by his side, might have been seen entering the neighbouring wood.

We say, might have been seen, but they never were again.

Whatever was the mystery, it remained undiscovered.

CHAPTER CXXVI.
KNIGHT ERRANTS.

Next morning, taking a farewell of their new-found friends, Dick and Tom continued their journey.

"This sort of thing is more amusing than profitable," remarked Dick, "and we must make up for lost time. That little tragedy was very exciting; but it cost time."

"All your own fault, Dick; you will always dip your fingers in other people's pies," drily responded Tom.

Then they rode on without further remarks until they came to a certain well-known cathedral town, where they were personally unknown.

Here they resolved to halt and look about themselves, thinking that by keeping their eyes and ears open they must learn something worthy of being attended to.

They put up at the "Duke of York," a very large hotel, where, however, there was accommodation for commercial men and such like.

They dined, and then took a stroll about the town to reconnoitre. They meant business now, and must lay their plans accordingly.

The town was quaint and old-fashioned. Around the cathedral were some very ancient buildings.

After surveying these for some time, they took a short cut to return to their inn, and found themselves in a very dingy street, which, however, had once been fashionable.

When half way down they came to a large mansion, evidently not many years ago both fashionable and elegant. The front door was carved, and the surroundings, though dingy, bore all the elements of grandeur.

It had still a brass knocker and an imposing number of windows, the lower ones, however, securely barred.

"There should be a history about that house," said Dick to his companion.

"I should say so. It has a look of faded grandeur about it," replied Tom, "which makes one think it belongs to a miser. I should like to see the inside of it."

"So would others," said a voice behind them, and, turning, they saw a young man, well but not richly dressed, who was also looking up at the mansion.

"Some mystery, eh ?" asked Dick.

"Yes, and a wicked one, that if not solved soon will wreck two lives !" the young man went on, bitterly.

"Might we learn it ?" Dick said, politely.

"Who knows ! Some idea might follow."

"There can be no harm done," the other answered, with some little hesitation in his tones.

Dick was quick in coming to a decision. He believed the other to be slightly embarrassed by a feeling that he could not take them to any suitable place.

Dick was nothing if not decisive.

"We are staying at the 'Duke of York,'" he continued, politely. "Will you join us at supper ? We should like very much to hear your story."

"You are very hospitable and friendly," said the other. "I should be uncouth to refuse your invitation."

Dick at once turned to seek the hotel, the stranger leading the way, as being better acquainted with the city than they were.

It was soon reached, and Dick ordered supper for them in a private room.

Dick noted that the domestics doffed their caps to the stranger, which seemed to indicate that if not wealthy he was respected.

A copious supper was at last disposed of, and then the three sat over their wine.

"I don't know why, gentlemen," said the stranger, "I should bore you with my sorrowful history, except that your kindness has won my gratitude and sympathy. I will, however, be brief.

"I am the only son and supposed heir of Sir John Harcourt, a baronet of good family," he began. "I was sent to Oxford and then on a short tour on the continent. My father had no other son ; but he had brought up a niece, my cousin Gladys, as if she were one of his own children.

"It will not surprise you to learn that we got very much attached, and, in fact, loved when we were very young.

"My father had but a moderate estate, which was entailed, bringing in only a very small income. But my mother brought my father a large fortune, which at her death became absolutely his, to will as he pleased ; and, besides, he had some large ventures in Virginia.

"Altogether he was a very rich man, and I had never any reason to believe that he would leave it away from me.

"I returned to England to find my father dead, leaving one of those inexplicable wills, which, while well meant, sometimes cause intolerable misery.

"Except a small provision for my cousin Gladys, all was left to me, on condition that before she reached the age of twenty-one I was to marry her.

"You will say there ought not to be any difficulty in doing that. You would think not, but ever since my return to England she has disappeared.

"Should she refuse me she retains her pittance, and that's all.

"Now comes that part which will explain much. If I *refuse* to marry Gladys my uncle Walter inherits all except enough to keep me in genteel poverty, *alias* starvation.

"My uncle must have poisoned my father's mind against me, made him believe in some evil deed of mine, because before I went my marriage with my cousin was all settled.

"Now comes the worst part of the story. My uncle was left guardian of my cousin. It wants but three weeks of her coming of age. If that passes without my wedding, that malevolent scoundrel takes all.

"At college he was a tyrant and a bully. Since that his life has been a secret ; but there is one mystery that would be solved if I could get into that house."

"And what is that, Sir John ?"

"I believe that in that house my cousin is imprisoned, and that she will not be let out until the fatal hour has passed," he replied. "Then this man will chuckle and claim that which is mine."

"Your uncle lives in that house ?" asked Dick Turpin.

"Yes, and has not left it for a year !" replied Sir John.

"Are there many servants?" inquired Dick.

"A man and a woman, I believe. But why do you ask ?" said Sir John Harcourt.

"Are you prepared to make a bold stroke for a wife ?" asked Dick.

"Yes ; but explain yourself."

"If you believe that your cousin is secreted in that old mansion," said Dick gravely, "I will undertake to break into the house with my friend here and search the premises, with or without your personal co-operation. There is a back entrance, I presume ?"

"Oh, yes," said Sir John, "by which an old domestic comes out at times to do marketing and so on. Besides, my uncle does not immure himself in that den always. He is never about in the day, but at night he goes out and mixes in some of the looser society of the place."

"What time does he go out generally ?" asked Dick, starting up.

"Well, about an hour later than this," the other answered, "and does not return much before dawn."

"Well, Sir John," said Dick, "if you will show us the way to enter I will undertake to search the house from top to bottom. If the young lady is there she shall be released."

"How can I ever prove my gratitude ? " asked the baronet.

"We are not rich men," said Dick, quietly, "and if we do this thing we shall be content to leave the reward to you."

"And it shall be liberal."

"Well, Sir John, this is our proposition," continued Dick. "Show us the back way, and when your uncle goes out, return here and show your-self to those who know you."

"Everybody knows me," said Sir John; "but I cannot venture into the coffee room amongst my equals."

"Because of the want of coin," laughed Dick. "You shall pay us when you like. Accept these as a loan."

And he thrust some guineas into the other's hand. Sir John coloured; but as he firmly believed in Gladys being restored to him, he accepted them.

Dick and Tom returned to their joint bed-room, and from their horse portmanteau took their masks, without which they never travelled.

Descending rapidly, they advised Sir John to secure a bedroom, and then went out.

The young baronet knew the way well, and they soon found themselves in a narrow street, with tall houses on each side, and several dark entries.

Sir John pointed out a back door by which servants were wont in palmier days to pass to and fro, and then led the friends up a dark passage, whence they could see all that passed without being seen themselves.

They had not long to wait. Before half an hour had passed a door was opened, and out came a man, his face half concealed by a slouched hat, and his form by a cloak. Closing the door carefully behind him, he moved away.

"That is my uncle," said Sir John.

"We have our reasons," continued Dick. "Do you return to the 'Duke of York,' and make your presence as prominent as possible. Don't in any way appear to be mixed up with what is practically a burglary."

Sir John sighed, but he saw that his new and extraordinary friends were right. He made no further opposition, but walked slowly back to the inn, where his presence was greeted with effusion.

He was personally as popular as his father had been before him. But none could make out the reason of that monstrous will.

Meanwhile our two friends, quite excited by the business before them, had easily picked the lock of the back door. This admitted them to an old-fashioned servants' hall.

Here they assumed their masks and produced a dark lantern, with which they examined the place.

Listening attentively, they heard voices, and, going down a small flight of steps, found them-selves in an underground kitchen, where an old man and an old woman were crooning over the fire.

They secured and gagged the old woman, and then, pistol in hand, bade the ancient serving man show them his master's apartments.

He was by no means an active man, but the sight of the pistols roused in him a nimbleness unknown for years.

His master's apartments—bedroom, dining-room, and library—were on the first floor, and were soon examined and ransacked.

After forcing the drawers of several bureaus, they came to one in which they found jewellery, notes, and gold to the value of some thousands of guineas.

"Now," said Dick in a terrible voice, "show us the young lady's room!"

"Oh, sir, my master will kill me!" the man gasped.

"Then he'll hang, which is a comfort. But if you don't want a bullet through your head, lead on!" responded Dick, putting the cold barrel of the pistol to his forehead.

He hesitated no longer. We will precede him.

In a small room in one of the upper storeys sat a young girl alone, the tears stealing down her pale cheeks, an expression of despair, sad in one so young, stamped over her features.

The room was plainly furnished, and over-looked the narrow street above alluded to. But it was barred. The blind was up, the window sash raised as far as possible, and the soft moon-light poured in freely, beautifying the humble apartment with a strange, sad brightness, and revealing every line of the girl's face as she looked out into the stillness of the night, as though she would fain gaze for ever into the star-lit sky.

She was of the middle height, and very pretty.

Suddenly the door opened, and turning she saw the old trembling servant and two masked men.

"Be not alarmed," said Dick, advancing and speaking gently to the girl, "we come from your cousin, Sir John, to take you away."

"Oh!" she cried, rising, and her face flushing with sudden joy, "can it be?"

"Yes, come quick!" said Dick, "lest your wicked uncle should return."

Gladys Harcourt required no twice telling, but putting on a shabby black hat and a lace scarf she followed them eagerly.

They lost no time in getting down, and were soon in the open air, where Gladys had not been for over a year.

She told them this, and both helped her along.

There was no vehicle at hand, so she had to walk to the inn.

Going in first Dick sought Sir John, and called him out of the coffee room.

"I've found her," said Dick, in a low tone, and next minute, no one being by, Gladys was clasped in her cousin's arms.

A door was open leading into a side room, and into this he took her, while Dick summoned the chambermaid. She knew him and his history, and understood at once.

"This is my cousin, Gladys Harcourt," he said, "let her have refreshments and a room."

He then rejoined the friends, and poured out his thanks.

"No thanks are necessary," answered Dick; "we are down here on our own business. We have done ours, and if while doing so we have been of use to you, we are glad. Now, don't talk of any reward. You will keep our secret."

"Yes! whatever it may be!" replied Sir John, very much astonished.

"Well, never say any more about this night's work," remarked our hero, drily. "My name is Dick Turpin, and my friend's Tom King. We've made a good haul from your uncle; and, simply finding the young lady by accident, released her at her own wish."

Sir John sat down, petrified with amazement. "Can this be true?"

"Oh, yes! the old man and old woman will speak as to the masks and pistols," said Dick, with a hoarse laugh, "and so will the young lady. And now, Sir John, farewell! If we have done you a service, forget it as soon as possible. We must be far away before morning."

Sir John was still almost overwhelmed with surprise and incredulity.

"I care not who you may be," he said, presently, holding out his hand, "but you have saved me from misery and wretchedness. Must you go at once?"

"Your uncle may return at any hour," replied Dick; "in our trade we cannot be too cautious."

"He never returns until cockcrow!" argued Sir John; "the house will close soon. We must have a parting glass."

The highwaymen went out to see to their horses, ordering them to be ready for daylight, when business would take them away.

The ostler was to well feed them, and promised not to fail, and the two returned.

Sir John, while thankful himself for the great mercy vouchsafed to him, could not help thinking what might have been but for his extraordinary meeting with these two desperate adventurers, who had solved the problem that had been gnawing at his heart for a year.

"Now, gentlemen," he said, when they were seated in a private room, with wine before them, "I tell you, it will be needless to fly, unless you wish it. As soon as it is fairly daybreak, I shall apply for a warrant against my uncle for the illegal detention of his niece."

"But, Sir John, it is a matter of much moment to us," urged Dick, comically.

"Don't do anything against your wills, you know," said Sir John, "but knowing the craven nature of my uncle, as I do, I venture to say, he will fly this place for ever before morning."

At this moment there came a great hue and cry. Several men dashed up to the house and asked for Sir John, as they had heard of his presence.

The young baronet came forward and was at once informed that Mr. Walter Harcourt, being fetched from his inn by his servant, learned that his house had been broken into, and a young mad lady, his ward, removed.

Mr. Walter Harcourt gave way to such a tempest of passion that he dropped dead in a fit.

The constable asked for instructions.

"You and old Sanders can remain in the house until morning," said Sir John, handing the officer a guinea. "Make yourselves comfortable."

And he returned to his friends, who were horrified at this sudden and tragic termination of their adventure.

But that the evildoer, foiled in his deed of crime, should die thus was no fault of theirs.

The coroner's court would bring it in "Died by the visitation of God."

Next day, Norton Falden rang with the news. The old man's sins had found him out. His avarice and cruelty had met with a punishment which none could say was not deserved.

But, after consulting his lawyers, Sir John found that he must lose no time in marrying. The days were passing rapidly.

They found that Walter had persuaded his brother, an old man who married late in life, that his son was keeping away in order to avoid marrying his cousin. Enraged at this he had made his strange will.

But Gladys now found plenty of friends, and ere the week passed she was married from the bishop's residence.

Dick and Tom could not stop for the solemn occasion, but went away after receiving the warm thanks of the young people, who earnestly and solemnly declared that they owed their happiness to the two highwaymen.

Satisfied with this adventure, which had brought them a clear profit of four thousand guineas, the two companions started for London.

It was long since they had made such a haul, and it was time they paid a visit to Jack Palmer's home.

After one night's stay in London, they went down to Jack's home and had a couple of jolly days, the *soi disant* farmer increasing his balance at his bank, which was getting very large, in such a way as to leave his family, if the worst came to the worst, well provided for.

CHAPTER CXXVII.

ON THE EVE OF DEPARTURE.

To Dick and Tom the idea of a visit to America was almost comic.

The far-off continent was a place of which they had scarcely ever heard before.

To learn that this country far away over the sea was inhabited by beings like themselves, with a mixture of blackmen and redmen, was very trying to the belief of the high tobies.

Hitherto, they had never heard of any foreign country, save France.

And this was a place inhabited by people who ate frogs, wore wooden shoes, and were papists, which, in the eyes of such excellent Protestants as Dick Turpin and Tom King was utterly incomprehensible.

France seemed familiar to them, and they were told that, on fine days, it might be seen from England, in the hazy distance.

But America!

It was too stupendous almost to be believed. Should they escape all dangers? should they ever come back? were the questions they asked themselves.

Well, they had the most perfect faith in the Blue Dwarf, and, as we know, some little confidence in themselves.

They must take the chance.

On their arrival in London from the farm house, they went to one of the rendezvous appointed by the Blue Dwarf, and found Tim Roach.

"Sail in two days," said that worthy.

Upon which Dick and Tom, before starting for parts unknown, determined to have a regular spree.

The prospect of being cooped up on board a horrible ship for an indefinite period, never seeing a field nor a house, to hear nothing but the roar of the sea and the wash of the waves, were far from a pleasurable notion to either Dick or Tom.

But they were making money fast, and could they only make up their minds to save—and both had a goodly nest egg (Dick's was a large one)—they might retire without fear of the consequences.

The sum realised by some highwaymen in those days was something fabulous. The money spent in riot and debauchery in a week would often have provided for fifty families.

"Light come light go" has always been the motto of those whose money came to them in a nefarious way.

But many modern ways of making money are infinitely more nefarious than taking it by force.

The cheating done by lawyers and brokers whose clients trust them, the hundred and one ways of levying black mail by men in power and with influence in any place of trust, the disgraceful sweating exercised in professions where such mean tricks were never supposed to have been heard of, are infinitely more despicable than highway robbery.

At all events, the man risked his neck, and was alway amenable to the laws of his country.

But for the mean, crawling thieves we speak of there is no punishment — not even that of their consciences, for they have none.

Dick and Tom were rather *blasé* of late. They had mixed in such good society that they did not seem so at home as heretofore in the haunts of vice and crime.

Well! they must go somewhere, and elected finally to try one of those gambling dens abounding near Drury Lane.

There was always excitement, at all events, to be met with in these places, and sometimes tragedies.

This modern Damon and Pythias had been too successful during the last few days to go in for any scheme simply for making money.

They would think only of enjoyment, pure and simple.

So they entered the junior Cocoa Nut, where a goodly collection of birds of prey and doves were always to be found, and discovered that at the early hour at which they entered there were many seats vacant.

Dick and Tom at once drew up to the green table and put down a guinea or two, with varied success. Nobody was playing for any stakes in particular, and the excitement was *nil*.

But as a rule it was a dangerous place. On many occasions half a dozen comfortable little patrimonies would change hands while a man was looking on.

Gradually it began to fill, and soon was crowded. One peculiarity of the Younger Cocoa Nut was that it admitted women, and by nine o'clock a third of the players were women, with perhaps as many lookers-on.

And if there were lips more tightly contracted than other lips, and eyes with a harder, greedier light in them than other eyes, those lips and those eyes belonged to the women.

The ungloved feminine hands had a claw-like aspect as they scraped the glittering pieces of gold over the green cloth; the feminine throats looked weird and scraggy as they craned themselves over masculine shoulders; the feminine eyes had something demoniac in their steely glare as they kept watch upon the rapid progress of the game.

Dick had got tired of playing, and looked around. He at once noticed that the prettiest and youngest woman in this golden chamber was a girl who stood behind the chair of a military-looking old man whose handsome face was a little disfigured by those traces which late hours and dissipated habits are supposed to leave behind them.

The girl held a card in one hand and a pen in the other, and was occupied in some mysterious process, by which she kept notes of the other's play.

She was very young, with a delicate face, in whose softer lines was a refined likeness to the features of the man she watched.

But while his eyes were both cold and grey, hers were of that dense black in which there seems such an unfathomable and mysterious depth.

What was she doing there? As she was the handsomest, so she was the worst-dressed woman in the room.

The flimsy silk mantle had faded from black to rusty brown, the straw hat which shaded her face was sunburnt, the ribbons had lost their brightness, but there was an air of attempted fashion in the trimmings of her dress.

The shabbily-dressed girl was looking out for some one. She watched her father's play carefully—she marked the card with unfailing fascination; but she performed those duties with a mechanical air.

The man played with the concentrated attention and the impassive countenance of an experienced gamester, rarely lifting his eyes from the green cloth, never looking back at the girl who stood behind him.

He was winning to-day, and he accepted his good fortune as quietly as he had often accepted evil fortune at the same table.

Then the girl's eyes brightened suddenly as she glanced upwards. The person she had been watching for had arrived.

The doors opened to admit a handsome man of five-and-twenty.

There was a semi-polite vagabondism about the half-indifferent, half-contemptuous expression of his face, with its fierce moustache and strongly-marked eyebrows overshadowing sleepy grey eyes—eyes that were half hidden by their long deep lashes, as still pools of blue water lie sometimes hidden amongst the rushes that flourish round them.

As this man came in the girl smiled, and then, turning to her father, told him she was tired.

"Well, then, give me the card and go away," the gamester said, peevishly; "girls are always tired."

The girl gave him the mysteriously-perforated card, and left her post behind his chair, but only to move away and watch the new arrival.

But where was her pleasure?

The young man on entering the room walked round the table till he came to the only vacant chair, in which he seated himself, and, after watching the game for a few minutes, began to play.

From the moment in which he dropped into that vacant seat to the time when he decided to leave the table, three hours afterwards, he never lifted his eyes from the green cloth, and seemed to be oblivious of anything that was going on around or about him.

The girl watched him furtively for some little time, and then went out.

The young man looked after her, but did not follow.

Dick Turpin was tired, but he had seen all this bye-play. He had gone into the supper room at last, and was seated in a window behind a curtain.

The handsome young man came in with another. He looked unutterably bored.

"Well, Hawkhurst," said his friend, "do you make any progress?"

"None, and I'm getting sick of it," answered the other; "the girl won't elope, and unless she does, I shan't get a penny of the money. Did the captain twig? He'd see her dead rather than let her marry me."

"And not far wrong," laughed the other.

"Well, neither he nor she shall ever know of this fortune unless she marries me. The captain is a gambler, a roue, but if he knew that he was heir to ten thousand a year and Castleton, I believe he's a gentleman at bottom," said the handsome young man, "and would whisk the girl off amongst his own set once more. But he has insulted me; he has refused me his daughter; she has refused to marry without Captain Castleton's consent, and she and he may go hang! I have the documents, and I will burn them rather than he shall ever know his luck. Let us to the Finish."

And he hurried down stairs, the other young man returning to speak to a friend and follow in ten minutes.

With an impatient gesture the first went on, followed by Dick and Tom.

He had not gone ten yards before he was tripped up and two heavy packets of papers taken from his pockets.

CHAPTER CXXVIII.

A WONDERFUL DISCOVERY.

Dick and Tom were too tired and had indulged in too many glasses to have very clear heads that night, so they decided to sleep upon it, and examine the papers at early morn.

Tom was a quick and apt scholar, and would soon solve any difficulties.

They got up, breakfasted early and frugally, as, from what the stranger Hawkhurst had said, they believed they had got hold of a great heir-at-law case.

They placed the papers on a table, and Tom King appreciated their importance as he read them out.

Here was a will leaving Castleton Manor and ten thousand a year to Captain George Lascelles Castleton, and the remainder to his daughter Charlotte, on condition that she married none of the Hawkhurst branch.

"Oh!" said Dick, "that is why he wanted to win the young lady to a marriage first."

"Yes," responded Tom, "and here are the marriage certificates of Captain George Lascelles Castleton and Dorothy his wife, with the certificate of the birth of Charlotte, and then finally a regular geneological tree. I suppose this Hawkhurst stole all this, and with his handsome face has been coming it over Miss Charlotte. What do you mean to do, Dick?"

"Well, Tom, I know a good deal of this Captain George Lascelles Castleton," said Dick. "He was brought up to look upon himself as the heir of Castleton. When his uncle died, no papers to prove his heirship could be found, and another man stepped into the estate. Driven to desperation, he turned gambler."

"And now?"

"We'll interview the joker and tell him what I know. Of course, Tom, we must have a goodly whack and go snacks," laughed Dick.

"Yes; when shall we go?"

"Soon," said Dick. "I happen to know where the Captain lives."

Captain Castleton had held that rank in a crack cavalry regiment; he lodged in some rather seedy drawing-rooms, and was at breakfast when Mr. Palmer and Mr. Markham were announced.

His daughter had gone out.

"You will excuse our abruptness, captain,"
said Dick; "but we believe we have good news—very good news."

"There can be none for me—it is all too late!" the other replied, gloomily.

"Excuse me, sir, for asking seemingly impertinent questions. But for some documents which have strangely disappeared, would you not be lord of Castleton Grange?"

"Yes," the other went on; "but they were stolen—destroyed."

"They were not, sir," was the answer; "they are all intact and safe. What would you give for them?"

"Anything in reason," gasped the other, trembling all over with anxiety.

"We will trust to your honour," said Dick. "I may appear impertinent," he added; "but if you received your inheritance you would leave London with your daughter and return to your proper station in society?"

"Most certainly," said the captain; "but you seem to know a great deal about me and mine. What know you of my daughter?"

"We were at the Junior Cocoa Nut last night," continued Dick; "but I must further question—you know a man named Sidney Hawkhurst?"

"Yes, indeed," replied the captain; "it is he who long since promised to get me back my own."

"He it is who has kept you out of it for a long time," was the grave reply.

"With what object?"

"He loves your daughter; at all events, her expected fortune!" said Dick, drily; "and, before he revealed the truth to you, wished to secure the young lady."

"The villain! the unmitigated villain! My daughter spurned him as he deserved."

"I fear not; but she has refused to wed him without your consent," was the answer. "I heard himself and a companion talking of the matter in the supper room. He said he would rather destroy the papers than give them up without the girl. Upon this, myself and friend, knowing the man well, played the amateur highwaymen, and eased my gentleman of all his ill-gotten plunder—and there it is!"

He placed it on the table before the captain.

Five minutes sufficed for the examination, and then Captain Castleton knew that he was among the rich gentry of the land.

"Come with me to my solicitor's," said the excited captain, hastily dressing; "you must explain the wondrous tale—I cannot."

He was ready in almost no time, and going out, after leaving a message for his daughter, they made for the solicitor's residence, which was not a hundred yards away, and, as it happened, he was disengaged.

"All right, Mr. Ransom," cried Captain Castleton, "everything is found. That scoundrel Sidney Hawkhurst had them all the time, but played fast and loose—to win my Charlotte. Pray, explain, Mr. Palmer!"

Mr. Palmer did, and then added:

"I knew that it would be difficult to get these documents out of such a consummate rogue by fair means, so we followed him out of the 'Cocoa Nut,' tripped him up, secured the important packets, and took them to Captain Castleton——"

"And gave them up without any stipulation of fee or reward!" added the captain—"but that must not be. What think you, Ransom—five thousand guineas?"

"Stop!" said Dick; "nothing of the kind. We know that we have rendered you, by mere accident, an essential service, but we shall be satisfied with a thousand guineas, when you come to your own."

"Draw up a binding agreement to that effect at once, Ransom, and let them have it, signed and sealed," continued Captain Castleton, impetuously.

"That will be acceptable," said Dick, "as myself and friend are both going to America, and may be absent some time. We hope, in the meantime, that all may be settled."

The agreement was drawn up, duly signed, sealed and witnessed, and then, leaving the lawyer to scan the papers with a legal eye, the captain, richer than he had been for years, with crisp bank notes and cheques in his pocket, turned back to his lodgings, to announce the good news to his daughter, and to celebrate the event by cracking a bottle.

But Miss Charlotte Castleton was nowhere to be found.

The captain turned pale as death.

"She only went to call on a friend," the alarmed father said, "I am ashamed to say—to borrow a trifle—for I lost last night. She should have been back an hour ago."

"Will you give me the address of the friend, captain?" said Dick, "I will run round. I fear that villain Hawkhurst has got hold of her. If so, we'll hunt him up. I know his haunts and a good deal about him."

The distracted father gave the address, and Dick started off to return in ten minutes with the news that Miss Castleton had been to Mrs. Withers, received half a guinea, and departed long ago.

"Lost! lost!" cried the unhappy father, "and all my fault."

"Don't lose all hope, sir. While I and Mr. Markham watch his movements, do you, captain, go to Doctors Commons and find if a license has been taken out. We will keep you well informed," said Dick, thrusting a couple of guineas into the other's hands, ere he dashed out.

Mr. Sidney Hawkhurst lived in a court out of Drury Lane, in a house which had once been fashionable, but which was now dilapidated and let out in tenements.

On asking for the tricky gentleman, they were directed to the second floor, but the Cerberus who lived in a little den at the entrance, pronounced his opinion, "not at home."

He thought, however, there was a young lady waiting for him upstairs.

This was enough. Tom King was despatched to warn the father, while Dick entered a public house and watched.

In about twenty minutes Mr. Sidney Hawkhurst, very much elated, and with a sinister smile on his handsome face, hurried into the house and rushed upstairs.

He was alone now, but doubtless a clergyman would follow.

Dick was wild with impatience, but at this moment Tom and the captain came in sight.

He lost no time in speaking, but led the way upstairs.

They were soon all three on the landing. The door was fastened, but one powerful blow from Dick's shoulders hurled it in, and there were Sidney Hawkhurst and Miss Charlotte Castleton seated on an old couch together.

"Thief, scoundrel, villain," cried the irate father, striking him in the face with his cane, "I have found you out at last!"

Charlotte Castleton simply cowered against the wall.

"To which allow me to add," said Dick Turpin, quietly, "Card sharper, filcher, and burglar!"

"What are you?" bellowed the infuriated ruffian.

"That matters not, my gentle cly-faker (pickpocket)," responded Dick, "I've baulked you here."

"Come out of this den of infamy, Charlotte," said the captain; "but before you do so, know that it is this miserable hound who has kept me so long out of my inheritance. He knew it all along—had the proofs in his possession, but wanted to marry you and secure your fortune, before telling the truth. Keep your distance, cur, ere I maim you for life!"

And he carried off his daughter, the rear being guarded by Dick and Tom.

Sidney Hawkhurst knew that he had played a fearful game, and lost.

He knew Charlotte Castleton well. Having found out his trickery, her love would turn to contempt.

The whole party were soon in the captain's poor lodgings. At sight of money, however, the landlady sent out to a crack tavern for lunch, which was served in style, and the meal heartily enjoyed by all but poor Charlotte.

The true state of affairs having been explained to her, she somewhat dried her tears.

Hawkhurst was clearly a mercenary villain, and as a set-off there was ten thousand a year, a house in town, a fine old castle in the country, and the prospect of society!

"You will make a sensation in society before the year is out, my dear," cried her father.

And so it happened, when Dick Turpin and Tom retired, Miss Castleton was tolerably consoled for the loss of her lover.

She might well be, for before the end of the second season she was the acknowledged *belle*, and had won the heart of the Earl of Babbington, whom she eventually married.

CHAPTER CXXIX.

As the Blue Dwarf had not as yet shown any sign, Tim Roach promised to let them know when they were wanted, and they were still free to enjoy themselves.

They resolved to just stretch their horses' legs over Hounslow Heath and a little beyond, and, having gained an appetite, to return and satisfy it.

Hounslow Heath was visited only with a view to stretching their horses' legs. They intended to return to Hampstead to dine.

They cantered along for some time, not forgetting to visit two of their favourite taverns, where they were well received, and, while they drank their stiff jorums of good Irish whiskey, heard the gossip of the neighbourhood.

It was nothing very new, not at all true, but, as the Yankee loafer remarked, "it don't sinnify."

There were no new residents about, but business was not particularly bad.

So they dawdled away the time, until, appetite being aroused, they might feel it advisable to take the road back to Hampstead.

It was just a pleasant ride before dinner, and the steeds were ready for a good spurt.

"D——" cried Tom King, suddenly, as his horse stumbled, and on rising showed that he had cast a shoe.

"It might have been worse," said Dick Turpin, with his usual cold-blooded philosophy; "yon's Jack Parker's, the blacksmith. I'll just take a gentle trot over the heath, and return in half-an-hour."

Tom grunted for all response, and then away went Dick, putting Black Bess on her mettle.

Nothing delighted the frolicsome mare more than to stretch her legs on that grassy heath.

Dick let her go at her own sweet will, and, as luck or ill-luck would have it, she took the course in the direction of the "Leather Bottle," then one of the most notorious haunts of highwaymen, but which in some unaccountable way enjoyed a special immunity from official interference.

But the superior authorities had thought fit to mark their feelings with regard to the "ancient flagon," as affected wits called it, by hanging the latest murderers, in chains, on a mound not very far from its door.

It really seemed to be as good as a sign-post, for many indeed came to see it, and all stopped to obtain further particulars at the bar, which brought grist to the mill of the landlord.

Of course, Dick could not pass without stopping to take the dust out of his throat.

He rode up to the door, dismounted, and entering, called for a pint of the best burnt sherry.

He was served very quickly, the interval being occupied by a brief conversation with the landlady, who was only too glad to see one so noted in the hierarchy of the tobies.

The liquor consumed, Dick bethought himself of his companion, and, going out, took charge of Black Bess.

At that moment his eye fell upon the gallows, where, hung in chains, was Abershaw, of jolly memory, who expiated his sins only a few days before.

Dick knew him well, and regretted him, and thought he would just have one look at him for old acquaintance sake.

He whistled to Black Bess to follow, and soon stood in front of the gallows, upon which he gazed with a sad, stern look.

"He! he! he!" laughed a shrill and malicious hag close to him.

Turning he saw Mother Grip.

"What want you, hag?" asked Dick, very much startled.

"I give you three years—then hang!" said the Hounslow witch.

Dick waited to hear no more, but, leaping on his horse, rode off to the other side of the heath, where he stopped until rejoined by Tom King.

As soon as he came, Dick led the way from Hounslow, nor stopped until he had reached his earlier destination.

Hampstead, with its quaint buildings, its upper and lower "Flask" and other favourite inns, was one of their dearest haunts.

The upper "Flask" is now a large private house on the right, just before reaching the heath, surrounded by a very high wall.

It was the scene of many an elopement and even duels in those days, and as much connected with divorces as another celebrated inn at the present day.

The author of "Pamela" laid many a scene in his novels in the locality.

Dick and Tom, however, did not stop on this occasion until they reached that famous hostelrie, the "Bull and Bush," then recently come into vogue, and much affected then, as now, by artists and poets with an eye to the picturesque.

On reaching this spot, attracted by its pleasant looks, they went in, entered the coffee room, and ordered refreshments.

These were served with the same punctuality and promptitude which ever since have won favour, and which prompted such men as Sir Joshua Reynolds, Hogarth, and lesser lights to visit there.

They were not alone. Seated at another table was an undoubted sea captain. He was enjoying his pipe and glass.

"Excuse me, sir," said Dick, politely, "but have you ever been to America?"

"Yes—and the Injies, and round the Horn," replied the ancient mariner.

"Well, sir," continued Dick, "we are bound shortly for America, and should like to hear a little about such outlandish places. Will you join us?"

"With pleasure, my hearties," said the other, coming with his pipe and glass to their table. "I come from these parts, and have just seen my youngsters; while they were getting dinner ready I thought I'd look round."

And he chuckled at the innocent deceit of going to the tavern being called a look round.

"What part are you going to?" he then asked.

"New York, first, and then to various parts."

"Well, New York's a nice place—only a few houses on an island, though," he remarked; "but it gets bigger every day. Ah! I mind the last time I went to New York I had a queer adventure. Would you mind hearing it?"

"One moment," said Dick, and, summoning the tapster, he ordered a bowl of punch, with plenty of rum in it.

The sailor chuckled.

"You know our lingo," he remarked.

"Oh yes," explained the other. "Seen a deal of life in my time—all sorts of classes."

Well, presently the bowl of punch was brought, the glasses filled, and then the sailor told his story.

It was so filled with technicalities that if told in his way it would weary the reader. We therefore condense the really interesting narrative.

It appeared that, from cabin boy to master, all the life of Bob Milner had been spent in the service of the same firm of shipowners, and that his life had been singularly uneventful.

In fact, this was his one story, and, like a good many other people, he was very fond of telling that one story:—

Some years before, he was seated in his snug cabin, lying at anchor in the Mersey, ready to start the very next day, early, for New York.

The captain was rather gloomy. It was a wild, wet night in September, and above him he could hear the wish-wash of the driving rain and the whistling of the wind in the rigging.

But this was not the cause of his gloominess. Just before leaving he had heard of an old friend and pal of his, Captain Jacob Anson, who had been found dead, half dressed, in his bath tub on the previous morning. He had been discovered face downwards in the water, which was only a few inches deep.

As one leg of his trousers was rolled up, it was supposed he had been finishing his bath by stooping and washing his feet, which position probably caused a fit, when he fell.

He was surprised to hear of his death in this way, for he had known the captain, as an old friend, to be a man of robust health, and very active for one of his years.

In the course of his roving sea life he had passed through many strange adventures and dangers. He had also many war experiences; he had been a midshipman and promoted for good conduct, but finally took to the merchant service.

Strange, indeed, it seemed that a man who had escaped so many grave perils should after all be drowned in six or seven inches of water in the bath !

While these thoughts were still passing through his mind he was interrupted.

"Captain," roared his first mate, Mr. Thompson, at the companion way, "here's a young man, in a shore boat, to ship."

"Ship !" cried Milner, in astonishment, "who on earth could have sent anyone away off here to ship at such a time? Tell him we have all the men we want."

But the stranger, gliding past the mate, came, all dripping wet, into the cabin, and stood before him.

Never had he seen a handsomer or trimmer-looking youth. His deeply-embrowned face, his attire, and the way he had of supporting one leg on the ball of his foot, made him pretty sure he was a sailor.

He held his Scotch cap in his hand, and the water trickled from his short ringlets down cheeks as smooth as a girl's. His eyes were round, and of a soft deep blue; but, looking into them, you might have detected a daring, care-for-nothing expression that implied he was not to be trifled with.

"And why are you so anxious to ship again?" asked Milner; "men just returned from a voyage, as you seem to be, do not usually care to get off again in a hurry."

He gave the captain a swift, keen look, who was startled by the tiger-like flash momentarily lighting those soft eyes of his.

"My money, sir, the earnings of a year, was all stolen from me in the boarding house where I put up for one night."

"That was hard."

"Yes, it was, sir," he responded, his eyes softening with a sad, gentle expression.

Milner felt sorry for the young fellow, and said he would ship him, while in the meantime he mentally but vainly asked himself where he had seen a face resembling his before.

But when he signed himself John Rogers on the ship's books, he was sure he had never seen anyone of that name before.

"There is some mystery about that boy," he said, after he had gone forward.

He had never been so much interested in a foremast hand before. He was indeed a good sailor.

Next day he sent him aloft to mend a shroud, where the maintopsail had chafed it, and to put leather sheathing around it. This task was performed with remarkable celerity, and in the neatest possible manner.

"Very well done, Jack," said Milner, and he gave his captain a pleasant, gratified look from his blue eyes that made his heart warm towards him.

He was so quiet and mild looking that before long some of his rough shipmates—all of whom were older than he—thought to domineer over him.

The upshot of this was, that one day he seized one of these tyrants, a big, strapping fellow, named Robert Martin, by the collar with one hand, by the wrist with the other, and, by a powerful, dexterous movement, hurled him across his hip, head foremost, upon the forehatch, where the man lay half stunned.

Here the matter should have ended. His over-awed adversary would never have molested him again. But, no; Rogers must spring upon the prostrate man and pound him with blows that fell like a sledge hammer until he was senseless.

He then snatched up a handspike.

"There, Jack, that will do," said the captain, sternly. The young man seemed to hesitate, then, with a tigerish gleam in his eye, threw down the heavy weapon, and walked away.

The time passed—voyages were serious things in those days—and nothing further happened. The men kept aloof from John Rogers.

They were within a day's sail of the destined port. Far away they could dimly see the line of the coast, but a strong gale, with a head wind, compelled the skipper to beat off the land under reefed topsails.

It was a dark, misty night, and the captain was on deck, when all at once, the spanker blew clear of the gasket, the rope holding it to the mast, and slipping about, threatened to carry away the gaff. In fact, the stays holding it now parted, and he feared every moment it would come down.

Jack was ordered aloft to secure the sail. He ran up the rigging like a squirrel, and Milner went below to put on his overcoat; when he came up he saw nothing of Jack, except his Scotch cap lying on the deck, while the gaff now hung down nearly ready to fall.

He ran to the man at the wheel, an old one-eyed Portuguese.

"What's become of Jack?" he inquired. "Did you see nothing—hear nothing of him?"

"I thought I heard a sort of cry behind me," he answered, "but it was so dark, I couldn't see anything."

"Great Heaven! I believe he has fallen overboard," exclaimed the captain.

He called all hands, and discovered that Jack indeed was missing. He lowered a boat, and looked for him in vain.

"He is lost !" was the general cry.

Milner suffered dreadfully about this affair, and reproached himself for sending the youngest sailor aloft to the gaff.

Just at daylight, a cruiser came in sight with English colours flying. She made directly for them.

"Ship ahoy !" was the hail from her deck when she was near enough.

"Halloa !" answered the captain.

"Is that the 'Ocean Queen?'"

"Aye ! aye !" was the answer.

"Please, heave to, and I will send a boat aboard."

On his heaving to, they sent a boat alongside, with a police officer in uniform.

"Want a young fellow about eighteen, shipped aboard your vessel at Liverpool," said the officer, while the men-of-warsmen stood by. "He wore a Scotch cap, blue jacket and trousers."

"I did ship such a lad," replied the skipper,

DICK TURPIN AND TOM KING TRY ON THEIR PRAIRIE OUTFITS.

" but he aint here now. What's he wanted for ?"

"For the murder of old Captain Anson, at Birkenhead !" was the answer. "Where's the young scoundrel ?"

Captain Bob Milner explained. The officer told him that he was the son of the captain's wife by her first husband. He had been seen to leave the captain's house in the early morning.

Then Captain Milner recollected. It was the likeness to Anson's wife he had recognised.

"If the scoundrel's dead," said the officer, " I think as how we've come on a fool's errand, and must let you go."

"Avast !" said Robert Martin, the man who had been aloft, and who, it will be remembered, had been so mercilessly pounded by Jack, who had come down from the mizzen-topsail yard, by means of a backstay, "just you wait. I was standing amidships when Jack went aloft to the gaff. All at once, although it was so dark, I could make out the outline of his form, as he slid down from aloft. Then he gave a sort of cry, and crouched in the black shadows, so that the man at the wheel couldn't see him, and sneaked along to the steerage hatchway. You'll find him behind the false bulkhead in the steerage. I'd a said nothing 'cause of what he did to me, but when I find him charged with murder, I do my duty by speaking."

The runner, guided by one of the men, went below into the steerage, and, dislodging the thick plank which covered the opening leading into the small space between the double bulkhead, they found Jack, so tightly squeezed that he could hardly breathe.

As he was brought on deck, securely handcuffed, the absence of surprise on the part of some of the men made the captain suspect that they, too, had known of his being concealed aboard.

Well, he was taken to England, and being tried, was convicted. Seeing that there was no hope, he made a full confession of his crime.

The captain had refused, on some excuse about his bad temper and disposition, to obtain for him a midshipman's warrant, and he was heard to swear he would be avenged.

Dick and Tom, who were deeply interested in the story, which was dramatically told, thanked the captain.

It had taken some time to tell, and as they wanted advice about an outfit, they thought a snack would be advisable.

Bob Milner acquiesced, and, the order being given, the conversation continued.

The skipper informed them that, as far as their journey up country was concerned, they should leave their purchases until they reached New York, only taking their ship's outfit with them.

Tom King, upon this, asked for a list of things required, so that their journey to Hampstead would not in any way be wasted.

A very pleasant afternoon was passed, and then the new friends parted.

Bob Milner, who had forgotten all about his dinner with his youngsters, and who was well primed, went off rather sheepishly, while Dick and Tom returned to town.

They found Tim Roach awaiting them with instructions to join the Blue Dwarf at Portsmouth on the evening of the sixth day.

They accordingly determined to procure their sea outfit at once, as Tim Roach intimated that

next day he should depart with a light waggon and luggage for the ship.

Though a lady did not carry a waggon load of furbelows in those days, yet, still, as they were going to a city where there were some high officials, even a lord being governor, finery to a certain extent must be provided for.

Having taken the advice of the captain of the "Ocean Queen," they had their boxes sent to the address indicated by Tim, and then gave themselves up to the society of some Circes of their acquaintance.

Next day they started for Portsmouth, which place they reached very quickly, and put up at the "Blue Posts."

Their first duty was now to secure the safety of their horses, by which they set great store. They knew a horse dealer of high character, who, in addition to selling horses, let them on hire.

To this man they told their story. They were going to America, a journey which might last six months or a year. During that time they wished their horses taken care of. They were willing to have them let to respectable persons who would treat them fairly and kindly, and would pay six months' keep in advance.

To this Mr. Luscombe at once agreed. He saw quickly what kind of tits they were, and declared they should never be ridden by anyone except himself or a friend.

They were in the counting-house alone—that is, the horse dealer, Dick, and Tom—preparing to pay the six months' keep.

"That's a beauty of yours," said the horse dealer, addressing Dick ; "if I didn't know better, I should say she was Black Bess."

"And what do you know about Black Bess, Mr. Luscombe ?" asked the valiant highwayman.

"She was born and bred in this stable," speaking generically of his varied establishments.

"Then I may as well tell you," said Dick, smiling, "that it is Black Bess."

" Ho !" cried the other, holding out his hand ; "then I'm proud to know the rider, and we'll wet this bargain as soon as we've settled the books."

The money was duly paid, the receipts given, and then the worthy horse dealer led his new friends into his private apartments, where he entertained them most hospitably.

In his eyes the owner of such a horse as that held a higher position than anyone else. No matter how or for what purpose he kept such cattle, in his eyes he was a hero.

After spending a pleasant half hour, they returned to the " Blue Posts " minus their horses, and going into the room appointed to captains, ordered dinner.

Our friends could accommodate themselves to any society, and knew, even when the liquor was in, how to exercise a careful amount of discrimination.

The doughty captains in H.M. service eyed them with haughty disdain, and some even ventured to insinuate that they were bagmen. But they did not look like individuals who could be joked with, and they had no mind to pick a serious quarrel with utter strangers, who came into the room by right of residence in the house.

But Dick and Tom found this quiescent attitude very dull, and as soon as their dinner was over rose and strolled out of the house in search of more lively companions.

Doubtless Mr. Luscombe would be glad to provide them with entertainment; but then, if he had recognised Black Bess he had also recognised the rider, and our friends had no desire to make their profession known too much.

Mr. Luscombe was, no doubt, a very worthy man and an excellent citizen, but they should consider him a man very much given to his cups, and hence apt to be free in his conversation.

It transpired that Tim Roach and a coachman had arrived, and put up at a more private and patrician hotel than the " Blue Posts," which was only patronised by noblemen when they wore a blue coat.

They wandered through the streets towards the " Hard," and looked out for some place where they might amuse themselves, however roughly.

They were about to enter a shabby-looking place whence emanated the sounds of a rasping fiddle, when suddenly they espied Captain Bob Milner crossing the road. Hastening up to him they shook hands, and heartily and readily accepted his invitation to go into a house with him where there were a number of men of his own class, to whom he introduced his Hampstead friends.

Here they were hail-fellow-well-met, and the talk and the smoking went on galore.

The skipper incidentally told them that he was appointed once more to command the " Ocean Queen," and that his best cabins had been taken for a young couple, their nurse and child, also for two other gentlemen in charge of an invalid, with a couple of servants, and further two gentlemen named Palmer and Markham.

" Palmer! that's me," said Dick.

" Markham! that's me," added Tom.

This was a remarkable coincidence which at once necessitated glasses round at the skipper's expense, and finally it was decided to order supper for all in a room upstairs at the back of the house, where they could make as much noise as they liked.

The supper was ordered, and would be ready in an hour.

It is useless to record the further events of that night, but when they rose rather late the next morning in their own room at the " Blue Posts"—how they reached there they knew not—they found orders to go on board at once.

This they did, and a few hours later they were sweeping out to sea, leaving Old England behind them, and bound for the land of the redskin, the buffalo, the rattlesnake, and alligator—a land which to Dick and Tom was quite unknown and legendary.

CHAPTER CXXX.
NEW YORK.

We are in the New York of the Knickerbockers, the Vanderbilts, the Van Ranssalers, and the Peter Stuyvesants, while the Dutch were governors of the State.

But from a purely Dutch colony it had become now partially English. Founded by the Hollanders, it had been conquered by Great Britain and gradually made British.

The New England States, with their cities of Boston, Philadelphia, &c., had at once invaded the State in crowds, and were proceeding to Yankeefy it as fast as possible, never expecting, however, what a mighty metropolis it would become.

New York, at the time of which we write, was a very different place to what it is now. A man, speaking of his residence, describes it as agreeably situated on one of the salt marshes beyond Corlear's Hook, subject, indeed, to be occasionally overflowed, and much infested in summer time with mosquitoes, but otherwise very agreeable, producing abundant crops of salt grass and bulrushes.

When it was visited first by the Dutch under Communipan it was called Manhattan by the natives, which name they speedily changed into New Amsterdam. At first it was nothing but a fort and trading station, but soon there grew up around a numerous progeny of little Dutch houses, all of which seemed to nestle most lovingly under its walls.

These were surrounded by a strong palisade, to guard against any sudden irruption of savages.

There was, however, excellent accommodation even then, before the days of the huge hotels of the present, for travellers, and Lord Elphick and his lady, with Lord Jermyn and Lady Jermyn and Colonel Grant, readily found apartments in an inn of a superior class.

Dick and Tom also found a place more suited to their calibre, to which they were directed by Captain Robert Milner—a mixture of the inn and boarding house as at present established in the same locality.

They were very tired when they reached their sanctuary, and retired to rest in a double-bedded room as usual with our friends.

They both woke tolerably early, and at once discovered they were in a strange land.

Somebody at the back of the house was singing in a nasal tone and with a queer pronunciation, which made the words almost incomprehensible to the two listeners, as follows:—

Oh, de sezan has arrove when de robin am a singing,
    An' de farmer gits his plow out to furrow up de ground;
De notes of de robin frew de forests am a ringing,
    An' de mule sticks his ears up at ebery little sound;
De grass am looking green 'long de aiges of de medder
    An' de turtle dove ar' cooin' in de maple on de hill;
An' de gander an' his mate are a walkin in love's shadder,
    An' de pickaniny darky goes a wadin' by the mill.

Both rose, and going to the window saw in a back yard a negro, a sort of black Sam Weller or Boots at the Swan, working away with cheerful alacrity at the boots and shoes of the establishment.

Blacks had been seen in England even long before that time, some having come over in the train of returned colonists; but at the time of which we speak they were very rare.

At all events, they had not come under the notice of Dick Turpin or Tom King.

" Well," said Dick, with a rather strong exclamation, " we are in a strange sort of place! Did you ever see anything so ugly in all your life?"

" Well, never; but the blackamoor is very jolly," replied Tom, " let's go down and see what sort of grub they give us."

They dressed, not without shaving, as usual—they were very punctilious John Bulls on this point—and went down to breakfast just as a shrill tinkling bell sounded the summons for the first meal.

The captain's table, to which they were attached, was copiously supplied—steaks, chops, fish, and vegetables in abundance. The food was washed down by jugs of cider and ale, with spirits for those who preferred it.

But the great characteristic was the copiousness of the meal, and quality, in which the Americans, especially the New Englanders, have not degenerated even unto this day.

"This is jolly. Do you feed like this, captain, every day ?"

"Yes," said Milner, "when we don't have something better. This is a rare country, sir, as you'll find. Going west, I think ?"

"When my friends have seen a little of New York," replied Dick, diplomatically ; "they've no end of letters. I believe we are free for several days."

But in the afternoon they were sent for by Colonel Grant and informed that they would have seen enough of New York in a week, and then, wishing to make use of their absolute freedom, they would go up country. He commissioned them through Milner to make inquiries and find a trustworthy guide, and to purchase necessaries.

"You see, Mr. Palmer," said the colonel, smiling, " we don't mean always to follow a beaten track, and so must have a waggon. I believe the correct thing will be a guide and two teamsters, and I think we'd better wear the dress of intending settlers. It will excite less attention."

"Very good, sir," replied Dick ; " we'll report to-night ;" and he went out to reconnoitre.

These two men had, since their employment by the Blue Dwarf, acted so faithfully and loyally that all were ready and willing to forget their terrible profession.

Indeed, the Blue Dwarf was not without a secret hope that they might take to the life of the West, and give up their habits of rapine.

Besides, Dick and Tom had proved so useful that if they were left behind they might get into some serious trouble, and Sapathwa be deprived of their services. So they were invited to accompany the party.

After an early dinner Dick asked for an interview with Captain Milner, and explained his requirements.

"Well," said the skipper, " I'd better ask the landlord ;" and he, being summoned, advised them to let him send for Indian Jack, as he was called, a half-breed, who was known as a scout out west, a mighty hunter, and a good guide everywhere.

It must be explained here that modern American slang was unknown at the time of which we write. " I guess " and all that sort of thing was not invented. Rough men spoke bad grammar, and pronounced many words as if there were no "g" at the end, as "singin'" for "singing," and so on, with a few other little eccentric expressions.

The present style is an invention of the period, nothing more, and a very bad invention.

Indian Jack was an Oneida half-breed. His father had been French and his mother Indian.

When he reached the inn his appearance at once impressed our friends.

He was tall and wiry. His complexion was as dark as that of a gipsy, while his dress was composed almost wholly of skins. He had a tunic of deerskin, a cap of the same, leather leggings above moccasins and soft shoes of deer hide ; hence the name of Leather Stocking, by which these men are so often called.

He had a long hunting knife in the belt of his tunic, and a hunting shirt, while his right hand grasped a long rifle that rested in the hollow of his left arm.

The landlord explained that a party of Eng-

lish wished to explore as far on the borders as was safe, and wanted a guide, a waggon to carry stores, a good team, and a teamster.

These two were of the party, indicating Dick and Tom, and they wished to dress and arm under his direction.

"They'll leave all to you, Jack, and pay liberal, take my afferdavy for that," said the landlord.

"Good !" said the guide, in a guttural but not unpleasantly harsh tone ; " Indian Jack is ready. Best buy waggon—sell again when done with, and the same with oxen."

"Well," remarked Dick, "I think so, too, young man ; but I'll consult the chief. If you have no objection, then, we'll see about clothes and a gun each, not forgetting knives."

"Good !" the other continued quietly, "since that's the locrum ; Jack ready when white man ready."

Both Dick and Tom rose and followed the half-breed, who was as brave, true, and honest a frontier man as ever stepped in untanned shoe leather.

He took them straightway to a man who supplied traders, hunters, trappers, and others with what are now called store goods, and introduced the new customers.

They were English, and rich. That was enough, and soon, after half an hour's interview, Dick and Tom wore disguises that would have baffled the keenest Bow Street runners in England.

They had on brand new moccasins of the very best untanned leather, leggings, which were, in fact, tightly-fitting trousers, reaching from the ankle to the waist, a hunting shirt from the knee to the neck, with light sleeves and a gorgeous crimson sash ; the edging of the tunic and leggings was ornamented with coloured strips of blue cloth.

From the sash hung a powder horn and hunting knife, while the head was surmounted by a broad-brimmed *sombrero*, or what is now popularly designated as a Buffalo Bill hat.

Mr. Ikey Solomons—such was his euphonious name—offered rifles as well, and as Indian Jack approved, they made this purchase also.

The whole was paid for liberally, the guide being too well known for extortion to be tried, and then the two returned to their inn, after ordering their own clothes to be sent on to the Hudson Tavern.

Bidding Indian Jack have whatever he pleased, Dick and Tom, with a comic twinkle in their eyes, went to the "New York Arms," made themselves known to the authorities, and went up to the first floor, to the apartments occupied by the exploring party, as they called themselves.

Knocking a little sharply, the two hunters of the west went in and stood before the astonished group. Colonel Grant and Lord Jermyn were seated talking together, the earl and Lady Laura occupied a lounge in loving proximity, while the Blue Dwarf sat half concealed by curtains artfully arranged to conceal his form.

"I presume you have made a mistake," began Colonel Grant, rising, and speaking a little haughtily.

"No, colonel," began Dick, taking off his hat ; " it's our first appearance as 'The Hunters of the Prairies' on any stage."

It was too much. In recognising in these two supposed Indian hunters Dick Turpin and Tom King, all burst out laughing. Shelton Seymour and Lady Laura were convulsed, while even Sapathwa smiled grimly.

"My lords, ladies and gentlemen," began Dick, with great gravity, "we have provided ourselves with our travelling costume, under the advice of Indian Jack, the guide, and have now come for your orders."

"Oh! excellent well," cried Colonel Grant, nearly choked, "splendid! but I think we'll try middle-class homespun. But as guides — it's magnificent!"

"Well, colonel, we only have done what you told us, and Indian Jack highly recommended," said Dick, who could stand being laughed at as well as any man; "but about the waggon and teamster. The guide recommends buying them and selling them again when you have done with them."

All nodded approval.

"The fact is, Mr. Palmer, you have done so well already, that we shall leave everything to your judgment," said Colonel Grant; "still, of course, get everything as cheap as you can."

"Thanks, colonel," said Dick. "I don't think that you will regret trusting me, sir."

"Certainly not; but one moment," remarked the colonel, coming up to him. "You must want money."

And he thrust a handful of notes into his hand.

"You can keep an account, you know," said the colonel, smiling. "Let us know about twelve how things are progressing."

Dick bowed all round, and then retired with Tom, both feeling as yet rather awkward in their new costume.

But they would soon be used to it, and this was so much the better, as it would be some time before they would change it for anything more civilised.

Next day they had their first view of the half human sons of the forest, who occasionally made their appearance in the streets of New York, fantastically painted and decorated with beads and flaunting feathers, sauntering about with an air of listless indifference; at other times, inflamed with liquor, swaggering and whooping and yelling about the town like so many fiends, which conduct usually ended in their being locked up.

"Nice boys to meet in the woods and prairies," growled Dick. "What does the colonel mean by taking us among them? I shouldn't mind handling a dozen of them poor creatures!"

Yet Dick lived to form a very different opinion of them.

But still, they had to go, and at the end of a week all the preparations were made.

Their first trip was to be the Katskill, or Cat Hills, so called because of the fact that during the time of the Dutch domination they were much infested by catamounts, as well as thickly peopled by bears, wolves, and deer.

They had a strong but light waggon, four powerful but not unwieldy oxen, the guide, and two trusty men of his selection, backwoodsmen.

These were ordered to hold themselves in readiness to start at any moment.

It was the evening of the seventh day after their arrival in New York, and Dick and Tom, more used to the place, had, under the charge of Indian Jack and the two subordinate guides he had hired, gone to one of those lower-class places of public amusement which were to be found in a seaport town.

Compared with London or Portsmouth, it was, however, slow. The united Yankee and Dutch mind had not as yet introduced gambling, except in such a mild form as "spoiled five" or "catch the ten."

They played as modern American old maids are said to play the most exciting games, with a limit of twopence-halfpenny. The loss of a shilling by one of these ladies, who are not poor, is considered a life-long calamity. One day a member of the set, having won eighteen-pence, her conscience smote her, and she vowed that gambling was dreadful, and she would never play again. She never did; but she stuck to the eighteen-pence!

"I hope we shall start soon," said Dick, as they left the gay and festive scene. "This sort of life will soon kill me. I don't see what we're here for!"

"S'blood!" replied Tom King, starting.

They were standing close to the port near the landing place for passengers. As Tom spoke a number of people who had just arrived came pouring out through a gate, escorted by blacks and other touts, inviting the travellers to seek various places where accommodation was to be had.

"Plenty of work," added Tom, "for there's Brian Seymour and Robert Woodstock!"

Dick Turpin fell back in surprise, but next moment, remembering his disguise, he stood his ground and looked.

Yes! the two indefatigable and persevering scoundrels were already on their track.

How could it be?

It was simple enough. Brian and Robert, for ever on the prowl after the young earl, had visited one of their favourite haunts on the road to Portsmouth, and seeing Dick and Tom pass had followed them.

By one of those singular accidents which do not often happen in a lifetime, the two men were flush of cash; they had won thousands from a young baronet, who had just inherited, and were able to follow on to Portsmouth.

Once in that well-known seaport, it was not difficult to find that a large and distinguished English party were going out to New York in the "Ocean Queen."

On inquiry they found that another vessel sailed in a week, and took their passages accordingly.

This gave them a week on board.

Amazed and astounded as he was, Dick never for one moment lost his presence of mind, but followed in the track of the two sleuth hounds of murder and rapine.

They put up at the "New Amsterdam House," one of the old-fashioned inns frequented by Hollanders.

It was only eight o'clock in the evening.

The two friends went at once to the residence of the earl and asked to see the colonel.

They were at once admitted, and found that gentleman, Lord Jermyn, and two English gentlemen of position under government, playing whist in a separate room.

The colonel saw at once that they had important news, but with an expressive look bade them sit down.

When it was finished, as it happened, the English officials rose. There was a ball at the governor's, and it was their duty to attend.

"Don't be late," they said, smiling, as they gazed at the visitors, whom they believed to be hired guides. "We shall expect you."

"Well!" said the colonel in a low tone.

"We must leave to-night. Brian Seymour and Robert Woodstock have traced us," said Dick, in quite a crest-fallen way.

Colonel Grant and Lord Jermyn gazed at one another with an appalled look.

"Impossible!" cried Lord Jermyn.

"They have just landed from the 'Indian Queen,' and have gone to the 'New Amsterdam House,'" said Dick. "My lord, they must have been on the scent and followed us to Portsmouth," added Dick, who had been reflecting deeply.

"I fancy so," replied the colonel. "Can we start to-night?"

"I think so, sir."

"Remain here, Dick; and you, Tom," continued the colonel, "go to the rendezvous and have the caravan ready for midnight. Lay it to English eccentricity; but it can harm no one."

Tom silently obeyed.

"I will have everything ready for removal," proceeded the colonel. "They have plenty of carts here. Do you in the meantime go to the 'New Amsterdam' and keep watch and ward. Who knows? Out in the wilds we may catch them napping; and, by heavens! if we do, I will end this persecution."

The "New Amsterdam" was not at all a select house. On the voyage out Brian and Robert had found this so, and became aware that it was frequented by a jolly lot—adventurers and the like—and where some fun was to be had.

Dick knew enough about the place to be aware that his going into the public room might attract attention, and cause comments to be made. But there was a drinking-bar in full view of the public apartment, and this he entered.

There were not very many men there; but they were of the humbler sort, and when Dick civilly asked them to drink—in fact, almost humbly, as a stranger would—they accepted without the slightest hesitation.

"Lot of strangers came in from the 'Indian Queen?'" he then said.

"Not many—only two here; but they seem tidy well off—piles of luggage. They do bring a lot from the old country," said one of the "loafers."

"Yes," said Dick; "I've only lately come from the old shop; but I didn't bring much truck."

"Goin' to try up country?" asked the man.

"Well—yes"—with a slight drawl. "I was what they call a poacher in England," he added, with a laugh, "and suppose I can shoot a deer here, and no questions asked?"

"Yes, sir, and 'bars, and catamounts, and deer. None of your blessed game laws here, sir, as when I was a boy," retorted the other.

"Been here some time?" asked Dick.

"Twenty year," was the answer.

Dick thought that his appearance did not indicate that he had done much for himself in that time; but he made no remark.

He, however, easily set the others talking by asking them to drink, and thus was able to hear a great deal that was passing in the sitting-room.

Brian and Robert were too much elated at the respect with which they were treated, as new arrivals from the old country, not to be drawn into the usual trap held out to all such persons.

They stood a grand supper, and when Dick last peeped in were too far gone to be dangerous that night.

The moment he discovered this the listener left.

He found everyone ready. All the luggage had been removed to where the waggon awaited them, and all was in readiness at the hour of midnight.

"Indian Jack," said Dick, who knew that the most consummate flattery with such a man was to trust him, "are we to be friends? You know that your pay will be anything you ask; but I wish us to be friends during the six months or more we may pass together."

"And so does Indian Jack!" was the quiet answer. "Money very good—make squaw happy—got lot of papoose—but friend better."

"Then, Indian—you are white enough to know the value of money—you shall be the richest man amongst the guides if you serve us well," said Dick. "We have bitter enemies just come from across the water. Take us where they cannot find us."

"Good!" answered Indian Jack. "Ready?"

"In ten minutes."

Colonel Grant had been wise in leaving all to Dick Turpin. With better chances the highwayman might have been a general.

He had one good quality essential to success. He could judge who were to be trusted.

Twenty minutes later the waggon was drawn out into the silent streets. Not a soul was to be seen—not a white man, a red man, nor black man.

The guide, on horseback, led the way. All the rest were mounted, and kept behind.

Lady Laura rode beside her young husband, wearing a short riding-habit.

Indian Jack had decided to take them into the heart of the Catskills.

This mountainous region, a part of the State of New York, contains some of the finest scenery in the world. Poets, painters, and descriptive writers—English, American, and foreign—have wasted words in their endeavours to paint its beauties.

In vain! It must be seen to be appreciated.

Hills, valleys, trees, thrown together in admirable and beautiful confusion—gullies, gorges, streams, in picturesque disorder—met the eye.

Through the lower flats of this region Indian Jack had decided to lead his party until he brought them to a spot with two qualities.

Where they could pass the night in safety and know when any foe approached.

Dick had fully explained that they were not afraid of open violence. All they had to fear was treachery.

The foe was utterly without heart or principle, and would shoot them from an ambush or crawl into their camp and stab them to the heart, just as the opportunity offered.

Indian Jack was nothing if not vain, and Dick, having discovered this, had won his heart in a way that was irresistible with a half-breed.

He had bought him a complete new suit of buckskin, a knife, a shot pouch, a powder horn, and the best rifle in New York.

Indian Jack felt a big man. There was no position in civilised life which he did not look down upon.

The caravan crawled until they were half a mile out of the town.

Then, to the utter amazement and confusion of the whole party, they found that there was a water channel before them.

All became aware that the city of Manhattan, New York, New Amsterdam, or whatever it might be called, was on an island, and that the mainland was a quarter of a mile off.

Dick stared; all the rest waited.

Indian Jack waved his hand for silence just as Dick was going to—well, let us say ejaculate.

"Come," said the half-breed.

And he led him to where two scows were moored, that is to say, two large barges, flat-bottomed and wide. In size they were as big as some small men-of-war.

He explained that this was their only way of reaching the mainland, and showed Dick a huge ferry rope to which the scows were attached.

Dick now resolved to trust Indian Jack in everything. First, the ferrymen, six in number, were roused. They stared at the strange company, but when shown a larger sum in gold than they had ever seen before in a lump in their lives, they agreed to do as they were told.

With a rapidity and ingenuity which surprised everybody, the waggon, oxen, and horses were put on board. Then the human beings followed.

After this the ferrymen set to work in a double way, and pulled on the line, while the four others, aided by Indian Jack and his two comrades, used huge and heavy sculls.

It was arduous work; but occasionally there was shoal water, and then they began to pole the scows, which prevented such a heavy strain on the rope.

The whole thing was an utter novelty to our friends, but no one expressed any surprise.

The one anxiety was to get away from the vicinity of the two murderous villains who had got on their track with such infernal perseverance and tact.

This extraordinary passage took two hours. It took some time to get the caravan ready again.

The ferrymen were quite glad to stop on that side all night—for a consideration.

As there were no other ferry boats they could not be followed that night.

As soon as the whole party were ready the caravan resumed its march.

CHAPTER CXXXI.

THE MOUNTAIN HOME.

The night soon cleared, but still the scenery could not be very well distinguished. They made out crags and trees, and tiny waterfalls, but nothing very distinctly.

One thing, however, was quite clear. The road was heavy in the extreme, and the caravan made but slow progress.

Still, there was very little to fear. By one of those heaven-sent chances which occur only once in a lifetime, they were on their guard. They knew that, in the first place, Brian and Robert were behind them, and that they had to face their malignancy and hate.

Secret assassination was the great thing they had to guard against.

Of course, neither Brian Seymour nor Robert Woodstock could have come to America without a good supply of money. But even they could scarcely realise the lengths to which these scoundrels would go to attain their ends.

They little thought that at that very moment they were closeted with two of the most utter, unhanged rascals in New York and its environs, plotting the murder of the earl and the abduction of Lady Laura and the child.

They were amply provided with money, which they had obtained by a daring crime. They had committed a burglary in a country house, where they were received and trusted as relatives of the Earl of Elphick. They had stolen the whole of the family plate and jewellery, on which they had raised a large sum.

They were to be feared indeed.

The caravan halted at four in the morning and camped.

They had comfortable tents; in fact, everything had been done on the grandest scale.

Dick, Tom, Indian Jack, and the other men had one to themselves, where they slept soundly until a good while after morning broke.

Dick and Tom thought they would just like a look round, and, entering the woods, followed on in the hope of finding an elevation whence they could get a good view of their surroundings.

Suddenly they started, and then stood still, as a weird sound fell upon their ears.

It appeared as if a lot of blacksmiths were at work in the forest. There was undoubtedly the sound of repeated knocking with picks or something at no great distance.

Pushing forward, they soon came upon a wild, weird scene indeed, worthy of the Hartz Mountains, where an evil spirit holds high revel on the Brocken.

There was a yawning cavern in the side of a rock, and within they could see fires and torches, and many men busily attacking the rocky sides and the earth with picks, iron wedges, and hammers.

Wondering what it meant, they advanced closer, to find themselves near a long, low, log house, with unmistakable signs of a drinking shop about it.

They at once entered, and found that their surmises were correct. There was a long bar provided with drinks of all kinds, while in front of the counter was a deal table, on which a sable servant was putting all that was needful for a breakfast.

They went up, and a fellow in a slouched hat, very stout and cheery, asked what they wanted.

"Two drinks," said Dick, "and if there's any to spare, something to eat."

"Sambo, two more knives and forks," the host said, and then supplied them with whiskey.

"New in these here parts, strangers?"

"Oh! yes," replied Dick, "passing through with a party. Looking around just to see for ourselves."

"No idea of settling?"

"None; we're from the old country, and are just seeing life."

The man was evidently satisfied. He feared they might be "prospectors," who might offend gold seekers.

The Catskill mountains were long believed to be rich in the precious metals. In fact, enough was found to give an appetite for more, and this grotto had yielded sufficient to make it worth Sam Perkins' while to start a groggery.

The diggers now came trooping in, rough fellows—English, Irish, Scotch, and Dutch, with canvas pants and red shirts.

Sam Perkins introduced the strangers in a way that at once relieved any fears the diggers might have had of rivals, and both Dick and Tom were heartily received.

As soon as the copious meal was cleared, Dick

and Tom ordered "big rummers" round, and the diggers swore eternal friendship. They had no time to lose, they said; in fact, were late, but begged their new friends to have a big drink, and put a handful of dollars in the landlord's hands for that purpose.

They left amidst the plaudits of the crowd, and reached the camp just as the caravan was ready to start.

They explained their singular rencontre, which was heard with great interest.

It was decided that evening to make only such stoppages as were advised by the guides and teamsters to be necessary for the repose of the animals.

The leaders were anxious to get over the prairies and plains to some safe hiding place in the hills, where they might secrete themselves, and give Brian Seymour the slip.

The guides said that at a distance of some four hundred miles—no distance at all in the new country—was a valley of great beauty and fertility, where they would find everything that man could wish.

It was in the Indian country, but the tribes in the vicinity belonged to the Delaware or great Mohican race, who were friendly and faithful to the English.

This, then, was an advantage, as Brian would never think of looking for them there.

Two more days sufficed to carry them through the Catskill mountains, and to descend to the fertile prairie, with here and there a scanty settlement of the hardy pioneers of progress.

From these they received a hearty reception, such visits being very few and far between.

Their progress over the prairie was now tolerably rapid, but still sixteen or eighteen miles a day was considered very good work.

Lord and Lady Elphick were, indeed, delighted. Mounted on excellent steeds, they rode here, there, and everywhere over the grassy plain, rousing the birds and small animals from the prairie grass.

They breathed health every hour, while the babe, the nurse declared, grew visibly.

It was Sapathwa's original suggestion, and all were grateful for it.

At the end of the third week they came in sight of the hills, which were not very lofty, but still very far off western spurs of the Alleghany Mountains.

They were, in truth, in verdure clad.

The track was tolerably clear, as if one or two waggons had passed that way before.

Presently they got into a kind of gully, where the rocks were perpendicular, and the earth strewed with big stones.

Through this the waggon was dragged, however, at a tolerable pace, the oxen pulling admirably. All along they had been well fed, and never overworked, so that they were ready and willing.

After a journey of about two hours they came to a kind of ledge, from which there was a sharp incline, and at the bottom a beautiful valley, all trees, shrubs, flowers, and running water.

"How lovely!" cried Lady Laura, "one could live here for ever."

"And wear homespun instead of silks, wooden bead necklaces instead of diamonds, and be presented to some Indian chief instead of to his Majesty," said her husband laughing.

"Well, I don't exactly mean for ever," the young lady retorted; "but wouldn't it be nice to carry it off to England and tack it on to our park?"

"Well, yes," continued Shelton, "that is rather a reasonable proposal for a woman. Eh! what's up?"

The teamsters were unhitching the oxen, and the guide explained that the slope was composed of what was called shingle, or loose stones, and that unless great precautions were taken, it would reach the bottom rather too rapidly, upsetting and scattering its contents on every side.

The remedy was to hitch on two oxen on each side, and so harness them as to keep the waggon back by sheer force.

All would have to dismount, the horses being led.

As soon as the oxen were hitched on properly, the guide got to the head of the waggon to help to control it, and then it was allowed to slide.

It was quite clear that but for the power of the teams the waggon would have been upset and probably broken.

As it was, a great deal of pulling and hauling was necessary to make the waggon go slowly. The wheels, too, were locked.

The horses went down easily, picking their way carefully. But the English party had to exercise great care, while the nurse would have fared but badly had not one of the guides helped her. The man, a sturdy Yankee, had taken a great fancy to her, and was most polite in his rough and ready way.

"Jane has made a conquest, Laura," said the young earl, laughing.

"I hope not," said Laura, quite alarmed; "she'll be leaving us for that fellow."

"Well, now, I call that selfish," retorted her husband; "you get married yourself, and don't want poor Jane to follow your example. Of course, we can get another nurse, a black girl, or even a squaw."

"Shelton, you are a tease; but I hope Jane will give us proper notice before she leaves," said Lady Laura.

At this moment they reached the bottom, and all re-mounted.

Indian Jack now proposed that they should ride forward and select the site of their location, while the waggon came slowly after.

Indian Jack was a pretty good judge of white men's taste, and at once led them to a choice and beautiful spot. It was about a hundred yards from the water, with a goodly lot of timber around.

Indian Jack pointed to a small mound with a flat place on top about forty feet across each way. There he suggested they should build a block-house, sufficiently strong to resist an attack, should any of the inimical Indians come that way.

This eventuality he did not much fear. The nearest Indians lived on the borders of a dense forest, replete with game, about four miles off, and these could be easily propitiated with blankets, powder, and cheap guns, which could, with all other necessaries, be procured from Port Laramie, further back in the hills.

These forts were really trading posts, well fortified, however, as a protection from warlike redskins and their miserable renegade allies. They were frequented by traders to buy skins, and there were dealers there who sold everything that was needed.

Colonel Grant, who tacitly led the whole party, at once declared that this should be their mountain home.

They would erect one block-house for the heads of the party, and another for the men, where they could drink, smoke, and sleep to their heart's content.

Indian Jack assured them that the woods would supply them with plenty of game, bear's meat, venison, turkey, and pig's meat, with no end of small birds; while the river would produce an endless variety of fish.

The guides would undertake to supply the camp with food, though, of course, they would do the same by way of amusement.

As soon as the waggon came up a halt was declared, and a holiday proclaimed for the rest of the day.

CHAPTER CXXXII.

AN INDIAN GOD.

Five days later there was a marvellous change in the scene.

A block-house and a long log hut had been erected, with a *corral*, or enclosure, for the cattle.

The men, all of them, were provided with heavy American axes. Knowing that the log hut had to be built, hammers and all other necessary tools had been provided.

The logs were a foot square. The windows, which were four in number, were a foot and a half each way, and had thick wooden shutters.

The roof was sloping, and made from stout planks cut with axes.

The log hut was built in exactly the same way, but was not quite so lofty.

Two days before, Indian Jack, the two teamsters, and Tom had started with the waggon for Fort Laramie, about nine miles distant, and were expected back about noon.

Dick and the two other guides had remained to finish the block-house, which had been built in two days.

They had plenty of game and fish, and lived admirably. They could get all they wanted except tea, sugar, and bacon, which our Englishmen could not do without. They couldn't drink the native whiskey, that is the heads; but Dick and Tom had to. Wine was kept for Lady Laura, our friends indulging in good "apple Jack," as the Americans called cider.

The waggon returned a little after noon, when everybody dined, and then the "plunder," as the Americans call goods, was apportioned among the two residences.

It was arranged that next day the two other guides should go into Fort Laramie with Dick, Colonel Grant, and Lord Jermyn to buy blankets, powder, and guns for the Mohicans, to whom they intended to pay a friendly visit.

Dick thought he would have a few hours' amusement that afternoon, and invited Indian Jack to show him some shooting.

Indian Jack, with whom Dick was a great favourite, acquiesced, and shortly after the two started, crossing the stream and going down the valley to where it widened into a thickly-wooded prairie.

Here they were sure to find game, and did so. Dick had the good fortune to kill a fine buck, with splendid horns, which Indian Jack cut up into joints, which, with the skin, he hung up on the branches of a tree, leaving the offal and inferior parts to the vultures and prairie wolves.

Dick brought down some wild turkeys, which were very good eating. Generally they are shot at night, when flying to roost.

All this, however, seemed very much like what he had done in England. What he wanted was something new. He was not long before he was mightily astonished.

As they picked their way through the grass, Dick suddenly came to a standstill, as he heard what sounded like the beating of a drum in the distance.

"Eh, Jack, what's that?" he asked.

"Come—see!" replied the dusky hunter, with a smile. "Keep quiet."

Dick followed his guide a considerable distance, until they reached the edge of a thicket, into which, motioning for silence, Jack led the other.

Reaching a hedge of cactus, behind which the noise continued, Jack signed him to look and make no noise.

And what did Dick see?

A magnificent bird, called the ruffled grouse, common in those days. It was this bird that was drumming.

The peculiar noise made by them while drumming is usually heard while the bird is standing on a log, but the log has nothing to do with the sound produced. The bird, while drumming, assumes an upright position and drops his wings until the flight feathers almost or quite touch the log, or other perch, on which he stands.

He then, by an intense muscular effort, makes quick, spasmodic beats with his wings. In doing this the ends of the wing feathers may, and perhaps sometimes do, touch the log. It is the intense quiver of the flight feathers as they come in contact with the still air in the short and intensely-rapid beats, that produce the soft, yet powerful and far-reaching sound.

No impact of a feather or feathers with a solid substance—especially a moss-covered log—could ever make the sound, soft as it is; and it seems to come to you from every direction, so that it requires a quick and practised ear to locate it correctly.

Dick looked in silence for some time, and then he spoke.

"Well, I'm blessed!" he said. "I must take that home," and he felt for his gun.

But the bird had vanished, and Dick was left staring blankly, while Indian Jack shook with suppressed laughter.

Dick made no remark, but followed the Indian in silence some little distance, until they reached one of those trees with wide spreading branches, the boughs of which begin two or three feet from the ground.

Suddenly Indian Jack gave a sharp, yelp-like cry, and pointed to the tree.

Dick quite startled, reached the first branch just as Indian Jack fired his rifle.

Then the Londoner saw a drove of little animals rushing at them, about two feet high, with little eyes, and with strong tusks like boars', only smaller and sharper than those seen in Europe.

Indian Jack in a moment went beside him and informed him that these were peccaries, the wild hogs of the prairie, some of the most vindictive and dangerous animals the hunter has to face.

The guide explained that once it sees a man it will never leave him; it lies down and waits. It is of little use to kill one after another unless all the boars are slain. The incautious hunter who faces it in the open is sure to be gored to death.

"What are we to do?" asked Dick, ruefully.

"Kill—one—two—three—keep firing, friend, hear——" was the answer. "When quite dark —go away."

Dick listened with perfect awe. He could scarcely believe that a drove of these little pigs could be so dangerous.

He, however, began, in common with Indian Jack, to fire at the little brutes. Several of them were killed, but the savage animals sat upon their haunches looking steadily at their expected prey.

"This is infernal!" said Dick, at last. "I've a great mind to get down and have a shy at them."

"Kill dead!" replied the guide.

Dick was wise enough to take the experienced hunter's advice, and remained still.

At fixed intervals they fired, until presently it began to get dark. But the persistent little brutes never moved.

At last, under the leafy arches of the trees it was quite dark, and they could no longer see the piggies.

But they could hear their sharp and savage little grunts.

Presently, however, that ceased, and they were about to descend, when the Indian fired another shot, which was answered by a shout at no great distance.

Then the two hunters came up and saw at once what the difficulty was. They could not help laughing at Dick's indignation at being treed by such little brutes.

When he got back, however, he ate some broiled peccary for supper. His employers were very much amused at the relation of his adventures, which he told with great vivacity and humour.

Next day Dick, the two hunters, the colonel, and Lord Jermyn started for Fort Laramie, which they found to be a very extensive trading post, with a wall eleven feet high and eight wide. The outside and inside were made of piles driven into the ground, the vacancy being filled with earth.

No Indian would venture to attack such fortifications with white men behind them.

The travellers were well received by the agents, some of whom were men of substance and position, with wives and families in the cities, where, after a few years, they retired.

The chief trader, Mr. Farnham, invited the two English gentlemen to his house, and was amazed to find that one of them was a lord. When told that they intended locating for a season, he asked permission to pay his respects.

Of course they would be very glad to see him and any of his friends.

Meanwhile, Dick and the others were buying all that was wanted of the minor traders, as the big ones merely purchased the skins and furs, which, when carefully prepared, are sent off to the nearest river, and shipped in scows to the sea.

Mr. Farnham was very intelligent and well informed, and gave them a great deal of information about the country and the Indians.

It was quite late in the afternoon when they rose to start, reaching home towards dusk of evening. A few days later Mr. Farnham and some of the other leading traders came riding over early, and were delighted to be introduced to two real live countesses.

Our people made them as comfortable as possible, and a very pleasant day was spent. The English and Americans fraternised, and Mr. Farnham invited them all to pay a visit a fortnight hence to the fort.

All the party became convinced that their American journey would be a very pleasant affair, little expecting the terrible trials they would have to pass through in that land, which would cause all they had suffered in England to seem as nothing.

But the knowledge of the future is mercifully concealed from us.

Two days later, they paid a visit to the great village of the Mohicans, who received them with great affability. They had been preceded by Indian Jack and the traders with pack horses loaded with the presents.

The whole tribe, male and female, old and young, turned out and gave them a grand reception, with speeches, which fortunately were short, as they had to be interpreted.

Then giving the whole party seats—the Blue Dwarf and Dick were absent—they gave them a great Indian spectacle. There was a war-dance, a game of ball—one of the gayest scenes in Indian life; after which there were foot races and other amusements.

When they rose to go, after a treaty of amity had been declared, binding them to defend their new friends *vi et armis*, all the young men mounted and accompanied them to within a mile of their residence.

The ladies, when their first fright was over, became quite delighted with the gallant young Delawares, who were as gentle in their way of speaking as the most refined gentlemen in their own country. Everyone has noticed this particular, especially in regard to the Delawares, the gentle race who were exterminated through their fidelity to the English.

Two more days passed, and then something happened which had a marked effect on their fortunes.

Sapathwa, confined perforce to the block-house in the daytime, was in the habit of going out at night, sometimes by himself, sometimes with Dick.

On the third evening after the visit to the Indian village, Sapathwa rose, after every one slept, from the corner he always occupied in the block-house, and went forth unarmed to wander through the woods—his favourite amusement in England.

Indian Jack saw him depart, but his orders were to take no notice of his proceedings, instructions he was only too ready to obey after obtaining one glimpse of his unearthly countenance.

When all hands were summoned to breakfast, it was found that Sapathwa was missing.

In an instant the camp was up and nothing else thought of. Everyone able to move dispersed to scour the neighbourhood.

Dick and Bill Simmons, one of the scouts, started together on foot. He knew not why, but seemed to think he should find him near the great Delaware village.

Sapathwa had spoken a great deal about the Mohicans, and expressed a great desire to study them, their habits and modes of thought.

They reached to within half a mile of the Mohican town, and there saw that a crowd was going towards the village, carrying something elevated on their shoulders.

Hurrying up and getting into the crowd, their astonishment may be conceived.

On wild men's shoulders was a platform of poles and skins, upon which, sitting erect on a stool, was the Blue Dwarf, looking more serene, proud, and contemplative than they had ever seen him before. He gazed down upon the hideous painted throng with a kindly smile of protection, keeping his countenance admirably, despite the hideously comic and distorted crowd below.

In front marched a medicine man, made up to look as fearful as he could imagine himself. Some shouted, some danced, some blew horns, and all who were not carrying their strange demi-god rushed helter-skelter with terrific yells.

Sapathwa saw Dick, and his lips whispered a faint sound.

"Do nothing! say nothing! Quite safe! Go!"

And they went without another word, and rushed back to report the astounding event which had occurred.

"Taken him for a god," said Indian Jack, grinning; "all safe; expect one from the rising sun."

All Indian races believe in the advent of a great saviour to their race from the East. This is believed to be some old tradition about the second coming of Montezuma.

Our friends were infinitely amused, but were in a way alarmed.

But a consultation was held, Indian Jack and Dick being called in, and it was finally agreed to claim him next day as their great medicine man, who had power to change himself into any shape he liked, and whose breath could wither the strongest man.

"Give him up quick," grinned Indian Jack, "when hear that."

And none had any doubt of the circumstance. Indians are very superstitious.

They are also born conjurors. In one or two tribes they have men who can do table-turning in a way which would shame the paltry professors of the "art" in Europe.

At an early hour the whole party was collected. Lady Laura, Lady Jermyn, the nurse and baby, with the amorous guide, were left at home.

All the rest mounted and rode at a rapid pace for the Mohican village. When they came within a couple of hundred yards, they drew rein and dismounted.

Indian Jack went forward, and walked into the centre of the camp.

His astonishment was great.

Sapathwa was taking his breakfast in public, waited on by some of the leading men.

He was seated in a tent, the sides of which had been drawn, so that all could see. The Blue Dwarf, still preserving his complacent gravity, accepted from two kneeling braves some broiled meat on a platter. It was cut, but the Indians had given him a knife and a pointed stick, which he was using very freely.

Another held in one hand a wooden goblet and a bottle, which Indian Jack knew well contained whiskey.

Several of the sachems sat looking on, evidently delighted with the imperturbable serenity of their new god.

When the Indian had waited some minutes, a slight sign summoned him to the side of one of the chiefs.

Sapathwa was putting away his platter, and in the act of drinking from the goblet.

Indian Jack announced the visit of the white men, and pointed out where they were approaching.

As they came up and saw what was going on, it was with difficulty they controlled their risible faculties.

But this would have spoiled all, as, except in the privacy of the domestic circle, Indians never laugh.

Greetings took place, and then the great sachem asked their business.

Indian Jack stepped forward and made a speech, in which he said all that had been agreed on.

He thanked the redskins for their kindness to the great paleface medicine man, and promised them a rich present of coloured blankets as a reward. He then further explained that they could not do without their conjuror.

The Indians looked grave. It was quite evident that they would part with their inspired captive reluctantly.

At this moment Indian Jack unfolded a particularly bright blanket in purple and gold, and threw it on the sachem's knee.

Some men sneer at dressy uniforms and the like; but the human mind is impressed.

A great writer has said, "Some years since when a great orator was made lord mayor, he used to wear a red gown and a cocked hat, the splendour of which delighted him as much as a new curtain ring in her nose and a string of glass beads round her neck charms Queen Quashee-ma-boo."

The great writer then calls this "twopenny splendour."

He was wrong. A lord mayor in evening dress would impress no one.

Then Indian Jack having announced that a hundred similar ones would be presented to the tribe in a few days, a murmur of satisfaction went round the group.

The great sachem then made a speech, expressed his desire to be at amity with their white brethren, and at once gave up their great medicine man.

All they asked was that they should be allowed to take him to the confines, where his horse would await him.

All agreed, and hurried away to avoid laughter, and be ready to receive their medicine man.

All mounted ready except Indian Jack, who stood waiting with a horse.

A few minutes elapsed, and then the sound of horns, with the accompaniment of some monotonous chant, was heard, and the procession came in sight.

It was exactly the same as before, but what chiefly astounded our friends was the stolid gravity of Sapathwa.

The outside of the stockade was reached, and then the transfer took place.

Sapathwa was assisted to mount his horse, and the whole party rode off at a sober pace, which was kept up until they were out of sight of the village.

Then Colonel Grant turned to Sapathwa. "How could you do it?" he asked; "how keep your countenance amid that gang?"

"They were not frightened at me, and they

were kind to me," was the rather bitter answer.

Colonel Grant made no reply, and the subject dropped.

The time passed pleasantly enough in excursions in the forest, picnics in wonderful places, rides to curious caves and mighty waterfalls, until at last the day came round for the visit to the fort.

All the heads were to go save Sapathwa, while the escort was to be composed of Dick, Tom, and Indian Jack.

It was a fine day, and a pleasant journey. Shelton and Laura enjoyed it especially.

The fort was *en fete*.

Flags and banners had been hoisted, and when the advancing *cortège* came in sight several old cannon were fired.

The gates were open, and were surrounded by a motley collection of loafers—Indians and whites and half breeds—who gazed with wonder at the gay throng.

Then the traders came out and received their guests, whom they led into the inside of the fort, where a pavilion had been erected for their accommodation.

At the steps leading up to this they all alighted, and were conducted into a gaily-decorated hall, where the banquet was laid out.

Some neatly-dressed women conducted the ladies to an apartment specially reserved, and then the attendants proceeded to spread the table.

The banquet was copious, and there were many delicacies, and even had there been deficiencies, they would have been made up for by the cordial hospitality of the givers of the banquet.

A very pleasant day was spent, and it was quite evening when the cavalcade returned, jocund and happy.

Would they have been in such high spirits had they seen, amid the hangers-on round the gate, two pairs of evil eyes fixed upon them as they passed, with a look of triumph and hate?

A week passed, and then one morning an Indian runner came to the white men's camp t bid them be careful.

It was rumoured that the Sioux, who dwelt i the hills at a distance of thirty miles, had hear of the wealth of the palefaces, and were pre paring for a serious attack on them.

Some loafing half-breed from the fort ha spread the news abroad.

The Mohicans sent a message to say that the would fight to the last gasp for their palefac friends; but what they had to guard agains were ambushes and surprises.

The runner was thanked, and an invitation h brought for someone to visit the camp an confer was accepted.

He then departed with presents galore, an was made quite happy.

It was then decided that Dick and India Jack should visit the Mohican village, wit powers to treat.

The rest would remain near the block-hous keeping a good look-out for enemies.

On reaching the village the Indian, withou any circumlocution, proposed that a number c young men should start in small parties for th Sioux territory, and that these should be followe up by a larger party, which Indian Jack an Dick would accompany.

They would then be able to get good informa tion as to the movements of the Sioux, and b prepared.

The sachem emphatically declared that if plundering expedition entered their territory t injure the whites, not a man of them woul leave that region alive.

While they were still conferring, Tom rode u to ask what had been settled.

Dick told him, and he at once rode back wit the news.

An hour later they started on an expeditio which, if a man had said a year ago he woul have joined in, he would have set him down a a lunatic.

They were to go on foot, make as long a marc as they could that day, rest until midnight, an then start for the neighbourhood of the Siou village.

END OF VOLUME II.